About

Cathy Williams is a g
perseverance as she had
her writing career, and f
has now fulfilled her ambition to pursue this most enjoyable of careers. She would encourage any would-be writer to have faith and go for it! She derives inspiration from the tropical island of Trinidad and from the peaceful countryside of middle England. Cathy lives in Warwickshire with her family.

Joss Wood's passion for putting black letters on a white screen is only matched by her love of books and travelling and her hatred of making school lunches and ironing. Fuelled by coffee and craziness, Joss is a hands on Mum and, after a career in local economic development and business lobbying, she now writes full time. Surrounded by family, friends and books she lives in Kwa-Zulu Natal, South Africa with her husband and two children.

Louise Fuller was a tomboy who hated pink and always wanted to be the prince. Not the princess! Now she enjoys creating heroines who aren't pretty pushovers but strong, believable women. Before writing for Mills & Boon, she studied literature and philosophy at university and then worked as a reporter on her local newspaper. She lives in Tunbridge Wells with her impossibly handsome husband, Patrick and their six children.

One Night...

June 2022
to Forever

July 2022
to Scandal

August 2022
to Marriage

September 2022
for Revenge

December 2022
to Seduction

January 2023
for Business

February 2023
of Convenience

March 2023
to Safety

One Night...
For Business

CATHY WILLIAMS

JOSS WOOD

LOUISE FULLER

MILLS & BOON

First Published in Great Britain 2023
By Mills & Boon, an imprint of HarperCollins*Publishers*, Ltd
1 London Bridge Street, London, SE1 9GF

www.harpercollins.co.uk

HarperCollins*Publishers*
Macken House, 39/40 Mayor Street Upper,
Dublin 1, D01 C9W8, Ireland

ISBN: 978-0-263-31846-3

This book is produced from independently certified FSC™ paper to ensure responsible forest management.

For more information visit: www.harpercollins.co.uk/green

Printed and Bound in Spain using 100% Renewable electricity at CPI Black Print, Barcelona

THE ITALIAN'S ONE-NIGHT CONSEQUENCE

CATHY WILLIAMS

CHAPTER ONE

FROM THE BACK seat of his chauffeur-driven car, which was parked a discreet distance away, Leo Conti took a few minutes to savour the edifice that dominated this tree-lined Dublin road. Prime location, perfect size, and with all the discernible signs of wear and tear that indicated a department store clinging to life by the skin of its teeth.

Frankly, things couldn't have been better.

This was the store his grandfather had spent a lifetime trying to acquire. It was the store that had eluded the old man's grasp for over fifty years, always just out of reach. Despite the vast property portfolio Benito Conti had built up over the decades, and the grand shopping complexes he had opened across the globe, this one department store had continued to hold sway over him.

Leo, raised by his grandparents from the age of eight, had never been able to understand why his grandfather couldn't just let it go—but then, being outmanoeuvred by someone you'd once considered your closest friend would leave a sour taste in anybody's mouth.

Which said something about the nature of trust.

Over the years Leo had witnessed his grandfather's

frustrated attempts to purchase the department store from Tommaso Gallo to no avail.

'He would rather it crumble to the ground,' Benito had grumbled, 'than sell it to me. Too damn proud! Well, if it *does* crumble—and crumble it will, because Tommaso has been drinking and gambling his money away for decades—I will be the first in line to laugh! The man has no honour.'

Honour, Leo thought now, as his sharp eyes continued to take in the outward signs of decay, was an irrational emotion that always led to unnecessary complications.

'Find yourself something to do, James,' Leo said to his chauffeur, leaning forward, eyes still on the building. 'Buy yourself a decent meal somewhere. Take a break from that fast food junk you insist on eating. I'll call you when it's time for you to swing by and collect me.'

'You plan on buying the place today, boss?'

A shadow of a smile crossed Leo's face. He caught his driver's eyes in the rearview mirror. James Cure—driver, dogsbody and rehabilitated petty thief—was one of the few people Leo would actually trust with his life.

'I plan,' Leo drawled, opening the passenger door and letting in a blast of summer heat, 'on having a little incognito tour to find out just how low I can go when it comes to putting money on the table. From what I see, the old man has died leaving a nice, healthy liability behind, and from what I understand, the new owner—whoever he is—will want to sell before the dreaded words *fire sale* start circulating in the business community.'

Leo had no idea who the new owner was. In fact he wouldn't have known that Tommaso Gallo had gone to meet his maker a mere month previously if his grandfather hadn't summoned him back from Hong Kong to buy the store before it went to someone else.

'Now,' Leo said, briskly winding up the conversation, 'off you go, James—and while you're finding yourself a nice, healthy salad for lunch, try and locate the nearest pawn shop, so that you can offload that array of jewellery you insist on wearing.' Leo grinned. 'Hasn't anyone told you that medallions, signet rings and thick gold chains are things of the past?'

James smiled and rolled his eyes before driving off.

Still grinning from the familiar exchange, Leo strolled towards the bank of revolving glass doors, joining the very small number of shoppers coming and going—which, on what should have been a busy Saturday morning in the height of summer, pretty much said it all about the state of the department store.

Four storeys of glass and concrete, heading for the knacker's yard. Mentally he dropped the price he'd had in his head by a couple of hundred thousand.

His grandfather, he thought wryly, would be pleased as Punch. He would have found it galling to have paid top whack for a place he privately thought should have belonged to him fifty years ago, had Tommaso Gallo been prepared to honour the deal he had promised.

Strolling away from the revolving doors towards the store guide by the escalator, Leo gave some thought to the tales about the now legendary feud that had been part and parcel of life as he had grown up.

Two friends—both from Italy, both talented, both seeking to make their fortunes in Ireland. One small, dilapidated shop, up for sale at a knockdown price. But sitting on a slice of street that both Tommaso and Benito had fast recognised would be worth a lot in years to come. The drift of business hadn't quite reached that part of the city then, but it would.

They could have done the sensible thing and gone into business together, but instead they had tossed a coin after way too many drinks. Winner to take all. A drunken handshake had sealed the bet that would prove the unravelling of their friendship—for Benito had won the toss, fair and square, only for his one-time friend to go behind his back and snap up the property before Benito had been able to get his finances together.

Bitter, Benito had retreated to London where, over time, he had made his own vast fortune—but he had never forgiven Tommaso for his treachery. Nor had he ever stopped wanting that one department store, which he really didn't need because he had quite enough of his own.

Leo knew that he could have worked a little harder to dampen his grandfather's desire to have something that no longer mattered, all things considered, but he loved his grandfather and, much as he didn't believe in emotions overriding common sense, he had to admit that something in him could understand the need for some sort of retribution after such an act of betrayal.

And also, from a practical point of view, it would certainly work in Leo's interests to have the place. Dublin would be an excellent addition to his own massive portfolio of companies. He had already agreed with his grandfather that once the store was back in Conti hands he, Leo, would do with it as he wished, with the proviso that the name Conti replaced Gallo.

Leo had argued with his grandfather, wanting him to allow him to pay for the purchase himself. Because there was no way he intended to leave it as a cumbersome department store, however iconic it had once been.

That sort of sentimentality wasn't for him. No, Leo wanted the place because he liked the thought of finally getting his foot into Dublin—something long denied him because he had never found the perfect property to set down roots.

Along with his own start-up companies Leo had acquired a string of software and IT companies, which he had merged under one umbrella and continued to run while simultaneously overseeing Benito's empire by proxy. He had only a handful of outlets for his highly specialised merchandise, where expert advice was on hand for the elite group of medical, architectural and engineering giants who used what he had to offer.

This site would be perfect for expanding his businesses into a new market.

His thoughts far away, he was already indulging in the pleasurable exercise of planning how he would use the space to its best advantage.

Naturally it would have to be gutted. Wood, carpet and dowdy furnishings might have worked back in the day—although to be fair Leo wasn't sure *when* that day might have been—but as soon as he got his hands on the store they'd have to go. God knew, the place was probably riddled with rising damp, dry rot and termites. By the time he was through with it, and the 'Gallo' sign had been unceremoniously dumped, it would be unrecognisable.

He looked around, wondering which decrepit part of the store he should hit first—and there she was.

Standing behind one of the make-up counters, she looked as out of place as a fish in a bookstore. Despite the fact that she was surrounded by all manner of war paint, in expensive jars and shiny compact holders, she herself appeared to be devoid of any cosmetics. Frowning at an arrangement of dark burgundy pots on the glass counter, and needlessly repositioning them, she was the very picture of natural, stunningly beautiful freshness, and for a few seconds Leo actually held his breath as he stared at her.

His libido, which had been untested for the past three weeks, ever since he had broken up with his latest conquest after she'd started making unfortunate noises about permanence and commitment, sprang into enthusiastic life.

Leo was so surprised at his reaction that he was hardly aware that he was staring like a horny teenager. Not cool. Not *him.*

Especially when the leggy girl he was staring at was definitely *not* a Page Three girl and even more definitely *not* the sort of woman he was attracted to.

She was tall and willowy, from the little he could make out under the cheap store uniform, and she had the sort of wide-eyed innocence that was always accompanied in his head with the strident ringing of alarm bells. Her skin was smooth and satiny and the colour of pale caramel, as though she had been toasted in the sun. Her hair was tied back, but the bits escaping were a shade darker than her skin, toffee-coloured with strands of strawberry blonde running through it.

And her eyes…

She abruptly stopped what she was doing and looked up, gazing directly back at him.

Her eyes were green—as clear as glass washed up on a beach.

The kick of sexual attraction, a lust as raw as anything he'd ever felt before, shot through him like a bolt of adrenaline, and Leo felt himself harden in immediate response. It was fierce enough to take his mind off everything that had hitherto been occupying it.

His stiffened shaft was painful, and he had to adjust his position to release some of the pressure. As their eyes tangled he thought that if she kept looking at him like that, making him imagine what it would be like to have that succulent full mouth circling the throbbing, rigid length of him, he would soon be desperate for release.

He began walking towards her, every hunting instinct inside him honing in on his prey. He'd never wanted any woman with such urgent immediacy before and Leo wasn't about to ignore the pull. When it came to sex, he was a man who had always got what he wanted—and he wanted this woman with every fibre in his body.

The closer he got to her, the more stupendously pretty she was. Her huge eyes were almond-shaped, fringed with very dark lashes that seemed to contradict the colour of her hair. Her lips, parted, were sensuous and full, even though their startled-in-the-headlights expression was teasingly innocent. And her body…

The unappealing, clinical white dress, belted at the waist, should have been enough to dampen any man's ardour, but instead it sent his imagination into frantic overdrive and he caught himself wondering what her breasts would look like, what they would taste like…

'Can I help you?' Maddie's heart was beating like a sledgehammer, but her expression was studiously polite as she met the stranger's openly appreciative gaze.

Man sees girl. Man is attracted to girl. Man makes beeline for girl because he has one thing on his mind and that's getting her into bed with him.

Maddie was used to that response from the opposite sex. She hated it.

What was even more galling was the fact that this particular man had, just for a second, aroused something in her *other* than her usual instinct to slam down the shutters hard the minute she saw a come-on situation on the horizon.

In fact, for a second, she had felt a stirring between her thighs—a tingling, tickly *melting* that had horrified her.

'Interesting question,' the man murmured, positioning himself directly in front of her.

The look in her eyes seemed to amuse him.

'Are you looking for make-up?' Maddie asked bluntly. 'Because if so you're in the wrong department. I could always point you in the right direction.'

In response, the man randomly picked up a jar from the precarious display she had been fiddling with earlier and twirled it in his hand.

'What's this if not make-up?'

Maddie removed it from him and swivelled it so that the label was facing him. 'Regenerating night cream, targeting a woman in her sixties,' she said crisply. 'Are you interested in buying it?'

'Oh, I'm *interested*,' he said, in a tone laced with innuendo.

'Well, that's all I'm selling, so if it's not what you're *interested* in you should probably keep moving.'

Maddie folded her arms. She knew she was blushing. She also knew that her body was misbehaving. Once cretly she wondered if the grandfather she'd never met might have attempted to contact her mother, only to have his efforts spurned. Parents were often more forgiving with their children than the other way around.

Her eyes misted over and she reached out and impulsively circled the man's wrist with her fingers—and then yanked her hand back because the charge of electricity that shot through her was downright frightening.

He raised his eyebrows, and for a second she felt that he could read every thought that had flashed through her head.

'No need,' he murmured. 'Have dinner with me.'

'I beg your pardon?'

'I'll pass on the face cream. Frankly, all those wild claims can't possibly be true. But have dinner with me. Name the place, name the time...'

'You're not interested in buying anything in this store, are you?'

Maddie's voice cooled by several degrees, because he was just another example of a cocky guy who wanted to get her into bed. She'd been spot-on first time round.

'And as for a dinner date... That'll be a *no*.'

Dinner with this man? How arrogant was he?

Her eyes slid surreptitiously over him and she understood very well why he was as arrogant as he was. The guy was drop-dead gorgeous.

Lean, perfectly chiselled features, dark hair worn slightly too long, which emphasised his powerful masculinity rather than detracting from it, a tightly honed body that testified to time spent working out, even though he didn't look like the sort of man who spent much time preening in front of mirrors and flexing his muscles. And those eyes… Sexy, bedroom eyes that made her skin burn and made her thoughts wander to what a dinner date with him might be like…

She forced herself to conjure up the hateful memory of her ex—Adam. He'd been good-looking too. Plus charming, charismatic, and from the sort of family that had spent generations looking down on people like her. Well, that whole experience had been a learning curve for Maddie, and she wasn't about to put those valuable lessons to waste by succumbing to the phoney charm of the man in front of her with his sinful good looks and his *I could make your body sing* bedroom eyes.

'Should I be?'

Maddie frowned. 'What do you mean? What are you talking about?'

'*Should* I be interested in buying anything here? Look around you. This is a department store that's gone to rack and ruin. I'm staggered that you would even have contemplated working here in the first place. The job situation in Dublin must be dire for you to have settled on *this*—and you've obviously had no on-the-job training because there isn't enough money to go round for such essentials as training programmes. I'm pretty sure that if I looked I'd find an array of out-of-date merchandise and demotivated sales assistants.'

'Who *are* you?'

Maddie looked at him narrowly. Was she missing something?

Leo met her stare and held it. He'd planned on a little incognito surveillance and he was going to stick to the plan—bar this little detour which, he thought, he could very well use to his advantage. She'd turned down his dinner date but he wasn't fazed by that. Women never said no to him for very long.

Although…

He frowned, because *this* particular woman didn't seem to fit the mould.

'Just someone browsing,' Leo said smoothly, and then he added, truthfully, 'I don't get to this part of the world very often and I wanted to see this store everyone seems to know about.' He looked around him. 'I'm less than impressed.'

The woman followed his gaze and said nothing, perhaps because she'd noticed those very same signs of disrepair. She seemed to suddenly realise that he was still watching her, his eyes narrowed.

'I can see that you agree with me.'

'Like I said, I haven't been here for very long—but if you're looking for something to buy as a souvenir of the store, there's an excellent selection on the second floor. Mugs, tote bags, lots of stuff…'

Leo suppressed a shudder at the image of tackiness created in his head. Had the place moved with the times *at all*? Or had progress being quietly sidelined as Gallo's money ran out?

He had a satisfying vision of what the place would look like under his dominion. High-tech, white glossy counters and open, uncluttered spaces, glass and mirrors, ranks of computers and accessories waiting to be explored—no irritating background elevator music and salespeople who actually knew what they were talking about.

'If you have lots of money to spend, then we offer a range of leather handbags which we manufacture ourselves to the highest possible standard. They're Italian, and really beautiful quality.'

'Sadly,' Leo said, easily giving voice to the lie, 'my finances would struggle to stretch to one of your leather handbags.'

She nodded. He didn't seem like the sort of broke, wrong-side-of-the-tracks kind of guy she had encountered during her life, but it was a fact that a good-looking man could look expensive in anything.

'But I could probably stretch to one of those tote things you mentioned…'

'Second floor.'

'Take me.'

'Come again?'

'I want you to do your sales pitch on me.'

'I'll be honest with you,' she said flatly, 'if this is another way of trying to get me to have dinner with you, then you can forget it. I won't be doing that.'

Leo wondered whether she would have had a change of heart had she known his true worth. Most definitely, he thought, with his usual healthy dose of cynicism. That said, he was a man accustomed to getting what he wanted—and the more he talked to her, looked at her, felt the pleasurable race of his pulses and the hard throb of his libido, the more he wanted to rise to the challenge of breaking down whatever walls she felt she had to erect.

For once, work and the reason he was in this sad excuse of a store had been put on the back burner.

'You're very arrogant, aren't you?' he murmured, watching her carefully as the slow burn of anger turned her cheeks a healthy pink. 'Do you think that you have what it takes to make a man keep banging on a door that's been firmly shut in his face?'

'How *dare* you?'

'You forget—I'm the customer and the customer is always right.'

His grin was meant to take the sting out of his words and make her realise that he'd been teasing her.

'That's better,' Leo said as her anger appeared to fade, then glanced at his watch to find that time had flown by. 'Now, why don't you show me this souvenir section of yours?' He raised both hands in mock surrender. 'And you can breathe safe in the knowledge that there'll be no more dinner invitations. You say you're new here… You can practise your sales patter on me. I'm just passing through, so you won't have to worry that I'll be gossiping behind your back with the locals, telling them that the new girl at the big store doesn't seem to know the ropes.'

Maddie looked down, but she wanted to smile.

So far she'd made no friends. It would take time for her to integrate. This interaction almost felt like a breath of fresh air. Naturally she wasn't going to be an idiot and go on any dates with any strangers—especially good-looking ones who obviously knew how to say the right things to get a woman's pulse racing. But he had valid criticisms of the store, and she would need those—would need to find out what customers thought when they entered. Customers would look at the place through different eyes from hers. It might actually be a good idea to encourage his opinions.

So he'd asked her out… Maddie didn't spend time staring at her reflection in mirrors, but she knew that she was attractive. It was something that had dogged her, for better or for worse. Certainly for worse when it had come to Adam, but she couldn't let the memory of that determine every single response to every single guy who happened to look in her direction. Could she?

Besides, setting aside the killer looks, the man still staring at her wasn't a rich creep—like Adam had been, had she only had the wisdom to see that from the very start. This guy was more tote bags than soft Italian leather.

Maddie felt a thrilling little frisson as she breathed in deeply and said, 'Well, I guess I could get someone to cover for me just for a little while.'

Brian Walsh was in charge of the store temporarily, and he was the only one who knew who she really was. He had worked there for over twenty years and was keen to see the store become again the place it had once been, so he was fully on board with her decision to evaluate the store undercover for a short period of time while she worked out a way forward.

'My…er…my boss is just over there. I'll ask his…er…permission…'

'Your boss?' he asked, his interest clearly pricked by the knowledge.

'Mr Walsh. If you don't mind waiting…?'

'I have all the time in the world,' he said expansively, deciding on the spot to tell James to head back to the hotel, just in case he found himself staying longer than anticipated. 'I'll be right here when you return.'

CHAPTER TWO

LEO COULD HAVE taken the opportunity to probe her about her boss—the man Leo would soon be putting through the wringer—but that, he decided as he watched her heading back towards him, could wait. His grandfather wanted the store *yesterday*, but tomorrow or the day after was just fine with Leo. There was no doubt in his mind that he would secure the store—so what was the harm in letting himself be temporarily distracted?

She moved like a dancer, her body erect, looking neither right nor left as she walked gracefully across the department store floor. He suddenly realised he didn't even know her name, and he put that right the minute she was standing in front of him again, her fresh, floral scent filling his nostrils and turning him on.

'Shouldn't you be wearing a name tag? Something discreetly pinned to your nice white outfit so that I know exactly who to complain about if you sell me overpriced face cream that makes my girlfriend's skin break out in spots?'

'You have a girlfriend?'

The interest in her voice pleased him.

'Because,' she went on quickly, the flush on her cheeks betraying the fact that she'd realised her slip, 'if you do, then you should have said. I could have pointed you in the direction of a whole different selection of face products.'

Leo glanced down at her. She was tall. Much taller than the women he was fond of dating. 'Alas, that's a position that's waiting to be filled,' he murmured. 'And it has to be said that, as presents go, anti-wrinkle, anti-ageing face cream wouldn't make a good one for any of the women I've ever dated in the past. So, what *is* your name?'

'Madison.' She kept her eyes professionally forward as the escalator took them up one floor and then the next, up to the second floor, where any visible effort at revitalisation had been abandoned. Here, the décor begged to be revamped and the displays craved some sort of creative, modern overhaul.

'Madison…?'

'But everyone calls me Maddie. We're here.'

She began walking towards the back of the floor while Leo took his time strolling slightly behind her, taking in the store's rundown appearance. He was surprised spiders weren't weaving cobwebs between the dated merchandise—although he had to concede the sales assistants they passed were all wearing cheerful smiles.

Attention distracted, he glanced at the arrangement of souvenirs, all bearing the Gallo logo. Absently he toyed with a canvas bag, and then he looked at her seriously.

'You're not Irish.' He dropped the bag and it dangled forlornly on its rack.

'No. Well, not exactly.'

Maddie looked at him and felt her insides swoop.

Even standing at a respectable distance away from her, he still seemed to invade her personal space. He was so...*big*...and his presence was so...*suffocatingly powerful*. Curiosity gripped her, and she wondered who exactly he was and what he did.

Where did he live? Why would a man like this be dawdling on a Saturday morning in this particular department store?

Alarmed, she cleared her throat, but for some reason found herself unable to drag her eyes away from his stunningly beautiful face. 'Australia. I'm Australian.'

'You've come from the other side of the world to work *here*?'

'Are you always so...so *rude*... Mr...? I don't even know your name!'

'You mean just in case you want to complain about me to your boss? My name is Leo. Shall we shake hands and make the introductions formal?'

Maddie stuck her hands firmly behind her back and glowered. 'I feel I can speak on behalf of my boss when I say that it's always useful to hear constructive criticism about the store, but your criticism isn't at all constructive, Mr... Mr...'

'Leo.'

She glanced around her and winced slightly at what she saw. 'I believe,' she said carefully, 'that the owner of the store passed away a short time ago. I don't think much has been done in terms of modernisation in recent years.'

'I have some experience of the retail market,' Leo said absently, his eyes still wandering over the shelves and wares around them.

Suddenly those eyes were back on hers and a smile tugged at his lips.

'This isn't a dinner invitation, but I see that there's a coffee shop on this floor. If you'd find it helpful, I could give you a few pearls of wisdom…'

'You've run a department store in the past?'

Leo grinned, his deep blue eyes lazy and amused. 'I wouldn't quite put it like that…'

'I get it.'

Maddie knew all about doing menial jobs to earn a living. She also knew all about the way people could look at someone attractive and misconstrue their place in the great pecking order. *She* didn't look like someone who should be mopping floors in a hospital on the outskirts of Sydney. If she had, her life would never have ended up taking the unfortunate twists and turns that it had.

She met his direct gaze and smiled.

That smile knocked Leo sideways. Just like that he wanted to drag her away from the tasteless display of goods, pull her into the nearest cupboard and get underneath that prim and proper clinical white get-up that wouldn't have gone amiss on a dental assistant. He wanted to kiss her raspberry-pink lips, crush them under his mouth, feel her tongue lashing against his, and then slowly, bit by bit, he wanted to get up close and personal with her body.

He suppressed a groan. She was still smiling, and his erection was getting more rigid by the second. He had to look away to catch his breath and focus on something innocuous. A stack of Gallo-label tea towels did the trick.

'You do?'

'I can understand. I've had lots of menial jobs in the past. Trust me—it's heavenly being here.' Maddie said it with the utmost sincerity.

Somehow they were walking away from the souvenir section towards the café.

Leo turned to her, his fingers hooking in the waistband of his low slung faded jeans.

'I'm thinking you'll probably get in trouble with the boss if you take time out to have a coffee with me.'

'I expect I might.'

The fierce antagonism that had filled her when she'd thought he was after her seemed to have evaporated. Somehow he'd managed to put her at ease. And Maddie wasn't sure whether to be alarmed at that development or happy about it.

Ever since Adam she'd made a habit of practically crossing the road to the other side of the street every time she spotted a man heading in her direction. Events had conspired to turn her social life, sparse as it had been, into a no-go zone. Men had been the first casualty of her experience with Adam and friends had fast followed, because her trust had been broken down to the point where it had all but disappeared.

But should she allow those experiences to follow her all the way to the other side of the world?

This was going to be her new home, and the last thing she wanted to do was to commence life in her new home as a crazy lady recluse.

Yes, warning bells had sounded when she'd first met Leo. But he wasn't rich, and as soon as she'd told him to back off he'd backed off. He wasn't from the area. He wasn't going to be around. He was also happy to talk to her about the store, and she could use a little impartial advice—even though he wouldn't know the reasons behind her wanting to hear what he had to say.

Sometimes nomads and wanderers—people who fell in and out of jobs— picked up life lessons along the way, and the very fact that they were streetwise gave them an added insight into life. Taking the path of adventure, untethered by the ropes that held most people down, brought its own rewards.

And, my word, was the man sexy...

She looked at him, every nerve-ending in her body tingling as he settled his fabulous eyes on her and allowed the silence between them to stretch to breaking point.

'How long are you going to be in this lovely city?' Maddie asked a little breathlessly, and Leo shrugged.

'Perhaps not even overnight,' he mused, harking back to his original plan and marvelling at the speed with which it had changed course along the way. Just as well as he was a man who could think on his feet and adapt.

At any rate, he'd probably seen everything there was to see with regard to the condition of the store, short of tapping on walls and peering into cupboards. He knew enough to settle the thorny matter of how much he should offer for the place and how fast he should move. He presumed the boss was ready to throw the towel in.

But that wasn't what was putting a smile on his face at the moment.

'It might be nice to…er…to have dinner with you.' Maddie blushed and glanced away.

'May I ask what's prompted the change of heart?' Leo asked wryly. 'Five minutes ago I was the devil incarnate for suggesting any such thing.'

'I…' Maddie took a deep breath. 'I haven't been in

Ireland long, and it would be…nice to have some company for a couple of hours. I've more or less stayed in on my own for the past few weeks.'

With her looks, Leo mused, solitude would have to be her chosen option—because she'd only have to step foot out of her front door and company would be available in any direction she chose to look.

But then that probably wasn't the sort of company she had in mind. The sort of company that came with strings attached. The sort of company she had assumed *he'd* been offering—and, frankly, her assumptions had been dead-on.

Leo wasn't surprised that her looks had made her wary of the attention she got—had made her guarded and cynical about what men wanted from her. It wasn't that different from the way his vast wealth had made *him* guarded and cynical when it came to the opposite sex.

He wasn't looking for commitment and he didn't do declarations of love. He enjoyed impermanence when it came to women.

Leo didn't know whether he might have gone down the normal route of marriage, two point two kids and a house in the country—or in his case several houses in several countries—if bitter experience hadn't taught him the value of steering clear of relationships.

His grandparents had been very happily married. His parents, he had been told, had likewise been very happily married—indeed, had been on something of a second honeymoon when a lorry, going too fast in bad weather, had slammed into their little Fiat and crushed it.

He had not been blighted by poor childhood memories or affected by warring parents or evil stepmothers. Alcohol, drug abuse and infidelity had been conspicuously and thankfully absent from his life. *His* cautionary tales stemmed from an altogether different source.

He shrugged aside this lapse in concentration as well as any niggling of his conscience, by reminding himself that he was as honourable as they came, because he was always, *always* upfront in his relationships. He told it like it was.

Sex and fun, but no cosy nights in front of the telly, no meeting the parents.

That said, he was a one-woman man, and any woman he dated would have all of him—if only for a limited amount of time. Largely, he was the one who usually called it a day, but he was perfectly happy if it were the other way around. He was the least possessive man he knew and he liked it that way.

He looked at Maddie in silence for a little while. She'd rebuffed him first time around, and he was sharp enough to pick up that little comment about how it would *'be nice to have company for a couple of hours'*.

'Tell me where you live,' he drawled. 'I'll pick you up.'

'You have a car?'

'I have a fleet of them,' he said, which was the absolute truth. 'Of course they're garaged in London—which is where, incidentally, I have my penthouse apartment—but if you tell me which make you'd prefer, I'll make sure it's delivered to me in time to collect you later. So, what's it to be? Ferrari? Range Rover? BMW? Or maybe something classic like an Aston Martin…?'

Maddie burst out laughing. The guy had a sense of humour and she liked that. She hadn't laughed for a long time, but now she was laughing so hard that tears came to her eyes.

Finally, sobering up, she said, still smiling, 'I'll meet you somewhere. I think there are some cheap and cheerful restaurants we could go to…'

'I'll give you my number. Text me. I'll meet you there at…what? Seven? What time does this place close?'

'Seven would be great. Now, really, I have to go…'

'One last thing…' Leo looked at her seriously. 'You need not fear that I'll make a pest of myself. I won't.'

Maddie reddened and an errant thought flashed through her head,

What would it be like if you were *to make a pest of yourself...?*

'Good,' she said nonchalantly. 'Because I've a lot going on in my life at the moment and the last thing I need is…is…'

'Fending off a nuisance?'

'I was going to say that the last thing I need is a relationship.'

At which Leo was the one to burst out laughing. He looked at her with his midnight-blue eyes, 'Trust me—relationships don't ever feature on my agenda. See you later, Maddie.'

And he was gone, leaving her standing as still as a statue, even though inside her everything was weirdly mushy, as though she'd just stepped off a death-defying rollercoaster ride and was struggling to get her bearings.

She spent the remainder of the day in a state of low-level excitement. She told herself that this wasn't a date. Not really. This was dinner with someone who'd made her laugh—because the alternative was yet another night in, going through the mountains of paperwork her solicitor had left for her, trying to work out the best approach to take when she went to see the bank manager for a loan the following week.

She was twenty-four years old! Where was the harm in acting her age? She couldn't remember the last time she'd felt young, and the tall, dark, handsome stranger had made her feel young.

And he wasn't going to be sticking around.

By seven that evening, as she stood outside the cheap Italian restaurant where they'd arranged to meet, the nerves which had abated at some point during the day were back in full swing.

She smoothed down the front of her shirt. No one could accuse her of dressing to impress. She was in a pair of ripped jeans, some flat navy ballet pumps and a tee shirt that was a little tighter than she liked and a little shorter than she might have wanted, exposing a sliver of flat brown skin. It, like the jeans, was faded and worn.

She'd had a brief flirtation with designer dressing. Adam had liked to see her in expensive gear and, much against her will, he had encouraged her into wearing clothes that he'd bought for her—expensive, slinky silk outfits and high, high designer heels.

He'd enjoyed the way everyone's heads had turned whenever she'd stalked into a room and Maddie had gone along with it, albeit reluctantly, because she'd loved him and had wanted to please him.

She'd sent the entire lot back to his flash apartment when their relationship had crashed and burned, and had promptly returned to the sorts of clothes she'd always felt comfortable in.

Leo, at least, would appreciate her choice of clothing, since they came from the same side of the tracks.

Feeling more buoyant, she pushed open the door to the trattoria and looked around, hoping she'd arrived before he had because then she could have a drink to steady her nerves, and also hoping that she hadn't, because to arrive early might suggest that she was desperate for male company. More than that—desperate for *his* company.

Nursing a drink at the very back of the restaurant, Leo had spotted her immediately. How could he not? The entire restaurant had spotted her at roughly the same time. Every male head swung round. Mouths fell open. In fairness to her, she didn't seem to notice any of this as she peered around her, squinting into the semi-lit depths of the trattoria, which was noisy, packed and uncomfortable.

In a room full of pale faces her honeyed tan stood out, as did her hair, flowing in a wavy mane over narrow shoulders almost down to her waist. Leo half stood and she walked towards him, weaving a path through the crowds until she was right in front of him.

'Been here before?' he asked, and when she shook her head he nodded and scanned the room. 'Do you think we'll be able to have a conversation or should we resign ourselves to shouting?'

'It's cheap and cheerful. And I hear that the food's good.'

She slipped into a chair and tried not to drink in his masculine beauty. She'd just about managed to convince herself that he couldn't possibly be as striking as she remembered, but he was even more so. He radiated a dynamism that made her shiver with awareness, and his exotic colouring only added to the potent appeal of his good looks.

Very quickly Maddie had a glass of wine to calm her nerves, even though common sense told her there was nothing to be nervous about.

Certainly he was sticking to the script. If his original dinner invitation had set her antennae onto red alert, actually being here with him was doing the opposite, dispelling any misgivings she might have been harbouring about his intentions.

He was charm itself. He chatted about the many countries he had visited—which made sense because he was obviously a guy who lived for the present and absorbed whatever adventures life had to offer. It was something she really admired. He was witty and insightful, and she found herself laughing out loud at some of his anecdotes, barely noticing the antipasti he had ordered for them to share.

'I envy you,' she said truthfully as plates were cleared, glasses refilled and bowls of pasta placed in front of them. 'I've never got to travel. I would have loved to, but my mum and I barely had enough to make ends meet and we would never have been able to afford it. I guess it's a lot easier when you only have yourself to consider, and I suppose you could always pick up jobs here and there to pay your way…'

'I do try and get myself an honest day's work when I'm abroad,' he said, almost uncomfortably. 'Tell me why you've run away from Australia.'

The abrupt change in the conversation caught Maddie off-guard and she stiffened—her natural response whenever she thought about her past. What would this complete stranger think were she to tell him the truth? He might be an adventurer, living off the land and shunning responsibility, but that didn't mean that he wouldn't be judgemental if she were to share her story with him.

The *whole* of her story.

Maddie found that she didn't want him to think badly of her. 'Whoever said anything about running away?' she hedged lightly, winding long strands of spaghetti around her fork and avoiding eye contact.

Leo raised his eyebrows wryly. He sat back and gave her the benefit of his full attention, which was enough to make her blush furiously.

Her glass-green eyes drifted to his forearms, strong and muscled and sprinkled with dark hair, and she wondered what it would be like to be touched by them, to have his hands roam and explore her body. Her heart picked up speed and she licked her lips, panicked by the way her body was insisting on slipping its leash and running wild.

'Well,' Leo drawled, his voice a low murmur that made the hairs on the nape of her neck stand on end, 'looking at the facts: you're on the other side of the world, without a network of fellow travelling friends, and working in a job that can't really be classed as career-building. You haven't mentioned anything about studying, so I'm thinking that's not relevant. Which leads me to think that you're running away from something. Or someone. Or both.'

Maddie laughed, but the tide of colour in her cheeks was more vibrant now. 'My mum died,' she said, twirling the stem of her wine glass and then pausing as he filled it with more wine. 'I'd spent some time looking after her. It was very unexpected. Bad luck, really. She broke her leg, and it was a very complex break, but it should have been okay.' She blinked furiously. 'Unfortunately the operation turned out to be a fiasco. She was confined to hospital for much longer than anticipated and then she needed a great deal of further surgery. Every time she felt she was back on her feet something would go wrong and back she would have to go.'

'How old were you when all this happened?'

'Just before my twentieth birthday,' Maddie admitted.

'Must have been tough.'

'Everyone goes through tough times.' She brushed off any show of sympathy because she was close enough to tears already. But she could see sympathy in the deep navy eyes resting on her and that was weird, because her very first impression of him had been of a guy who was as hard as nails.

Something about the predatory way he moved, the cool, lazy self-assurance in his eyes, the arrogant set of his features… But then being wary of the opposite sex, suspecting the worst before the worst could happen, had become a way of life for her.

'*You* must have,' she said lightly, blushing. 'Gone through rough times, I mean? Or at least had one or two hairy encounters! Isn't that part and parcel of being a nomad? A side effect of living life as an adventurer?'

Leo was enjoying the tinge of colour staining her cheeks. *Australia.* Hence the golden hue of her skin. Next to her, the other women in the restaurant seemed pale and anaemic.

He shrugged, adept as always at evading any sort of real sharing. 'Sisters? Brothers?' he asked. 'Anyone out there for you when your mother was ill?'

'Just me.' Maddie realised that somewhere along the line food had been eaten and plates cleared away. She couldn't remember when exactly that had happened. 'My mother was from here, actually...'

'Ireland?' Startled, Leo caught her eyes.

'As a matter of fact, she was.'

Maddie wondered what he would think if she told him that she was the owner of the very store he had been busy criticising only hours before. He didn't look the type to scare easily, but men could be funny when it came to women being higher up the financial pecking order than they were.

'Hence you're returning to your motherland...?'

'I thought it made sense. I wanted to get out of Australia after...after everything...'

Leo didn't say anything, but his gaze was penetrating.

The waiter had approached, asking them what they'd thought of their meal, pressing them to sample some dessert but they both politely declined, asking only for the bill.

Maddie reached into her rucksack, withdrawing a wallet and extracting notes.

'What are you doing?' he asked with a frown.

'Paying my way.' Maddie looked at him, surprised at his reaction to what she thought was perfectly obvious.

'When I go out with a woman *I* foot the bill,' Leo asserted.

She stiffened. 'Not this woman. I pay my half. That way I'm in no one's debt.'

'The price of a cheap Italian meal doesn't put you in my *debt*.' Leo tossed a handful of euros onto the silver platter—enough to cover the meal with an overly generous tip.

'Have you never met a man who knows how to treat a woman?' he asked, rising to his feet.

Maddie thought of her ex-boyfriend. Adam had *loved* paying for things for her. Flowers, chocolates, expensive meals out—but with the lavishing of gifts had come the manacles of control, the compulsion to turn her into something he wanted. And underneath all that had been his superiority—thinking that by making her into his doll he was asserting ascendancy over her, owning her.

But she'd remained the girl from the wrong side of the tracks, and sure enough that was something that couldn't be buried under gifts and presents. Inevitably she'd learned a valuable lesson in the perils of ever thinking that someone rich and well-connected could ever be anything but condescending and manipulative.

Anyway, all those wildly expensive gifts had made her feel horribly uncomfortable, and she certainly didn't like the idea of Leo or anyone else paying for her. As she had found to her cost, there was no such thing as a free lunch.

'Are you asking me if I've ever met a man who knows how to reach for his wallet and buy me pretty baubles?' She slapped a few euros on the table. The waiter was going to be very happy indeed with the extravagant tip coming his way. 'Because if that's what you're asking then, yes, I have. And it didn't work out for me. Which is why I prefer to keep things simple and pay my way.'

She stood up, and Leo shrugged, but his deep, dark eyes were assessing and thoughtful.

'Far be it from me to tear someone away from her closely held principles,' he murmured.

They headed outside, walking in the balmy summer air in no particular direction.

Except with some surprise Maddie realised that her

legs were somehow moving towards the honeycomb of streets where her grandfather's house was. It was on the outskirts of the city centre and, whilst the location was to die for, the house was not nearly as grand as some of the others and was in a state of disrepair.

The old man, so she had been told by her solicitor, had gradually downsized over the years, more and more as his healthy income had been whittled away to next to nothing, lost in gambling dens and crates of whiskey.

Maddie had wondered whether the absence of his only child had perhaps fuelled that spiral of despair, which had made her even more motivated to accept the challenge that had been bequeathed to her.

She stole a sneaky glance at the towering, over-the-top, sex-on-legs guy next to her and suddenly felt ashamed that she had snapped at him for trying to be a gentleman when in all likelihood he couldn't afford it any more than she could.

'Sorry,' she apologised sheepishly. 'You hit a sore spot there.'

Leo paused and looked down at her, holding her eyes with his, his expression speculative.

Her body trembled as she gazed back up at him, her eyes undoubtedly betraying her want.

'I'll be on my way,' Leo murmured, breaking eye contact to stare up the road which was still as busy now as it had been hours previously. New York was not the only city, it would seem, that never slept.

'Leo…' Maddie breathed.

She wanted him. She didn't know whether it was because she was lonely or because the unexpected stirring of attraction had reminded her that she was still young after all. Maybe he had unlocked some realisation that she couldn't remain a prisoner of her past for the rest of her life.

Or maybe he was just so damned sexy that she simply couldn't resist the pull of raw, primal lust.

Two ships passing in the night, she thought…

'Do you want me to kiss you?' Leo asked on a husky murmur, still not touching her.

'No!' Thank goodness they had managed to find themselves in a quiet corner of the otherwise busy street.

'Then you need to stop looking at me like that.'

'Like what?'

'Like you want to eat me up…like you'd like *me* to eat *you* up.'

'Leo…'

'We're both adults,' Leo delivered on a rough undertone, 'so I'll be honest. You're spectacular-looking and I want you more than I can remember wanting any woman for a long time. I want to touch you. I want to taste you…*everywhere.* But I don't do long-term and in this instance we're talking a one-night stand. A one-night stand to remember, but still a one-night stand. If you don't like that, then walk away, Maddie.'

'I always promised myself that I would never have a one-night stand,' Maddie said, by rote, but her body was certainly not walking away. Indeed, it was staying very firmly put.

Leo shrugged, holding her gaze.

Confusion tore through Maddie, because she wasn't lying. She'd never been a one-night stand kind of girl. From a young age her looks had attracted attention, and she had learned very fast that attention from the opposite sex more often than not bypassed the important stuff—like getting to know her, giving her credit for having a brain and seeing beyond the fact that she was, in Leo's words, 'spectacular-looking'. Adam had only served to cement those lessons in her head.

But…

But, but, but...

'Would you like to come in for a cup of coffee?' she hazarded.

Leo's eyebrows shot up. He refused to let her hide behind the cup of coffee scenario. 'You want me. And I want you. I'll accept the offer of coffee, but I'm not interested in a push-pull game of one step forward followed by two back.'

'Nor am I.' She tiptoed forward, filled with a sense of heady daring, and brushed his perfect mouth with hers.

CHAPTER THREE

After a brisk walk away from the city centre, they found themselves in a tree-lined avenue filled with mansions.

'I don't live in one of these.'

Maddie didn't look at him as she said this but her cheeks were flaming red. She wasn't lying, but she was uncomfortably conscious of the fact that she had played fast and loose with the truth.

She consoled herself with the obvious justification that launching into a garbled, long-winded explanation about inheritances and distant relatives was not relevant, given they were not going to be in one another's lives for longer than this one night.

Which brought her full circle, questioning what she was doing. A one-night stand? Her proud, stubborn, fiercely independent mother would have had a heart attack on the spot, because she had drummed it into her only child that you had to choose carefully when it came to giving your body to someone else.

'You'll make mistakes,' Lizzie Gallo had told her daughter, 'but it's still important to go into every relationship thinking it could be the one.'

Reflecting now on that advice, Maddie had to concede that her mother might not have ended up where she had, if she'd a one-night stand with Maddie's father rather than running away with him, only to be abandoned the second he realised that the fortune he'd banked on Lizzie's father providing wasn't going to be coming his way.

Disinheritance in the name of love hadn't been his thing. He'd stuck around just long enough to determine that there was going to be no reconciliation between daughter and rich daddy, and then he'd scarpered.

'But I gave it my all,' her mother had said, in one of her rare moments of honesty—because Lizzie Gallo had never been someone to moan and look backwards. 'And, for me, that was the main thing. You climb into bed with someone for a few hours and, believe me, you won't feel great when you climb out of it so that you can do the walk of shame back home.'

Well, that, Maddie reflected, sneaking a sidelong glance at the virtual stranger who had somehow managed to ensnare her into jettisoning all her principles, had not exactly served her well when it came to Adam.

She'd thrown herself into her relationship with Adam and given it everything. She'd been so in love with the idea of being in love that she'd missed all the warning signs of a relationship that had been made anywhere but in heaven.

This time... *This time she knew what she was getting into.* No girlish fantasies and romantic daydreams about Prince Charming only for Prince Charming to turn out to be Mr Toad. She was with a guy who wasn't interested in laying down roots and who'd made it perfectly clear what he wanted.

She felt the bloom of longing between her legs and swallowed down a rush of powerful excitement.

The houses they were passing now were getting smaller and finally, at the end of the elegant road, she swung up the only drive that was unkempt.

'Not what I expected.' Leo glanced at the edifice of what must once upon a time been a rather charming cottage but now looked like something from the Land that Time Forgot.

'What did you expect?'

Maddie unlocked the front door and pushed it open into a hallway that was worn, but still carried the hallmarks of the house it had once been. A flagstone floor, an old-fashioned wooden umbrella stand, a sturdy banister leading upstairs, and worn paintwork with great big discoloured patches from where she had removed dark, lugubrious paintings.

'Something a little less…imposing…'

'Does that bother you?'

'Why should it?'

She'd turned to look at him and Leo could not resist the urge to touch, to feel the smoothness of her cheeks. He ran an exploratory finger over her striking cheekbones and then outlined the contours of her full mouth. When she shivered, he smiled with undisguised hunger.

'I don't know how you do what you do to me,' he murmured, trailing his finger down towards her tee shirt and stopping just where the shadow of her cleavage began, 'but all I want to do right now is rip those clothes off you and take you right here, right now…'

Maddie's breath caught in her throat and she unconsciously arched her body up, so that her small, high breasts pushed towards him in a bold invitation for him to touch.

It was clear she wanted him—so badly that it was a physical ache—and her whole body shuddered as he slipped his hand underneath her tee shirt and then cupped her breast briefly, before tugging the lacy bra to one side so that he could feel the softness of her skin and the tightness of her nipple.

Positioning himself in front of her, Leo reached under the shirt with both hands, pushing up her bra completely to free her breasts, all the while keeping his eyes firmly pinned to her face, because he was absolutely loving the mesmerised hot burn of desire in her bright green eyes.

He stroked her nipples with the pads of his thumbs and her lips parted on a sigh of pleasure.

'Liking it?'

'Don't stop.'

If *he* couldn't understand the primal urgency of his reaction to her, then the same must be said for her. Leo didn't need any more encouragement. He removed her tee shirt in one easy movement and for a few seconds just looked at her perfect breasts, no more than a handful, tipped with rosy buds. His erection was hard and heavy and painful, and he had to breathe in deep to control the fierce sweep of lust.

Her head was flung back, her eyes closed as he slowly backed her towards the staircase, and then she was standing, holding on to the banister, her body beautifully positioned for him to attend to her naked breasts.

Which he did.

He suckled one stiffened nipple, licking and teasing it with his tongue, while he readied the other for his ministrations with his fingers. Her soft moans were doing all sorts of wonderful things to his body and right now he couldn't get enough of her. It was remarkable.

Leaving one throbbing nipple behind, he gave a repeat performance on the other, drawing it deep into his mouth while his tongue continued to torment her.

Maddie reached down to undo the button of his jeans but Leo stopped her.

He would have liked to kid himself that this was to do with his mastering the situation and taking his time, but he had to admit wryly to himself that it was more to do with breaking things off briefly so that he could gather his crazily scattered self-control. Any more touching and he would have to fight not to explode without warning.

'What about the coffee?' he reminded her shakily, and Maddie blinked, roused from her slumberous enjoyment and clearly desperate for him to carry on touching her.

'Coffee?' she parroted weakly, which actually made Leo burst out laughing.

He kissed her on the mouth—a teasing, gentle kiss that made her squirm because it was so tender.

'You can't promise a man coffee and then renege on the offer…'

'Of course not.'

Maddie grinned and slung her arms around his neck to pull him towards her, before shuffling her heated body back into her bra and tee shirt while he watched with avid, devouring hunger. Then she reached out to pepper his sexy mouth with little, darting kisses before slipping her tongue in.

'You're a witch,' he muttered against her mouth.

In the grip of a situation he could never have predicted, Leo followed her towards the back of the house and into a kitchen which, as with the rest of what he'd seen, was in dire need of attention.

'Tell me what you're doing in a house like this,' Leo said, his eyes returning to her slender frame, her back towards him as she made them both mugs of coffee.

Maddie stilled, but only for a fraction of a second, and then she said lightly, 'I can thank a relative for the use of this house. It's not much, but it's brilliant just having a roof over my head. Even a roof that springs leaks when it rains. You should see the corridor upstairs. I've learned just where to position the buckets and pans.' She spun round to hand him his mug. 'You never told me whether it bothers you?'

'I believe I said, why should it?'

'Well,' she said, 'you might get it into your head that I'm a snob because I happen to be staying in a house like this. You might think that we're from different worlds and that wouldn't be the case.'

'Whether it's the case or not,' Leo countered smoothly, 'it doesn't really matter, does it? We're here to enjoy ourselves, not analyse one another's beliefs.'

He let her lead the way into a sitting room, where she opted for switching on one of the lamps on the table rather than the overhead light.

The sofas were deep and squashy, but there were an abnormal amount of small tables and a feeling of a place stuck in time. Leo had no idea where this helpful relative was, but he sincerely hoped he was on an urgent spending spree to replace the furnishings.

He placed his cup on one of the many tables and sat next to her on one of the sofas. Sprawled against one end, he crooked his finger and she wriggled up towards him. He swivelled her so that she was lying against him, her back pressed against his body, nicely pushing down on his hard, thick erection.

He took her coffee from her and settled them both into a more comfortable position.

If this house belonged to him, he decided on the spot, he would put a floor-to-ceiling mirror on the opposite wall for an occasion such as this, when he would have enjoyed nothing better than seeing their reflection, watching the little changes on her beautiful face as he touched her.

He removed the tee shirt once more, wondering why she had bothered to put it back on in the first place when it was always just going to come off again, and cupped her breasts in his hands, playing with them and working her up bit by bit.

Looking down at her, with the soft, flowery scent of her hair filling his nostrils, Leo could see the faint blush of her skin. She was still golden, but paler where her clothes had protected her from the sun, and against the paleness of her breasts her nipples were deep rosy discs. He badly wanted to suckle on them again but he would wait.

At least, he reflected wryly, he wasn't on the verge of coming prematurely. A temporary reprieve from the unthinkable.

She was wearing button-fly jeans and he began undoing the buttons one at a time until he could glimpse her white knickers.

'Take your jeans off,' he murmured. 'I'd do it myself, but my hands are otherwise occupied at the moment.'

He moved them back to her breasts as she wriggled

out of the jeans, leaving her underwear on. The jeans fell to the floor and then she squirmed a little, like a cat preparing to settle on a feather cushion. She reached up and began to turn around, but he stilled her with his hands, silently instructing her to stay as she was.

'I'm hanging on to my self-control by a thread,' he confided. 'Turn around and I won't be able to predict what might happen. Your eyes do something to me…'

Maddie laughed. And as his hand moved from breast to ribcage she parted her legs and whimpered with pleasure.

'I wish I could see your face,' Leo said huskily, and she laughed again.

'I'm glad you can't. I'd be embarrassed.'

Leo grunted. He was accustomed to flamboyant women who weren't easily embarrassed—and certainly not by antics between the sheets. He found her diffidence a turn-on.

Gently he slipped his hand underneath her white panties, felt the brush of downy hair against his fingers, and as he slid one long brown finger into her wetness he couldn't prevent a groan of pure sensual enjoyment.

He found the throbbing bud and she moaned as he began playing with it. She parted her legs further and he cupped her briefly before carrying on with what he'd been doing.

Maddie feverishly wriggled out of her underwear. Sensation was tearing into her and she found that she could scarcely breathe. When she looked down to see the motion of his hand as he played with her she wanted to pass out from the sheer erotic pleasure of it.

Letting go of the last of her inhibitions, she gave herself over to what he was doing to her body. The rhythmic stroke of his finger against her core was taking her higher and higher, and her breathing was staccato as she moved against his hand, bucking and arching, and then, as a low groan was wrenched out of her, she toppled over the edge and spasmed against his fingers in an orgasm that went on and on and on, an unstoppable spiral of pleasure.

Spent, Maddie lay against him, her eyes closed. And then, as she floated back to earth, she turned around and straddled him.

Strangely, she wanted him even more now, but she would have to give her body time to recover. She linked her fingers behind his neck and smiled.

'That was…wonderful…' she confessed.

Leo placed his hands on her waist. He could very nearly circle it with his hands, she was so slender.

'For me too.'

'I'm sorry. It was selfish of me to come, but I couldn't hold off.'

'I didn't want you to,' he said roughly. 'You'll come again, but next time I'll be deep inside you, and when you do I'll see your face and watch when the moment happens.'

Maddie blushed, because she had never indulged in this sort of sexual banter, and the way he was holding her gaze was such a turn-on that she could almost come again without him having to touch her.

She buried her face against the side of his neck and felt a pang, something so sharp and painful that she almost drew back—a pang of *missing.*

She swept that silly feeling aside and this time *she* was the one to touch and arouse. She stripped him of his clothing, looked in wonder at his impressive size. When she ordered him to lie back on the sofa, he laughed.

'I guess we should migrate upstairs to a bed,' she said at one point, in between licking him, teasing him with her mouth and kissing him.

'Why? This sofa does very nicely indeed…'

Was that because a sofa somehow carried on the one-night stand theme? Maddie wondered.

She lost herself in the wonder of his glorious body. He was lean and strong, and the dark hair on his chest felt like a declaration of masculinity. He was all man. Alpha male to the very core of him. And she couldn't get enough of his body, of *him*.

This time things moved at a pace that allowed them to explore one another as if they had all the time in the world.

Where his fingers had been, his mouth explored. He tasted between her thighs until she was practically crying for him to take her all the way. She tasted him as well, and his hands curled into her long hair, directing her so that she knew what felt good for him—although she quickly discovered that she seemed to have a second sense for pleasing him.

Or maybe it was simply the fact that the novelty of this situation had made him so aroused that whatever she did and wherever she touched it would have the same dramatic effect.

Leo wanted to hang on. Hell, it shouldn't be a problem. He was a master when it came to self-control in the bedroom—a guy who knew how to orchestrate sex and time it to perfection. Not so now.

He couldn't hang on. He couldn't find his self-control or *any* kind of control for that matter. He couldn't think. He just had to have her before he splintered into a million pieces.

Whatever world he had entered, it was in a different league from anything he had ever experienced in his life before. Savage want poured through his body in waves that carried the ferocity of a sledgehammer, knocking him for six and wiping out his formidable composure.

The disconnect between his head and his body had never been greater, but all that was forgotten when he thrust into her and felt her body arch up to meet his, moulding and fitting against him as smoothly as a hand fitted into a glove personally made for it.

Leo felt as though she had been fashioned for him, her body so perfectly tuned to his that the straightforward business of making love was elevated into an experience beyond description.

His climax was the most powerful he had ever had, and he only surfaced when it was over and his body was well and truly spent. Then he turned her to face him so that their naked bodies were pressed together.

'Maddie…' The self-control that had been left at the front door now made its presence known. 'We didn't… *hell…*' He groaned aloud and raked his fingers through his hair. 'It's never happened before but I didn't use protection. Are you…this is not be a question I should ever have to ask…but are you on the pill?'

Slumberous green cat's eyes focused on him and she frowned. 'No. No, I'm not.'

How could she have taken a chance like this?

But then, he thought, she'd taken it for the same reason he had. Because lust had been so much more overwhelming than common sense. Their bodies had been on fire and the notion of protection hadn't even registered.

'There's not a lot we can do now…' She sighed and squirmed, the heat of his body already scattering her thoughts and fogging her mind.

Leo was astounded at the speed with which he was prepared to immerse himself in that vague assurance, but he reminded himself that he had friends who'd taken months, and in a couple of cases years, to achieve what he'd always been scrupulous in protecting himself against.

He placed his hand on her waist and shifted. This was a one-night stand. Right about now he should be getting his act together and telling her that it was time for him to go.

'Maddie…'

'I hope you have a good trip back to…to…'

Maddie was quick to silence any little voice that wanted to promote something more than the one-night stand that was on the table.

She feathered a kiss on his mouth. 'To wherever it is you're going next.'

'London.' Leo cleared his throat. 'I'm going straight down to London from here.'

'Well, in that case I hope you have a very good trip back down to London. Say hi to Big Ben for me.' She traced an idle pattern on his hard, naked chest.

'It's possible,' Leo inserted gruffly, without batting an eyelid, 'that I could explore Dublin for a few days, however…'

It could work. He could do a few background checks on the store, fill in the blanks. It wouldn't hurt. And while he was here he could wine and dine this woman who had just made the earth move for him. Wine and dine on a budget, of course, bearing in mind that she thought that he was in the same financial bracket as she was.

The thought held a great deal of appeal for Leo. He wasn't ready to chalk this heady experience down as a one-night stand. He was a man who had always had everything he wanted—and certainly every woman he had ever wanted. Having it all, however, had definite downsides…one of which was a jaded palate. Maddie, from the other side of the world, was like a dose of pure, life-giving oxygen.

Doubtless this sense of exhilaration would wither and die after a couple of nights, because they had absolutely nothing in common and sex, however earth-moving, was just sex after all, but in the meantime…

He pulled her back towards him, wanting her all over again. The more he thought about it, the more appealing was the idea of playing truant for a couple of days, of taking time out from life as he knew it.

'Really? You might stay here for a while?'

Maddie felt as though a cloud she hadn't even realised had been there had suddenly lifted to reveal a bank of unexpected sunshine.

'There's nothing more exciting than exploring a new city.'

'That would be lovely,' Maddie said.

Leo grinned. 'Let's go for a bit more enthusiasm,' he encouraged,

Maddie hesitated. She'd geared herself up for a one-night stand, at the end of which she'd wave goodbye to this stranger who had filled her life with joy for a brief period of time. A two-or three-night stand posed a few more issues, and top of the list was the fact that she hadn't been entirely truthful with him.

'Okay.' She smiled and wriggled against him, and felt the jut of his erection against her belly. 'I'd really like that. But there's something I feel I ought to tell you…'

'Please don't tell me that you're a married woman with a jealous husband hiding in a cupboard somewhere.'

'Of course I'm not!'

'Then what?'

He gently pushed her onto her back and rose up over her, nudging her with the tip of his throbbing erection, swiping it slowly against her core until she was losing track of what she wanted to tell him.

No condoms? No problem. There were myriad ways to pleasure one another without penetration, and in the morning they could stockpile protection.

'I'm not quite who you think I am. I mean, you've got the major details, but there's one little thing… You know the store?'

'The store?' Leo nudged a little further into her moistness, clearly only half registering what she was saying because his body was already taking over and deciding where its priorities lay. *Not* in a heart-to-heart discussion.

'Where we met.'

'Ah, *that* store. What about it?'

'I'm not actually a shop assistant there.'

'No? Shoplifter?'

Maddie laughed. In the short space of time she'd known him she'd found that he had a brilliant sense of humour.

'Owner, as a matter of fact.'

Leo stilled and slowly pulled back so that he was staring down at her, scarcely believing his ears. *'Owner...?'*

Sensing the shift in atmosphere, Maddie laughed nervously. 'It doesn't matter,' she assured him. 'I haven't suddenly turned into a crashing snob.'

'Owner? Please explain. I'm all ears.'

He slung his muscular legs over the side of the sofa and began getting dressed.

Maddie didn't try to stop him—if he wanted to leave then he should leave—but she felt as though a black hole had opened up beneath her feet.

'My grandfather owned the store.'

Maddie was beginning to feel uncomfortable now, and disadvantaged because she was still naked and vulnerable. So she too began to sling on the clothes she had earlier discarded in such excited haste.

From having their bodies pressed so closely together they might have been one, they now stood awkwardly in the dimly lit living room, facing one another like sparring opponents in a ring.

Maddie had no idea why or how this had occurred. But past experience had taught her the wisdom of developing a tough outer shell, and it came into effect now, stiffening her backbone, lending defiance to her glass-green eyes.

'I'm listening,' Leo said softly.

'I never met him. He and my mother fell out before I was born and never reconciled. But when he died a short while back he left the entire store to me, along with this house.' She gestured to encompass the building in which they were standing. 'And a few other bits and pieces. I'm sorry I wasn't upfront with you, but I didn't see the point of launching into my back story.'

'I had no idea…' Leo said slowly.

Tommaso's granddaughter. This changed everything, and already the shutters were falling into place. He didn't believe in age-old enmities, and he certainly didn't believe in taking sides in a feud in which he had played no part, but something stirred in him—a sense of injustice done to his grandfather. Was this what they meant when they said that blood was thicker than water?

That aside, he intended to buy the place—whoever or whatever stood in his way—and the woman standing in front of him now was no longer the lover he wanted to keep in his bed but his adversary in a deal he intended to close.

'I don't see that it changes anything.' Maddie winced at the plea hidden behind her words.

'It changes *everything*,' Leo said softly, heading towards the door.

'Because you've found out I'm not impoverished?' Maddie threw at him, half following, but only because she was so angry and bewildered.

'You'll find out why soon enough…'

Pride held her back and killed the questions rising fast inside her, but when she heard the front door slam she sagged onto the sofa.

She didn't care. He meant nothing to her! She wasn't going to beat herself up about her decision to go to bed with him and she certainly wasn't going to waste time asking herself what he'd meant by that parting shot.

CHAPTER FOUR

MADDIE HAD HUNDREDS of steps to take and a veritable long and winding road to go before she could ever begin to return the store she had inherited to its former glory. But, despite the fact that she had no formal training in business, she discovered she had an innate talent for the work and enjoyed the straightforward process of planning a way forward.

If you could call climbing a mountain straightforward…

Certainly over the next fortnight work occupied her mind to the point where she could almost come close to forgetting about her encounter with Leo.

Almost but not quite.

In the quiet hours she spent in the house, meticulously working out how to pull it apart so that she could put it together again, he invaded her thoughts like a stealthy intruder, finding his way into all the nooks and crannies of her mind.

She had no regrets about what they had done. She had taken a risk and lived in the moment and she had enjoyed every minute of it. But she had to ask herself whether she had somehow inherited her mother's gene for always picking the wrong man. First Adam and then Leo.

With finances for moving forward with the store's

overhaul now in place, thanks to a sympathetic bank manager who was as keen as she to see the store resume its rightful place as the leading light in the city centre, there was just one hurdle left to overcome.

'There's a buyer waiting in the wings,' her lawyer, Anthony, had told her three days previously, 'and he is prepared to be hostile to get the store.'

'Over my dead body.'

The house had been remortgaged, dozens of valuable paintings and artefacts which had been bought when her grandfather had been living in boom times had been sold, and sufficient capital acquired to support the loan from the bank. Maddie had got little sleep while putting it all together, and she wasn't going to have the rug pulled from under her feet at the last minute.

But Anthony had told her that with a good enough offer on the table he would find it hard not to advise a sale. He had then gone into the complexities of the money she was being lent, and interest rates and time frames, and Maddie had zoned out, focusing only on the fight that lay ahead of her.

More than ever, as she fought to get things in order, it seemed to her that she was doing something the grandfather she had never met had intended her to do.

She'd never known what it was like to have any sort of extended family. Her mother had been tight-lipped on the subject of her own family, which had been diminished to just her father by the time she had left for Australia with the man who would eventually turn out to be precisely the fortune-hunter she had been warned against.

Maddie had always secretly felt saddened at the thought of her grandfather perhaps trying to keep in touch. Who knew? Her mother had died relatively young. Perhaps if she hadn't she would have eventually swallowed her pride and returned to England.

Just being in the house where her grandfather had lived had warmed Maddie towards the man she had never known. In her mind he had been a kindly gentleman who had been big-hearted enough to leave all his worldly goods to her.

No one was going to deprive her of her legacy and everything that was wrapped up with it. This slice of her past had completed her—filled in the dots about where she had come from. It wasn't just a business deal for her. It was a reconnection with the past she had never known, and it was giving her a sense of direction and purpose in a life that had always held a lot of unanswered questions.

Which didn't mean that she wasn't feeling sick to her stomach as she and Anthony strode into the imposing glass house on the outskirts of the city centre where a meeting of the buyer's lawyers had been arranged on neutral territory.

'Where are we?' she asked nervously as they entered the building and were faced with grey modernist splendour.

She'd dressed in her most serious outfit, bought especially for the occasion—a sober grey suit, a crisp white shirt and very high black heels that would give her the advantage over any hostile bidder because in her heels she was at least six foot tall. Provided she didn't sit down, she was sure she would appear a sufficiently commanding figure and be able to announce to the assembled crowd that she wasn't someone to be messed with.

She could tell that Anthony, who only just reached her shoulder, approved of the tactic.

She had also pinned her chaotic hair back into a neat chignon that had taken for ever to do and had almost made her late.

'We're within the hallowed walls of one of the most influential companies in the country,' Anthony adjusted his tie a little nervously. 'Mostly building and construction, but recently diversifying into electronics and smart installations in new-builds.'

'Impressive.'

'Our buyer obviously has a lot of connections if he can snap his fingers and arrange for the meeting to be held here. I've done my background research and he's made of money.'

'Well, money isn't everything. Maybe he's trying to intimidate us.'

Maddie told herself that scare tactics weren't going to work, but she was as nervous as a kitten as they were escorted along a cool marble walkway that circled an impressive courtyard, which was visible through banks of glass. When she looked down she could see a few figures dotted around a central fountain, enjoying the sunshine even though it wasn't yet lunchtime.

Then, looking ahead, she saw opaque glass, and as their escort stood aside she entered a long, brightly lit room. *Quite a few men*, was Maddie's first thought. All kitted out in regulation charcoal-grey business suits.

Except one.

One man dominated the space around him and was head and shoulders taller than every other man there. He was not wearing a suit. Black jeans and a black polo shirt, short-sleeved. The epitome of *I don't give a damn what I wear* cool.

Leo.

* * *

Leo had been expecting her, but he still felt a sizzle of something as she walked into the room, towering over the short man next to her, so strikingly pretty that every single male in the room fell silent.

His white teeth snapped together in a surge of something primitive and proprietorial.

He'd had her. She was his.

His woman.

Except, he thought as logic reasserted itself, she wasn't, was she? She was his opponent. And, as such, no time must be wasted on thinking about all her delectable, distracting assets.

His midnight-deep eyes roved broodingly over her. She was wearing the most boring outfit in the world, but even that couldn't stand in the way of his imagination which had already taken flight.

He mentally stripped her. Got rid of the dreadful suit and the prissy top. Unhooked whatever bra she was wearing and pulled down her panties. Why had she tied her hair back? The urge to see it spilling in colourful splendour over her slender shoulders was so powerful that he had to steady himself.

It had been over a fortnight.

He hadn't been braced to walk away from her but walk away he had—because, with him, business always came first. Always had, always would.

There wasn't a woman in the world who could damage that sacred pecking order.

But he knew that he was getting excited just looking at her and thinking about what she'd felt like under him and over him and touching him and inviting him to touch her everywhere.

That sign of weakness enraged him, and he broke the mental connection by stepping forward and walking straight towards her.

It took willpower she had never known she'd possessed to hold her ground and not fall back as the one man she had never expected to see again sauntered towards her.

What on earth was going on?

Maddie knew that whatever impression she was making it wasn't that of a confident businesswoman in charge of the situation. More a gaping goldfish, stranded and gasping for air.

'I don't understand…' She stared at Leo, her breathing rapid and shallow, as though she'd been running a marathon, her nostrils flaring as she inhaled the clean, woody scent of him.

She'd thought about him so much that she could scarcely believe that he was standing in front of her—especially as none of it seemed to make any sense.

Leo didn't say anything for a few seconds, and when he did speak it was to tell the assembled crowd that they could leave.

'I'll deal with this privately,' he said dismissively. 'When the transaction is agreed you can prepare the required paperwork.'

'Maddie… Ms Gallo…' Anthony approached her with an expression of concern—only to meet Leo's cool navy eyes.

'Maddie will be as safe as houses with me,' he said, addressing the much shorter man in a kindly voice that made Maddie's teeth snap together in anger because it was just so…*patronising.*

'Now, wait just a minute…er…'

'Leo. You know my name. You just don't know my surname. Conti.'

'You're…you're…' Her brain was moving at a snail's pace.

Yes, Conti was the name of the man who was planning on pulling the rug from under her feet. Maddie vaguely recalled that much sinking in when Anthony had explained the situation to her. She'd been far too wrapped up in feeling angry that someone could just swan along and try and snatch the store away from her before she'd even had a chance to do something with it.

The men in suits were quietly leaving the room. Maddie was conscious of their departure, but only just—because she was gradually putting two and two together, and by the time the door closed on the lawyers who had come to draw up a deal she had no intention of agreeing to she was fit to explode.

'You *lied* to me!' she burst out, galvanised into action and storming over to the window, then storming back towards him, hands on her hips, eyes spitting fury.

Leo stood his ground and met her tempestuous gaze head-on, without so much as flinching.

'Did I?' he drawled, moving towards the table at the back of the room to pour himself a glass of water, taking his time.

'You let me think that you were…you were… What were you doing in my store in the first place? Oh, don't bother answering that! You'd come along to have a look at what you wanted to get your hands on!'

'I like to see what I'm sinking my money into, yes.'

'I'm leaving!' She spun round, shaking, and began heading towards the door.

She didn't get there, because two strides in she was stopped by his hand on her arm.

Her whole body reacted as though a shot of high-voltage electricity had been injected straight into her bloodstream. The heat from his hand would have been enough to stop her dead in her tracks even if no pressure had been applied.

Her body remembered his and that terrified her.

'How could you have lied to me!'

Leo met her vivid eyes. 'Stop playing the crucified martyr, Maddie. Have you conveniently forgotten that you weren't exactly forthcoming about who *you* were when we were climbing into the sack together?'

'That was different!'

'How? Enlighten me?'

'I thought you might have been scared off because I happened to own the store! *Ha!*'

'Is that right? And if I'd told you who I was…would we have ended up in bed?'

'I'm getting the picture, Leo. You're rich and powerful and you were scared that a poor little salesgirl might have decided you were a promising candidate to get involved with…'

'Is that so far-fetched?'

Maddie stared stubbornly at him, too angry to give an inch on this, even though she could see that he might, conceivably, have a point.

Not that it mattered! What mattered was that he was not going to get his rich, powerful paws on the store her grandfather had left her.

'Well?' Leo pressed, his tone making it clear he felt she was equally guilty of deception to suit her own purposes.

'If you knew me *at all,*' Maddie snapped, 'then you

would know that the fact you're rich doesn't work in your favour. If you'd told me from the start who you were and what you were worth I would have run a mile! I've had enough experience of rich creeps to last me a lifetime!'

Leo's eyes narrowed.

He'd loosened his grip on her arm but he was still holding her, and the look in his eyes was saying he wanted to do so much more than just hold her.

Their eyes locked and she felt a shift in the atmosphere from blazing anger to the slow sizzle of sexual awareness.

She found that she was holding her breath.

'Don't,' Maddie whispered.

'Don't what?'

'Look at me like that.'

'You mean the way you're looking at me? As though the only thing on your mind now is the thought of my mouth on yours?'

She wrenched herself free from his grasp and took a few shaky steps back.

'Don't kid yourself!'

She wrapped her arms around her body to stop herself from shaking like a leaf. He was so big, so powerful, and she was so drawn to him that she had to make a conscious effort not to stumble back into his hypnotic radius like a zombie under the spell of a master magician.

'Like I said, I don't go for guys like you!'

Guys like him?

Leo was enraged to be categorised and written off. He was even more enraged that his body was reacting to her like a sex-starved, randy adolescent when his brain was telling him to drop any pointless back-and-forth conversation and get down to business.

'That's not what you were saying a fortnight ago, when you fell into my arms like a starving person suddenly presented with a five-course spread.'

The erection pushing against the zipper of his jeans was as hard as steel and he abruptly turned away, giving himself time to get his runaway libido under control.

'I made a mistake with a rich man,' Maddie flung at him in a trembling voice. 'I got involved with someone I thought had a conscience and a moral compass and I discovered that, actually, rich people don't operate like that. Rich people are above the law, and they don't give a damn who they step on because they know they're never going to have to pay the price for what they do!'

Leo stared at her through narrowed eyes. 'You're judging me by someone you happen to have been involved with who...*what*? Did a runner? Hit on your best friend?'

'If only,' Maddie said bitterly. 'Oh, Adam White was a lot more destructive than *that*!'

She seemed to catch herself and fell silent, breathing evenly as if to stifle the emotions which had definitely got the better of her.

'It doesn't matter,' she told him coolly. 'What matters is that I'm not going to be selling you the store and I don't care how much money you throw down on the table.'

'Sit.'

'I'm perfectly fine standing.'

'Let's put our brief liaison behind us, Maddie. What's at stake here has nothing to do with the fact that we slept together. We're both adults. It happened. Neither of us knew the full story when we climbed into bed. Or should I say when we occupied the sofa in your sitting room.'

The evocative image his words conjured did nothing

to lessen the surge of his unwanted attraction. Leo carried on without skipping a beat, but he had to divert his eyes from her face. Even the fact that she was glaring at him couldn't diminish her pulling power.

'There's no point playing the blame game. Okay, so you might have run a mile if you'd known how rich I was.' He shrugged indifferently. 'And maybe I didn't advertise my wealth because I've had experience of what it's like to be targeted by women who only have one thing on their mind.'

'Oh, please,' Maddie muttered sarcastically.

Leo raised his eyebrows to look at her. 'You think I'm lying?'

'Don't pretend that you don't know how attractive you are—with or without your stupid oversized bank balance!'

Leo shot her a slow, curling smile and the atmosphere was suddenly charged. She flicked her tongue over her upper lip and the gesture was so *sexy* that Leo found himself stepping towards her.

She didn't pull back. She couldn't, because her legs had turned to lead. She almost whimpered when he was only inches away from her, but fortunately pride kicked in and instead she drew a steadying breath and tried to clear her mind from the fog enveloping it.

'Tough, isn't it?' Leo drawled huskily, and the low, velvety timbre of his voice sent shivers racing up and down her spine.

'I don't know what you're talking about.'

But she was mesmerised by his eyes and the sheer beauty of his face. He had the most amazing lashes, she thought distractedly—so long, so thick. It was just another detail to take in and store.

She balled her hands into defensive fists and made a concerted effort to drag her wayward mind back from the brink—which was a very, *very* dangerous place for it to stray.

'Oh, you know exactly what I'm talking about, Maddie. The thing our bodies are doing right now. Don't try and pretend that you don't want me to touch you right here, right now, and damn the consequences.' Then he drew back abruptly and said, his voice brisk, 'But that's not going to do. Business before pleasure, I'm afraid.'

He grinned and her humiliation was complete.

How could she have allowed herself to forget that this was her enemy? Another rich man who had lied to her? A man who wanted to take what was hers and was willing to do so by whatever means he deemed fit? A bully, in other words.

She blinked and glared and wanted nothing more badly than to wipe the grin from his face—not least because it just ratcheted up his outrageous sex appeal.

'I suppose,' Leo drawled, stepping away and sauntering towards the window, where he proceeded to glance out before returning his full attention to her face, 'your lawyer, or your accountant, or whoever that little man was who came in with you, has explained the deal that's been put on the table?'

'I didn't pay much attention to that because I'm not interested in selling.'

'Big mistake. You should have. Sentiment is all well and good, but money is what does the talking—and I'm prepared to put however much money down on the table I have to if it gets me what I want. And believe me when I tell you that my supply of cash is bottomless.'

He'd gone into that store fully prepared to pay the

least amount of money for the place he could, but he was fast revising his original plan because she was stubborn and—for reasons that frankly confounded him—she wasn't going to roll over and play dead because he wanted her to.

He felt a sense of grudging admiration, because people, as a rule, were prone to caving in to him in the face of any show of determination, such was the range of his power and influence and the force of his personality.

She, on the other hand, looked as close to caving in as his art teacher had looked when, at the age of ten, Leo had asked to be let off detention because the dog had eaten his project.

'Maddie, you could have your dream life with the money I'm prepared to offer. Frankly, as it stands, I would be handing over far more than the place is worth. Because in case you haven't noticed it's falling apart at the seams and it's lost its customer base. One more poor season and the whole house of cards will come tumbling down.'

'I've sorted out the finances and I have a business plan to get it back up and running.'

'Impressive. I had no idea you had experience in bringing ailing companies back from the brink.'

'This is more than just a game for me, Leo. I never met my grandfather and yet he placed his faith in me to transform the store.'

'The store that *he* ran into the ground because of his fondness for the bottle and the nearest gambling den.'

Maddie stiffened. If he thought that he was going to get to her by insulting her grandfather then he was mistaken. Yes, Tommaso Gallo had drunk too much and gambled away his fortune, but she was convinced that

that was because he had lost his only daughter. That was what misery could do to a person.

'Why are you so keen to have it, Leo?' She shot him a look of helpless frustration. 'Why can't you just buy something else? Somewhere else? I mean, it's a *store.* If you're sarcastic about *my* lack of business experience, then how much experience in retail do *you* have?'

She realised that she actually had no idea what he did for a living or where his money came from.

Leo was staring at her thoughtfully. Her sentiments seemed to be skewed. Did she somehow see herself as the beneficiary of a kindly old Father Christmas figure? She'd never met the old man, and clearly had no idea of the sort of person he was.

Should he break the glad tidings that Tommaso Gallo and Father Christmas had about as much in common as a rattlesnake and a mouse?

He decided that revelations could wait until another day. He pushed himself away from the window and flexed his muscles as he prowled through the vast conference room, finally sinking into one of the leather chairs and swivelling it so that it was facing her.

'I wouldn't keep it as the same type of traditional retail store.'

Strangely, despite her high heels and the fact that, standing up, she was towering over him, he had shed nothing of his dominance. If anything, she felt awkward standing, so she in turn sat at the very end of the long, walnut table.

At least she now felt more businesslike. 'What would you do to it?'

'I want a foothold in Dublin,' Leo said flatly. 'This store is exactly where I want to be and it's exactly the right size. I have a portfolio of companies and it would continue being a store, but exclusively dealing with my targeted software, adapted high-tech computers and specialised training stations.'

'An electronics shop?'

Leo frowned. 'The retail market is saturated, Maddie. Too many people are buying too many products online. You'll never find a better offer than the one I'm prepared to give you. Take it and don't fight me.'

'Surely you can source another big store to gobble up!'

'You have your personal reasons for wanting to hang on to your white elephant. I have my own personal reasons for wanting to take it from you.'

'What are you talking about?'

'You don't know much about old Tommaso, do you?'

'You *knew* my grandfather?' Confused, Maddie stared at him in consternation. 'How *old* are you?'

Leo smiled drily. 'I'm not an eighty-year-old man rescued from looking his age thanks to plastic surgery.'

'I didn't think you were.'

'And no, to answer your first question, I never met the old man.'

'Then how do you…? I don't understand.'

'My grandfather and Tommaso were friends back in the day. Did your mother never talk about what went on between them?'

'No. No, she didn't.'

'Not a word?'

'I think that part of her life was something she walked away from, and when she walked away she made sure never to look back. I knew she'd fallen out with my grandfather over her choice of partner, and had exiled herself on the other side of the world, but beyond that I really don't know anything about either of my grandparents. *Or* their friends.'

'Well, he and my grandfather were, once upon a time, very good friends. Indeed, they landed in Ireland searching for the same thing,—their fortunes.'

'What was your father called?'

'Benito. Benito and Tommaso. Two friends as tight as thieves until a simple bet tore their friendship apart.'

'A *bet*?' Maddie shook her head. She had no idea where this was heading, but her gut instinct was telling her that wherever it was it wasn't going to be her idea of a dream destination.

'One bet over a certain small shop. The toss of a coin. My grandfather won the bet.'

'But…'

'I know,' Leo purred with an undercurrent of coolness. 'You're asking yourself how it is that Tommaso ended up with the iconic store in Dublin when he lost the bet. I'll tell you how. Your grandfather betrayed Benito. While he was planning what to do with the shop Tommaso hit the bank, secured a loan and made the deal in record time—and then he put his hands up in mock surrender so that he could take his punishment safe in the knowledge that he'd got what he wanted. So you see—you have *your* reasons for hanging on and I have *my* reasons for making sure to loosen your grip. My grandfather has wanted that store for decades. It's just about the only thing he has left to want. He's never stopped trying to get it, and I intend to make sure he gets it before he dies.'

Leo thought that technically, the store wasn't *quite* the only thing his grandfather had left to want. The pitter-patter of tiny great-grandchildren's feet was also high on the old man's wish list—but that was something that wasn't going to happen.

Not given to introspection, and certainly not given to rehashing a past he wanted to forget, Leo was suddenly reminded of the one and only catastrophe that had provided him with the most valuable learning curve he had ever experienced.

Forget about deals and money and what one power broker might be saying to another power broker in order to undermine him. In the great scheme of things, how did *that* figure? No, *his* learning curve had been at the hands of a woman.

He'd been twenty-three, cocksure and confident that he knew all there was to know about women. She'd been ten years older, and what she knew hadn't yet registered on his radar. She'd been sexy, offhand, and she'd made him work. She'd made him work all the way up the aisle into a marriage that had ended before the ink on the certificate had had time to dry.

The alluring, enigmatic sexy woman he'd married had turned out to be a wily fortune-hunter who'd known just what tricks to play on a young rich kid with too much self-confidence and too little cynicism.

After two years she'd relinquished her band of gold in exchange for financial security for the rest of her life.

Leo still kept a picture of her in his wallet—because everybody needed a reminder of their youthful folly.

Afterwards, he'd wondered whether he hadn't been subconsciously ripe for the picking because his grandmother, desperately ill at the time, had been so keen for him to settle down. He'd gone into something and it hadn't been with his eyes wide open.

Thankfully his grandmother had died before she

could witness the true horror of Leo's divorce proceedings and all mention of those pitter-pattering little feet had been dropped, but Leo knew that it was something his grandfather still secretly longed for. He still nurtured a burning desire to see his one and only grandson settled with some plump homely wife who would be there to keep the home fires burning.

Not going to happen.

But number two on the list *could* happen.

'I don't believe you.' Maddie glared at him defiantly. 'The world doesn't need another electronics store. My grandfather's place adds to the history of this city and I'm never—repeat, *never*—going to sell it to you or to anyone else. And I don't care *how* much money you throw at me!'

She was furious on so many levels that she could scarcely breathe. Furious that he had tried to destroy the image she had in her head of her grandfather. But of course he would try any low trick in the book to get what he wanted! Furious that he was so unfazed by every single thing she'd said to him. And furious that he still had that stupid, *stupid* effect on her even though she absolutely *hated* him!

'Is that the sound of a gauntlet being thrown down?' Leo drawled, enjoying the hectic colour in her cheeks and wanting more than anything else to kiss her into submission in just the sort of crazy, macho way he really should have no time for.

'Yes, it is!'

'Fine.' Leo shrugged and began sauntering towards the door. 'In that case…game on.'

CHAPTER FIVE

LEO LOOKED AT the report sitting in front of him. It was slight, but significant. Three pages at most. In the week since he'd seen Maddie he'd had time to reflect on what approach he wanted to take with regard to the store.

'I won't rest until I have it.'

That was what his grandfather had declared only days before, when Leo had presented him with the obstacle in his way in the form of one very beautiful, very stubborn and ridiculously fiery girl from the other side of the world.

'It's a matter of pride. I was fair to Tommaso when he started haemorrhaging money because of the gambling and the drinking. I knew about his wife, knew how unexpected her death was and how hard it'd hit him, and I felt sorry for what the man was going through. We'd been friends, after all. But time and bitterness and pain had turned him into a vengeful old man. He would rather have seen the store fall into rack and ruin than sell it to me—even though I offered way above market price for it—just like he sliced his daughter out of his life rather than forgive and move on. Forget what the granddaughter says about hanging on to it because it's part of the city's heritage. Rubbish! Tommaso couldn't have given a damn about heritage! He refused to sell through sheer spite. He never forgave me because I refused to accept what he had done—refused to accept that he had betrayed me and I'd called him a dishonourable cheat!'

Leo was quietly pleased that his grandfather had still insisted on the purchase. Had he not insisted it was possible that he, Leo, would have shrugged and walked away because he couldn't be bothered with the fight. He would have simply bided his time, waited a couple of years until the place was collapsing—because how successful was it going to be, really, when Maddie hadn't the first idea about running a business—and moved in for the kill.

But she'd thrown down a gauntlet. That was something Leo had never been able to resist.

And more than that… The thought of Maddie being the instigator of the challenge frankly thrilled him.

He hadn't been able to dislodge the woman from his head, where she seemed to have taken up semi-permanent residence. Walking away from her might just have been more frustrating than walking away from the purchase.

And now, in front of him, he had just what he needed to get what he wanted. The trump card, in a manner of speaking. The ace of spades.

To play it or not to play it…?

He would see how their meeting went.

This time he had invited her to his own offices in London. No accountants would be present…no high-powered lawyers.

'We need to talk,' he had drawled when he had called

her two evenings previously. 'I have some information you might find of interest...'

He had heard the hesitation in her voice when she had demanded to know what he could possibly have of interest when she had already said all there was to say on the matter.

He'd had his doubts that she would show up, in which case he would be prepared to simply go and get her, but to his surprise she had texted him only a few hours ago to confirm the meeting and added,

I have something to tell you as well.

When he had tried calling her she had failed to pick up.

And now here he was, and he hadn't been so invigorated in as long as he could remember.

When his PA buzzed to tell him that his visitor had arrived and was waiting in the foyer downstairs, he relaxed back into his chair and smiled to himself, savouring the tingle of anticipation.

'Show her up in fifteen minutes.'

After all, a little bit of mind-games never went amiss...

Downstairs, Maddie was trying hard to squash the painful sensation of nausea rippling through her in little waves. It was like seasickness except far, far worse.

What did Leo want to see her about? What did he have to say that he thought might be of interest? Would he offer more money?

As things stood, Anthony was already getting cold feet about her plan to keep the store, and she'd had to endure a long, meaningful chat about the importance of at least *considering* the very generous offer Leo had made. There was only so far the very loyal investors would agree to it, he had said. In the end they were only human, and if enough money was thrown at them, they would start leaving the sinking ship in droves.

Maddie knew that she would have to be as cool as a cucumber and stand her ground. Except…

She felt another wave of nausea and knew it had nothing to do with the financial discussions ahead of her. Feeling faint now, she closed her eyes briefly and tried not to relive the shock of finding out that she was pregnant.

How *could* she have been so reckless? She'd thought the chances were slim when they'd made love, but the possibility of pregnancy had begun nibbling away at the edges of her mind. Beneath all the angst over the store, and her even greater angst at her chaotic feelings towards Leo, there had been a dragging fear that that one slip-up might have had repercussions.

Even so, she'd been convinced when she'd done a test that she couldn't be *that* unlucky. Wasn't there a limit to how much bad luck one person could have in a lifetime? Surely she'd used up her allowance?

Seemingly not.

Little did he know, but one more euro on the table and she would have to relinquish her dream of resurrecting the store and carrying on the legacy her grandfather had left her.

How could she gamble on making a success of something she had never done before when, with a baby inside her, taking a gamble was the one thing she couldn't afford to do now?

But Maddie wasn't going to think of worst-case scenarios. Not yet.

She sat.

She waited.

And she grew more and more nervous with each passing second.

If he'd wanted to intimidate her he'd chosen his venue well, because this was luxury on a scale that was practically unimaginable. Looking around her, she could tell that even the tiniest of details, like the potted plant on the smoked glass table in front of her, was pricey.

The *people* looked pricey! All young and beautiful in sharp suits, scuttling to and from the bank of elevators on a mission to make more and more money.

She jumped when someone suddenly stood in front of her and told her to follow.

She'd been sitting around for over a quarter of an hour, but instead of the delay giving time for her nerves to settle it had had the opposite effect.

'Mr Conti apologises for the delay in seeing you,' said the forty-something woman with the severe hair cut but kindly face as she preceded Maddie to one of the elevators.

Maddie very much doubted that, but she remained silent, too overawed by her surroundings and too wrapped up with what she was going to say to Leo to say anything at all.

But even in her distraught, anxious daze she couldn't help but notice the details of his vast offices—the smell and feel of money beyond most people's wildest imaginations.

The lift was a deep walnut with smoked glass, and

when it stopped they were disgorged into a huge glass space where workstations were separated by glass partitions and exotic plants. It was predominantly white, and there were a lot of sleek, wafer-thin computers on desks where everyone was hard at work. In fact, no one even glanced across as they walked away from what almost looked like a greenhouse with industrious worker bees towards a more intimate area.

The offices of the CEO were private, and concealed behind walnut and chrome doors. Nerves building to a peak, Maddie nearly turned tail and ran when they finally paused in front of them, closed at the very end of the plush, wide corridor.

'Don't be nervous.' The PA turned to her with a smile and a wink. 'Deep down, he's a lamb.' She paused. 'Well, perhaps *lamb* isn't quite the word I'm looking for, but he's scrupulously fair.'

'I'm not nervous,' Maddie lied, her teeth all but chattering.

Her stomach was in knots as she was propelled through a vast outer office—grey, white and glass—through an interconnecting door and then she was there. Standing in front of him while behind her the door quietly clicked shut.

Maddie stared. She couldn't help herself. The real-life Leo Conti was so much more powerful, so much more breathtaking than the two-dimensional one who had dominated her thoughts for the past couple of weeks since she had seen him.

Her mouth went dry and every single coherent thought vanished from her head, zapped into the ether by the devastating effect he had on her.

'Why don't you have a seat?' Leo said politely.

He wondered whether she was looking at him like that on purpose. Was she trying to turn him on?

Just like that his thoughts veered off at a tantalising tangent.

She wanted the store and, as she'd said, that *want* was wrapped up in all sorts of motivations that had nothing to do with money.

What if she'd decided that stubborn refusal and a fight was the wrong approach to get what she wanted? What if she'd decided that a more powerful weapon was sex?

The drab outfit, a replica of the one she had worn at the last meeting she had attended, certainly didn't advertise a woman prepared to bare her all as a means to an end, but strangely it was even more provocative than if she'd worn a mini-skirt and stilettoes.

Leo toyed with that pleasurable notion in the space of the few seconds it took for her to sink into a chair which was strategically slightly lower than the one in which he was sitting.

He imagined her coming on to him, offering herself to him. He pictured that interconnecting door being locked and his PA dispatched while he stripped her, very, very slowly, and took her even more slowly on his desk…on the sofa in his outer chamber…on the floor…

Sudden craving surged through him and he had to breathe evenly and focus—although even focussing he still found himself overly absorbed at a scenario he had not once considered.

Would he back off the deal in exchange for that luscious body at his disposal?

Sex and women had never—not once—come ahead of business for him, but in this instance Leo found himself giving serious consideration to breaking that sacred principle.

Angry with himself, he shook his head and looked at her coolly from under lowered lashes. 'You seem to be having a problem accepting the deal I've offered you.'

'Is that why you called me in? To go over all this? Do you think you can intimidate me if there isn't an army of lawyers and accountants around?'

Maddie wanted to sound firm and in control, and she wondered whether he could detect the nervous wobble in her voice.

She'd spent ages wondering when she should break the news of her pregnancy to him. Or even if she should tell him at all! Not only had he been a fleeting visitor in her life but he had entered it under false pretences. Was that the sort of man she wanted as an influence on any child of hers?

He might do crazy things to her body, but wasn't he just another mega-wealthy guy who believed that life was his for the taking? Arrogant? Superior? Not above stamping on other people if it suited them? Hadn't she had too much experience of men like that to invite one into her life simply because she'd happened to fall pregnant by him?

She had had enough of a shock—was now facing enough of an altered future. Did she want to further compound the situation by telling Leo?

Of course there was a chance that he might just shrug and walk away from the whole situation, but what if he didn't?

He would be around *for ever.*

The pros and cons had gone round and round in her head in the space of a handful of hours, but the reality was that she had known from the very second she had seen that pink line that there was no way she could keep the pregnancy from him.

She knew what it felt like to grow up without a father. It was not something she would recommend. Not unless she had very good reason to go down that route.

Her mother had made her choices and Maddie had known that those choices had been difficult and irretrievable. Her own father had been a bastard—a coward and a fortune-hunter.

Leo, whatever else he might be, was none of those things.

So, as she waited to hear what he had to say, for his conversation to play out before hers could begin, she knew that her nerves stemmed from her own revelations to come rather than whatever it was he had summoned her into his office to impart.

'You should have a look at his.' Leo reached towards a slender file and pushed it across the desk to her.

Business was business. That had always been his mantra. Even if she *had* agreed to see him so that she could somehow seduce him into doing what she wanted, there was no way he would succumb to the temptation. At any rate, the defiant tilt of her head was *not* the body language of a woman gearing up to use her feminine wiles on him, and Leo knew that, however pleasurable it had been to play with that tantalising thought, he would have thought a great deal less of her had she chosen to go down that road.

So what choice did he have but to play the cards in his hand?

He watched carefully as she took the file and opened it. He noted the pallor in her cheeks, followed by hot colour as she read and then re-read the report he had received a couple of days ago.

When she'd finished reading it, her head remained lowered, even though she'd quietly closed the file and kept it on her lap.

Deep-seated unease coursed through him, unfamiliar and disconcerting. Leo had no idea what to do with those feelings because he'd never had them before.

This wasn't playing dirty. This information hadn't come into his possession via bribery or blackmail. It was documented, and it had been sourced in five seconds flat by the man he'd instructed.

So why did he now feel like a cad? Why was that lowered head doing all sorts of things to his conscience?

Leo scowled. 'Well?'

'Well, what?' Maddie looked at him. Her eyes were filled with unshed tears. 'Is this why you summoned me to come and see you? I'm surprised you aren't surrounded by your army of lawyers so that they can pick me apart and then spit me out. Because that's why you've got this, isn't it? So that you can use it against me. So that you can force me to sell to you under the threat of making this information public. How *could* you, Leo?'

Leo flushed darkly. 'This information is in the public domain, Maddie.'

'That doesn't mean that you should use it to scare me into doing as you say.'

Suddenly restless, Leo rose to his feet in one easy movement and began pacing his office, finally returning to his desk, perching on the edge of it right in front of her.

'Tell me what happened.'

'Why?' Her green eyes flashed.

'Because I want to hear.'

Leo sighed and raked his fingers through his hair. It felt as though life had been a lot more straightforward before this woman had entered it. Under normal circumstances, with ammunition available, he certainly wouldn't be hanging around asking for back stories.

But he could see that she was trying hard not to cry and that cut him to the quick. The report was simply factual. There would be more to it than was written in black and white.

Maddie glared at him and hesitated. Inside, anger warred with pride. He looked as though he really wanted to hear what she had to say, but how could she trust him? This was the guy who had pretended to be a pauper because it had suited his purpose at the time.

'Please, Maddie.' Leo surprised himself but he meant it. 'What's there is the skeleton of a story. Fill it out for me.'

'How did you know what to look for?'

'I didn't. But I always do very thorough background checks on people and companies before I put money on the table and start signing papers.'

'And if you come across something dodgy you use it against them? Is that it?'

'It's standard business practice to make sure all the facts are on the table. Any fresh-faced accounts manager might have a gambling problem, and that's something that would require close scrutiny of the books. I'm not a big, bad wolf. I'm doing what anyone else would do in my situation.'

Maddie looked down at her fingers and then met his hooded gaze. 'When my mother died,' she began, avoiding sentiment and keeping strictly to the facts, 'I was all over the place. I'd had to abandon my university dreams to look after her, as I think I told you. I therefore left school with a lot of dreams but not much hope of realising any of them, or even of getting a halfway decent job.'

She drew in a deep, steadying breath and detached herself from the remembered emotion. Leo was gazing at her levelly, his expression neither sympathetic nor unsympathetic, merely interested.

'I made money doing menial stuff, and eventually found a well-paid job working for a lovely elderly lady in one of the most expensive suburbs in Sydney. I lived in—which suited me because I saved on rent. In return I took care of her, and I also helped her with an autobiography she was writing. Through her I met Adam, her grandson. He was handsome and charming and… Well, the whole package, really. Or so I thought. We began dating. I was cautious at first. I've had experience with boys wanting to go out with me because of the way…'

She blushed and he looked at her with amusement, as if he'd never heard any woman so obviously wanting to play down her attractiveness.

'Because of the way you look?' he inserted smoothly, and she gave a jerky nod.

'I really thought we had something good,' she said bitterly. 'I really believed that life was being kind to me after all I'd been through with my mum. Anyway, that's by the by.'

She gathered herself, told herself that this wasn't a confessional in front of someone who was going to give her a big bear hug before telling her that everything was going to be all right. This was a story that she wanted to relate because she refused to be defined by the cold, harsh facts without him hearing what was behind those facts.

They might be on opposite sides of the fence now, but they'd also been as intimate as it was possible for two people to get. Something inside her didn't want him to be left with the wrong impression of her.

At which thought, she firmed her soft mouth and ploughed on. 'Lacey—the lady I worked for—started getting forgetful shortly after I started with her. Small things at first, and I didn't think anything of it. Not enough for alarm bells to start ringing. But then it seemed to progress quite fast—although it's possible that I just didn't notice anything to begin with because I was in recovery from Mum's death.'

She sneaked a glance at him. Was he bored? Maybe trying to sift through the information so that he could find her weak spot? She recalled what his PA had said about him being fair and realised that, however angry she was with him, she *did* think that he was fair.

'And then?' But Leo had some idea of what was going to come, and he knew that it would all be wrapped up with the ex she had fled from.

'A very valuable necklace went missing. It was worth…well, more than I can say. Adam and his sister blamed me. I tried to tell them… I couldn't believe that the guy I'd thought I had a future with could turn on me—could believe that I was nothing more than a common thief and a liar.'

She broke eye contact and stared without blinking for a few seconds, gathering herself.

Angry at a man he'd never met in his life, and held captive by the strangest surge of protectiveness, Leo thrust a box of tissues from his drawer towards her. She snatched a few without tearing her eyes away from the wall.

She sucked in some air and crumpled the tissues in her hand, then looked at Leo levelly.

'No one believed me,' she said simply, 'and Lacey was so forgetful that no one took much notice of her at all. There was a missing necklace, and I was a poor girl from the wrong side of the tracks, so therefore there was no question that I was guilty. The police were called in and I was formally charged with theft.

'I was staring a prison sentence in the face, or at least the threat of one, when one of the police officers, having chatted to Lacey, brought in a medic. She was diagnosed with Alzheimer's. Shortly after that, by a stroke of luck, the necklace resurfaced. It had been in the pocket of one of her skirts. She must have removed it and stuck it in there when she was out in the garden. I was unconditionally cleared of all charges—but mud sticks and all I wanted to do was run away. The whole episode… I felt dirty, disgraced, even though I'd done nothing wrong. The questions…the suspicions…and then the horror of what could have happened if that diagnosis hadn't been made—if one person hadn't noticed what no one else had… It was all too much.'

She laughed shortly.

'So you were right when you said that I must have been running away from something.'

'And the ex?'

'What about him?'

'Did he come crawling back to apologise, clutching flowers and the engagement ring you were hoping he would eventually put on your finger?'

Maddie stiffened with pride. 'I broke off all contact with his entire family and with him. He got the message loud and clear that I wanted nothing more to do with him.'

'But he hurt you?'

'What do you think?'

'Then suddenly, out of the blue, you discover that you're the sole beneficiary of old Tommaso's dwindling fortune…'

'It's my chance to do something with my life, to move on, and I'm going to take it.'

Did she mean that even now that circumstances had changed? Leo had detected the shadow of a hesitation in that declaration. She said she wasn't going to cave in and sell to him. She'd shouted that from the rooftops. But there was an inflection in her voice that made him wonder just how adamant she was about that.

He'd increased his offer. The diminutive lawyer who had traipsed along in her wake must have opened her eyes to the advantages of taking what had been put on the table.

He looked at the folder, still resting on her lap, his dark eyes lazy, thoughtful, speculative.

Maddie followed that lazy gaze. It didn't take a genius to figure out that he knew just what he had to do to get her where he wanted her. She'd been exonerated of all charges, her name fully cleared, but any brush with the law would be enough to have bankers and shareholders running to the table to snatch at the deal Leo had thrown down—even if she *had* emerged as pure as driven snow from the unfortunate episode.

'You're going to use this information against me, aren't you?' she said quietly.

Leo, who had decided to do no such thing, allowed a telling silence to develop between them.

'Do you think it would be fair for all parties involved in this deal—all the people who stand to gain or lose by the decision you and I make—that they remain in ignorance of what's taken place?'

It was a valid enough question as far as Leo was concerned, even though he knew without a shadow of a doubt, as he watched the emotions flicker across her beautiful face, that he would bury the report—bury it so well that it would never see the light of day.

'I see.' Maddie stood up. 'I wonder why I expected anything different.'

'Sit down!'

'Don't you *dare* tell me what to do! I should have guessed that all rich men are exactly the same. They may talk differently and walk differently, but in the end they're all the same. They're all prepared to go the extra mile when it comes to getting what they want.'

'That is outrageous!'

'Is it? Okay, Leo, you win. I'll take whatever deal it is you want to offer. I'll accept the money and I'll go away—because the last thing I need is to start a new life over here with my past following behind me like a bad smell!'

'Stop being hysterical and *sit down*! Whoever said anything about my using this information? I admit under normal circumstances I wouldn't hesitate, but in this instance…'

Maddie barely heard a word he was saying. Her heart was beating as fast and as hard as a sledgehammer and she was breathing so rapidly that she thought she might hyperventilate.

Which was the last thing she needed in her condition.

And suddenly the whole point of this meeting surged back to her consciousness and she stared at him.

'Are you going to sit down?' Leo demanded, vaulting upright and swinging round his desk so that he was staring down at her. 'And before we go any further let's get one thing straight—I am *nothing* like that scumbag you got mixed up with! I don't lead women up any garden paths and I damn well would *never* shout guilty until proved innocent!'

'But you *would* drag my name through the mud even though I *am* innocent!'

'Have you heard *a word* I've said to you?'

Maddie stared fiercely at him. Without even realising what she was doing, she rested the flat of her hand against his chest, warding him off but wanting badly to draw him towards her.

She sprang away, shocked at how he could scramble her brains even when she was in the midst of a ferocious argument.

'I am *not* going to use any information against you, Maddie, so you can relax on that score. It doesn't mean that I won't get the store from you, because I will, but I won't be making any of this sorry business public knowledge in order to further my intentions.'

Maddie stared. Her hand still burned from where she had rested it against his chest. *She was turned on by him.* There was no ignoring the hot dampness between her thighs and the pinching of her nipples.

Maybe it was her hormones, she thought wildly. Her responses were going every which way. She had come here planning on being cool and contained, but very quickly all those good intentions had unravelled and now here she was, screaming at him and not listening to a word he was saying.

He wasn't going to use the information he had uncovered. That didn't matter, however. This meeting had disclosed something very important—something she couldn't just look away from in the hope that she might be wrong.

She still wanted Leo more than she'd ever wanted anything or anyone in her life before.

No matter what she thought of him personally, her body still craved his touch and that terrified her.

So the fighting would end.

She would hand over the store to him and she would tell him about the baby.

But once the store was his, contact would be effectively broken. She would take the money and she would sell her grandfather's house and leave Ireland for good.

Maddie didn't think that a fully paid up member of the successful bachelor club would travel far and wide to see a child he had never committed to having in the first place. She would be able to step back from something that felt a lot like fire. The life she would build would not hold the legacy she had inherited, but it would have something else—something equally important. A child. Plus, she would have more than enough money to support them both.

'You don't have to fight me for the store, Leo. I told you. It's yours for the taking. You can get your lawyers to talk to Anthony and they can sort out the sale.'

Leo took a step back and tilted his head to one side, as though listening for a noise he couldn't quite hear. Yet.

'And your change of heart stems from…?'

Maddie backed towards the door until she was pressed against it. 'I have more on my plate now than just the store.'

'Explain.' Leo took two steps towards her, the depth of his navy eyes skewering her temporarily to the spot.

'I'm pregnant, Leo.'

She stared at him and watched the colour drain away from his face. He was a man who'd been slammed by a train at full speed and was finding it hard to breathe.

The outer office was empty. Maddie could tell that much. She realised Leo must have dismissed the PA, knowing that his chat with her was going to be highly personal, involving sensitive information about her past.

'I don't believe you.'

'I'm pregnant. So you can have the damned store! I'm going now. I'll give you a chance to digest what I've said. But the store is yours and that's the main thing. Isn't it?'

With which parting shot she pulled open the door and shot out of his office, walking briskly without a backward glance towards the elevator that had earlier whooshed her up to his office.

CHAPTER SIX

MADDIE DIDN'T MAKE IT. Not quite. As he followed her into the elevator she spun round, the look on her face evidence that she hadn't heard him behind her.

'Leo…'

'You don't get to do this, Maddie.'

'Do what?'

'Detonate a bomb in my life and then make a run for it.'

'I wasn't making a run for it.'

'We're going back to my apartment and you're going to tell me in words of one syllable what the hell is going on!'

But Leo knew what was going on. He'd taken an appalling chance and now the chickens had come home to roost. She wasn't lying. She wasn't the sort. He was going to be a father, and it was a nightmare so all-encompassing that he had to absorb it in stages.

After all the lessons he'd learnt from the five-second marriage that should never have happened, and which had ended up costing him an arm and a leg and certainly a great deal of pride, he'd blithely had unprotected sex with a woman because he hadn't been able to resist.

After a decade of playing it safe, never taking

chances and avoiding anything that smelled like a honey trap, he'd blown it all with a woman he'd known for less than a day.

But, by God, the sex had been amazing.

Leo was infuriated that that ridiculous thought had the nerve even to cross his mind when what he had to deal with was the fact that life as he knew it was over.

He wondered, briefly, whether she had engineered the whole bloody mess—but that suspicion barely lasted a second. Somehow, however cynical he was on the subject of women and what they would do when it came to getting their hands on pots of gold, there was something fundamentally honest about Maddie.

His mouth twisted as he followed that thought through to its logical conclusion.

She was bone-deep honest, and while he would happily have said the same for himself—despite his ruthlessness when it came to business dealings—he knew that she distrusted him. He'd ferreted out information about her, and even though he'd told her that he wasn't going to use it, the fact that it was out there, in his possession, had awakened that distrust of him.

Added to that was the small technicality of him keeping his true identity under wraps when they'd first met, and it was little wonder that she was desperate to find the nearest exit.

Tough.

He hadn't banked on this, but he wasn't a man who dodged any bullet.

He looked at her with brooding intensity. Never had he felt so restless, and yet, confined in their ten-by-ten metal box, he had no choice but to deal with the riptide of emotions flooding through him without moving a muscle.

She was keeping her eyes studiously averted. She looked as though she would break in two if he so much as reached out and touched her.

'I'm not going to your apartment with you,' Maddie said as the elevator doors opened, disgorging them back into the foyer where she had sat earlier, awash with nerves.

'Well, sorry to be a party-pooper, but if you think you're escaping back to Dublin before we can talk about this...this...*situation* then you've got another think coming.'

'You need time to mull it over,' she said, and her voice held an urgent, panicky undertone. 'You need time to digest.'

Leo didn't bother to dignify that suggestion with an answer. Walking out of the building, he was simultaneously calling his driver and keeping an extremely watchful eye on the bombshell dragging her feet alongside him. If she was searching for the most effective way of vanishing, then she was out of luck.

To his satisfaction, he saw that James, on the ball as always, was pulling to a stop in the black Jag. Leo opened the back door and propelled Maddie in without skipping a beat.

Maddie barely knew what was happening. One minute she was racking her brains to try and think of a way of avoiding Leo and his crazy suggestion that they go to his apartment to talk, and the next minute she was somehow in the back seat of a car, which was being driven by a young man with curly dark hair and lots of gold jewellery.

She was almost distracted enough by the sight to forget *why* she was in the back seat of Leo's car. Then it slammed back into her with force and she turned to him and hissed, 'You can't do this. You can't just… just…*kidnap me...*'

'Kidnap you? Stop over-dramatising, Maddie. And instead of wasting your energy trying to fight me, just accept that I intend to have this conversation you're obviously desperate to avoid.'

'I'm not *desperate* to avoid anything! I just thought that you might need time to…to…'

'Get to grips with the grenade you've just detonated in my life?'

Maddie looked at him furiously. Conscious of the strange driver at the wheel, Maddie resorted to resentful silence—which Leo did not attempt to break.

She wished she could read what was going on in his head. What was he thinking? She'd imagined that when she broke the news he would be furious. Shocked to start with, but then furious.

She had pictured herself backing out of his office, leaving him to plot how he could get rid of her and a baby he hadn't asked for as quietly and efficiently as possible. She hadn't envisaged a scenario in which she was being driven to his apartment.

In silence.

The drive took half an hour, and then she was treated to the splendour of London at its finest as the car pulled up outside a redbrick Victorian mansion, with very precise black railings and a row of perfectly groomed shaped shrubs edging the shallow bank of steps that led up to a pristine black door.

It turned out that his penthouse apartment ranged

across the top two floors. In a daze, she followed him into a wide, ornate hallway, where a porter made sure uninvited riff-raff were kept out, into a mirrored lift and then straight up into his apartment.

The lift was obviously for his use only.

Inside, greys and creams blended with wood and dull chrome. On the walls, impressive abstract art provided splashes of colour. It was all very open-plan, and configured in such a way that the most was made of the soaring ceilings and the two floors were connected by a glass and iron staircase.

Leo was walking towards a sitting area dominated by two oversized white leather sofas and Maddie followed him.

'When did you find out?' he asked without preamble. 'And there's no point perching on the edge of the sofa as though you're about to turn tail and run. You won't be going anywhere until we've discussed this…this…nightmare.'

'It's not a *nightmare*…'

'Well, it's certainly not a dream come true. When did you find out?'

'Yesterday.'

'And your plan was to show up in my office, hand me the keys to the store, inform me that you were carrying my child and then what? Head for the hills? Disappear under cover of darkness?'

Maddie reddened because, roughly speaking, he wasn't too far from the truth.

Eyes narrowed, Leo said coolly. 'It's not going to happen.'

'Which part?' Maddie asked faintly.

'The trade-off. I get the store, you get to run away. *Not* going to happen.'

'Leo…' Maddie breathed in deeply. 'We had a few hours of fun. Neither of us planned on having to deal with any consequences…'

A few hours of fun? Leo was inexplicably outraged to hear himself dismissed as *a few hours of fun*. He knew, rationally, that this was exactly how *he* would have categorised most of his exploits with women. Maybe slightly more than just the few hours, but essentially the same sentiment. Fun on the run.

That didn't make it any more acceptable.

'You didn't bank on my getting pregnant,' Maddie said, ignoring his glowering expression and ploughing on, 'and I get it that you're a bachelor through and through. The last thing you need or want is the sort of lifelong commitment that a child brings—especially when you didn't ask for this situation. No one wants to find that their nicely ordered perfect life has suddenly turned into a *nightmare*.'

Leo knew that she made sense. He was a committed bachelor. She wasn't to know why that was so deeply ingrained in him, but she had hit the nail on the head anyway. She had also been right when she'd said that the last thing he'd ever have asked for would be the lifelong commitment of a child—a duty of care stretching into infinity.

'I *didn't* ask for this,' he grated, 'but I'm honest enough to admit that no one held a gun to my head and forced me into having unprotected sex with you.'

'It doesn't matter. It's happened, and I'm not going to be responsible for lumbering you with a burden you didn't ask for.' She angled her head stubbornly and firmed her mouth. 'Well?' she pressed into the silence between them. 'You're not saying anything,'

'I'm waiting for you to finish what *you* want to say.'

Maddie breathed out a sigh. 'That's good.'

She cleared her throat to move on to stage two of the speech she had prepared in her head. It was a rough outline of the only solution she could think of, bearing in mind that she, herself, was still coming to terms with the fundamental change to her life looming on the not too distant horizon.

'If I sell the store to you then I will have more than sufficient money to make a life for myself and the baby. You won't have to take on any lifelong financial commitment. In fact you won't have to take on any commitment at all. In this day and age, single parent families are the norm.'

'I'm touched by your thoughtfulness and generosity,' Leo drawled. 'I can't think of a single other woman who, given the same circumstances, would be so overjoyed to see me walk scot-free.'

'Well...'

'Maybe it's because of your father.'

'What do you mean?'

'The stupendously low opinion you have of men.'

Maddie reddened. 'I'm giving you the option of not having your life ruined—'

'That's a very emotive word. *Ruined.*'

'So is *nightmare*,' Maddie countered, without batting an eye.

'Well, we won't be using either, because I won't be walking away scot-free. You're assuming that I'm the type of guy who's so self-interested that he's happy to get a woman pregnant and then leave her in the lurch.'

Maddie stiffened. 'What are you saying?'

'I may not have asked for this situation, but now that it's arisen walking away from it isn't going to be the solution I'll be taking.'

'You want the store.'

'It's bricks and mortar. I'm prepared to put that particular want on the back burner.'

'But I can't handle the responsibility of turning the place around when I'm going to have to deal with pregnancy and a newborn!'

'You can't handle it *alone...*'

'Even with help from a team of managers and workers...'

'Of course we'll have to discuss what the way forward with the store should be,' Leo mused, rising to his feet in one lithe, graceful movement to stroll towards the high-tech open-plan kitchen, where he proceeded to get them both something cold to drink.

Bewildered, Maddie twisted round to follow him. The accoutrements of a businessman had been shed along his way. The sleeves of his shirt were rolled to the elbow, and she hadn't noticed but he had slipped off his leather shoes and socks and was barefoot. He looked so stunning, so sophisticated...*so completely out of her league.*

She thought of Adam and her foolishness in falling for someone else who had been out of her league. She thought of the way he had stood back, siding with his family, accusing her of theft and not caring that her whole life was unravelling.

She thought of Leo, accessing that private information. Even if he had decided to withhold using it against her to get what he wanted she knew that he would have considered that option because that was the kind of man that he was.

She didn't know what was going on, but she felt a shiver of apprehension slither down her spine.

'Leo, I have no idea what you're talking about,' she confessed, having accepted the mineral water he had poured for her only to place it on the glass coffee table next to her.

'Don't you?'

'*What* way forward with the store?'

'Like I mentioned to you before, the day of the dinosaur department store, jack of all trades and master of none, is coming to an end.'

He was covering the room in ever-diminishing circles and finally he was standing directly in front of her, navy eyes unreadable, oozing just the sort of unfair sex appeal that made a nonsense of her attempts to get her brain in working order.

Maddie frowned. 'I don't know where you're going with this. Yes, I would have loved to have held on to the store, kept it as it was, but if you have it then what you do with it is no longer my concern.'

'You haven't *listened* to me, have you, Maddie?'

'I…'

'I'm not buying the store. Neither am I going anywhere. You're pregnant, and this completely changes the basis of our relationship.'

'But, Leo, we don't *have* a relationship.'

'You're the mother of my unborn baby. What do you call *that*?'

Faced with this direct question, which seemed to beg a sensible answer she was struggling to provide, Maddie could only stare at him speechlessly.

'Believe me,' Leo said heavily, moving to sit on the chair adjacent to her, stretching out his long legs at an angle and then relaxing back with his fingers linked on his stomach. 'I hadn't banked on any of this happening. But happen it has, and as far as I can see there's only one sensible solution that's going to work. I will have to marry you and legitimise my child.'

Maddie's mouth fell open. Before she could say anything he held up one assured hand, as though to stop her before she could interrupt. Which she wasn't about to do because her vocal cords had seized up.

'I won't lie to you, Maddie, marriage has not been on my radar. I'm a red-blooded male and I've had my fun, but I haven't been tempted to turn fun into anything more serious. You have your past, and that's shaped you. I have mine.'

'What? What past? This is exactly what I'm talking about. I don't know anything about you! How can you sit there and start talking about marriage when we don't know one another? It's crazy.'

'Crazy it may be, but we're in the most intimate situation it's possible for two people to be in.'

'And, as you've just said, you've never considered marriage! So how on earth do you expect me to react when you sit there now, telling me that's the only solution to this situation?'

'You're looking at this in the wrong way—putting an unnecessarily negative spin on it.'

'What do you mean?'

'Marriage in the conventional sense of the word isn't something I believe in, and there's no point in my pretending otherwise.'

'"The conventional sense of the word"? Would that

be the convention of two people being together because they're in love?'

'The world is littered with kids who end up in therapy because of parents who got married because they thought they were *in love.* Your mother,' he inserted shrewdly, 'thought *she* was in love, and absconded to the other side of the world in complete defiance of common sense only for the marriage to end in tears.'

Maddie flushed. 'That's not the point.'

'It's precisely the point. You had all contact with this country and your grandfather severed because of your mother's headstrong pursuit of *love.*'

Maddie didn't answer because he had a point. 'You're twisting everything to suit your argument,' she muttered, shooting him a fulminating look from under her lashes. 'I didn't see this side of you when we…when I…'

'When you were overwhelmed with lust and jumped into bed with me?'

'You're *so* arrogant. I should have known that you couldn't be a carefree wanderer. Someone like that would have been a lot more humble, a lot more down-to-earth. He wouldn't have had an ego the size of a cruise liner.'

Leo grinned, because in spite of the tenseness of the situation he was enjoying her dry sense of humour and the way she wasn't caving in to him. *Yet.*

'One of those humble, down-to-earth, carefree wandering souls would have hit the high seas the minute you told him you were pregnant. Generally speaking, perpetual Peter Pans don't cope well with the thought of being tied down. Which brings us back to the matter in hand. What I'm proposing is a union for the sake of our child. A practical solution. Something that makes sense.'

'Oh, wow, Leo. You're *really* selling it to me,' Maddie said acidly. 'I always dreamed of love and marriage and then the pitter-patter of tiny feet. Now you're presenting me with marriage, the pitter-patter of tiny feet, and forget about love because love doesn't count for anything.'

'You thought you'd found love with a loser who turned on you because he thought you were a thief. So much for the myth that love can survive through thick and thin. Convince me that love is all that matters when your mother learnt the hard way and so did you. Love is all a crock of—'

'Stop!' Maddie stood up to pace the room. 'Look…' She breathed in deeply. 'I know you mean well, and you have good intentions, and your offer is very generous, but I can't think of anything worse than being stuck with someone with whom I have no emotional connection.'

Stuck with? Was she actually *trying* to enrage him?

'But this isn't about *you,* is it?'

'Not entirely.' Maddie reddened. 'But it's not all about our child either. Yes, every child deserves two parents—but only if those parents are happy and committed to one another.'

Leo could no longer contain his impatience. 'Strip back the jargon and how many couples tick all the boxes?' Restless, he stood up to prowl the room, just as she was, until they were facing one another like opponents in a ring.

'I don't care about how many couples tick the boxes or don't,' Maddie muttered stubbornly, tearing her eyes away from his ridiculously beautiful face. 'I care about whether *I* would be able to tick the boxes with my partner.'

'Oh, bring on the violin music!' Leo fought down the urge to thump something in sheer frustration. How was it that he was having to wage war in an effort to persuade someone to share a life of obscene wealth and privilege?

'I couldn't bear the thought of being married to someone because he felt responsible for a situation he hadn't banked on.'

'Are you telling me that you would rather jeopardise the well-being of a child for your own selfish concerns?'

'It's not selfish.'

'You of all people should be able to understand the limitations of a life with only one parent. Yes, it's common. Yes, single parent families are a statistic. But you are turning down the option of *two* parents. Do you think our child will thank you for that in the years to come?'

Maddie glared, buffeted by the pull of his arguments, all of which made perfect sense in a way, but…

'We don't *love* one another,' she cried in protest.

She thought of those moments they'd shared and was embarrassed at how powerful her instinct was to read into them a bonding and a meeting of minds that hadn't been there. There had been something about that brief time they'd spent together that had made her feel as though she'd found her soulmate.

'What happens when we get bored with one another? What happens when you start resenting the fact that you're tied to someone you don't want to be with?'

'I don't see the point of conjecture. We have to deal with the here and now.'

'How can you be so...*practical*?'

'Because one of us needs to be.'

'I can't marry you. Yes, I *know* I should be hardened and cynical—but I'm not.'

Leo could recognise defeat as well as the next man. He'd approached the situation from the only perspective that made sense and had automatically assumed that she would fall in line—because, frankly, what woman wouldn't? He'd failed to take into account the fact that it was fair to say in the short space of time he'd known her she had been nothing like any of the women he had ever gone out with. So why should she react with any degree of predictability?

Too late he was recognising that she was as headstrong and stubborn as a mule, and as capable of digging her heels in as strenuously as he was.

'Are you telling me that you'd like to spread your net and see what you can catch while you're pregnant with my baby?'

'Of course not! What man is going to look twice at a woman who's having someone else's child?'

'You'd be shocked,' he muttered in a driven undertone.

When he thought of her putting herself out there, finding some loser who was only interested in spinning her some line so that he could crawl all over her body, he saw red. But he was quick enough to realise that any show of anger wasn't going to cut it. The more he tried to cajole and badger her into seeing things from his point of view, the more she was going to backpedal and see him as the bad guy, trying to force her into a loathsome life of undiluted luxury.

'Okay.' He held his hand up in a gesture of surrender

that made Maddie narrow her eyes suspiciously. 'Let's move on to another pragmatic approach to the situation. One that excludes what I still maintain is the most desirable solution. You don't want marriage? Well, I can't frogmarch you up the aisle, bound and tied. But we're going to have to approach this calmly.'

He patted the space on the sofa next to him and she sat down and twisted to look at him.

His dark, dark blue eyes immediately made Maddie feel hot and bothered, but when she looked away all she could see was the taut pull of his trousers over his muscular thighs, the bronzed forearms liberally sprinkled with dark hair, the way that dark hair curled round the matt gold of his watch strap… She felt faint.

'Go on,' she managed to croak, noting that he had dumped the marriage solution faster than the speed of light when she'd provided him with a get-out clause.

'I will want to be actively involved in everything from this point onwards. And I certainly will not risk you doing a runner by buying the store from you. You want it. It's yours. That way I am assured that you won't be leaving the place any time soon.'

'But you live here…in London…'

'And naturally I'll continue to oversee things here. But I can run my empire from anywhere in the world, such is the nature of communications these days. And Dublin seems to be an extremely charming place in which to settle… Nice restaurants, spectacular scenery, friendly locals…'

Leo thought that he could usefully live there for a few months and use that time to source an alternative location for his business… Or he might just explore the outskirts of the city and put in place the makings of a golf complex which he had been toying with for some time. It would be a little holiday, in a manner of speaking.

Naturally his grandfather would be curious as to his sudden change of location from London to Dublin, and the absence of a deal on the store, and in due course Leo would explain all. If Maddie was wary of *him*, then being confronted by his grandfather, whose thoughts about children being born out of wedlock were firmly rooted somewhere in the Victorian era, would have her running for the hills.

And, up close and personal, he would be able to keep an eye on her. She had dug her heels in and refused the marriage solution, but there was more than one way to skin a cat, and Leo was in little doubt that she would see the wisdom of that solution once she began to struggle with the technicalities of running a store…when the difficulties of being a single parent loomed all the more glaringly.

Because he would be there right next to her—a constant alternative waiting in the wings. He would get the girl, he thought, even if he had to play the waiting game for a bit.

'But you don't… You don't have anywhere to live here…'

Maddie wondered what it would be like to live with him, to wake up next to him every morning and go to sleep with the warmth of his body against hers. And then she immediately killed that stupid fantasy, because nothing could be further from reality.

This was never going to be a love story with a happy ending.

'That won't be a problem.' Leo shrugged. 'I'll buy somewhere.'

'*Buy* somewhere?'

'You'd be surprised how fast a house can change hands when enough money is put on the table,' Leo said drily. 'I don't foresee a problem.'

'I won't do a runner. How can I when I'll have a store to oversee? There's no need for you to decamp to Ireland.'

Leo spread his arms wide in a gesture of magnanimity which made her think of a predatory shark, trying to convince a school of minnows that, no, it wasn't *in the least bit* interested in gobbling them up.

'Like I said, whether you do a runner or not, I intend to be here for you every step of the way.' He shot her a slow, curling smile. 'You'll have me around twenty-four-seven—without the inconvenience of a wedding ring on your finger...'

CHAPTER SEVEN

MADDIE LOOKED AT the half-finished building work which she had tentatively begun on her house six weeks previously. It was just another aggravating headache added to the pile of aggravating headaches which had been slowly but steadily mounting ever since she had confidently declared to Leo that if he didn't want to buy the store from her then she was overjoyed, because she would be able to rebuild her family's legacy and return it to its former glory.

Niggling problems had arisen at the store. Missing stock, inadequate paperwork for suppliers which had only just come to light, a persistent leak in one of the departments on the top floor, which the plumbing team had ominously told her *'looked bad'*... After that she had dismissed them, so that she could consider her options.

Several members of staff had also chosen to quit, following the announcement of her ownership, and replacing them was proving another headache because everyone seemed to think that there was no chance the store was a viable employer—even though she had personally sat in at all the interviews and done her best to persuade them otherwise.

And now this.

Maddie sighed and contemplated the exposed plasterboard and the flooring which had been ripped up—but not in its entirety. Which meant that half the kitchen floor was comprised of the original tired tiles and the other half of bare brick and wood, with enough gaps to let in several families of rodents.

The fridge had been disconnected, and now the builder had phoned to say that he wasn't going to be around for the next week because of a 'personal emergency'.

Maddie looked at her phone.

Leo.

She didn't want to think of him but she did. She couldn't help herself. True to his word, he had been around a lot. Phoning her. Arranging to meet her for lunch. Insisting on doing the occasional grocery shop with her because he wanted to make sure she was buying food that was nutritious.

She refused to invite him back to her house, just as she discouraged his visits to the store. She wanted and needed her independence. She'd turned him down and for good reason. The last thing she wanted was to drift into a state where she found herself depending on him, and she knew that was a real danger because he was just so damned *present.* The perfect gentleman.

There had been no mention of marriage, nothing that could be construed as being remotely sexual... He was just strong, reliable, and annoyingly, infuriatingly *helpful.*

Maddie knew that she should be grateful that he'd never overstepped the mark.

She didn't want him in the house? He shrugged and took the hint with alacrity.

She was vague about him visiting the store? He acquiesced with another of those non-committal shrugs of his.

He treated her as though she was made of porcelain, and the only time she'd sensed that he was having trouble backing down was when she had absolutely refused to see his private doctor on a weekly basis because it was 'better safe than sorry'.

All in all, he had treated her with tact, consideration and a detached courtesy. And, however much she told herself that that was a *good* thing, she hated it.

On the spur of the moment she dialled the hotline number. For the first time since he had given it to her weeks ago.

In the middle of a high-level meeting, attended by a select handful of people who had come to see him because he had no intention of spreading himself thin by going to see *them*, Leo raised one imperious hand, at which all conversation stopped.

Maddie's name had flashed up on his screen, and since it was the first time she had deigned to call him he had no intention of ignoring the call.

Frankly, he'd grown tired of waiting. To start with he'd expected her to phone him within a few days—if only because *he* called *her* with tiresome regularity, and whatever had happened to good manners and meeting halfway on the effort front?

Then, when no phone call had materialised, he'd banked on that changing just as soon as she'd unearthed all the problems at the store. Hadn't he volunteered to help her often enough?

Several weeks later and he'd all but given up.

'Leo,' he said now, without preamble.

'Sorry, I'm disturbing you,' Maddie apologised, the reluctance in her voice making it clear how uncomfortable she was having given in to the temptation of calling him.

Leo looked at the room full of important people who had gathered there for his convenience. 'Not in the slightest.'

'It's just that…'

'Tell me what's wrong.' He half turned, making a motion with one hand to inform the gathering that they were to continue without him and indicating that his second-in-command would host.

'Nothing's wrong… It's just that…well… I'm here at home…' Maddie gazed with despair at the half-finished kitchen, in which cooking no halfway decent meal had been possible for the past two weeks. 'And I'm having one or two little problems… It's nothing, really… I shouldn't have bothered you.'

'I'm on my way.'

Leo killed the phone call before she could launch into a long-winded monologue of apology.

For the first time in his life he knew what it felt like to be worried. He was worried now. He'd never met anyone as stubbornly determined to be self-sufficient as Maddie, and the fact that she had confessed to having 'one or two problems' was a source of high-voltage concern—because *'one or two problems'* could range from a chipped nail to the sky falling down.

No, he thought, scrap the chipped nail and go straight to the sky falling down.

His Ferrari was equipped to deliver him to her house in record time, and he rang the doorbell and kept his finger there, already planning on breaking the door down if she didn't answer it within ten seconds.

She answered it before brute force became necessary.

'What's wrong?' were his opening words as he strode past her into the hall and then spun round on his heel, eyes narrowed, inspecting her from head to toe for visible signs of distress.

She was as stunning as she always was. Very slightly showing her pregnancy now, but it was hardly noticeable under the jogging bottoms and the baggy top.

Distractedly, Leo marvelled that she could take the most unfortunate of outfits and turn it into something intensely sexy.

He shifted impatiently as his body began to undermine his common sense. As it was wont to do with predictable regularity. She'd laid down her parameters six weeks ago—turned his marriage proposal down and all but said that she deserved someone better than him, someone more suitable, someone who came with the full package.

Forced into a corner, and obliged to bide his time, Leo knew that he couldn't risk undermining his own objectives by giving in to the temptation to put that will power of hers to the test.

He focused on her face, but there was no reprieve there because the connection that lured him in wasn't just about the way she looked or the way his body reacted to hers. Something ran deeper, like a powerful underwater current, and that pull operated on a completely different level.

Leo frowned, as he always did when this kind of thinking ambushed him, not quite knowing what to do with the confused jumble of feelings he couldn't seem to pin down and box up. He spoke to her on the phone and her voice did something to him. It was bizarre, a little perplexing. He didn't care to dwell on it.

Instead, he thought about those sidelong glances when she'd thought he wasn't looking. He could have done something about that, but he'd backed away. Push her even a little at the wrong time, he'd reasoned, and she would be off. And he wasn't going to risk that happening just for the sake of staunching the painful ache of desire that took him over whenever he was around her.

For someone as accustomed as he was to the transitory nature of lust, Leo was a little shocked at how much he still wanted to touch Maddie. Even when she wasn't around she was in his head like a burr. Was it because she had been elevated to a position never previously occupied by any other woman? Mother of his unborn baby. Or was it because the physical side of their relationship had not been allowed to follow its natural course and wind down to its inevitable conclusion?

Maybe it was a mixture of both. Leo didn't know. He just knew that he seemed to be engaged in a permanent battle to keep his hands off her.

Maddie chewed her lip—and then she did the absolute unthinkable. She burst into tears.

Panicked, Leo pulled her to him and held her close. He smoothed her hair and mumbled softly. Just when he needed a handkerchief he discovered that he didn't have one, so he wiped her cheek with his knuckle and listened to her tell him that nothing was wrong, that she didn't know why she was crying and that it could only be hormones—and actually she shouldn't have called him.

'Talk to me,' was his response to all that.

'I feel overwhelmed,' Maddie confessed in a small voice, getting her crazy crying jag under control but not pulling out of his embrace 'The store… The house…'

Since Leo had only heard about developments at the store second-hand, and hadn't been to the house at all, he took a chance to look around him, then beyond her, to the open door through which he glimpsed the chaos of what remained of the kitchen.

Swearing softly under his breath, he edged her away from him. 'Why didn't you tell me?'

He wanted to sweep her off her feet and carry her to the scene of the crime, but rather than spook her with caveman antics he shuffled, still holding her, until they were both in the kitchen. He settled her into one of the chairs that hadn't been rehomed somewhere else while work was being carried out.

Or not, judging from the state of things.

He inspected the shoddy, half-finished mess.

An unusable kitchen.

Leo looked around for another chair and then, not finding one handy, did the caveman thing after all and swept her off her feet as though she weighed nothing. He carried her into the living room, which contained most of the displaced contents of the kitchen.

'I repeat,' he said, gently depositing her on the sofa and then dragging a chair over so that he could pin her to the spot without any room for manoeuvre, 'why didn't you tell me about this sooner?'

'They said it would only take two weeks.'

'Name of the company?'

'Well…'

'Maddie, just tell me who you employed to do this job.'

She fumbled with her cell phone and passed it to him, so that he could see the details of the company she'd used, and then, silencing her with one hand while he phoned them, she listened as he let rip.

No shouting, no bellowing and no threats. His voice was soft—dangerously soft—and the threat was implicit. 'One week,' he said, 'and don't make me regret giving you that long…'

And then he made her tell him, leaving nothing out, what was going on both in the store and the rest of the house.

The store would come together. At least he had a foothold of sorts there, and could make sure no disasters occurred. The house, on the other hand…

'The kitchen is effectively out of bounds?' he said finally, and Maddie nodded sheepishly.

'So how have you been able to eat?'

'I… Well…'

'You're pregnant, Maddie. I don't want to hear any evasive non-answers. Yes, I have taken you out for dinners and the occasional lunch, but in between… Tell me what your diet has been. Because from the looks of it there have been no cooking facilities here for some time.'

Leo had never thought that being the Great Protector could feel so good.

'A little over two weeks…'

'That's plenty long enough when you're supposed to be putting nutrients into your body.'

'I've been eating,' she mumbled sheepishly, but he read in her eyes that it had been a long time since she had seen a homecooked meal.

'This isn't going to do,' Leo said flatly. 'I can't stop you jeopardising your *own* well-being by living off preservative-stuffed junk food, but I *can* and *will* prevent you from damaging the baby you're carrying!'

She pulled herself together and said primly, 'Once everything's in place my eating habits will return to normal. I love cooking. I would never not eat, and you don't have to tell me that this isn't a good time to have an erratic diet. I'm not an idiot.'

'Again, you should have told me sooner.'

'I didn't think the builders would just up and disappear.'

'You're stressed, and stress is the last thing you need right now.'

And, he thought, she couldn't accuse *him* of contributing to the source of her stress, considering he had done nothing but kick his heels for the past few weeks, gritting his teeth in silent frustration as she became more and more entrenched in her determination to prove how self-sufficient she was.

There were times when she seriously made him want to tear his hair out.

'Let's go upstairs,' he said abruptly, coming to a decision and not giving himself time to have any rethink.

Maddie's eyes widened. 'For what?'

Leo looked at her in silence for a few seconds. 'What

would you like it to be for?' he couldn't resist asking, his voice as soft as silk.

He lowered his eyes, annoyed with himself and with the prompt response of his libido to the thought of having her. More than anything he would like to see her changing body…ripening with his child.

'You're going to pack your bags,' he said gruffly, 'because you're leaving here today. With me.'

'What?'

'You recall I mentioned that my grandfather is cruising in the Caribbean and had stopped off to stay on one of the smaller islands? Well, the villa on that island belongs to me, and I intend on taking you there. Unfortunately there will be no meet-and-greet with him, as he's now enjoying the splendours of the open seas, but it's a great place to unwind—and you need to unwind.'

Leo couldn't disguise a certain amount of relief that Benito had left the island. In due course he would meet the woman who would become his future granddaughter-in-law, as far as he was concerned, and Leo hadn't disillusioned him. It was a bridge to be crossed when he got to it. But he would certainly be thrilled to think that they would be going to the villa together—as a couple.

'Leo, that's ridiculous! I can't just…just leave for a holiday while everything here is in disarray!'

But the thought of doing that dangled like a carrot in front of her.

'Leave everything to me,' Leo said, rising to his feet and heading out towards the hall and the staircase while Maddie shot up and tripped along behind him.

'I can manage just fine on my own,' she said, dutifully registering a protest vote.

He spun round to stare at her with incredulity.

'No, Maddie, you can't. The house is a mess. You haven't been eating. You've hired a team of builders who have obviously got the message that they can do as they please because you're too stressed out to stand your ground. You're too proud to ask for help. Whether you like it or not, you're going to pack two bags of summer clothes and we're going to fly out to my house first thing in the morning. Now, I can either pack those bags for you, or you can pack them yourself. When the bags are packed you're going to come back with me to my place, spend the night, and forget every single worry that's been dragging you down.'

'Since when did you become so bossy?'

Leo dealt her an amused, crooked smile.

'Sometimes being bossy is the only thing that works when you're dealing with a woman who digs her heels in so far that she refuses to ask for help even when she discovers she can't pull them out. Now, the bags...?'

Maddie gazed out of the window on the plane to the bank of clouds below. Everything had happened so fast that her head was still spinning. Put simply, Leo had taken over and, like a juggernaut, had bulldozed every single obstacle until she had left behind a trusted foreman who was going to supervise the work on the house with a rod of steel. And as far as the store was concerned he had moved in some of his own people.

'The store is yours,' he had told her before she'd been able to object, 'but you need the right resources to run it. I'll make sure you have them.'

Maddie had accepted without hesitation. Pride was one thing, but other people's livelihoods depended on her doing what she had set out to do with the store, and it had been proving more time-consuming and difficult than she had imagined. Pregnant, and with her head not entirely focused on the store, she had been distracted. And in the evenings she was very, very tired. Too tired to commit to the gruelling hours necessary at this stage in the process of taking the store out of the doldrums. And there was a limit to how much she could ask her trusted employees to do.

Leo would not take advantage. She knew that. She'd spent the past few weeks coming to terms with the fact that he was a man who was true to his word—a completely different species from Adam, with whom she had first so rashly compared him.

Leo was honourable to a fault. His proposal to her had been the ultimate act of selflessness, because he didn't love her, had never planned on having any sort of relationship with her after that one heady night of sex, and had never factored marriage to any woman into his agenda. He had his reasons, and she was guessing that he'd been hurt just as she had, but that aside she'd always known that he was not a guy in it for the long term. Yet, he'd bitten the bullet and proposed because he'd felt it was the right thing to do.

Not once over the past few weeks had he tried to bully her into marrying him either. He had obeyed all the *Do Not Trespass* signs she had posted without complaint. And that was pretty amazing, because she had thought that there was something fundamentally restless and impatient about him that would have had him crashing through any signs that didn't suit him.

She would not come back to find that the store had been converted into an electronics shop. Not that there was any chance of that anyway, because they would only be away for ten days.

She sneaked a sidelong glance at him. He was working, frowning slightly as he read through whatever was on his screen. He was perfectly still and yet he exuded the sort of energy that made her think of a resting tiger.

Ten days in his company…

How on earth was she going to cope?

Her heart picked up speed. Being in his company was a balancing act, and only now, with all the usual distractions removed, was she recognising that balancing act for what it was. A breathless mixture of excitement and apprehension, a forbidden longing that defied logic, and a need to get close to the fire even though it was dangerous.

It was okay when she was only seeing him now and again, only hearing that dark, velvety voice a couple of times a day. It was okay when there were other people around to dilute the force of his personality. But she quailed at the thought of being with him in an empty house.

'You never said…' She cleared her throat. 'Does anyone live in the…er…villa?'

Leo saved what he had been reading with the press of a key and angled his big body towards her in the first-class seat, which was generous but still somehow felt cramped to him.

'Anyone like who?' he drawled, amused by the delicate flush that had spread across her high cheekbones.

He'd expected her to fight him when it came to this trip because she seemed to want to fight him on everything, but she had conceded quickly and with a hint of relief.

Life was tough when you had no experience of the big, bad world of business—and when you'd made it your mission not to ask for help from the one person who could help you. Maddie was finding that out for herself and, whilst he was furious that she had allowed the situation to get out of hand before coming to him, he knew that he had finally found a way in to her.

He'd played the waiting game and he'd soon got fed up with it. It wasn't his style. Now that waiting game was over. He would show her just how good her life could be with him in it.

There was no way he was going to let her go down any road that saw him being pushed into second place in the parent stakes—arranging visits and watching from the sidelines while some other guy took the reins.

But any threat of a custody battle wouldn't do him any favours. Leo was very realistic about that. He worked long hours and, whilst he might have bottomless funds when it came to providing financial security, it would be crazy to think that a live-in nanny would be any match for Maddie. No sane judge would rule in his favour. He wouldn't contemplate any such course of action. Because if he did, and subsequently lost, the price he would end up paying would be high.

Time had not been his friend. But he intended to make sure that it would be from now on, and being with her, a little voice said, wasn't exactly going to be a hardship. She had the oddest talent when it came to lifting his spirits, even though *accommodating* and *acquiescent* were two words that could never be used to describe her. and he'd always plumped for those two things when it came to the opposite sex.

'Staff?' Maddie ventured, wondering what sort of

staff manned a villa that was empty most of the year. 'You haven't really said much about it. How big is it? And why on earth do you have a villa on an island in the Caribbean if you hardly ever go there?'

'Investment,' Leo said succinctly. 'I tend to use it as a company retreat. Occasionally as a bonus holiday for high achievers. So, yes, there's staff. When it's empty they come in twice weekly, to air the place and make sure nothing's amiss, but it's used fairly frequently so they're kept busy much of the time. They're all on hefty retainers, so they're there whenever I need them.'

'Wow. Sometimes…'

'Sometimes?'

'Sometimes when you say stuff like that—like when you said that you would stay in Ireland and buy a house and it wouldn't be a problem because you could throw money at it—I realise just how *different* we are from one another.'

'Different doesn't necessarily mean incompatible.'

'Leo, before I went to work for Lacey I scrubbed floors. My mum worked all the hours God gave to make ends meet. She didn't get a penny from my grandfather…'

No surprise there, Leo thought. Old Tommaso, if his own grandfather could be believed, had forgotten how to spend money unless it was on drink or horses. He certainly wouldn't have been sending any to the daughter he'd excommunicated because of her lifestyle choices.

He'd made it quite clear—and indeed Leo had read the letter sent to his grandfather years ago, after his last purchase attempt of the store had hit a brick wall—that selling the store was as pie in the sky as welcoming back his wayward daughter.

'Too proud to ask, I'll bet…' Maddie said sadly.

'Really?'

'She could be stubborn.'

'The family resemblance is duly noted,' Leo remarked wryly.

Maddie blushed. 'I've never had a holiday, and when I came over here it was the first time I'd been on a plane.'

'We grew up in very different backgrounds,' Leo conceded, 'but we share some very similar traits. I've never known any woman as bloody stubborn as me, or as determined to set a course and stick to it.' He looked at her narrowly. 'Occasionally a person has to dig beneath the surface.'

'You're only saying that because I'm pregnant with your baby and you have to find *some* positives.'

'If that bastard ex of yours was around,' Leo said grimly, 'I'd flatten him.'

Maddie pinkened with pleasure at the possessiveness in Leo's voice. 'He did me a favour. He made me careful about trusting people.'

'He took away your confidence, and for that he deserves to be ripped apart limb by limb.'

'I'm just being realistic. Anyway… You haven't said… Will the house be staffed?'

'There will just be the two of us.' He shrugged, 'So there won't be any need to have the place swamped with staff. There will be a discreet service—a skeleton staff—and they, naturally, will not live in. No need for you to do anything at all on the domestic front, and I feel we're perfectly capable of taking care of our own breakfasts,'

'Of course,' Maddie said faintly. 'I've been doing that

all my life. I think I've got my technique well-honed when it comes to putting some cereal in a bowl or boiling an egg and making some toast.'

Leo's mouth twitched with amusement. 'I find it tiresome if there are people hovering when I want privacy…'

Maddie wondered what sort of privacy Leo had in mind, and had to soothe herself with the timely reminder that he was no longer interested in her as a sexual being. She was carrying his child and had now entered a different category. He'd gone from wanting her to wanting to make sure she was okay—which was a completely different thing.

But she wanted him to care because of *her* and not just because of the fact that she was carrying his baby. She wanted to crawl into his arms and have him hold her because he wanted to—not because he was concerned about her stress levels because of the baby…

She pushed the thought away.

'You won't have to think about anything while you're out there, Maddie,' he continued.

'That's a big promise, Leo.' She laughed, surprised at how relaxed she felt in his company—but then, when she'd first met him she'd felt relaxed as well.

For a moment he wasn't Leo the billionaire, who'd wanted her store and was now stuck with her because of the pregnancy, but the Leo who had charmed her with his wit and humour and mind-blowing sex appeal.

'I've never been in a situation where I haven't had to think about *something*, so I'm not sure how I would cope with that.'

She blushed when he fixed his amazing eyes on her with thoughtful, speculative intensity.

'You haven't had an easy life,' he conceded, 'but now you're pregnant, and your days of having to stress and worry are over.'

'I'm not a piece of china.' But the protest was half-hearted.

'You are to me.'

Maddie blushed a little more, rattled because there was something intimate about what he was saying—even though she knew that he was just reiterating what he'd said from the beginning, which was that she was his responsibility now that she was pregnant, whether she liked it or not.

She cleared her throat but couldn't quite meet his gaze. 'I shouldn't complain anyway. I have a lot to be thankful for, thanks to my grandfather's legacy. I have the store, and a roof over my head, and sufficient money to have secured the bank loan. I just wish,' she confessed, 'that I could have met him.'

'Tommaso?' Leo looked at her, startled. 'Why?'

'What do you mean *why*?' Maddie asked. 'I never knew my dad. My mum ran away from her family—precious little of it as there was—and severed all ties. There was always just me and my mum. And, yes, she used to say that we were two against the world, but I would really have liked it to have been *lots* of us against the world. Two is such a lonely number… I knew I was never going to meet my father, and I never wanted to, but I would have loved to have met my grandfather—especially as I think that he probably wanted to meet me, to have Mum relent…'

'What gives you *that* idea?'

'He left everything to me,' Maddie said flatly. 'Why else would he have done that?'

'Because it's the Italian way,' Leo said drily.

'You're so cynical, Leo.'

'He was never going to leave his dwindling fortune to the local cat sanctuary.'

She looked away, her chin at a defiant angle, heated colour still tingeing her cheeks.

Leo could see that Maddie wanted to believe the best of Tommaso—was desperate to forge a link with the grandfather she'd never known—and taking care of the store was part of that. She obviously had no idea what the wily fox had really been like, and on the spot Leo decided that that was something he would never reveal. Let her keep her dreams.

Besides, instigating show-downs and arguments wasn't part of his agenda.

He relaxed and said soothingly, 'To the best of my knowledge, he was no animal lover. And perhaps you're right—perhaps it was his way of reaching out to you from beyond the grave…'

'You think so?'

The urge to burst out laughing died on his lips as he took in the earnestness of her expression, the *hope*. Not for the first time, he cursed the old bastard who had stubbornly refused to make amends with his only child—and with the grandchild he had never seen.

'I'm sure that's exactly how it was,' he said gravely.

Leo had always wanted the store—had promised his grandfather he'd get it—but he knew that he wasn't going to stamp out Maddie's curiously romanticised dreams to get his way, and knew that his grandfather would understand. Frankly, the prospect of a great-grandchild would be a heck of a lot more exciting to the old man.

'Mum never talked about any of it. She was way too proud. I sometimes wonder whether I should have pressed her more for answers.'

'Why didn't you?'

'I knew it would upset her.'

'Understandable,' Leo said in a low, roughened undertone. 'And of course it's only when we're older that we have the confidence to tackle our parents on an adult footing. Respect often gets in the way of interrogation, and I guess by the time you came of age you were wrapped up in having to deal with much bigger issues because your mother was ill.'

Maddie looked astounded at his understanding of just where she was coming from.

'Don't beat yourself up over that,' he said, more briskly. 'I find it never pays to dwell on the past. In less than four hours you're going to be at my villa, without a care in the world. I have everything at the store under control, and my team will be reporting daily on work to your house.'

Returning to his laptop—because there was such a thing as too much touchy-feely, *let's get the tissues out and have a good old cry* bonding—he glanced at her out of the corner of his eye and saw, with great satisfaction, that when she lay back and closed her eyes all traces of anxiety had been wiped clean from her face.

CHAPTER EIGHT

MADDIE HAD NO real idea what to expect at the end of the nine-hour trip—mostly by plane, but for the final leg on the small speedboat which had been waiting for them at the marina. But any awkwardness at being so far removed from her comfort zone with Leo was dispelled in her speechless wonderment at the stunning island on which they finally found themselves.

Evening was fast approaching, and as they were taken from one marina on the main island to be deposited at another marina on its much smaller sister, she could just about appreciate the scenery as it was gradually absorbed into darkness. Burnt orange skies turned to violet, then finally to star-pricked black, and she saw lush vegetation, soft, rounded hills, a main road that was just big enough for two cars to pass side by side, and banks upon banks of gently swaying coconut trees, tall and spindly and graceful.

'It's stunning,' she breathed, her head swinging from left to right as the car which had been waiting for them, and which Leo was now handling like an expert, bounced along the uneven road.

There was virtually no traffic at all. But lights from occupied houses could be glimpsed as they went along.

This was the enclave of the super-rich—an island on which they could relax without fear of paparazzi or nosy neighbours with binoculars.

Somewhere close to the marina they had left behind was a small but functioning town, where the essentials could be purchased and where several high-end restaurants catered for the island's wealthy visitors, and for anyone else who wanted to travel by boat from the main island and enjoy the top-rated cuisine.

Leo explained all this as they drove towards his villa. His voice was low and soothing, and the melodious background noise of the sea was achieving the impossible and making her forget all about the stress she had left behind in Ireland.

Leo had promised her complete rest and relaxation and he was already delivering on that promise big-time. She hadn't felt this rested in a long, long time.

Sneaking a sideways glance at his strong profile as he concentrated on driving, she felt her body respond in the way she had tried so hard to train it not to do. Her breathing slowed and her eyelids fluttered and she was assailed by total recall of how those strong hands had felt roaming all over her body.

She pushed those thoughts away to the back of her mind because they were inappropriate. She and Leo had to grope their way to a new and different footing, and getting turned on by him had no place in that scenario.

They would share a child and have a cordial but detached relationship. There could be nothing else for them. Because she could never and *would* never marry anyone who had to be dragged up the aisle like a prisoner in handcuffs. She deserved better—no matter what he said about two parents being better than one. She *knew* that two parents were better than one! But only if those parents had married for the right reasons.

What if *her* parents had decided to stick together because of *her*? Would her childhood have been picture-perfect with a disillusioned and bitter mother and a father manacled against his will? He would only have wanted marriage for the fortune he'd anticipated getting out of her mother, and would have suddenly found himself anchored down because of a child on the way.

Needless to say that was a fairly impossible scenario to imagine, because her father hadn't had an ounce of responsibility running through his veins, but still…

And yet for all that sensible reasoning, with the balmy night air outside and the foreign sight of a velvety black sky dotted with stars, Maddie *was* turned on—as though a dimmer switch had been buzzing in the background and had suddenly been turned to full beam.

She shifted, and was alarmed at the suffocating sense of *want*.

It was almost a relief when the car rounded a bend and there was the villa, lit up on the outside. It was ranch-style, with a massive outer veranda that seemed to circle the whole impressive building like a necklace. They drove into the courtyard, with Leo making innocuous conversation about the island and what she might expect by way of entertainment.

Which was very little from the sounds of it.

'I hate clubs anyway,' Maddie said distractedly as she stared at the villa and tried to get her head around how much her life had changed in the space of a few months.

She rested her hand on her stomach and for a few seconds wished that the perfect life she'd always dreamed of had materialised. With a baby on the way and financial security, and finally feeling well and truly over her stupid, ill-advised ex, things should have been so good—but what promised so much on the outside was riddled with rot on the inside, and she couldn't get away from that.

Leo didn't care about her. He was doing all this because of the baby. If it weren't for the new life she was carrying he would have waged a no-holds-barred attack on her in order to get the store, and the single night they had shared would have been a distant memory.

He didn't care about her.

But she cared about him.

She shivered and tried to unravel that thought so that she could pick it apart and make a nonsense of it. But it had formed and it refused to budge.

She cared about him.

She might have thrown caution to the wind and slept with him for all the right reasons, but she had remained connected to him after sex, even though she'd barely been aware of it.

And then finding out she was pregnant… That had opened a door and allowed all sorts of things to enter—all sorts of emotions that she hadn't been able to staunch. She'd seen beyond the billionaire. And once that had happened she'd been seduced by all the complex sides of him that showed him to be honourable, decent, fair…

She'd fallen for those traits.

She'd fallen for the guy who had stepped up to the plate when it had mattered and had backed off when she had told him to.

Maddie had to remind herself strenuously of all the reasons she had told him to back off, because in a moment of weakness, as he drew to a stop and then turned to look at her, his beautiful face all shadows and angles, she wondered what she had done.

He'd proposed marriage and she'd turned him down flat. Why? Had he been right? Had she been selfish?

She could do a lot worse than marry someone who was *not* the sort of ruthless money-making machine she had written him off as being. And who knew? He could come to love her. Couldn't he?

Maddie hated having those thoughts, because she knew how dangerous they were.

'Hello?' Leo interrupted drily. 'I've lost you. Please don't tell me that you've suddenly decided to get cold feet because you're going to be sharing a villa with me.'

'Huh?' Maddie blinked.

Leo contained his impatience. 'Separate quarters,' he told her abruptly, swinging out of the car and feeling the blast of late-evening humidity, hearing the orchestra of insects which was so much part and parcel of this part of the world.

Never had he had to curtail his energy and his driving need to act as much as over the past few hours. It was frustrating. He was the father of her child and prepared to do the decent thing. He was ready to sacrifice his freedom for the greater good. He couldn't understand why it was so damned hard for her to see that and accept it.

He prided himself on being a pretty unemotional guy, but now he was having to deal with irrational mood swings. One minute he was optimistic, determined to work his way into any cracks he could see, to find a foothold and frankly exploit it. The next minute he could smell her retreat and was at a loss as to whether to push forward or stand still. There was a helplessness to this situation that he found maddening, and it took all he had to tame his urge to *do something.*

His work was suffering. For the first time in his life he wasn't able to focus with the level of intensity he was so accustomed to. He was, for once, impotent. Unable to stamp his authority and get what he wanted, what he *knew* was right. And he *thought* about her. Without warning he would think about the sound of her laughter, or the way she sometimes looked at him out of the corner of her eye, or the things she said that could make him laugh out loud because her sense of humour so often mirrored his.

It was doing his head in.

'Separate quarters?' Maddie parroted.

'You needn't worry that your privacy is going to be invaded in any way,' Leo gritted, not looking at her but heaving the suitcases out of the car and preceding her into the villa. 'Although I should warn you in advance that there's no one here at the moment. We're both adults, and I didn't think it was necessary to have members of staff hovering here past their bedtime because we need chaperones.'

Maddie flushed, clearly apprehensive that he might not be able to restrain himself around her. Where would she have got that idea? Considering he'd backed right off and hadn't shown the slightest interest in her since she'd turned him down.

'Absolutely!' She smiled brightly and changed the subject. 'The villa is gorgeous, Leo. I'm surprised you don't want to retire here permanently!'

'Sun, sea and stars has never been my thing for longer than five minutes.'

Leo grinned that sexy grin that made her quiver inside.

'You're more wine, women and song?' Maddie quipped, following him into the villa and doing a complete turn as she absorbed her surroundings.

Cool shades of cream complemented wood and the bold silkscreen paintings on the walls. White shutters would keep the glare of the sun out. And as she wandered, agog, towards an expanse of glass towards the back of the villa, she glimpsed manicured lawns, lit up just as the front was.

When she turned around it was to find Leo looking at her—although he looked away as soon as their eyes met.

'Hungry?' he asked.

'A bit.'

'Kitchen's through here. Food will have been prepared and there will be no shortage of anything.'

'This is the most amazing house I've ever been in,' Maddie breathed, frankly awestruck and working hard to remember every socialist tendency that should be fighting to play down the shameless splendour of the villa.

Leo paused to look at her again, head tilted to one side. 'Funny, but I no longer notice my surroundings,' he mused truthfully.

'That's because you've always had far too much money,' she said sternly, and he burst out laughing, his navy eyes appreciative.

'I never thought I'd ever hear those words leave any woman's mouth.'

'Then you've been mixing with the wrong type of woman.'

She wasn't looking at him as she said this. She was

shamelessly peering out through the glass doors, squinting into the darkness, intrigued by the glimpse of an illuminated infinity pool.

'What sort of women do you think I *should* have been mixing with?'

Maddie started, because he had come up behind her and she could see his reflection in the glass—a towering, impossibly forceful presence that gave her goosebumps. The urge to sink back against that hard body was so overpowering that she inhaled deeply and stared blindly, trying hard to block him from her line of vision.

'Well?'

Leo stepped closer towards her. He had managed to angle the conversation into a place that felt highly personal, and suddenly he seemed determined to explore all those places she was trying to keep hidden from him—places where desire and lust were locked away.

'I—I don't know,' she stammered.

When she turned round it was to discover that he was even closer to her than she'd thought. But if she stepped back she'd bump into the glass. She was trapped with only inches between them.

Maddie could feel the heat emanating from his body in waves, and like a dose of incense it went to her head and made her feel giddy. She licked her lips and tried to think straight.

'Tut-tut,' Leo chided softly. 'You can't just make sweeping statements and then refuse to back them up. Do you think I should have been going out with earnest young women who like nothing better than to spend an evening discussing books?'

Maddie shifted and blushed. She tried to imagine Leo with a woman fitting that description and honestly couldn't think of *any* woman who wouldn't want to rip his clothes off within five seconds of occupying the same sofa as him.

'Well, they would have been better than women who like you for your money.'

'What makes you think that earnest young women who like discussing books wouldn't want me for my money? Wouldn't be impressed by all of this?' He spread his arms in an all-encompassing gesture, but his fabulous eyes remained firmly fixed to Maddie's face. 'After all, *you* are.'

Maddie glared at him and Leo laughed.

'But I do know that you weren't attracted to me because of my bank balance,' he murmured with satisfaction. 'Were you?'

Maddie muttered something inaudible. He was pinning her into a corner, standing just a fraction too close to her and looking at her just a little too intently and with slightly too much sexy humour for her to be comfortable.

Sex was off the menu!

But then she mentally kicked herself for even thinking that that would be going through his head. Leo was good at making her think all sorts of forbidden thoughts just by doing what he was doing now—getting just a little too much under her skin. He probably didn't even realise what he was doing!

Restless in her own skin, Maddie stared down for a few seconds and fidgeted.

'I really like that about you…'

Leo placed one finger under her chin in a barely there touch and Maddie immediately looked up, bright green eyes meeting deepest blue.

Suddenly she had somehow managed to turn into a swooning Victorian maiden—the same swooning maiden who had been bowled over by him, enough to leap into bed with him before he'd even finished asking. And as far as impulse decisions went, how clever had *that* one been? Considering she was standing here now, pregnant with his baby?

And yet…

When Maddie went through those 'sliding doors' and thought about the other road she might have gone down, she knew that she preferred this one.

What if he hadn't been after her store? What if he had genuinely been who he'd said he was? Or *implied* he was? A sexy guy just passing through—another rolling stone looking for adventure?

One night of passion and that would have been it. She would never have lain eyes on him again. She couldn't get her head around the enormity of that, because he had managed to become such a huge part of her life—always there in her thoughts in one way or another.

With the less attractive option—and the reason why she had to stand firm against the pulsing tide of craving that threatened to breach her defences the second she took her eye off the ball—came the realisation that under normal circumstances, and without a baby on the way, she *would* have met him again.

They would have had their one night and then she would have met the real Leo—the billionaire who wanted what she had and would stop at nothing to get his hands on it. He wouldn't have been toting her off to this fabulous villa in a tropical paradise. He would have been sitting, steely eyed, on the opposite side of a boardroom table while his team of lawyers tried to prise the store away from her. He wouldn't have given a damn about the sentiment wrapped up in her need to do something with her legacy. She would have been disposable.

Unfortunately nothing could stop the ache inside her when their eyes locked. It was as if he had somehow programmed her brain to ignore common sense. She could give herself a thousand bracing lectures about why she couldn't afford to let her body do the talking, but the second he did what he was doing now—looking at her *like that*—she was all lust and craving and weak-kneed desire.

'You bucked the trend,' Leo continued in the same musing low voice, as rich and as silky as the finest chocolate. 'You thought I had nothing and you weren't bothered. In fact what bothered you was thinking that you might have more than me...'

'I'm suspicious of rich guys after Adam,' Maddie breathed. 'And besides, I was raised not to place too much importance on money. I guess, when I look back, that was my mother's response to being disinherited. She'd given up everything for love. She couldn't start telling me that the only thing that mattered was money. But she must have found it so hard—especially in the beginning, when she could still remember what it was like to have everything she wanted at the snap of a finger.'

'Like I said...you bucked the trend...'

Maddie was mesmerised by his eyes, weakly unable to tear her gaze away. She blinked and gathered herself against the riptide pulling her under. 'Poor Leo. What a daily strain it must be, having to beat back women who want nothing more than to do whatever you want and fall into bed with you.'

Leo laughed and stepped back—which at least meant that she could breathe without fear that her airways would start closing up.

'Fortunately,' he drawled, 'I'm made of stern stuff, and I've found that I can handle that thorny dilemma reasonably well. Now, shall I show you to your quarters? You can shower and then join me for something to eat. It's late, but you need to fatten up.'

Wrenched out of her heated torpor, Maddie took a few seconds to establish that Leo was back to his usual self—casual and courteous and practically whistling a merry tune as he spun round and began sauntering off into the bowels of the sprawling villa.

She tripped along, soon catching up with him. She'd packed only one suitcase, which he'd retrieved from the airy hallway. When she reached for her carry-on he tut-tutted in a fashion that made her teeth snap together in frustration and took it from her.

'I'm not completely helpless, Leo,' she said, her mouth downturned and resentful because she knew that, however appropriate it was, this was not how she wished to be treated by him.

'In my eyes you are,' he purred, ignoring her tight-lipped expression and favouring her with a smile that was an annoying combination of ruefulness and pure charm. 'I hope this will do…'

He pushed open a door that led to the most wonderful bedroom Maddie had ever seen. The white wooden shutters were closed, but she knew that when they were open the light would flood in, because they covered the expanse of one entire wall. The king-sized bed was draped in the finest of mosquito nets, and the room was cooled by air-conditioning that was virtually silent. The décor, like in the rest of the villa, was pale. Cream walls, light bamboo furniture and an oversized squashy pale lemon sofa next to a door that led directly out onto the veranda that circled the house.

Leo was striding to another door, which he pushed open in the manner of an estate agent keen to show a prospective buyer all the home comforts.

'En-suite bathroom,' he said, and Maddie walked towards him and peered into a room the size of the apartment she had shared with her mother in Sydney.

Through an archway leading from the bedroom was a spacious sitting area, complete with a giant flat screen television and all the accoutrements of an office—which was the only indicator that the villa was used for work purposes much of the time.

He returned to the bedroom and stood to one side of the huge bed. 'Think you'll be comfortable?'

Maddie stared at him, mouth dry, and tried to get her wayward thoughts back in order—because seeing him there next to the bed was resurrecting all sorts of unfortunate memories.

She half closed her eyes and pictured his lean, muscular body splayed across the puffy white duvet, bronzed and hard and *naked.*

'It's perfect,' she croaked, jerkily heading to her suitcase and flipping it open so that he would get the message that it was time for him to leave.

Which he did.

'If you need anything…' Leo pointed to a bell which she hadn't noticed on the table next to the bed '…summon me…'

'Really?' Maddie almost smiled at his use of the expression. Without thinking, she added, half to herself,

'And what would you do?' Then she realised what she'd said and reddened.

'*You're* here to do nothing,' Leo told her, straight-faced, 'so basically I'll do whatever you want.'

The quiet charge of electricity thrummed between them.

'Oh? You'd cook and clean for me?' Maddie quipped, perversely tempted to keep him in the bedroom now that he was clearly itching to leave. 'Somehow I can't picture you doing *any* of that stuff, Leo.'

'Cleaning might be a problem,' he conceded with amusement. 'But I could definitely rise to the challenge of cooking—although there will be no need for that, bearing in mind I have round-the-clock staff who are paid to take care of those duties.'

For the first time in living memory he didn't flinch at the vision of domesticity that presented itself to him. He had a strangely satisfying vision of her resting on the sofa in his living room, heavy with his child, while he brought her home-cooked food.

He'd never cooked anything that hadn't come with printed instructions on the packet in which it was wrapped, but he was sure he could rustle up something and he rather enjoyed playing with that thought. Maybe in due course he would invest in a recipe book. Who knew? His life was changing, and it was going to change even more dramatically after the baby was born. Could he say with any certainty that he *wouldn't* be spending evenings in, wearing an apron and brandishing a spatula in front of the stove?

He grinned. The faster you accepted the inevitable, the better off you were. *Fact.*

He was pro-active, creative, solution-orientated, and

he seldom wasted energy pushing boulders up hills when they were very likely to come rolling right back down.

If you worked with what you'd got, however troublesome, you usually ended up coming out the victor. And, since Leo intended to come out the victor in this scenario, he was proud of the unusual tramline his thoughts were travelling along.

'Of course,' Maddie said politely.

'Although,' he mused, 'I might relieve them of some of their culinary duties.'

He wondered where the pots and pans were kept. It was an area of the kitchen he'd never felt the need to explore.

'Why would you do that?'

'Necessity,' Leo said succinctly. He lowered his eyes and looked at her lazily, each syllable leaving his mouth replete with intent. 'You will find that I'm a man who doesn't take shortcuts when it comes to the things that matter to me. My child will top that list. Having someone else prepare food will naturally work occasionally, but I'll do much of that myself.'

'You will?'

'What sort of father do you think I will be?'

'I—I haven't really given it much thought,' Maddie stammered, caught on the back foot at this unexpected tangent.

'I'm sure you have,' Leo responded wryly. 'Just as I'm sure that I don't emerge in those thoughts with flying colours. You think I would be an unsuitable rich husband who fails to live up to the storybook image in your head, and a likewise unsuitable rich father who thinks that money can take the place of time.'

'I've never thought anything of the sort!'

'Of course you did. At the risk of disillusioning you, I intend to be a hands-on father. My work life will be tailored to accommodate my child. I didn't envisage myself in the role of a father until it was sprung on me, but now that I am I will be giving it everything I have.'

He patiently waited for her to pounce. He almost felt that he knew her better than she knew herself.

Maddie shuffled as she sifted through what he was saying. Okay, so maybe she *had* been guilty of type-casting him as the wealthy but absent parent—but was that her fault? Workaholics were never interested in the small stuff, were they? Since when could she have expected the most eligible bachelor on the planet to willingly immerse himself in nappy-changing duties?

Was he just saying that to make a good impression?

No, why should he?

'So cooking practice might be just the thing.' Leo paused and looked at her after a moment's silence. 'And of course,' he continued, 'it would carry on, I imagine, even after I have found someone…'

'Found someone?' Maddie looked at him, disorientated. 'What are you talking about?'

'Well,' Leo said crisply, all business now, wrapping up their little *tête-à-tête* just at the point when she was hanging on to his every word, her heart beating like a crazy, caged bird inside her chest, 'you don't think that while you're roaming the streets in search of Prince Charming I'm going to be sitting in my apartment keeping the home fires burning as I pine for the marriage that never was, do you?'

Leo let the silence settle between them like a piece of lead dropping into still water, only to send concentric ripples across the surface, turning the stillness into a frenzy of motion.

He was by the bedroom door now, and he lounged against the doorframe, his lean, rangy body relaxed and at ease.

'Of course not!' Maddie was aware of her voice sounding a little less stable than usual and she cleared her throat.

'Good!' he said brightly. 'Because I won't be.'

'Although I really don't think it's acceptable for any child to be exposed to a constant carousel of women coming and going,' she protested stoutly, and Leo raised his eyebrows with an expression she understood completely. She was quick to clarify. 'I have no intention of entertaining a series of men in front of any child of mine!'

'And you have my word that I will likewise be extremely discreet in all *my* relationships.'

He watched as she fidgeted and stared at him. For a few seconds he was distracted by the lushness of her parted mouth and the soft little breaths coming from her. It surprised him how many of her mannerisms he had absorbed over time—right down to the way she had just tossed her hair back in a gesture that was proud, feisty and unconsciously sexy.

He had no intention of stressing her out. He had brought her here so that she could *de*-stress. But neither was he going to spend this valuable one-on-one time tiptoeing around her and waiting patiently for her to come to her senses.

When they returned to London and Benito was back from his cruise, he would condescend to meet the mother of his much longed-for grandchild, and Leo intended the picture to be complete, with wedding bells chiming in the not too distant future if not immediately imminent. He knew that Benito Conti would be bitterly disappointed to be presented with a complicated scenario of joint custody and visiting rights.

'The only woman our child will meet will be the woman who will become his or her stepmother.'

A dull pain spread through Maddie, making her limbs heavy. She suddenly wanted to be sick, because this very likely possibility was one she had not considered in much detail. She'd been far too wrapped up in standing her ground and refusing to compromise on her principles.

'I know you'll agree with me that our child would benefit from that.'

'So you wouldn't object if *I* found someone else?'

'What could I do?'

Leo gritted his teeth and controlled the insane thought that he would be tempted to pummel whoever she happened to find, which had to be double standards at their very worst.

'As you pointed out, isn't that the way of the world these days? Split families and children being ferried from one set of parents to the other? Half-brothers and stepsisters and stepfathers and Christmas celebrated ten times a year so that everyone can get a look-in?'

Maddie didn't reply, because she was busy wondering what this wife-to-be of his would look like. It was galling, but true, that whilst as a single mother her ranking on the eligibility scale would plummet, he, as a single father, would discover that his had hit the stratosphere.

There was nothing a woman loved more than a guy

with a baby. It brought out every maternal instinct in them. Throw *rich beyond belief* and *sinfully sexy* into the mix and Leo would be lucky if he could get two steps out of his penthouse apartment before finding a queue of eager candidates waiting to interview for the job of perfect stepmother to his child. *Her* child!

'But enough of this,' he concluded. 'Towels should be in the bathroom, and there are more beauty products in the cupboard than on the beauty counter at the store. I gave very precise instructions as to the stocking of essentials while we were here.'

'Okay…' Maddie said, in a daze.

'No routine out here. I will continue working for much of the day, but I'm sure I can find time to show you around the island. Primarily, though, you're to do as you please. Come and go as you want. You may have spotted the swimming pool? You'll find it quite stunning. It overlooks the ocean. If you need anything at all, there's the bell…'

He grinned and gave her a little half-salute, but she was too distracted to respond in kind. Instead she nodded, and found that she actually needed to force herself to breathe when the bedroom door had closed quietly behind him.

CHAPTER NINE

'I'VE MADE A SCHEDULE,' Leo said, brandishing a printed sheet of paper as Maddie walked into the kitchen the following morning at a little after nine.

'You should have woken me up,' she said, sniffing and clearly detecting the smell of bacon. 'I never get up this late.'

'It's important that you get your rest.' He ushered her to a chair and sat her down. 'Sleep well?'

'Have you...*cooked*?'

'"Cooked" is a big word. I prefer to say *dabbled*. I thought I'd give the staff some time off while we're here. After all, in my role of *father* I'm going to have to function without a team of people picking up the pieces behind me all the time.'

Leo had had time to think. She disliked the notion of marriage as a business transaction. She wanted romance. She wanted to be swept off her feet by the perfect guy. He wasn't the perfect guy for her, and he wasn't going to pretend that he was. He wasn't going to wax lyrical about love. But he *was* going to show her what he was made of when it came to fulfilling his responsibilities.

As a bonus, he would also be showing her what another woman might find appealing. Goodbye Leo the womaniser and hello Leo the dutiful dad with apron and spatula. And, of course, the baby…

All's fair in love and war, he thought and finding solutions to problems was his forte, whatever the problem might be.

This was his solution and he was going to bring everything to the table.

'So what did you…er…*dabble* in?' Maddie asked.

'Bacon. Eggs. Bread.' He brought two plates to the table and continued doing whatever he was doing with his back to her, a tea towel slung over one shoulder.

He looked drop-dead gorgeous, and Maddie had to stare. He was wearing low-slung khaki shorts and a faded tee shirt and he was barefoot. With his back to her, she could appreciate the long lines of his lean body, the strength of his muscular legs, the width of his broad shoulders.

It didn't seem fair that a man in old clothes with a tea towel over his shoulder should look so mouthwatering.

Any woman looking at him right now wouldn't be able to resist.

Stick a baby in a high chair next to him and he'd have to beat them away with sticks.

She felt queasy thinking about it.

'Have you ever done anything this…ambitious… before?'

Leo produced a big white plate on which some charred bacon sat, spread across four fried eggs.

'Timing may have been an issue,' Leo declared, fetching a heaping mound of toast, 'but practice will make perfect. Eat up. You need to get nutrients into you after the fiasco with your kitchen. By the way, I got an email this morning. Things are already moving on that front.'

'Really?' Maddie helped herself to a slice of toast and then to one of the less dangerously overcooked rashers of bacon. 'But it's only been a matter of a day…'

'I said I'd sort it, and it'll be sorted in record time. I snap my fingers and people jump. Now, about this schedule.'

'Schedule?'

'I don't want you feeling bored while you're here.'

'Leo, I don't think it would be possible to feel bored here. There's the pool and the wonderful gardens to explore, and I'm very happy to wander into town and have a look around. I don't want you to think that you have to put yourself out for me.'

Leo paused, fork raised to his mouth, and looked at her. 'Wander into town?' In that little flowered sundress that made her look as pure as the driven snow and as sexy as the hottest siren? Over his dead body. No one would guess that she was pregnant. She'd be knee-deep in lecherous men within seconds.

'A tour of the island.' He swept aside her contribution and carried on eating. 'I have a boat docked in one of the sheltered bays. Nothing fancy.'

'You keep a boat here? Whatever for, when you hardly use the villa?'

'Guests at the villa are welcome to use it. It gets used. How are you on the swimming front?'

'I'm not exactly a fish…'

'I thought Australia was all about the outdoor life…?'

'Swimming lessons are pricey. I'm a self-taught swimmer. I get by, but I wouldn't put money on my chances of surviving in a riptide.'

'Then it's just as well,' Leo said smugly, 'that I'll be there every step of the way to keep an eye on you. Fortunately I'm a first-class swimmer.'

Maddie rolled her eyes. He was determined to treat her like an invalid. She should protest, but there was a warm, cosy feeling inside her created by the attention and she was rather enjoying it.

She'd never had attention—not really. Her mother had loved her, but she had been so busy working to make ends meet that there hadn't been time for lots of bonding sessions, and for the last few years of her life *she* had been the one requiring attention.

Then Maddie had gone into the business of caring for Lacey. And when Adam had come along, she had basked in the glow of thinking that she was loved. But, looking back, she could see that Adam had dressed her like a doll to be showcased, and had never shown that he loved her for who she was when she wasn't draped in the latest fashions and expensive jewellery. She could see now that he had been so conscious of the disparity in their status that cossetting her had never even occurred to him. She'd been arm candy. Nothing more.

There had been no other relatives in her life to lean on—no siblings, no doting grandparents, no aunts or uncles or cousins.

So what was the harm in accepting a little pampering from Leo?

'So, if you get your swimsuit…' He stood up briskly. 'I'll meet you in the hall in say…half an hour?'

'We should tidy the kitchen.'

'Leave all that.' Leo removed the plate from her hand. 'I'll deal with it later, once we're back from our day's activities.'

'We're going for *the day*?'

'Unless you have an unavoidable appointment?'

'No, but…'

Don't do this, don't be so nice that I start regretting my decision.

'What about work?'

'I can't remember the last time I had a holiday. A few days off isn't going to kill me. And, anyway, I'm keeping on top of things via email.'

Maddie was amused and a little relieved to find out that there would be no burnt offerings for lunch, because forty minutes later they were swinging by one of the few restaurants in the town, where he collected a picnic hamper and a cooler bag of drinks.

It was hot, the sun beating down from a cloudless turquoise sky, and the island was so small that it was possible to see the distant strip of sea from either side of the car as it bumped along away from the town.

Fringes of coconut trees lined the small ribbon of road, stretching into the distance—banks of them like upright soldiers on parade.

Every so often she would see a flash of deep blue sea, and then, after twenty minutes of driving, they were ploughing down a rocky incline and pulling into a cove.

It was a private beach, small but perfectly formed. Backed into the shrubbery among the coconut trees was a small cabin, and moored to one side was the boat he had told her about.

'How many properties like these do you own?' she asked as he swung round to help her out of the Jeep.

'A handful. All investment places. Some used slightly more than others.'

'Don't you get tired of London? Want to escape to some place like this?'

'I've never been good at escaping,' Leo confessed. He looked at her and then brushed some of her hair away from her face.

'If you were born into money…'

She bent down to pull off her sandals and Leo drew in a sharp breath, causing her to look up, catch his eyes on her cleavage and the black swimsuit holding in her pouting breasts, which were bigger and fuller now with her new pregnant figure. She looked away and quickly straightened, hopping a little because the sand was hot.

'Then surely you must have had loads of opportunity to do whatever you wanted…'

'I must have been born with an over-developed responsibility gene. That sand's hot.' He swept her off her feet and carried her to the cabin. 'Make sure you apply lots of sunblock. I'm going to fetch the hamper and we can relax for a while before we take the boat out.'

Maddie looked at him for a while, silent and speculative. He *did* that. He only told her what he wanted her to know. He never spoke about anything personal and she wished she could get into his head and prise out his secrets. He knew all hers!

'Okay.'

She shrugged. She was going to enjoy the day and enjoy being away from the chaos of the house and the weight of running the store.

The cabin was small but exquisite, as lovely as anything money could buy. She opened the few doors and peered into two bedrooms and two bathrooms, a bedroom and another bathroom on either side of a wooden-floored sitting area and an open-plan kitchen. Lots of squashy sofas and low tables.

She replaced her dress with a sarong and rubbed sunblock all over. She was used to the sun, having lived in Australia, and knew that taking chances was never a good idea, even though she tanned easily.

She looked in the full-length mirror and saw a girl who looked radiant. Her skin had deepened over the summer to the colour of a latte—her Italian ancestry shining through. Her hair was almost down to her waist. When she turned to the side she could see the small but definite bump of her tummy.

The biggest change to her appearance, though, was that the misery of the past few years and the horror of what had happened to her before she'd left Australia were no longer etched on her face.

She looked...*happy.* She was pregnant after a one-night stand, the house she had inherited had been all but dismantled the last time she'd set eyes on it, and the responsibility of running the store was a weight that couldn't be underestimated because other people's livelihoods were at stake, and yet she was *happy.*

Happy to be right here, right now, with a man who wasn't in love with her and never would be. Just happy to be around him.

It was a frightening thought, and it made her heart beat fast—because there could only be one reason why she felt so content, despite the many things that should be concerning her.

Leo didn't love her, but that didn't mean *she* hadn't fallen for *him*—because she had. He'd got under her skin, and now that he had lodged there she couldn't prise him away.

Ever since she'd become pregnant he'd been a rock, and never more so than now. He was determined to prove just how solid he could be and it was a seductive tactic—because it was making her rethink the decision she had made.

Still pensive, she went out to find that he had set up camp under a canopy of coconut trees. She took a few seconds to absorb the setting. Powdery white sand sloping down to crystal-clear water as blue as the sky above it…rocks and coconut trees embracing the cove…the brightly painted boat now bobbing in the water to one side…and Leo, hunky and sexy and willing to cook her breakfast because he felt she needed looking after.

Had she been seeing everything from a skewed perspective? Instead of bemoaning the fact that he was protective because of the baby she was carrying and not because of *her*, should she instead just be seeing his drive to be protective as something to be lauded? As an indication of his strength of character and his fundamental decency?

Her formative experience with men had come in the form of her father, who had jumped ship and bailed on wedlock the second he'd discovered that her mother came without the dowry he'd banked on. And then Adam, who had treated her like a mannequin and then dumped her when she'd been accused of theft because he'd thought that someone who didn't come from his class couldn't possibly have principles.

And yet, despite her experiences, she realised she'd put a lot of faith in love. Heck, she'd dug her heels in and turned down Leo's marriage proposal because he didn't love her.

But what she'd failed to appreciate was that there

were all sorts of counter-arguments for the deal he'd proposed that made a lot of sense. Including the fact that not marrying him meant she'd have to face the idea of him not being in her life after the baby was born.

Leo glanced across and saw her standing there, looking at him pensively. She quickly looked away, out towards the water, but she wasn't fast enough to miss the appreciative glance he cast over her rounded stomach, which he was seeing for the first time. She suddenly realised how little the wisp of floaty fabric tied around her waist did to cover her.

'Have you remembered the sunblock?' he asked, with a hint of some deeper thought in his voice.

Maddie remembered that her feeling resentful because his concern was solely directed with the baby in mind should not be on the cards, and so she smiled and nodded.

'It's practically a criminal offence to go out without sunblock in Australia. You're really well prepared for a day at the beach, Leo.' She eyed the picture-perfect oversized towel, the hamper, the fluffy beach towels rolled into sausage shapes.

'I'm going to put the food inside,' he responded. 'Then what about a bit of sailing?'

'Are you sure…'

'That I'm a master sailor? Yes.' He grinned. 'You'll be safe with me.'

But my heart won't be, she thought as he disappeared into the cabin, and reappeared almost immediately, hand outstretched to lead her to the boat.

She felt a frisson as their fingers linked and then as he helped her in, settling her under the canopy and taking the wheel.

Maddie leaned back and closed her eyes, and as the boat chugged off in a very sedate manner she smiled, letting the wind blow her hair all round her face.

It was too noisy with the engine running to talk, and she liked that because she needed to think. She needed to do something with the churning in her head. She needed to sift through the tangle of confused thoughts and put them into some kind of order.

She needed to ask herself whether she had made the right decision in turning him down and whether it was too late to reverse that decision.

She half opened her eyes and drank him in. He'd unbuttoned his shirt and it whipped behind him, exposing the bronzed perfection of his torso. His swimming trunks were baggy, riding low on his lean hips, and he was steering with one hand, dark sunglasses in place.

He took her breath away.

He would take any woman's breath away.

If they were married, though, she wouldn't have to deal with the pain of watching him take those other women's breath away.

She walked towards him and stood right next to him, slinging her arm casually around his waist.

Leo stiffened, but didn't glance down at her.

'I'll anchor in a couple of minutes,' he said roughly. 'If you're not confident in the water you can stick to the side of the boat. The ladder will be down. You can climb up any time you get nervous. Or you don't have to come in at all. Although…' He breathed in the scent of her and felt a rush of desire. 'I hope you do. The water here is warm. If you're feeling brave, we can grab a couple of snorkels and see what's there.'

'Should I be scared?'

'Never with me around.'

He killed the engine and it spluttered into silence. When he drew back to look at her she was shading her eyes against the glare, her face upturned to his.

'You *do* make me feel safe,' she confided truthfully. 'And I know I haven't said this before, but I really appreciate everything you're doing for me now that I'm pregnant.'

Leo wondered whether she knew what that arm round his waist had done to him and how those glass-green eyes were affecting him.

'Good!' he said heartily. 'Swim?'

He turned away before his arousal became overpowering and paused on the edge of the boat, desperate for some cold water to kill his rampant libido.

'Definitely!' Maddie laughed and untied her sarong, and then faced him, still smiling.

She was the most beautiful thing he'd ever seen, and Leo dived into the sea before he let loose a groan of desire. He swam underwater, his powerful body sleek and brown as he sliced through the water and surfaced wiping his face.

She was tentatively taking the steps down and he swam towards her to help.

'I can manage!' Maddie laughed, but she did curve round and link her fingers behind his neck briefly before letting go and doggy-paddling by the ladder. 'This is as good as it gets with me. I can swim *a bit…*'

'Hang on to the ladder. I'm going to get the snorkels. There's a lifesaver ring you can hold, to make sure you don't feel out of your depth.'

'I won't need that,' Maddie teased breathlessly, 'Not when you're here and you've said that I can trust you.'

Hell, she was doing it again...turning him on when she obviously didn't mean to...

Five minutes later they were snorkelling, and Maddie was clearly having the time of her life.

It was strange that she'd never done anything like this before, especially as she'd lived in a country famed for its Great Barrier Reef and its exotic underwater life.

She got a bit braver the longer they were in the water, venturing further out holding on to Leo. She only reluctantly returned to the boat when he tapped her and told her how long they'd been swimming.

'That was amazing,' she confessed excitedly, removing the snorkel and shaking her hair, before flipping it into a makeshift braid that hung like a wet burnished gold rope down her back. 'I could do that every day!'

Leo grinned. 'Then we'll have to do something about that,' he drawled, towelling himself dry and slinging the damp towel across his shoulders.

Their eyes met and he didn't look away. Nor did she.

When she walked towards him—carefully, because a boat was not the steadiest surface in the world—he didn't move a muscle. He waited. As still and as watchful as a jungle animal on high alert.

He was picking up all sorts of signals and he didn't know what to believe and what not to believe. But when she stopped right in front of him and looked up at him he knew exactly what to believe.

'You shouldn't,' he said roughly.

'Shouldn't what?'

'Stand there looking at me as though you want me

to strip you bare and make love to you right here on this boat.'

Maddie looked down, suddenly shy. She was pregnant with his baby, and yet here she was *shy*?

'Is that what you want, *cara*?'

He tilted her chin and met her apple-green eyes steadily.

'Do you want me to do this?'

He trailed one long brown finger along her cleavage and she shuddered and let loose a stifled little gasp.

'What about this?'

He reached to the straps of her swimsuit and hooked his fingers under before he slowly began pulling them down, watching her carefully, getting more and more worked up with every passing second.

It was his turn to stifle a groan of pure pleasure as her breasts were exposed, pale orbs with those delectable rosy nipples, bigger and darker now, just as her breasts were fuller and heavier. He was startled to see that his hands were shaking as he rubbed the tips of her nipples with the pads of his thumbs. The swimsuit had bunched up at her waist and he badly wanted to take it off completely, but he hesitated.

'Is this what you want?' he demanded unsteadily. 'Because it's what *I* want…'

Maddie nodded, and Leo did what he wanted to do. He pulled off her swimsuit and then devoted himself to her body, tasting it, working his way down while she remained standing, holding on to the steel pole supporting the canopy. Her head was flung back and her mouth was half open as she moaned, a low, guttural sound as his mouth found the patch between her legs and he burrowed there, nuzzling before gently parting the folds of her womanhood so that he could slide his tongue into her slick groove.

Maddie plunged her fingers into his springy hair, arched her back and *enjoyed*. She opened her legs wider, sank against his tongue, bucked as it teased her and came explosively against his mouth, twisting and crying out while the sea breeze blew strands of hair across her open mouth and warmed her breasts.

'I can't stop wanting you,' she gasped, finally collapsing against him and letting him carry her down the stunted row of stairs that led to the small living area on the boat. There was no bed, but there was a long, upholstered bench seat, and he lay her down and stood up to look at her nakedness.

'And I you,' he growled.

Leo couldn't get his shirt off fast enough, and then the swimming trunks. And he couldn't take his eyes off her rosy flushed face. He was captivated by the way she lay there, idly stroking her breast with one hand, mesmerised by her swollen stomach.

'Is this safe?' he asked, sinking onto the bench seat alongside her and wishing he'd had the wit to install something more accommodating.

'Of course it is!' Maddie laughed and kissed him. 'I just need you, Leo. I need you to come inside me...'

Leo needed no further encouragement. Some foreplay? *Yes*. He suckled her breasts and idly played between her thighs. He wanted to devote more time to both, but he couldn't because his animal cravings were too intense.

This was his woman—ripe with his child. A surge of possessiveness and fierce pride rushed through him as he pushed into her, taking her in long, hard strokes, only just holding on for her to reach her peak before coming inside her, pouring himself into her and crying out with the pleasure and satisfaction of it.

He'd never experienced anything like it in his life before. He couldn't let this woman go. He couldn't let any other man hold the child she was carrying. The only man who would ever hold this baby would be him.

He was obviously a lot less New Age than he'd imagined.

'Marry me, Maddie.'

The silence was the length of a heartbeat and then Maddie nodded, still flushed from lovemaking.

'Okay.'

Leo dealt her a slow, slashing smile that took her breath away. 'You changed your mind?' he said, knowing he should leave well alone but needing to hear why she had come round to his way of thinking.

A post-coital rush of heated acquiescence would inevitably lead to a sober rethink in the cold light of day.

'I changed my mind,' Maddie said. 'In an ideal world, this isn't how I saw my life going—marrying a man for the sake of a baby. But it's not an ideal world and you were right. I should be the first to recognise that. I've seen how attentive you can be, Leo. You would make a great dad. That's enough for me.'

It would never really be enough, but it would have to do. And in time, who knew...? Perhaps he would come to love her the way she loved him.

'Are you sure?' His navy blue eyes were thoughtful. 'Sure you can do without the fairy tale? I'm not built for the business of falling in love, Maddie.'

Maddie didn't skip a beat, because she'd made her decision and she was going to stand by it. She adored this man, and she would always nurture the hope that his heart would open up to her, but she would never let him see that. He wanted a business transaction, and that was what he was going to get.

'I know,' she said, and shrugged. 'Maybe I'm not either. Now, let's not talk any more. Have I told you that I can't seem to get enough of you…?'

Maddie swept up the trail of clothes on the floor. On the bed, Leo was half dozing, half looking at her, sated after a bout of extremely satisfying early-morning sex.

'You're very untidy, Leo. Is that one of the bad habits of coming from a wealthy background? You're so used to people tidying up behind you that you've forgotten how to do it yourself?'

But her voice was light and teasing. The past three days had been the best three days of her entire life. He made her feel so safe, so secure, so *cherished.* Maddie knew that it was dangerous, but she could just *feel* something between them. He said he didn't 'do' love, but surely he wouldn't be so attentive and tender if he didn't feel at least *some* of what she was feeling. Surely!

He had never spoken about what had turned him off all the things that propelled most normal people into marriage, for better or for worse, and she hadn't asked. They had their pact and she wasn't going to start rocking any boats. She was going to play the long game.

She picked up his shorts, tutting, and shook them, dislodging his wallet from the pocket. It flew open, discharging its contents. Platinum cards, business cards, cash and…

Maddie frowned and stooped to retrieve the picture

that had fallen out along with everything else. She held it up to the light.

Staring back at her was a fair-haired woman with full lips and bright blue laughing eyes. There was something knowing about those eyes. And an undeniable sensuality. The woman was looking down at whoever was taking the picture and her lips were parted…teasing, tempting.

Maddie shivered—because now she *knew*. She walked over to Leo, who had sat up, and showed him the picture.

'Who's this?' she asked lightly.

Leo stilled. He reached for the photo without bothering to look at it and stuck it on the bedside table.

She'd hoped he would say it was no one of any importance, but a steely resolve had washed over his features when he turned back to her.

'That is my ex-wife.'

CHAPTER TEN

'YOUR EX-*WIFE*,' MADDIE said woodenly, folding her arms, colour draining from her face faster than water going down a drain. 'You were *married*. And you didn't think that it was important enough to tell me?'

Suddenly restless, Leo vaulted upright, gloriously and unashamedly naked. He grabbed the nearest item of clothing, which happened to be his boxers, and stepped into them.

'How is it something that impacts on us?' His voice was cool and toneless, and that said more than words alone could ever say.

That woman in the picture was his wife, who had meant so much to him that he couldn't even let her name pass his lips. *This* was the mysterious reason why he wasn't interested in love. Because he'd been there before. He'd given his heart to someone else and he no longer possessed one to give to anyone who followed.

All Maddie's dreams and hopes about time working its magic and building the sort of love in him for her that she felt for him had been castles in the sand, now washed away by grim reality.

"How is it something that impacts on us?"'

Maddie stared at him with incredulity and Leo had the grace to flush.

'It's in the past.'

'But don't you think it's a past you should have *told* me about? I mean, you know all about mine...'

'You chose to tell me,' Leo pointed out, with the sort of remorseless logic that set her teeth on edge. Caught on the back foot, Leo always fell back on his automatic instinct to defend himself.

'I chose to share my past with you.'

'The implication being that I should return the favour?'

'Most normal people would.'

'Haven't you deduced by now that I don't play by the same rules?'

Yes, Maddie thought miserably, yes, she had. She had just opted to ignore it.

She flung on her dressing gown and stared down at her bare feet, at the pale pink of the polish she had put on her toenails the evening before.

'Where is she now?' she asked stiffly, wondering if she should be on the lookout for the sexy blonde he had loved popping out from the nearest wardrobe or lurking behind the bushes wearing nothing but that sexy, *sexy* smile.

'Things didn't work out.'

'"Things didn't work out"? But you still keep a picture of her in your wallet?'

What sort of response *was that?* What did *things didn't work out* even *mean*? Obviously whatever had happened he had been bitterly hurt and fatally scarred.

'Where are you going with this, Maddie? That part of my past has nothing to do with us. You have to trust me.'

Maddie swallowed back her hurt. She had agreed to marry this man and she loved him. He had his past, just as she had hers, and marrying him would mean living with that and dealing with it, but she couldn't live without him.

She knew what would happen if she got into a flaming row with him over this. He would vanish. To his office or out in the Jeep to a beach, or into the garden… Anywhere just as long as she wasn't there, because he wasn't going to deal with her hysterics.

Dealing with her hysterics and her jealousy wasn't part of their business transaction.

'I'm going to have a bath,' she said, turning away.

Leo nodded and said nothing. What was there to say? He had closed the door on that slice of his past and he wasn't going to re-open it. What would be the good in that? Maddie would have to trust him.

But he had glimpsed that shattered expression on her face as she had turned away and something inside him had twisted painfully.

He didn't wait for her to emerge. Instead he flung on some clothes, headed down to the pool and washed away his restlessness by swimming lap after lap after lap until every muscle in his body was aching.

When he returned to the villa it was to find her in the kitchen, seemingly back to normal.

'Where were you?' she asked from where she was standing by the stove, putting on a saucepan with some butter, ready for the eggs that stood on the counter nearby.

It must have taken so much for her to act as though nothing had happened, but she managed it.

She also managed to smile at him.

'I'm making us some of those eggs we bought at the market this morning.'

Leo looked at her, trying to gauge her mood and feeling a little disconcerted that there was nothing to gauge. If she'd been hurt by his silence then she'd recovered fast. He frowned, not knowing how that speedy recovery made him feel.

'Okay. Great. I was in the pool.'

He hovered, for once indecisive. Should he revive the subject of Claire? He frowned, because it wasn't like him to backtrack on any decision once that decision had been made—and he'd made the decision not to start babbling on about his past, on which the door had been shut.

'It looks lovely out there,' Maddie said gaily, a broad smile pinned to her face.

She sounded like a Stepford Wife. All that was missing was the gingham apron.

'Anyway, breakfast will be ready in about five minutes. Does that give you enough time to change?'

Leo grunted and disappeared, duly reappearing in under five minutes in a pair of faded blue Bermuda shorts and a white tee shirt, barefoot as always. He couldn't see the point of wearing shoes in the villa when the floor was so warm.

He gritted his teeth and wondered how it was that he was about to bring up a subject he had only minutes before sworn to avoid.

'About Claire...'

Maddie looked at him seriously. Really? He wanted to talk about his ex? Did he think that she actually *wanted* to hear about how much he had given himself to a relationship that hadn't worked out? Did she need an explanation as to why he could never give again?

No way. That would not only be a dagger to her heart, but a dagger twisting and swivelling and causing maximum damage. *Thanks, but no thanks.*

'No,' she said.

'No?'

'I don't want to talk about her. Like you said, that's your past and this is the present. We both know why we're going into this…er…arrangement. We both know that it's not the sort of marriage that most people dream about. But it's the right thing for us to do. I know that. Like I said, I've seen for myself what a good dad you would make, and we might not be a traditional couple, with all the traditional hopes and dreams, but we get along all right and that's the main thing.'

Said out loud, it sounded like a poor excuse for a union. But then she thought of her life without Leo, and the horror that image conjured up reaffirmed why she was doing what she was. He would never love her. He hadn't been lying when he'd said that he just didn't have it in him. But she would always love *him*.

She was surprised to see that Leo didn't look relieved and elated that they were on the same page. The look on his face was more…*dissatisfaction.*

He swept aside her response. 'We have something else going for us.'

'What's that?'

'This.'

He pulled her towards him and kissed her. Kissed her until she was drugged with wanting him and on fire to have him touch her the way only he could.

When he did this—kissed her and held her and let

his body do the talking—she forgot everything. Forgot the fact that she was in love with a man who'd given his heart away to someone else. Forgot that she felt like a hypocrite, hiding her aching heart under a cheery smile.

She grunted with pleasure as he pushed down her shorts so that he could caress her swollen belly.

Her pregnancy fascinated him, and his fascination thrilled her. He slid his fingers lower, taking his time to caress her intimately with slow, rhythmic movements that left her panting with pleasure.

He whispered in her ear what he wanted to do to her, where he wanted to touch and feel and taste, until Maddie was giddy with desire. Then, still taking his time, he sat her on the edge of the table and she supported herself, hands stretched out behind her, palms flat on the smooth, polished wood.

He tugged off the shorts, taking her knickers at the same time, and pushed up her tee shirt so that he could see her breasts. Then he undid his zipper and dropped his shorts to the ground.

Her eyes were closed and she sighed and moaned softly as he slid into her, angling her body so that he could take her in a few thrusts. Quick, hot sex that swept away everything in its path.

'I can't get enough of you...' he growled, when they were both sated and normal business had resumed—although the eggs were burned and had had to be chucked.

Enough of the sex, Maddie completed in her head. But she couldn't get enough of that either. And that, if she was going through the *pros* checklist, counted for a lot.

'Well, you'll have to make do for the moment,' she told him lightly. 'We've made plans for today. I'm looking forward to seeing that cove you were telling me about.'

Another bright smile. Her jaw was beginning to ache from the effort of those bright smiles.

Leo kissed the tip of her nose.

'And then back to Dublin,' Maddie said, tidying up, thinking of the house she'd left behind, which she knew was now in great order because Leo had been showing her daily updates of the work that was being done. Only the attic needed a bit of sprucing up.

'But not like before,' Leo reminded her. 'This time back to Dublin as a couple.'

Maddie choked down a painful lump. 'Yes,' she mumbled, looking away, 'as a couple…'

It was another two and a half weeks before Maddie finally made it up to the attic—the final thing on her to-do list. With Leo's support, everything that had seemed difficult and daunting had become manageable. He had helped in ways that he had said were small and incidental, but when she examined them later she saw they were huge and fundamental.

The house was near completion and new staff had been hired at the store and renovations had begun. The cobwebby elegance of a past era was being replaced by a modernist vision, but it was going to stay as the store it was meant to be.

The attic was her final as yet unexplored territory, which was why now, at a little after six in the evening, with Leo due to come over in an hour, Maddie was sitting on the ground surrounded by…*stuff*.

Boxes of old bills, receipts, random scraps of paper with names on them, which she deciphered as being the names of horses or dogs or whatever it was her grandfather had been wont to bet on. And then there were the pictures. These Maddie took her time with, looking at them one by one. Pictures of her grandmother, her mother—photos dating back decades.

She was barely aware of Leo, padding up the winding narrow staircase that led off from one of the top bedrooms to the enormous attic.

'You can help,' she announced, pausing to look at him and then struggling to tear her eyes away, as always happened.

He'd come straight from work. He'd already located premises for his offices, and magically everything had been completed with supersonic speed. His faith in the power of money had not been misplaced.

'Okay. I'll arrange for a clearance company. They can come in and remove the entire lot. I've never been in such an unmitigated disaster zone in my entire life.'

'I've got some photos here, Leo.' She shuffled over to where he had taken up residence on the floor and sat next to him, going through the pictures, marvelling at the past unfolding in front of her. Her mother had been quite remarkable-looking—as had her grandparents.

'He went bad after your grandmother died,' Leo said neutrally.

'Your grandfather told you that?'

'There was bad blood between them before that, with the acquisition of the store premises, but I believe there was some scattered correspondence between them for a while after. When your grandmother died the old man went down a different road.'

'You've not mentioned any of that before,' Maddie murmured absently, sifting through the photos and at the bottom finding a slender stack of envelopes. Maybe five.

Her mother's handwriting was on them, and Leo reached out to take them from her.

'Maddie...'

But she was already opening the first letter and Leo's jaw clenched as he read it over her shoulder—read the pleading note from Lizzie Gallo to her unforgiving father, and knew that the other letters would be along the same lines.

'Leo...' Maddie whispered, turning to look at him. 'I thought...'

'You did,' Leo said gravely.

He stroked her hair away from her face, noted the way her eyes had glazed over, the quiver of her mouth. If the old bastard had been around he wouldn't have seen the light of another day.

'You knew?'

He nodded on a sigh. 'Yes,' he confessed. 'There were words between Tommaso and my grandfather a long time ago. Probably shortly after your mother had decamped to Australia. Who knows whether she did that to get away from the toxic atmosphere in the house? Tommaso never recovered from Susan's death. My grandfather got in touch about buying the store. He got a letter back. I won't bother to tell you what it said. I imagine you can guess the gist.'

'That he would never sell the store—just like he would never forgive my mother, even though she'd begged for forgiveness. She had it so hard in Australia. Worked her fingers to the bone to earn money for both of us. And he refused to give her anything.'

'He was a bastard.'

'You never said…'

'You had your dreams and I wasn't going to shatter them,' Leo told her.

'I don't want the store,' Maddie whispered. 'It was never a legacy of love.'

'You don't know that.' Leo sighed. 'Things change when you're facing the grim reaper. Who knows what was going through the old man's head when he made that will?'

'You think?'

'I do think. Your mother was stubborn, and so was he. He couldn't bring himself to forgive, but he must have lived a life of regret—hence the gambling and the alcohol.'

'Why didn't you say anything?'

'I couldn't hurt you, Maddie.' He drew his breath in. 'I could never hurt you,' he continued in a roughened undertone.

He shifted so that he was looking directly at her. The lighting in the attic was dim—just shafts of watery sunshine filtering through the glass of the four Velux windows on the slanting roof.

'I need to tell you about my ex-wife. About Claire.'

'Please don't, Leo. I… I… No, please don't. I understand how you feel. Things didn't work out and it hurt you so much that you still can't bear to talk about it. You loved and you lost and, lest you forget, you keep her photo in your wallet. I get it. I just don't want the details.' She smiled weakly. 'There's such a thing as too much information.'

'Silly fool,' Leo said tenderly. 'Is that what you think?'

'What else? No one hangs on to a photo of someone they couldn't give a hoot about.'

'I keep that photo as a reminder of the biggest mistake I ever made,' he said heavily, and Maddie's eyebrows shot up in surprise. 'I was young and cocky and I fell for an older woman.' He grinned crookedly. 'I was a cliché, in other words. Except I was rich, so I could *get* the older woman. But she turned out to be a fortune-hunter who had spotted in me the perfect opportunity to feather her nest. And, rich young buck that I was, I fell for it hook, line and sinker. I married her and it lasted about two seconds. It was the most expensive mistake I ever made. She took the money and vanished as a wealthy divorcee, and after that…'

'You threw away the key to your heart?'

Maddie wanted to keep grounded, but inside she was taking flight, heady with the realisation that her assumptions had been unfounded.

'I threw away the key to my heart,' Leo concurred. 'And I thought that it was for the best. No love and no pretending that I was capable of it. I never banked on *you* coming along.'

'Say that again?' Maddie held her breath and tried hard to look puzzled and yet empathetic when inside her heart was racing and her mouth was dry.

'I never banked on you coming along. I never banked on falling in love. *Really* in love. In love so that I can't think of life without you in it, Maddie. In love so that if anyone tries to hurt you, I will kill them.'

'Leo…' Slowly, she smiled, heady and deliriously happy. 'You're saying all the right things.'

She reached out and ran a dusty finger across his cheek.

'I love you so much. I knew that you wanted a pragmatic relationship, and I knew that was the last thing

I wanted, but I also knew that I would rather have that with you than have anything else with anybody else. I never thought I would fall in love with you—not after everything I'd been through—but I did. Bit by bit I came to see you for the wonderful man you are. Thoughtful, kind, considerate, funny…'

'Scintillating…sexy…'

'Egotistical…untidy…terrible at cooking… The memory of that steak you cooked for me last week will live on in my head for ever…'

'Hey! That last one's going too far!' Leo burst out laughing. When he'd sobered up, he said, seriously, 'I would get down on one knee, Maddie, but I'm already sitting. Will you marry me? For the *right* reasons? Because I love you and need you and can't live without you?'

'Just try and stop me!'

Maddie flung her arms round his neck. She was living her own fairy tale. Whoever said that they couldn't come true?

The wedding was low-key. They both wanted to exchange vows before the baby was born, so less than three months later a very pregnant Maddie walked up the aisle in a picturesque church on the outskirts of Dublin.

Leo's grandfather, beaming with pride, was in attendance, accompanied by a female friend whom, he confided to Maddie, he had been seeing 'off and on' for over a year and a half.

'I've never mentioned it to Leo,' he said, 'because I'm an old fool, and you know how matter-of-fact that grandson of mine can be. Didn't want him pooh-poohing the whole thing. But all that's changed, thanks to you, my dear. The minute I met you I knew that you were the one who was going to change him for the better. No, maybe *better* isn't the word I'm looking for—because no one could ever accuse Leo of being anything but an honourable man. Maybe change him for the *softer*, if that makes any sense.'

Maddie didn't tell him that there hadn't been that much to change after all, because there had been a softie buried deep down all the time.

By now she had made friends in Dublin. Other mums-to-be, several members of staff at the store, who were all now energised as the store finally began to pay dividends.

It had been a two-pronged effort—one that had been shared between her and Leo. She had listened to his ideas for introducing a dedicated electronics department, which was loosely based on his original idea for what he had intended to do with the store, but scaled down considerably. In time, he would source a suitable location and expand operations there. He had given way to her with the rest. She had laughed when he'd suggested lending a hand when it came to choosing sexy lingerie for the women's department.

'It would definitely work,' he had murmured one evening, when they'd both been warm and sated and wrapped round one another in bed after some very satisfying lovemaking, 'if you try on each sample piece for me to inspect…'

The store had brought them together and now, for Maddie, it was something special—something more than just concrete and stone—and it would be for ever. She quietly hoped, and so did Leo, that it would be a legacy they would be able to pass down to their children, and their children's children, that its story would be told over and over until it became the backdrop to their lives. A very happy and wonderful story, despite its inauspicious beginnings.

There were no relatives for her at the small wedding—no brothers or sisters or aunts or uncles—but Maddie didn't mind. She had the most important person in the world there. She was marrying the man who had spotted her once upon a time in a store she had been battling to hang on to, and the rest, as he fondly told her, was history.

After the wedding they went on a flying honeymoon to a five-star hotel in Cornwall, and they had a wonderful time in driving rain and under heavy grey skies, wrapped up in woollens, as happy holding hands there as if they'd been on the most expensive trip to the Maldives.

'When the baby comes and you can travel comfortably,' Leo promised, 'we're going to go sailing down the Grenadines. Until then...' he looked up at the leaden skies and grinned '...we're going to enjoy the wonderful English countryside in typical English weather. It'll stand me in good stead for when we move out to the country.'

Having done up her grandfather's house to the highest possible standard, Maddie found herself reluctant to live there.

'I can forgive my grandfather for the sin of pride,' she'd admitted, 'but I can't forget. And I'll always wonder what life would have been like for me and Mum if he'd just relented and forgiven her for running away.'

'Too arrogant and too stubborn,' Leo had murmured.

'Those were traits he had even as a young man, according to my grandfather, and they probably became out of control the older he got and the lonelier he became. And don't forget he was gambling and drinking heavily. Those two things would have turned his brain to mush and wreaked havoc on his ability to think clearly.'

So they'd found a lovely little house, close to the very church where they'd married. And, of course, there was Leo's London place, which was every bit as luxurious as she remembered. But Dublin, he confessed, had grown on him.

Flora Madison Conti was born three days after her due date with no fuss at all.

Dark-haired and green-eyed, she was sweet-natured and, within hours of coming into the world, already the apple of her father's eye.

Their real honeymoon, taken when Flora was a little over three months old, was as perfect as anything Maddie could have hoped for, and made all the better when she received news that the store, for the first time in over a decade, had shown a profit.

Maddie thought that if only her mother could have seen her she would have been bursting with pride that her daughter had married for love—and also highly amused that Maddie was now in charge of the very store from which she had once been exiled.

Now, with Flora asleep, Maddie was in the kitchen in their beautiful little house, with her very domesticated alpha male husband due back at any second.

She heard the key in the lock and the sound of the door opening and her heart skipped a beat. Leo never failed to command her attention.

He strode in and smiled as his dark eyes rested on

her. Sitting there, with her long toffee-coloured hair swept over one shoulder and her golden skin glowing, she was the very picture of everything any man could ever hope for.

He was lucky, and he knew that he was. He had resigned himself to a life without love and he couldn't believe how naïve he had been in thinking that he could ever have been happy in a union that was devoid of it.

'Flora asleep, my darling?'

'She is...' Maddie stood up and walked towards him, and with every step closer her pulse raced faster and her pupils dilated. She felt the push of her breasts against her bra. 'And I've cooked us something special.'

'Tell me I haven't forgotten a special day... The anniversary of the first time you thought I was a wandering explorer...? Or maybe of the first time you realised that you were head over heels in love with the only man you'll ever need...?'

He grinned and pulled her to him, kissed her with lingering thoroughness.

'Sweet,' he murmured. 'Like nectar. Now, this special meal...will it wait?'

'Leo...!'

But Maddie giggled and tingled as he unhooked her bra and cupped her breast in his hand as though weighing it.

'Is that a plea for sex? Because if it is, then your wish is my command.'

'Is that *all* you think about?'

'It's all I've been thinking about since about...oh... three this afternoon. Highly inappropriate, given that I was in a high-level meeting at the time.' He stood back and looked at her, his beautiful eyes tender and serious.

'But I think about other things too. I think about how much I love being married to you and how bloody happy you make me. I think about how much I'm looking forward to growing old with you and sharing my life with you. And I think about my stunning little baby girl.'

'That's a lot of thinking for a top businessman like you,' Maddie said, and laughed.

'And that's not all I've been thinking about…' Leo murmured as they headed up the stairs to their bedroom suite, which was next to the nursery where Flora was fast asleep.

'No?' She was breathless as they entered the bedroom and he quietly shut the door behind them, not bothering to switch on the lights.

She began undoing the buttons of his shirt until it was open, and then she rubbed his flat brown nipple with the pad of her thumb, making him shudder at the delicate touch. When she rested her hand on the bulging erection pushing against his trousers, he stifled a moan.

'Tell me what else you've been thinking about…' She guided his hand to her loose skirt and then encouraged him to explore further, to touch her under the floaty fabric, through her lacy underwear, to feel her wetness on his fingers.

'You mean aside from what you want me to do to you right now?'

On cue, he slipped his big hand under her knickers and began rubbing between her legs with the flat of his hand. He wasn't in any rush to take things faster just yet. He kept on rubbing, before slipping a finger deep into her, loving the way her muscles contracted at the intimate contact.

'Keep that up and I won't remember what it is we're talking about,' Maddie panted unevenly.

'Okay…' Leo slid his finger to find the nub of her core and transferred his attention there. 'Here's what I've been thinking. What about making another baby, my darling? Right now?'

Maddie giggled and sighed and looked at him from under her lashes, her whole body on fire as he continued to devastate her senses with his finger.

'And that's why I adore you,' she breathed. 'You can read my mind…'

* * * * *

ONE NIGHT, TWO CONSEQUENCES

JOSS WOOD

I really believe that editors make books better –
especially my books! – and I've been really lucky
to work with some wonderfully talented people.
So, this book is dedicated to Flo (who taught me
so much), to Laurie (who loved this book from
the start), and to Charlotte (who now has the
unenviable task of keeping me on the straight
and narrow). Thank you for believing in me and
my books and for loving my characters and the
complicated situations I place them in.

CHAPTER ONE

REMY DRAYCOTT LOOKED at the open brochure in front of her as she sipped her glass of Belleaire Chardonnay. So this was the town of Bellevue, she thought, looking across the swish wine bar through the floor-to-ceiling windows onto the main street of the town. Cosmopolitan, sophisticated, quietly rich, it had an air of European elegance.

She liked it. A lot.

From what she'd seen so far on her brief tour of the towns of the Napa Valley, Bellevue—right at the north end of the valley—seemed to be a mixture of the best of the rest. It had take-your-breath-away views of the Palisade Mountains, a smidgeon of the old-world charm of Calistoga, a little of the casual elegance of St Helena and, if she had to judge by the superb gourmet burger she'd eaten for lunch at the glossy diner down the street, the same passion for food as Yountsville.

It was a pity she was only passing through… The town was begging for her to stay a little longer, explore a little more.

No, she couldn't, she thought, pushing temptation away. For the first time in—well, years, she actually had a deadline to be in a place at a specific time. And the reminder of why she had to be in Portland in three days' time had her throwing back the rest of her wine and signalling the barman for a refill.

In seventy-two hours, give or take, her mother was due to give birth to her half-sibling and Remy had promised to be there. Not in the hospital waiting room or waiting at home, like a normal person, but in the delivery room itself. With her mum—*obviously*—her grandmother, *and* her brand-new stepdad, who was just seven years old than herself.

Remy lifted her glass to her lips. She was amazed and terrified and confused about the entire situation.

Amazed that after a lifetime of being a single parent—well, that wasn't entirely true… Grandma Rosie had been her other parent in every way that counted—her intense, brilliant and fiercely feminist mother had settled down with a high school sports coach. Terrified for her because she was, in medical terms, an elderly mother—which essentially meant that a lot more could go wrong in a forty-four-year-old body than in a seventeen-year-old one. And confused because… Well, there was more than a quarter of a century's gap between her and her nearly here sibling.

Twenty-seven years… That was more than confusing—that was a tad bizarre.

It was all very weird and unsettling. Remy desperately hoped that Jan would take a different approach to raising this child than she had to her. Dear God, she could only pray. Just be *normal*, she told her still baking sibling. Normal would be perfect.

Remy felt the mood in the wine bar shift, felt the energy change. Grateful to be distracted from her thoughts, she turned her head to look at the new arrival into the elegant space. The man had stopped to talk to a couple sitting at a table close to the front door. His back was to her, so she admired the broad shoulders the white dress shirt covered, and the spectacular butt beneath the tailored, expensive black suit pants.

Finished with that conversation, he moved on to the next

table, shaking hands and kissing cheeks, and Remy waited for him to turn around so that she could see his face. She rested her chin in the palm of her hand—at ease, as always, with flying solo.

In the corner a short brunette strummed a guitar and crooned into a microphone, while a group of women her age sat in a booth, laughing raucously and slamming tequilas. Groups of people were gathered around the horseshoe-shaped bar, and Remy couldn't help noticing the interested and predatory female eyes tracking Hot and Sexy's progress to the bar. In a room brimming with handsome and successful men he had the ability to capture a lot of attention without doing much at all.

He eventually made it to the general vicinity of where she was sitting and Remy could—finally!—see that face up close and personal: wavy dark brown hair, almost black, a long nose, and deep-set, mysterious eyes. Strong jaw, sexy mouth.

Oh, yeah. Very hot. Incredibly sexy.

Remy tipped her head as he was pulled into yet another conversation and noticed that while he didn't seem to say much when he did people listened. *Really* listened. Even in silence he exuded confidence and control. More than his face or his body—both of which were panty-droppingly attractive—it was that control and confidence that intrigued her. Alpha male, she decided quickly: powerful, wealthy, in charge.

She'd known many alpha men. They had littered the offices, bars and pavements of New York. 'Arrogant' and 'entitled' hadn't turned her head for a long, long time. He did. And she had to wonder why. Something about him made her lady bits quiver—and quivering was a *not* a good thing. Not good at all.

She was passing through Bellevue and she didn't need any distractions. This man, she realised instinctively, was the type who women made themselves look silly over, changed their plans for, embarrassed themselves with.

Remy was too smart to do any of the above.

Too smart, period.

Bo Tessier had noticed her as soon as he'd pushed through the glass doors to his family's wine-tasting bar in the heart of Bellevue town—a venue that both locals and tourists flocked to for their evening entertainment. Her elbow was propped on the bar and her hand held up her head. Her hair was a long fall of rich brown messy, loose curls, shot through with chestnut streaks too subtle to have come out of a salon. She had sculpted cheekbones, a stubborn chin, and a body that was long and lean—almost scrawny.

'You heard that Bella passed away?'

He pulled his attention away from the beauty at the bar and looked down at the expectant faces at the table he was standing next to. He'd been answering the same question all day. Yes, of course he'd heard that Bella Abram, his neighbour and owner of Bella's Folly—a Queen Anne mansion on five acres, bordering the east side of Belleaire—had passed away in her sleep the night before last.

'We're wondering who will inherit. Bella was quite well off.'

And there was the other comment he'd been hearing all day.

As for the heirs—who knew? Bella had kept the valley entertained with her many torrid affairs, but she'd never married, and since as far as anyone knew she was the only child of only children…dead end. When her heir was identified he'd be first in line with an offer to purchase. He could do without her monstrosity of a house, filled with rubbish, but he wanted that land. More land meant more vines, and there would be space for tunnels to grow organic exotic fruits and vegetables to supply their restaurants—and others in the area.

He was very aware that the land, being on the main tourist route leading into town from the more southerly towns in the Napa Valley, was also a prime spot to be developed. Belleaire did *not* need a housing estate or a golf course or a shopping mall on its doorstep. He couldn't think of anything worse.

Extricating himself from the conversation, he moved towards the busy bar as a tourist group seated in a circle rose and, gathering their jackets and bags, drifted towards the exit. Bo stepped up to the bar and raked his hand through his hair.

'Your usual, sir?' the barman asked, and Bo nodded.

The barman scuttled across the area behind the bar and Bo winced when an expensive bottle of whiskey nearly slipped from his hand. Resisting the urge to climb over the bar and pour his own drink—he'd worked behind this bar during his college years—he drummed his fingers against the surface before abruptly stopping when he recalled his sister Ginny's words.

'You intimidate the hell out of our staff, Bo. You're so distant, so unapproachable. Loosen up, smile at them occasionally. Crack a joke, compliment them.'

Years ago—before he'd lost Ana and long before he'd assumed the enormous responsibilities of running the Belleaire Group—he would have found that easier to do. These days he didn't have the time or the energy or the inclination to soft-soap people into doing their jobs.

Communication was not his strong point—as Ginny frequently reminded him.

'You can only take strong and silent so far, brother darling. No man is an island and all that…'

Bo gave a mental shrug. It worked for him, and since he worked crazy hours running their multimillion-dollar group of companies, comprising vineyards, a winery, farms, a hotel, restaurants and more than a few wine bars, he didn't see the point in fixing what wasn't broken.

Bo lifted the glass of whiskey on ice and closed his eyes as the first sip slid easily down his throat. His business might be built on wine, but there was nothing like a good shot of Irish whiskey to soothe.

Looking across the bar, he caught the eye of the barman again. 'Has my cousin been in?'

'Eli has come and gone, sir. He waited for you, but said to tell you that he'd catch up with you in the morning.'

Out of the corner of his eye he saw the woman's head lift, knew that she was listening to their conversation. He felt her eyes on his face, sensed her interest. He didn't mind—hell, she was gorgeous.

But many, *many* gorgeous women strolled in and out of this wine bar, through the tasting rooms back at the vineyard, through their restaurant, their art gallery, hotel...his office, his life. He never picked up random women. If he required female company—he was only thirty-five and he frequently did—he had a couple of women on speed dial. Women he knew, liked, was comfortable with. Women who understood that he only wanted a couple of hours' strings-free fun.

Bo placed his forearms on the bar and looked at his foot resting on the gold rail, resisting the temptation to look her way and initiate conversation. He should be heading back to the estate, to the first of the four luxury houses they'd had built when they'd decided to turn the Belleaire mansion and family home into a boutique hotel. The houses were tucked into the east end of the estate, beyond the vineyards, and were far enough away from each other so that he didn't feel as if he was living in his sister's or his cousin's pockets. The fourth house, smaller than the rest, they kept for visiting family and friends.

He had a full day tomorrow, a crazy week ahead, and he was nuts to be even *considering* chatting up this beauty with shadows under her eyes. He knew instinctively that she wasn't his type. He liked women like himself: cool, collected, calm. He could tell from the short sundress she wore with kick-ass cowboy boots, from her curly down-to-the-waist hair and make-up-free face, that this woman was a free spirit.

He always ran as far and as fast as he could away from free spirits, adventurers, women who marched to the beat of their own drum. He preferred women who were uncomplicated, undemanding, easy-going. Calm… He really liked calm.

He just knew that this woman was anything but…

So toss back your whiskey and get out of here, Tessier. And there's no point in running pickup lines through your head. You are not going to use them on her or anybody else.

Smart, very successful—rich, if she had to judge by his subdued designer threads—and a little or a lot lost, Remy thought. His broad shoulders looked tight and his thumb tapping against his tumbler suggested tension. His hair held the furrows of frustrated fingers raking through it.

She recognised stress when she saw it—after all, she'd once been the living, breathing embodiment of it—and she sympathised. He needed more than one hastily thrown back whiskey and some conversation. He needed to relax, to laugh, and probably a healthy bout of really good sex.

She could help with one and two, and she couldn't emphatically state that three was out of the question. She was *that* attracted to him…

Here's hoping you have a sense of humour, cutie, because if you don't I'm about to fall flat on my face...

'You are just the way I like my coffee. Tall, dark and strong.'

He half turned towards her and she sucked in her breath at her first proper look at his eyes, which were gunmetal-grey, framed by dark, spiky lashes.

His straight, dark eyebrows pulled together. 'Excuse me?'

Remy made a clucking noise and pretended to think. 'Didn't work? Well, what about this…? I've been looking for a man with a VCR and I've finally found the perfect one… That's a Very Cute Rear, by the way.'

He rolled his eyes but she saw humour flash in them. *Thank God.*

His strong face remained impassive, and if it hadn't been for that flicker of fun she'd noticed she would have run for the hills.

'Seriously?'

Remy flashed her naughtiest grin. 'Really cheesy, huh?'

That sexy mouth tipped up just a little at the corners. 'Very.'

'Okay—last one. Aren't you the guy who's going to buy me my next drink?'

He stared at her for a moment, before releasing a smile which took him from cool and remote to vaguely accessible.

Oh, cutie, you definitely need to smile a lot more.

'Not great, but tolerable.'

His voice was low, melodious, and as smooth as the expensive whiskey he was drinking, she thought as he turned away to order her a drink. Then he took the vacant seat next to her and, as she'd expected, blinked when he noticed her eyes. Instead of commenting on the pale golden colour, as so many people did, he just crossed his arms, big biceps pulling the sleeves of his dress shirt tight across his arms. She longed to loosen that perfectly knotted red tie, to undo the top button of that blindingly white shirt. She wondered what he would look like in lived-in jeans and a T-shirt…how he looked naked. Fantastic, she decided.

'So, do those dreadful pickup lines usually work for you?' he asked, his eyes unreadable again.

'You bought me a drink, didn't you?' Remy pointed out.

'This is true.' He pushed the glass of wine in her direction. 'Got any others?'

'Pickup lines? Sure.'

'Hit me.'

'They *are* pretty dreadful,' she warned him, her expression inviting him to flirt a little, laugh a lot.

'I don't know…the VCR one was dated *and* dreadful.'

Remy tapped her finger against the bar and pretended to think. 'Okay, what about…your body is a wonderland and I want to be Alice?'

He groaned.

'Could you please step away from the bar? You're melting all the ice?'

There was that smile again.

'Are you a dictionary? Because you just gave me the definition of gorgeous?'

Yeah, the smile's growing bigger. C'mon, I know it's in there somewhere.

'You're so hot a firefighter couldn't put you out.'

His unexpected laughter rumbled over her and Remy couldn't help her shiver, which was quickly followed by heat flowing through her veins. She'd got him to smile properly, to laugh. She felt as if she'd won a seriously important prize.

She sent him another dazzling smile. 'I'm Remy.'

'Robert, but most people call me Bo.'

Robert was too uptight, too formal, Remy thought as she took a sip of her wine, but she supposed it suited his cool, calm, Lord of the Manor attitude. 'Bo' suited the laughing man she'd seen behind the stick-up-his-ass façade.

And she really found *that* man far too attractive.

This is a good time to get up and leave, Draycott. Before you do something really stupid like inviting him to inspect your panties—which just happen to be red and barely there. Take your reality pill, honey. Remember the last time you had sex? Which happened to be your first and only one-night stand? Two years ago? It was so unfulfilling that you swore you'd never do it again... Is this ringing any bells yet?

It was, but she really, *really* didn't want to listen to Sensible Remy. She wasn't any fun…

'How long are you staying in Bellevue?' he asked, distracting her from her crazy thoughts.

Remy looked at the functional, no-frills watch on her wrist. 'Ten hours or so? I'm hitting the road at first light. Do you live in the area?'

He nodded. 'Are you travelling alone?'

She knew that he was fishing—could see the attraction she felt echoed in his eyes. 'Yep, just me.'

'It's a nice holiday…touring the wine country,' he replied, his tone so bland that she wondered if she was perhaps reading him wrong.

Then his hand moved across the bar and his thumb stroked over the pulse-point of her wrist, which instantly bolted at his touch.

Holy hell, she was playing with fire, she thought, staring at his strong, broad hand on her pale wrist. Unable to pull away from his touch, so simple and so devastating, she used her other hand to pick up her wine glass and lubricate her mouth.

'So, how has your trip been so far?'

Same voice, but his eyes were on her mouth and the gunmetal-grey had turned smoky with passion. How could he keep his voice so smooth while she was a maelstrom of nerves and lust and attraction? *Kiss me, already*, she wanted to beg.

No begging allowed, Sensible Remy whispered in her ear.

'Oh, I'm not on holiday… I'm a professional vagrant.' That sounded better—a little breathy but there had been words in a sentence. Pretty impressive, really.

His thumb on her wrist stopped. *Noooo!*

'Want to explain that?' he asked.

She couldn't. All she could think about was the effect he was having on her and her desire to get him naked, to have her hands on that warm, muscled, masculine flesh. There was no way to verbalise that three years ago she'd lived in New York, that her doctorate in computer science had landed her the position of youngest Chief Information Officer of a Fortune 500 company. *Ever.*

She'd had an apartment in Manhattan, worked eighty-hour weeks, had an ulcer the size of a fist and had been prone to panic attacks. She'd been discontented, unhappy, unfulfilled. Bitchy, demanding, impatient. She could never tell him that it had taken her landing up in hospital to realise that she was working herself to death. And for what? A fat pay cheque and her mother's approval?

Could he even *begin* to understand why she'd given up everything because she hadn't liked what she'd been doing or who she'd been doing it for? That she'd run? To Europe, and then Africa, Asia? And when she hadn't found what she was looking for in foreign places—that nebulous, indefinable something that would make her life make sense—she'd come home to see if she could find it by travelling through her own country.

Seeing that he was still waiting for an answer, she shrugged and bit the inside of her lip. 'I've been travelling for a long time.'

'Why?'

She tipped her head and shoved her tongue in her cheek. 'I'm trying to *find* myself—to work out why I *do* the things I do and *make* the choices I make.'

His lips quirked at her dramatic tone. 'Any luck with that?'

'Absolutely none,' Remy replied in a mournful voice. And even while she was mocking herself she silently admitted that she was starting to become slightly concerned that she never would.

'And how do you support yourself and your gas habit?'

That amazing thumb had resumed its rhythm on her wrist. She could no more pull her hand away than she could adjust the temperature of the sun.

Savings, investments, property… She'd worked so hard that she'd never had time to spend any of her ridiculously huge salary. She earned enough in interest and dividends and rental, and from the occasional virtual consulting job she took, to allow her to keep travelling for a long, long time. If she was really lucky she would find whatever it was that she was looking for soon—in Portland, maybe, or in the next town she visited.

'When I need to I find work.' There were always IT consulting projects popping into her inbox—some of which she took on, if they were interesting enough.

'Doing…?'

'This and that… I'm a hell of a cook—and, for the record, a really bad waitress.'

He laughed again and she felt her womb contract. Why was getting this hard-eyed, hard-bodied man to laugh such a kick? Such an incredible turn-on?

'Good to know.'

'So…what do *you* do?'

Bo lifted his eyebrows. 'What do you *think* I do?'

The corners of his mouth lifted in a sexy little smile.

Was he flirting? He was so contained that she couldn't be sure, but she'd give him the benefit of the doubt.

'I'll play that game. Well, you look marginally intelligent,' she teased. 'Accountant?'

Bo pulled a face. 'Ugh!'

She pulled a face too. 'Lawyer?'

'Double *ugh*!'

She tapped her finger against her lip. 'So, not an accountant or a lawyer? I'd still say that you're in management.'

'Yeah.'

And she just knew that he was the top branch of a very tall tree. She couldn't imagine him taking orders from anyone. He was too controlled, too alpha…not her type at all. As a long-term prospect, she clarified. Along with her career she'd also given up on love and her dreams of happy-ever-after with a nice man followed by a couple of kids. She'd finally—*finally!*—learnt that, despite what people said, love, trust and approval were conditional—very much dependent on what she delivered.

So three years and two months ago she'd stopped playing that game, and she now kept any new relationships simple. Most of them were transient and fleeting anyway, due to the fact that she was constantly on the move.

And this was pure sexual heat shimmering between her and Bo: passion, lust and incredible chemistry.

Remy lifted her head from watching his thumb on her wrist—so fascinating, so thrilling!—and her eyes slammed into his. She swallowed at the heat and passion rolling through them and sighed when Bo lifted his hand and that magical thumb brushed her full bottom lip.

'So sexy,' he muttered as his other hand gripped her thigh.

Remy looked down at his hand and could easily imagine those tanned fingers on her breast, that wide hand sliding over her hip, under her bottom, lifting her to him…

Then he leaned forward and his mouth touched hers… warm, wonderful. Remy, shocked and surprised and utterly turned on, had to grab at his biceps to keep from falling off her stool. Bo steadied her by holding her waist, and she could feel the ridges of his fingers through her thin cotton dress.

Remy held on to his wrists and, wanting more of his deliciousness, pressed her mouth back onto his. He tasted like whiskey and breath mints and his lips were a surprise. Warm, firm, dry… *Confident*. That word again. What *he* was to his core and what *she* only had a glossy, thin layer of…

His hand moved to her spine, kneading as he worked his way up to her bare shoulders, moved around to touch her face. His thumb skated over her cheekbone as he deepened the kiss, his tongue sliding into her mouth.

Remy's eyes flew open at the bolt of lust that spiked through her. Where had *that* come from? She couldn't remember when last she'd been kissed with such mastery, such complete and utter self-assurance.

She wanted more of this—more of him. Now. Tonight. One night of passion with a man she knew would rock her world.

Grabbing every last bit of courage she had, she made herself pull back from him, determined to be sensible just for a minute.

'This sounds like an extraordinarily personal question, and I know you can lie when you answer but I hope you don't. Are you married? Involved?'

Apart from those hot, tumultuous eyes, he looked as calm and collected as before. Keeping his eyes locked on hers, he drained his drink. 'No.'

'Good.' Remy nodded. 'It's one of my little rules.' She

shrugged a slim shoulder and forced herself to say the words. 'Been tested lately?'

Bo remained unruffled. 'Yep. I'm good.'

'Me too, but I'd still expect you to use a condom.'

'Noted.'

'Okay, then.'

Remy, hoping, praying, that she wasn't making the biggest mistake of her life, stood up and draped her black leather bag over her slim shoulder. She was as nervous as hell—couldn't believe that she'd had the…well, the courage to do this. Knowing that laughter would loosen the tension between them, she deliberately looked down at his feet before flashing him a naughty grin.

'You know what they say about men with big feet. Want to prove that to me?'

His shout of laughter had more than a few customers looking their way.

Yeah, laugh, cutie, Remy thought as they left the bar. *You sound amazing.*

'You okay?'

Bo's voice rumbled across her skin and Remy nodded, rubbing her head against his shoulder.

'Wonderful, thanks.'

And she genuinely was. Sleeping with Bo was nothing like the last one-night stand she'd had, and she was thrilled that it was so much more. There were no regrets this time—no feelings of guilt, no resentment at not being satisfied.

She felt relaxed and calm and, weirdly, *safe*.

She'd hit the one-night stand jackpot, Remy thought on an internal smile. Very good-looking, and his body, under those sharp threads, was droolworthy. Long, lean muscles, ripped abs, broad shoulders… And he smelled divine.

He was the best lover she'd ever had by a million miles.

Sex with Bo had been fun and, strangely for an ONS, a little romantic. That had never happened to her before. With all her previous lovers her mind, ever analytical, had always ruled and she'd never allowed herself to fall into that space where she stopped thinking and just enjoyed. But instead of the fast and furious she'd expected, Bo had spent long, luscious minutes worshipping her body, allowing her to do the same to him. It had made what should have been a quick encounter deeper, more personal…softer.

Why was it that the one man who'd managed to show her how sex should be, who had been able to satisfy her beyond anything she'd believed possible, was the man she'd never see again?

Remy watched as Bo raised his wrist and looked at the bright dial of his watch, the roman numerals visible in the nearly dark room. This was it. In fifteen minutes—maybe twenty—he would slip out of her bed and then out of her life. She shouldn't want a little more time with him but she did: just an hour, or a day or two, here in this magical town.

Remy brushed her hand through the light, crisp layer of hair on Bo's chest. She rubbed her cheek against his shoulder before succumbing to the urge to bury her face in his strong neck, silently asking him to stay exactly where he was. She'd barely finished the thought when she felt the tap of his fingers against her hip, and she pulled her head back to look at him.

'I must go. I have to be up in a couple of hours.'

Remy sat up and managed a small smile as he swung his legs around to sit on the edge of the bed. 'I'm leaving early too.'

He reached behind him and squeezed her calf. 'I'm not going to ask you where you're going because I might be tempted to follow. I had a great time.'

Remy, holding the sheet up above her breasts, risked placing her hand on his shoulder and turned her intended caress into a quick pat. 'Me too. I thought we'd spontaneously combust that first time.'

His deep, sexy chuckle danced across her bare skin. 'We shouldn't have started kissing in the lift. We gave that other couple quite an eyeful.'

Remy frowned, confused. 'There was another couple in the lift?'

Bo stood up and pulled his boxers on. Placing his hands on his hips, he looked down at her, his mouth twisted into a wry smile. 'Yeah, there was.'

Remy tossed her head and didn't break contact with his mesmerising eyes. They were the most amazing shade of grey, edged with a ring of black. 'Well, sorry… I was kind of distracted.'

His eyes deepened and looked smoky again. 'I like the fact that I can make you lose track of your surroundings.'

Remy had to smile at the very self-satisfied smirk on his face.

When he'd headed to the bathroom Remy scuttled out of bed, rummaged in her suitcase and eventually found a pair of sleeping shorts and a roomy T-shirt. In the mirror on the opposite wall she saw her reflection and pulled a face at her very messy hair and make-up-free face. She wasn't looking her best, but what was the point of fussing over what she looked like when he was heading out through the door?

Out of her life.

One night. His staying any longer was not an option.

She shouldn't want him to stay at all.

Bo stood in the generic hotel bathroom and stared at his reflection in the large mirror above the basin. *This is a one-night stand,* he told himself, *a one-time deal.*

So what if it had been some of the best sex of his life? He'd spent two hours with her and they had done it…he could hardly believe it…*three* times. He wasn't in his dotage, but that was excessive even for him. He hadn't been able to stop touching her, seemingly desperate to make every second count.

He didn't want to walk back out there, pick his clothes up off the floor and walk out of her life. For the first time in far too many years he wasn't racing to leave, wasn't feeling the noose around his neck, the let-down after good sex with no emotional connection. All he wanted to do was to climb back into her bed and slide on home.

But that would not be sensible or practical and definitely not wise. Apart from the fact that she intrigued him—which he didn't like—they were out of condoms. Although if he didn't leave—*now!*—then he wasn't sure he'd be able to control himself.

Bo flipped on the cold tap and ducked his head under the spout, hoping the cold water would shock some sense into him. Why was he thinking about her like this? She was sex, pure and simple—a good time, and that was it!

She'd offered, he'd accepted, they'd both had fun—the *end*. He should be walking out through the door with a fat smile on his face.

She'd been a superb lay—the best two hours of his life…so why wasn't he feeling any better? Bo rubbed a towel over his hair and his hand over his jaw, now covered with dark stubble.

Since Ana he'd consciously, deliberately, kept all his sexual encounters casual and this had been supposed to be the most casual of all. A pretty girl—a tourist—someone he wouldn't see again. How much more casual could he get? He didn't know her surname, where she was from, what her cell number was, but she was the first woman in five years who'd managed to reach inside his gut and twist it into a knot.

And that was why he purposely, deliberately, strode

back into the room and quickly yanked on his clothes. The quicker he left, the quicker he could go back to thinking straight…

Remy had left the bed and got dressed and Bo was thankful for the small mercy that she wasn't still naked; that would have made leaving a lot harder than it already was. Than *he* already was…

He sent her a quick look. She sat on the corner of the bed, her long legs crossed at the knees. She looked cool and composed, so he walked over to her and dropped his head to kiss her high on her cheekbone, knowing that if he didn't keep it light he wouldn't be able to resist temptation…*again.*

'Thanks, Remy. Have a good life.'

'Yeah, you too.'

Bo yanked open the door, closed it behind him and shook his head. If someone had told him earlier that walking away from her would be difficult he would have told them that they had rocks in their head. Walking away was *never* difficult…

Except that this time it really was.

CHAPTER TWO

Six weeks later

In Portland, Remy stood in the smallest bedroom, which her mum had turned into a nursery for Callum, and kept her eyes firmly fixed on her baby half-brother's face. Only the fact that her mother would kill her if she woke Callum kept her from running into the dark Portland night, screaming like a psychotic banshee.

She was on the edge of sanity and there were more than a few contributing factors…

Six weeks in her mother's orbit was about five weeks and five days too long. As it turned out Callum slept a lot, and Jan had had plenty of time to nag her adult child.

'When are you going to pick up your career? You have an obligation to use the brains God gave you for something more worthwhile than catching flights, learning another way to cook fish and then blogging about it. All that education wasted. You are *not* fulfilling your potential.'

Below those comments were the unsaid implications… *You disappoint me. I expected more. What you* do *is important—not who you* are.

But she now had a bigger problem than her mother's nagging her about her life…

Remy looked down at the plastic wand in her hand and pulled another two out of her back pocket. One displayed a plus sign, one showed two lines and, just to make sure she got the message, the third had the word ‘pregnant’ in the display window.

She was going to have a baby.

This couldn’t be happening…

She was going to have Bo’s baby. The stranger from Bellevue. Her one-night, blow-her-head-off stand.

Remy slid down the wall and rested her head just below the butt of the happy giraffe painted on the wall. *God!* Why, oh, *why* was this happening to her? She *couldn’t* be pregnant—she didn’t *want* to be pregnant—but she held the irrefutable proof in her hands. And *how*? Bo had entered her only once, maybe twice, without a condom. On neither occasion had he been close to his happy ending… The man had had incredible self-control and he’d used that control to bring her to orgasm after orgasm during the night.

But apparently one of his super-sperm had sneaked out and had been hell-bent on finding its own happy ending. With *her* egg.

Remy muttered a series of silent curse words as tears pooled in her eyes.

In his wooden crib Callum snuffled and Remy tensed, thinking that he was about to wake up. She stretched her neck to look at him. Crap! She was going to have one of… of *those*! They didn’t even look all that interesting to have around; all Callum seemed to do was cry, eat and sleep.

She wanted to send hers back… Why didn’t life come with a remote control? *Whoops, didn’t mean to do that—rewind. Don’t like that channel—swap.*

Remy banged her head lightly against the wall. *Life doesn’t work that way, chicken.* She couldn’t duck, ignore or rewrite her life or her past…no matter how much she’d like to.

Remy stared at the carpet between her knees. She was

her mother's daughter in more ways than one: stupid when it came to condom use, apparently, but brilliant academically.

Like her brainy mother—a professor in mechanical engineering—she'd been in an accelerated learning programme most of her life and at sixteen had started at the same Ivy League college Jan was a lecturer at. She'd spent her entire undergraduate degree years feeling that she was an exhibit, her mum's pet project…paraded around when she was in favour, held at a distance when she wasn't.

After completing her PhD in computer science she'd been headhunted by Tiscot's, the biggest media and PR company in the country, to be their Chief Information Officer at a stupidly massive salary. Her desire to please and to achieve had followed her into the workplace, and she'd given the company, and her boss, more than a pound of her flesh—part of her soul as well.

Her life had been consumed by work, and such dedication, obsession, such *stupidity*, had caused her ulcer to perforate and she'd landed up in hospital—which had given her some much needed time to think.

Lying in that hospital bed, she'd never felt more alone. She'd had no visitors—why would she? She had no friends—and the only flowers she'd received had been from the firm, probably ordered by the junior receptionist. Long, long hours on her own had given her the time to examine her life and she had come to accept that she was twenty-five, lonely—because she never made an effort to make friends—perpetually single—because she never took the time to date—and desperately unhealthy because she never took the time to eat properly.

She was also burnt out and possibly depressed. And every time she thought about returning to Tiscot's the flames of hell fired up in her stomach.

That had been a freaking big clue that she'd had a choice

to make: she had to change her life or allow hell to move permanently into her stomach. She'd chosen to save herself and her sanity and had walked away from her corporate, high-pressure, immensely demanding job.

From New York she'd flown to England, but that hadn't quite been far enough to silence her mother's voice in her head constantly reminding her that she was making a huge mistake, that she was being a coward, a cop-out. That she wasn't good enough, wasn't working hard enough, wasn't achieving enough.

The rest of Europe had still been too close, so she'd headed for Asia, and by the time she'd got to Africa Jan's voice had been quieter. But sadly it still hadn't disappeared entirely.

Leaving her corporate life had been the right decision, Remy thought. And she'd seen some amazing places, met some extraordinary people. But travelling hadn't filled all the holes in her soul. She was still looking for…

Remy racked her brain. Why couldn't she define what she was seeking? Why did she have this belief that she would only know what it was when she found it? It wasn't love, or a man, or a relationship—love was conditional, an iffy emotion that wasn't steadfast and true. And, as she'd been shown all her life, it could be used as a weapon or a bribe. She had spent her life chasing it, catching it and then having it ripped from her grasp. She was *so* over it.

As a result, she didn't buy in to the premise that love, or a man, would make her happy. So what *would*? She wished she knew.

Was she looking for a new job? Possibly. A new passion? Definitely.

What she *hadn't* been looking for was pregnancy or incipient motherhood. That was taking her whole turn-over-a-new-leaf attitude a forest too far.

But a baby was on its way, she was keeping it, and

she had to adjust. She had to make plans—start thinking for two.

But before she could make plans she had to tell Bo—tell him that she was pregnant and expecting his child. Bo deserved to know he'd fathered a child, and her child needed to know who his or her father was. She knew this because nearly thirty years ago, in a rare display of loss of control, her mum had gone to a party, got totally high, and couldn't remember exactly who she'd slept with that night.

As a result Remy didn't have a cookin' clue *who* her own father was.

Telling Bo was the *one* thing she was sure of. She owed him that. She supposed that she would also have to tell her family…which meant—unfortunately—having a conversation with her mother.

Remy sighed and pushed her hair back off her face as she stood up. That was going to be fun. Jan would respond as if she'd told her that she was intending to juggle with vials of something lethal. It was going to be ten times worse than telling her mother that she had given up her job to go travelling to 'find' herself.

Way. Way. Worse.

Unlike travelling, she couldn't just give up a baby and resume the life Jan had spent so much time planning.

Remy walked over to the crib and stared down at the tiny, tiny little bundle who was her mother's latest little project. *Unfair,* Remy thought, biting her lip. Her mum loved Callum and she loved her. Sort of…

'I'll try to shield you as much as I can, little brother, but I'm warning you she's a force of nature. Don't be too smart, okay?' she murmured, touching the back of her knuckle to his satin-smooth head. 'I'm going to leave Portland now—tonight. I've got to get out of here. And, no, I'm not quite brave enough to tell her yet.'

'Tell her what?' Jan asked from the doorway, her arms folded against her already flat stomach.

Her body wouldn't *dare* rebel and hold on to its baby fat a minute longer than it should, Remy thought.

Remy pushed the pregnancy test wands back into her pocket, hiding them, before turning to face her mum. 'Nothing much,' she lied. 'Just that I'm leaving. It's time.'

Jan nodded briskly. 'Good. I was about to suggest the same thing. But before you go I want to tell you about a VP position that I hear is vacant at Repcal Tech. It's a step down from where you were before, but beggars can't be choosers…'

Back in Bellevue, Remy thought as she pulled into a spare parking space in front of the diner on the corner of Main and First. Looking down, she saw the open notebook next to her on the cracked bench seat of her old Ford 150. There were just two bullet points on the blank page.

Fill up with gas.
Find Bo and tell him you're pregnant.

Easy-peasy, lemon-squeezy, she assured herself. Once she told Bo that he was going to be a daddy and that she expected absolutely nothing from him she could move on again. He would be upset at the news—and then grateful when he heard that she intended to let him off the hook, happy that she didn't need or expect anything from him. Then she'd leave…

She had, she reckoned, another three months of travelling before she had to make some hard decisions—like where she wanted to live, what she was going to do for the rest of her life.

That's what happens when you let yourself play with fire, Draycott. You get burned, dummy.

Or, in her case, pregnant…

Remy grabbed her leather tote bag and left the car, slamming the heavy door shut behind her. She had been travelling for hours and she was hungry and desperate to use the bathroom.

Remy pushed open the door to the diner and sighed when she saw the packed tables and booths. Apparently lunchtime on a Saturday was chaotic. She used the facilities and washed her hands and face, taking some time to run a brush through her hair, to swipe on some lip gloss. This was Bo's town, after all, and she didn't want to run into him looking as if she'd been dragged backwards through a bush.

And if she *did* run into him, how should she tell him?

Hi, remember me? Thought you'd like to know that I'm pregnant.

Funny thing... You know when you slipped inside without a condom? Well, it had a pretty big consequence...

Or her favourite.

I'm pregnant. It's yours. Bye.

Remy sighed at her pale reflection in the bathroom mirror before whirling away and heading back into the diner. Food always made her feel better. She'd have a bacon and blue cheese burger and then she'd tackle the problem of finding out exactly who Bo actually was and how to get hold of him. Once she did that her duty would be done and she could move on.

There still wasn't an empty table in the place, so Remy looked over the customers to see who would be most receptive to sharing a table. Years of travelling had robbed her of any lingering shyness and she could talk to anybody, anywhere. There were two good-looking blondes, one male, one female, sitting in a corner booth. They looked enough alike for her to assume that they were siblings. And, since they weren't lovers, they shouldn't mind her horning in on their private time.

Her mind made up, Remy walked across the room to the booth and flashed them her biggest smile. Ooh, the blond guy was *very* fine: muscled and masculine, with a gorgeous pair of deep brown eyes.

Rein it in, Draycott. The last time you flirted with a hot man you ended up with a lot more than you bargained for.

So Remy dialled down her smile and gestured to the empty seats. 'I'm absolutely starving and I was wondering if I could share your table. Please?'

The elfin face of the woman was tilted up and she smiled back. 'Sure…' She scooted up on the bench and patted the empty space next to her. 'Take a seat. I'm Ginny, and this is my cousin Eli.'

Eli leaned back and gave her a long, lazy smile.

Yeah, definitely flirting material… Except that he didn't do anything for her. The eyes were brown, not grey, his hair was too light and his smile was too open.

'I'm Remy.'

'Are you passing through?' Eli asked.

'I might be around for a couple of days—a week, maybe.'

It didn't seem that big a town—surely it wouldn't take that long to track Bo down? Maybe she could ask Eli and Ginny if they knew him. But later, after they'd all eaten.

She gestured to their half-eaten plates of food—salad for her, burger for him—and to their cooling coffee. 'Don't let me interrupt your conversation, please.'

Remy quietly ordered her food from a waitress as the cousins resumed their discussion around organic farming. Remy, not knowing anything about farming, and even less about organic farming, tuned out and leaned back and closed her eyes. Lord, she was tired. Soul-deep tired… Thank goodness she'd booked a room at the hotel down the street before she'd left Portland. After her burger she'd check in and maybe just lie down for a little while.

'Did you see the sample menus from the chef candidates that were faxed through from LA?' Ginny was asking.

'Yeah…not that I read them,' Eli answered.

She'd said the magic word 'menus' and Remy couldn't help tuning in.

'I bet you he didn't explain the brief properly—the vision of the restaurant,' Ginny grumbled. 'They're too far out. We don't want Turkish eggs and caviar omelettes…'

'What are Turkish eggs?' Eli demanded.

'Poached eggs, basically,' Remy murmured, unable to help herself. 'Although I do mine with mint, chilli and smoked paprika. Seriously yummy.'

'Maybe we *do* want Turkish eggs on the menu,' Eli told Ginny.

'Well, I don't want caviar omelettes. Caviar omelettes do *not* belong in the type of place we are opening at Belleaire,' Ginny said obstinately.

Belleaire… Remy thought. The fancy wine estate on the outskirts of town. Were Eli and Ginny two of the three family members who owned and ran the upmarket, famous estate which was prominently featured in all the tourist brochures?

Okay, she wasn't going to pretend that she wasn't listening any more. 'What type of restaurant are you opening?' she asked, intrigued.

Ginny pushed her coffee cup away and half turned to face Remy. 'A family place—breakfasts, teas, light lunches. Fresh, healthy, light, interesting food that's not… *pretentious*. I want people to be able to relax, to bring their kids there, but still be able to get a nice meal, a decent glass of wine.' She pulled out a sheaf of papers from her bag and slapped them onto the table. 'My brother is currently interviewing candidates for the manager-cum-chef position and he's asked them to send through sample menus for what they would do if they were offered the position.'

Remy gestured to the papers. 'Can I look?'

'Are you a chef?'

Remy shook her head. 'No, but I *am* a cook and I adore food. I've done about a million cookery courses.' She skimmed through the menus, tossed most of them aside and kept a couple in another pile. She tapped her finger against the slim pile. 'These here are the best of a bad bunch, but they're still not great.'

Eli folded his arms and his biceps bulged. Nice arms, wide chest, flat stomach… But still she felt nothing. Weird.

'What would *you* do?'

She blinked at him. 'About what?'

'If it was your place? You obviously know food, and you seem to be familiar with the dishes on those menus.'

'Oh…' Remy thought for a minute, her face cupped in her hands. 'Um…interesting salads. Couscous and butternut, watermelon and feta—things like that. Soups with crusty, gorgeous bread. Hearty dishes like lamb stew, lasagne and chicken casserole. Classic puddings with one or two exceptions to keep things interesting. A specially designed menu for kids—but I'd avoid burgers and hot dogs. Fish and chips, a chicken pasta dish—meals that kids like and mums like them eating.'

Remy didn't notice the long look Ginny and Eli exchanged. Instead her eyes were on the waitress, who was walking in their direction with what was, hopefully, her burger. She was so hungry she could eat a horse.

'Are you looking for work?' Ginny asked.

'Sorry? What?' Remy sighed her disappointment when her burger went to the table two up from them.

'We're looking for a chef-manager to set up the bistro and you seem to know what you're talking about,' Ginny explained, her face animated with excitement.

'Uh… I wasn't planning on sticking around,' Remy replied, her mind whirling.

She was here to talk to Bo and then she was on her way. But setting up a restaurant, designing a menu, building something from the ground up, sounded like a whole bunch of fun.

Throughout her life, and despite trying many different activities on her travels, food had seemed to be her only constant. When she was a child, battling to reconcile her intellect with her emotions, Grandma Rosie had often hauled out her baking bowl and flour and put her to work. Baking calmed her and it and cooking was still her favourite means of stress relief.

When she'd started travelling she had finally had the time to indulge her passion; she'd started to blog about food and spent an enormous amount of time seeking out the best food markets, learning how to cook the local foods.

She'd taken a course in how to cook Thai food in Bangkok, had done a confectionery course in London, a *cordon bleu* course in Marseille. Sushi in Sydney. Chinese in… Sydney again. She seemed to gravitate towards the food industry, but she didn't want the pressure of working in a professional kitchen.

If she weren't pregnant she wouldn't hesitate to take Ginny up on her offer. But after seeing Bo she needed to keep moving while she still could. Some time in the next four months she had to find a town or a city she wanted to live in and—*ack!*—a job. Or, better, a business that covered her daily expenses and allowed her flexibility and freedom.

A cupcake shop? An ice cream parlour? An old-fashioned tea room?

And where? In Portland? Close to her mum and to Grandmother Rosie, who'd helped raise her?

'Do you have another job? Somewhere to be?' Ginny

demanded, breaking into Remy's thoughts. She pointed a finger at her. 'I can see that you are intrigued and interested, and life is too short to spend your time doing stuff you don't like.'

She knew that—that was why she didn't have an ulcer any more. A baby, but not an ulcer.

'I *am* interested…it *does* sound like fun.' Remy tipped her head, thinking quickly. 'Maybe I could spend a week or so here, look over the space and draw up some sample menus. I could possibly cook a couple of dishes that you can sample. I can't commit to a taking a job right now—to *anything* right now—but I'd be happy to give you guys some ideas, so that when you do employ someone you can tell them what you want and not have to rely on their taste.'

Ginny clapped her hands in delight. '*Would* you? That sounds amazing. Of course we'd pay you for your time.'

'Hell, I'd pay you to cook for me,' Eli stated. 'So, how long have you been travelling for?'

'Ages.' Remy smiled at him and his returning smile showed interest. She checked inside herself again… No flutter, no tingle—nothing. *Damn.*

Eli must have seen something cross her face, because his eyes laughed at her before he softly spoke again. 'Huh, I must be losing my touch. That doesn't happen often.'

He said it with such genuine regret and confusion that she couldn't hold his arrogant statement against him. So she shrugged and smiled, genuinely regretful. 'Sorry.'

'I've lost track of this conversation,' Ginny muttered.

'I've lost track of my burger,' Remy stated, desperate to change the subject. 'Oh, good—it's on its way.'

The waitress slipped her plate in front of her with a murmured apology about the delay. Remy waved her away—and then blanched as the smell of fried onions hit her nose. Swallowing down her sudden nausea, which she attributed to her being on the *very* wrong side of ravenous, she cut into her burger and pulled it apart. She'd ordered it rare, as she always did, and the patty was perfectly cooked, oozing juice.

Her stomach climbed up into her throat and Remy slapped her hand over her mouth.

Ginny frowned. 'Hey, are you okay?'

Remy shook her head and pushed her plate away. She had to get out of here. *Now!*

Scrabbling for her bag, she stood up, teetering on her feet. Eli flew up and grabbed her arm, keeping her from doing a face-plant on the floor.

'I think I'm going to be sick,' she muttered to no one in particular.

From a long way away she heard Eli speaking to Ginny. 'Maybe you should take her to wherever she's staying, Gin, and I'll settle the bill.'

Before she knew it the pint-sized Ginny had a surprisingly strong arm around her waist and was guiding her out of the restaurant.

So...okay, then, she thought as she sucked in fresh air. Maybe she *wasn't* going to be one of those lucky women who got to skate through pregnancy.

Bo looked at his watch. He had ten minutes before his meeting with Ginny and Eli, and he was thinking, as he always did, that he was lucky to have his sister and his cousin as full partners in the family business. They fought like cats and dogs, but implicitly trusted each other, and each of them had their strengths, their place in the business.

His was the business brain and he kept the whole ship sailing smoothly, Eli made the exceptional wines the business was built on, and Ginny was the farmer, the viticulturist: responsible for looking after the vines and the land, the olive orchard and the vegetable gardens that supplied the mansion hotel and the restaurants with fresh produce.

On paper and in the eyes of their staff he was the boss, but in reality they operated as a rough sort of democracy. Any major decisions were made collectively, through negotiation and compromise. Sometimes that negotiation and compromise sounded more like shouting and arguing, but whatever worked…

And it *did* work. Better than any of them would have believed when they'd inherited equal shares of the winery, house and land after their beloved grandfather had passed on ten years before. He and Ginny had supported Eli when he'd informed them that he needed to travel, to visit other wine-producing countries, and he and Eli had trusted Ginny's instincts to restore the Belleaire mansion to its former glory when they'd decided to turn it into a hotel. They'd both stood at his side when he'd buried his wife of six months…

Ana.

So little time as man and wife and he ached remembering that their marriage hadn't been the happiest time of their relationship. As always, before he forced those thoughts away he consoled himself with the reminder that he'd known her and loved her one way or another all his life. She'd been his childhood friend, his first girlfriend, his prom date. They'd broken up during college but had reconnected in their mid-twenties when she'd become his live-in lover, his fiancée, and finally, for far too short a time, his wife.

And, to date, the only woman he'd ever loved. Would ever love.

Ignoring the issue that cropped up after they married, he deliberately remembered that they had suited each other perfectly. He was ambitious and dynamic and driven, able to take control and to be in charge. He had grounded her. She'd been sanguine and scatty, easy-going and happy to let him do what he did best—which had been to make the decisions and to chart the course of their lives. They'd been the perfect example of opposites attracting, and lightning, Bo thought, shoving his hands into his pockets as he stared out of his office window at the sun setting over the western vineyard, didn't strike twice. He'd had the real thing. The *only* thing…

They said that memories of the people you'd lost faded, but even after four and a half years Bo didn't need to look at the large black-and-white photograph that dominated the credenza next to his desk to visualise Ana. The long blonde hair he'd used to love wrapping around his fists as he slid into her, her dirty laugh, her wide blue eyes. Sometimes he swore he could still smell her…

She was still as much a part of him as she had been… she always would be. Love didn't die with death. Or because of a rolling, on-off six month argument.

'I'll love you to the end…' he'd told her as the light of life had faded from her eyes, as she'd lain in his arms, battered and broken, in that driving rain. She'd needed to hear it and he'd needed to say it.

She'd managed a final tiny smile. 'Promise?'

'Yeah. Always.'

He glanced at the photograph and his heart contracted. He was still in love with his wife—would always be in love with his wife. Despite everything that had happened, he'd never stopped loving her. As a result he liked women but he didn't engage with them emotionally…financially. When you'd had something so amazing nobody else could compete—and he wasn't prepared for them to try.

And if the fact that he was still in love with his wife wasn't enough to put him off getting involved with a woman, then his job was. His career demanded eighty-hour weeks or more—when would he have time to date, for a relationship?

Nah, he was happy to play it cool, skimming along the surface…

Then his thoughts veered off on a tangent, as they often did lately, and the image of Remy—naked, looking down at him, her pale eyes warm with laughter—appeared behind his retina. Remy, his hot-as-hell, over-before-daylight, one-night lover. He could remember every kiss, every touch, every smell and he wished he could forget. One of these days he'd stop thinking of her…of that mind-blowing night.

Hopefully it would be sometime soon, so that his life could go back to normal. He hadn't seen another woman, hadn't had sex for six weeks, and it was time—way past time—to replace those hot memories of the champagne-eyed witch with the very bad pickup lines.

A hand slapping his desk jerked him back to the present. Eli and Ginny were on the other side of his desk, looking at him expectantly. When had they come in? He hadn't even noticed.

'Hi…what's up?'

Ginny and Eli exchanged a long, weird look. 'You called us to a meeting, Bo,' Ginny said, pushing her hair behind her ears. 'Are you okay?'

That would be a negative.

'Sure,' he lied, hating the feeling of operating on only one or two cylinders. He ran a multimillion-dollar company—it was time he acted like the super-sharp businessman he was reputed to be. Remembering his wife was normal—to be expected, even—but daydreaming about a hot night with a woman he wouldn't see again was not. It was utterly ridiculous…

Irritated with himself, he located the file he needed from a pile to his right and tossed it across the table to where his sister and cousin were now sitting.

Dropping into his leather chair, he leaned back and placed his feet on the corner of his desk. 'Bella's Folly.'

Ginny leaned forward, clasping her hands around her knees. 'The land with no owner?'

'That we know of. If there isn't a will, then the estate will pass on to her nearest relative. If there is a will, then it's simple. Either way, we need to find the heir first,' Eli said, placing his ankle on his knee.

'Yeah. There is going to be a *lot* of interest in the property.' Bo leaned further back in his chair. 'Moving on from one folly to another… The renovations for the bistro and coffee shop are nearly finished, and I'm flying to New York tonight and will be back tomorrow evening. I need to see some customers, talk to some distributors, and I'll also interview a couple of chefs for the position of the bistro chef/manager while I'm out there.'

Eli frowned. 'No candidates from California?'

'A couple,' Bo answered. 'These are better qualified.'

'We met someone today who had real potential. Someone who knew food and whom we really liked,' Ginny mused. 'She could be just what we're looking for.'

Bo lifted his eyebrows. 'Is she applying for the job?'

Ginny pulled a face. 'She's not sticking around that long—which is a pity, because I think she would've been perfect for the bistro.'

Comme ci, comme ça... Bo shrugged. 'I'll find someone in New York.'

Ginny shook her head. 'Just remember that we need the right *personality*. Someone who will fit in here at Belleaire with us. We want someone who is warm and funny, who can talk to kids and adults alike. Someone who has brilliant people skills and a solid sense of humour,' Ginny insisted.

The last person *he'd* come across with a solid sense of humour had turned out to be the best sex of his life.

Better than Ana? Really?

Different from Ana, he quickly amended. Very different.

I thought we were done thinking about her, moron?

'It would be nice if she was a looker, too.' Eli added.

Remy had been a looker...

Enough, Tessier!

Bo looked at his watch. 'I need to get going. Don't do anything stupid while I'm away, okay?'

Eli sent Ginny a sardonic look. 'How old are we? Ten?'

'One of these days he'll realise that he isn't actually the boss of us,' Ginny replied.

'Somebody needs to keep you two in line,' Bo told them, and held up his hand as mouths opened to protest. 'Yeah, I know. I'm arrogant, annoying and bossy.' He smiled at the two people he loved best. 'Now, get out of my office. I've got a lot to do before I head to the airport.'

Eli and Ginny, not in the least offended, stood up. Ginny, being Ginny, walked around his desk to give him a hug goodbye. It didn't matter if he was going away for two days or two years. Ginny would hug him as if he was leaving for ever.

CHAPTER THREE

THE BELLEAIRE WINE estate was dominated by a triple storey blue stone mansion—and how could it not be? Remy thought, pulling to the side of the broad, Spanish-oak-tree-lined driveway so that she could spend a minute admiring the house.

It had turrets and bay windows galore, balconies and buttresses, and was three storeys of pure whimsy. It looked like a grand old lady who'd had too many glasses of wine at suppertime and had decided to kick up her heels and dance a jig. It was loud and ostentatious and a tad over the top—and she absolutely loved it.

Her type of mansion, Remy thought.

The entrance to the hotel was just behind a massive square fountain, and there were discreet signs directing visitors to the art gallery, the craft shop, the potters' studio. In the other direction was the tasting room, and if she looked to the land there were rows of vines as far as the eye could see, heavy with grapes. It was late summer and autumn was on its way. Some of the trees were starting to turn and she knew that the harvest was fast approaching.

Remy, as directed by Ginny, took the path to the gallery and walked through the luscious gardens to her destination. God, it was pretty. How lucky were Ginny and Eli to own this, to be part of this? Remy looked around. The place was elegant, rich, tasteful…and Remy was *still* surprised that Ginny had invited her to see Belleaire up close and to join her and Eli for supper that night.

Remy felt heat in her cheekbones, still felt humiliated and foolish. After her mortifying display in the diner she'd shrugged off Ginny's company in the hotel reception area and stumbled up to her room, deathly tired and intensely humiliated, and had instantly dropped to her knees in front of the toilet.

She hadn't really left that bathroom since. God knew how she was going to manage eating with Eli and Ginny… She was still living on crackers, apples and cheese—none of which she could keep down. Dinner would be a nightmare. Right now, her best plan would be to tell them she was pregnant and that she'd just have a soft drink with them—she couldn't even drink wine on a wine estate, for Pete's sake!—and leave early.

Passing the art gallery, she saw another building with a sign stating that it was the Blue View Bistro and she grinned. Belleaire, Bellevue, Blue View…that worked, she thought. She pulled open the door and stepped into the large, mostly empty space.

On the wall closest to her was an artist's impression of what the restaurant would look like and Remy approved of the bright colours, fun artwork and welcoming vibe. There would be vintage mismatched chairs and tables, modern light fittings, and couches and chairs grouped in amongst the tables. It would be a fantastic mix of old and new… *Damn*, she wished that she'd be able to see it when it was done.

'Remy, you made it!'

Remy looked towards the bright voice and saw Ginny coming out from an area that was to be the bar. Surprising her, Ginny kissed both her cheeks before looking up into her face.

'How are you feeling? Better? I hope so. Come into

the bar area. My cousin and brother are having an argument about bar stools. You're still looking very pale and washed out.'

Great. Good to know. 'Um…'

'What was it? Stomach flu?' Ginny guided her over to the door to the bar and yanked it open.

Well, here goes, Remy thought, stepping into a room dominated by a massive bar. She'd consider it a practice round for when she told her child's sexy father. And, dear Lord, he'd been *so* sexy…

Focus, Remy.

'Uh, no. I'm pregnant, and that was my very first bout of morning sickness—henceforth to be known as all-day sickness.' She kept her eyes firmly on Ginny's face. 'Actually, I came to tell you that I can't do supper. I can't keep much down. The reason I'm in Bellevue is to tell the father that I'm pregnant with his baby.'

'Remy?'

It was the voice from her dreams—the one she still heard in her ear, against her skin. The one she heard in the memories she relived over and over again every night. That deep rumble, capable of sending heat to her womb, prickling her skin.

'Bo?'

He was dressed in battered jeans and an open-necked white shirt, sleeves rolled up to reveal raised veins on those tanned forearms. He was here—all six-foot-something of pure, pissed off male.

He got up slowly and she saw that his eyes were slate-grey and hard.

'What did you just say?'

What *had* she just said? She was so flabbergasted by his presence that she couldn't remember… Oh, hell. Pregnant. His baby.

Oh, heavens, why did these things keep happening to her?

Remy bit her bottom lip and folded her arms across her chest, thinking about damage control. 'Um…obviously I didn't mean to tell you like that…'

'You're *pregnant*?' Bo shouted, and she winced as his words bounced off the walls.

'Yes.'

Was it hot in here? she wondered as the floor rose and fell. Along with heat there was suddenly no air. Instinctively she reached out her hand and grabbed the edge of the bar to keep from falling over. She saw dots behind her eyes, felt the blackness coming closer.

The last thing she heard before crumpling to the floor was Eli's amused comment. 'Well, now, isn't *this* interesting?'

When she came to she was on the floor, her back against a solid male chest and two strong arms criss-crossed over her chest. She sat within the V of two legs, long thighs pressing against her own. She felt warm and secure and so very, *very* tired. Ginny was on her haunches in front of her and had a damp linen napkin in her hand, which she lifted to run across her forehead.

'Hey, you're back,' Ginny said quietly, her expression concerned.

'What happened?' Remy asked weakly.

Eli dropped to her level, rested his arm on his bent knee and handed her a quirky smile. 'Well, sunshine, you kind of announced that you were pregnant with Bo's baby and then you dropped like a stone.'

'When did you last eat? Are you getting enough rest? Vitamins?' Ginny demanded.

Remy pushed her hair out of her eyes. 'Bo…?'

She felt those strong arms tense before she heard his voice in her ear. 'Still here.'

Thank God. No, that wasn't right… She shouldn't *like* being in his arms. Shouldn't feel as if she was finally where she was meant to be…

Get a grip, Draycott!

He wasn't her man…this wasn't her place…

'Are you still feeling like you're going to faint?' he demanded, moving his hands to hold her hips.

She winced at the irritation in his voice. Well, it wasn't as if she'd done it on purpose. She touched her forehead and shook her head. 'No. I think I'm fine.'

His fingers dug into her skin. 'Be sure. I don't want to have to catch you again.'

Remy angled her head so that she could look at him. His mouth was drawn into a thin line and his jaw was rock-hard with tension. 'You caught me?'

'The man can move when he has incentive to do so,' Eli said in an amused drawl.

'Shut up, Elijah,' Bo snapped, and he scooted backwards and stood up.

Reaching for Remy's hands, he pulled her up into a standing position and kept a hand on her elbow—she supposed, to keep her from falling. Which was at odds with the furious expression on his face, which suggested that he'd like to boot her off the nearest cliff.

Could she blame him? Remy sighed. Not really. She had delivered her tilt-his-world-upside-down news with absolutely no finesse and then fallen to the floor.

Then again, his wasn't the only world that had been affected. He, at least, got to walk away. She didn't have the luxury of that choice. So Remy straightened her shoulders, lifted her chin and looked him dead in the eye. 'I'm pregnant. You're the father. That's all I wanted to say.'

Remy saw her bag on the table, so walked over to it

and pulled it over her shoulder. She dredged up a smile for Eli and Ginny.

'Sorry I spoilt your evening, and for fainting…for dropping this bombshell like I did. I seem to make a habit of looking like an idiot around you. So…I'm going to go now.'

Not waiting for their response, she turned and walked to the door leading to the restaurant, fighting back tears. *Why?* It wasn't as if she'd expected anything from him, and she didn't need anything from him. She wove her way between the tables and finally reached the front door. Pulling it open, she stepped outside and sucked in deep breaths of warm, early-evening air.

Placing her hand on her still flat stomach, she gave it a quick pat. 'Well, it's you and me, babe. And we'll be fine.'

Remy turned as the door behind her was wrenched open and Bo stalked out.

'Remy!'

Remy tipped her head as Bo walked down the path towards her. Oh, dear… The branch was back up his butt: he was now cool, calm and thoroughly in control. Unreadable eyes and a 'let's fix this' expression on his face. He stopped a foot away from her and she was reminded that this was a powerful man in his prime.

'We need to talk,' he stated.

'I think we've covered the high points,' Remy said.

'We haven't even started,' Bo replied, his voice low but determined. He placed his hand under her elbow. 'Let's go.'

Remy wrenched her arm out of his grip. 'I don't think so!'

Bo looked upwards, as if he were searching for patience. 'We need to talk and we are *going* to talk. You don't get to drop into my life again, tell me that you're pregnant and that I'm responsible, and then just walk out again. That's not how it works!'

Remy twisted her lips and looked down at her toes.

Of course they had to talk—she knew that—but just not right now. Not when she was feeling weak and foolish and so very, *very* tired. She just wanted some distance from him—to regroup, to stop thinking about how gorgeous he looked in those casual clothes, how much she wished she were in his arms, touching him, being loved by him.

These pregnancy hormones were playing havoc with her emotions. She just needed some time, some space… She needed to *think*.

Lifting a hand, she looked at the vineyards beyond his shoulder and forced words out. 'We'll talk…but not now. I have a cracking headache and I am really tired. Maybe tomorrow?'

Bo just looked at her for a long, long time before nodding. 'You do look like hell—and like a puff of wind could blow you over.'

Remy sighed her relief. 'Okay, then. I'll see you—' She squawked in dismay when Bo slid her bag off her shoulder and immediately slid the zip open. Like a typical man, he shoved his hand inside and rooted around. 'Hey! Give me my bag! What do you think you're doing?'

He pulled out her truck keys and dangled them in front of her nose before shoving them into the front pocket of his jeans. Remy just stared at him, not believing that he could pull such a Neanderthal stunt.

'You… What…? *Arrgh!* Why?'

Bo sent her a cold smile. 'I'm confiscating your keys because I have a sneaking suspicion that you might drive away and keep on going. And if you did I wouldn't know where to start looking for you. Talking of which…' He pulled her purse out of her bag and turned his back to her when she lunged for it. He quickly found her driver's licence and his height kept it out of her reach. 'Horrible photo of you… Remy Draycott, twenty-seven, formerly of the Upper West Side, Manhattan. Fancy…'

'Put it back.' Remy felt the enamel flying off her teeth as she ground them together. She watched as Bo replaced her driver's licence and closed her wallet, dropping it back into her bag. She tapped her foot and sent him a belligerent look. 'Are you done?'

'For now.' Bo wrapped the strap of her tote around his fist in that uniquely male way of carrying a woman's bag. He gestured to the path, silently suggesting that she start walking. 'We're going back to my place and we're going to talk. I'll bring you back to your truck later.'

'Give me back my keys and my bag and I will meet you tomorrow—at whatever time suits you.'

'*Now* suits me—and I don't trust you not to run,' Bo told her, his expression uncompromising. 'Frankly, I don't trust you at all.'

Remy watched, every sense on high alert, as Bo walked from the kitchen back to the lounge, a tumbler of whiskey in his hand and a cup of chamomile tea in the other. He placed her cup on the side table next to her and then, instead of sitting down on one of the long, plump leather couches that sat at right angles to the chair she was curled up in, he sat directly in front of her, on the handcrafted wooden table, and rested his forearms on his thighs.

She liked his open-plan wood and steel house, she thought. It was light and airy and he had good furniture. It needed a bit more colour, some art, some character, but it had a nice foundation.

Pity its owner was a pill.

She was still mightily unimpressed with him and his 'I'm confiscating your keys' and 'We're going to talk' statements.

Grunt. Grunt.

He was exactly the type of arrogant, domineering jerk she kept her distance from under normal circumstances.

Brusque, bolshie, bossy. She'd been raised in a feminist household by discussion and debate—with her mother always eventually getting her way—and it had been three years and a million miles since anyone—let alone a man—had presumed to tell her what to do.

She wasn't used to it and she didn't like it—and it didn't matter that he was unfairly gorgeous! All *that* meant was that he was perfect to frolic with.

But to deal with? To be the father of her baby?

Not so much…

Note to self: *Bad, bad—terrible—idea to fall pregnant by a man you do not know. Not good at all.*

Remy rubbed her hand across her forehead as she kicked off her sandals and tucked her feet under her bottom, turning so her cheek could rest on the back of the leather chair. She was comprehensively and utterly exhausted. She supposed she'd better get used to it, she thought. It was only going to get a lot worse.

Bo placed his glass on the coffee table and took her hand, holding it firmly in his when she tried to tug it away.

'What are you doing?' she squawked as lightning danced across her skin.

Bo placed the pad of his thumb into the valley between her hand and her thumb and squeezed. Remy nearly spilled her tea as pain radiated from the joint into her hand and up her arm.

'Stop! Jeez, that *hurts*!'

'Stop being such a baby,' Bo told her, keeping the pressure constant. 'I'm going to hold it for another thirty seconds, with a ten-second rest before we go again.'

Remy tugged, found she still couldn't dislodge his hand, and glared at him. 'And the point of this would be…?'

'Your headache. This is a pressure point. Your headache will go in a minute or two.'

'Rubbish!' Remy scoffed as he released the pressure.

But the weird thing was that her head *did* feel…well, lighter. It was still pounding, but not quite so badly.

Auto-suggestion, she told herself. It had nothing to do with those strong masculine fingers holding her hand.

'Ow! *Dammit!*' she howled when he resumed his torture. Although she had to admit that it was a sweet sort of pain…a healing pain. 'How did *you*, Mr Stick-Up-His-Ass, learn *this*?' she demanded.

'My wife was an acupuncturist and very into alternative medicine. I picked up a couple of tricks along the way,' Bo answered.

His eyes flickered with an emotion she couldn't identify. Sadness? Guilt?

He'd said that he was single and she believed him. So what had happened? There was only one way to find out.

'What happened to her? Did you get divorced?'

'Widowed. She died five years ago.'

Remy sucked her bottom lip between her teeth. 'I'm sorry…' she murmured.

'How's your head?' Bo asked, not bothering to be subtle about his desire to change the subject.

Remy frowned when she realised that her headache was practically gone. 'Huh? I can hardly feel it.'

'Good.'

'Thanks,' Remy said, tugging her hand out of his grasp. 'So—you wanted to talk?'

Bo, not saying anything, just stared at her for a long while and she struggled not to squirm. Those eyes should be considered a weapon of war, she decided. They could slice and dice with precision and icy control.

'We used condoms—how do you think this happened?'

She heard the disbelief in his voice and tried not to feel insulted. 'You don't remember that on round number two you slid on home *before* you put a condom on? You did the same thing on round three.'

She had a brief moment of pleasure when his eyes widened. He was obviously recalling that they *had* had unprotected sex. *Brief* unprotected sex, but enough to cause havoc in their lives.

Bo rubbed a hand over his jaw before waving at the air in the general direction of her stomach. 'And that was enough to…?'

'Obviously,' Remy replied. 'Look, Bo—I get that there are a million questions running through your head, but let's cut to the chase. You're the only guy I've slept with in more than two years. So, yeah, we can do the dog and pony show, argue about whether the kid is yours or not, but a paternity test will prove it is.'

She sighed.

'I know that you only signed up for a night of uncomplicated sex, not to be Daddy of the Year, so you don't need to worry about this… I'm perfectly happy to take this on single-handed.'

'Excuse me?'

Remy narrowed her eyes at his whippy voice. She tried again. 'You don't need to feel obligated.'

'We're discussing my child—not a freaking dinner engagement!' Bo said on a low growl.

Remy wasn't a fool. She saw that this was a man on the edge and thought that silence might be a good idea.

'Two years, huh?' Bo eventually commented.

That was what he thought was important? *Seriously?* Men!

'Give or take. It's definitely yours, Bo.'

Remy bit her lip as Bo's fingers tightened around his tumbler. Any more pressure and the glass would shatter in his hand.

'Do you want this child?' Bo asked abruptly.

She thought about lying to him, about putting a brave

face on, but she was too tired to try. 'Mostly. The idea of having a child is all so new and it's still sinking in.'

'Have you considered an abortion?'

Although she'd expected the question, along with the others about whether he was actually the father, a wave of disappointment drifted through her. She might not actively want the child—his child—but she couldn't contemplate doing away with the conglomeration of cells that would eventually become the perfect mixture of him and her.

When she didn't say anything Bo jumped into the conversation. 'Look, if you say this kid is mine, and the tests prove that it is—well, I'll raise it…her…him…if that isn't what you want to do.' Bo rubbed a hand over his face. 'Just don't get rid of it, okay?'

Remy looked astonished. 'Why would I do that?'

'It's been known to happen,' Bo snapped.

Remy saw something pass through his eyes—something under the veneer of calm that suggested deep pain and a healthy dose of panic. She'd given him every possible option to step away from her emotionally, yet he still stood there, processing the situation.

'You're not behaving as I expected you to,' she whispered, trying to contain a yawn. Nobody had so far.

'I never read the manual on how to react when you're told that a one-night stand is pregnant with your child,' Bo replied.

'You're so calm and collected. I expected you to be shouting and swearing.'

'You're pregnant, and you say that I am the father. We can't change that so we have to deal with it.'

'Well, I feel like I've been hit by a two-by-four,' Remy muttered.

'You *look* like you've been hit by a two-by-four,' Bo shot back. He stared down at his whiskey glass. 'Are you expecting me to suggest that we get married?'

Remy's mouth fell open in surprise. 'You're kidding, right?'

Bo just looked at her, his gaze steady.

'Why would you ask that?' Remy demanded. 'I don't *want* to get married!'

'I didn't ask you to. I asked whether you were *expecting* me to ask. Big difference.'

'Why would you even raise the subject?'

'Because some people would think it's the right thing to do.'

'In the last century, maybe!' Remy retorted, flummoxed at the thought of being this man's wife.

What would that be like? she wondered. How would it feel to be able to play with his body day in and day out?

Marriage, she reminded herself, *is more than sex, you moron.*

Marriage—any relationship with a man as strong-willed as Bo—wouldn't be a partnership or anything close to it. If he was anything like the other strong, corporate alpha men she'd met then it would mean that he'd want to control her, harness her. She'd been under her mother's thumb all her life—she wasn't going to swap one type of control for another. She'd never give *anyone* that much power over her in any way: work, personal life or anything in between. It was a vow she had no intention of breaking—ever.

'Are you crazy? I'm not getting married just because I'm pregnant! We don't even *know* each other!' Remy stated emphatically.

Bo just kept looking at her, his expression unreadable and his eyes steady. 'Again, I didn't ask. But I *will* take care of you and the child.'

'I don't need taking care of!' Remy enunciated each word clearly. 'I don't need *anything* from you.'

'Then you shouldn't have bothered to tell me and we could've avoided this conversation.' Bo leaned forward and his eyes pinned her to her seat. 'But you *did* tell me, and I'm not the type of guy who will stand on the sidelines while you make all the decisions about my child's life.'

Remy, not even remotely intimidated, narrowed her eyes. 'This is *my* child and *I* make the decisions. This was a courtesy visit—nothing else.'

'Like hell it was. Do not even *think* about leaving town; I will not be happy if I have to track you down.'

Remy rolled her eyes. 'And how do you intend stopping me?'

'Any way I have to.' Bo placed his empty glass on the table next to him and slapped his knees. He glanced at his watch and stood up. 'I need to make a call, and then I'll take you back to your truck.'

'Yay—because I am *so* over arguing with you,' Remy murmured, her eyes drooping closed. 'You're lucky I'm feeling so tired, because if I weren't I'd be tearing into you for being a high-handed, bossy, arrogant jerk! When I'm feeling better, I will.'

'I'm *so* scared.' Bo's tone was pure sarcasm.

'You should be.' Remy forced her eyes open to glare at him. 'I'll just close my eyes for a minute or two while I wait for you…'

Within seconds she was out like a light.

CHAPTER FOUR

BO CAST A glance across to his right. Instead of seeing the sleeping passenger he'd expected Remy was wide awake, and those pale eyes, witch-like in the low light of the car's interior, were watching him.

'Slick car.' Remy stated in her sex-on-legs voice.

Bo flicked another glance in her direction and wondered whether he was imagining the note of criticism in her voice. Yeah…the car was German and expensive and fast. He worked damn hard and ran a successful company and he believed he deserved a toy or two. Before Ana had died he'd loved his Ducati, but he hadn't been on his 'Cat' since.

'You have a problem with German sports cars?'

'Not generally. I usually have a problem with the men who drive them,' Remy replied, rubbing both hands over her face. Before he could reply, she held up a hand. 'Sorry… I'm not trying to pick a fight.' Remy blew out another long sigh and looked out of her window as they turned onto the main road to Bellevue. 'So, this must have been a hell of a day for you, huh?'

That was putting it mildly. 'I never expected to see you again and now you're back with a baby. *My* baby.'

That made him wonder, for the hundred and fourth time, how he'd lost control—the control he was so famous for.

'I'm still wrapping my head around the fact that I messed up by not using protection…' He hesitated for a brief moment, blindsided with the hot memory of how incredible she'd felt as he'd slipped into her. He cleared his throat. 'That tiny slip has had far-reaching, life-changing—life-*creating*!—consequences.'

Fate was laughing its ass off at him.

Remy placed the side of head on the window. 'Did you and your wife want kids?'

He never discussed his wife with his lovers—ever. Actually, he never discussed Ana at all. He thought he'd feel resentful and annoyed at her question, but it was just another surprise in a night of surprises that he didn't.

He cleared his throat and managed a one-word response. 'I did.'

He caught the searching look she sent in his direction. He wondered what her reaction would be if he told her that Ana had been vehemently opposed to having children and had casually informed him—on their honeymoon!—that she'd aborted a child shortly after she left college. The lost baby hadn't been his, thank God, but finding out about her antipathy towards children—he thought he knew everything about her—had been a shocking post-wedding present. He'd spent the next six months trying to change her mind but he'd underestimated her stubborness and the issue had driven a wedge between them.

'It must be tough that instead of having a child with the wife you loved you're having one with me—a woman you hoped never to see again.'

Actually, so much had happened tonight that he hadn't really had time to think about that until she brought it up.

'I—'

God, what had he been about to say? That he'd *wanted* to see her again? That he'd thought about her more than he should have? That she'd left an indelible impression on him?

He had—and she did.

Bo pushed a weary hand through his thick hair. Today had been a flip-your-life-over day, a massive turning point. 'It's been…*challenging.* I'm having a child with a complete stranger—a woman I've spent less than twelve hours with.' His glance was filled with irony. 'A woman who seems to be stubborn and independent and iron-willed.'

'That's me,' Remy murmured, her voice free of heat but lacking conviction.

What did *that* mean? That she *wasn't* as independent and strong-willed as she portrayed herself to be? Bo rubbed the back of his neck. He was too exhausted for these mental mind games, he realised.

'You can still walk away from this situation,' Remy reminded him.

'As much as you'd like me to do that, it's not going to happen. If you are carrying my baby, then I'm in this for the long haul.'

His baby…inside her because he hadn't been able to resist the impulse to experience what she felt like without the barrier of latex between them. She'd felt like nothing on earth—amazing—as if he'd come home…

No, home had been *Ana,* he mentally corrected himself.

Despite his frustration with his wayward thoughts Bo shuddered with lust. Ruthlessly he pushed away those hot, sexy, make-him-hard memories.

'*If* I am carrying your baby…' Remy repeated his words. 'You still have doubts that it is yours?'

Logic dictated that he should—that he should be suspicious and wary. He didn't know Remy at all. He'd shared one night with her and for all he knew this could be a mother of a trap. Maybe she'd slept with someone else and was trying to pin it on him. Or she'd slept with a whole lot of guys and thought that he was the best bet for coughing up the dough.

But…

He sighed heavily. *No.*

Just…no.

As much as he would have liked to believe that she was snowing him, he'd seen the truth in her eyes when she'd told him that he'd been her first lover in two years, that he was definitely the father. He knew that he would see the truth in her eyes right now if he looked for it. It was his kid. But she didn't want anything from him and fully intended walking this road alone.

Like hell, Bo thought.

'I believe that I got you pregnant,' Bo said as they entered the outskirts of Bellevue. 'And because I do believe it you should start realising that this is my kid too, and there is no question about whether I want to part of the child's life. I *will* be part of his…her…life.'

The thought was terrifying. And exciting. Of course it was. This baby would be the first of the new generation of Tessiers, and he didn't want his child bouncing from town to town with its free-spirited 'It will all be okay I can do it on my own' mother.

Its free-spirited but *feminist* mother, who didn't seem to grasp the concept of co-parenting or the fact that he would be part of her—correction—part of the baby's life!

His baby would have a home, stability, consistency, immediate and constant access to a parent. All the things he hadn't had as a child. He'd loved his parents, and in their own way they had loved him and Ginny, but they hadn't been a model of responsibility or domesticity. Their own needs and their need to save and uplift the poor, the sick and disadvantaged of the world had come first, and he and Ginny had been supposed to get with the programme and suck it up.

A French school in Equatorial Guinea and they couldn't speak French? Learn! Jumped by a bunch of ten-year-old thugs in a *barrio* in Rio? Fight back! Malaria in Indonesia? Sweat it out!

When it came to child-rearing his parents had believed in the 'toss 'em in at the deep end and make 'em swim' school of thought. They'd sink or they'd swim. Bo had made damn sure that both he and Ginny swam. And the need to protect his loved ones was a childhood trait that had followed him into his adult life and into his marriage.

Children needed stability and protection and roots, and if Remy couldn't provide that—how could she with her vagabond lifestyle?—he would.

He hadn't been able to save Ana from herself. He'd never wanted her to get her own superbike, but she'd wheedled one out of him and riding their powerful machines through the valley had been one of their favourite things to do. Until that day…

He'd warned her—twice!—that she had to slow down in the wet and misty conditions. She hadn't. Which had led to her taking a corner too fast. The bike had slid out from under her and she'd slammed into a concrete barrier. He'd held her in the rain as she slipped away…

Don't go there... Bo snapped his attention back and pulled up in front of Remy's hotel, parking in an empty space and staring up at the pretty façade.

'We need to have a proper talk,' he said, keeping his voice low. 'A serious "let's work this out" talk.'

Remy picked her handbag up off the floor as she nodded. 'I know. Just not tonight.'

No, not tonight. They were both at the end of their tethers and nothing good would come out of discussing this further right now.

Bo pulled in a couple of deep, calming breaths and ran his hand through his hair as he climbed out of his Mercedes to walk around the car and open Remy's door.

She lifted her nose. 'I don't need you to open doors for me.'

He sighed. *God, another argument?* 'Cut the feminist crap, Remy. I'm going to open doors and let you walk into rooms first and pull out your chair. If we have a son, so will he. Get used to it.'

She looked surprised at his crisp response, but she eventually put her hand in his, allowing him to help her from the low-slung car.

Bo kept her fingers linked in his, liking the contact, knowing he shouldn't, but too frazzled to care. He placed his other hand on her hip and watched the attraction flare in her amazing eyes. Standing so close to her, he instantly forgot that they were about to be parents, that she was only back because of the baby, that they didn't know or particularly like each other… He just needed to taste her, to feel her breasts pressed into his chest, her small hands touching his skin.

Pale eyes clashed with his and their mouths were a hair's breadth away from each other…so close. Temptation whirled and swirled and Remy's lids half closed, her chin tipping up as if to encourage him to dip his head, to take a nibble, a bite.

God, he wanted to.

The high-pitched shriek of a car alarm pierced their sexual fog and the moment evaporated. Remy placed her hand on his chest and took a step back, her face morphing from turned on to backing off.

It took a minute for her to speak. 'I think this situation is complicated enough without us adding another layer of crazy.'

Bo rubbed the back of his neck, unable to argue. He still wanted her, but they had far bigger problems to deal with.

'Thanks for the lift.' Remy said. A shrug of her shoulders followed her words. 'But I could've driven myself back here.'

'You would've put yourself in a ditch, you're so tired. I'll make a plan to have your truck delivered in the morning. I'll have the keys left at the front desk.'

Remy yawned. 'Okay. Well…goodnight.'

'We'll talk again in the morning,' Bo assured her, and watched as she walked towards the entrance.

Leaning his hip into the door of his vehicle, he folded his arms and stood there for a long time after she'd disappeared inside. Oh, yeah, they'd talk. She needed to fully understand that he intended to be part of this process and would do whatever he had to.

He'd support her until the child was born—pay her medical expenses, her rent, pay for her food. When the baby arrived they'd renegotiate the future. But for now he had to protect Remy, look after Remy, because by protecting her he was protecting his son or daughter and he wasn't losing again…

He wasn't losing anyone he loved, anybody close or emotionally connected to him.

He wouldn't ever remarry, and he'd couldn't fall in love again, but in a roundabout, crazy way he'd been given the one thing he still craved. That he'd always craved.

A child. A little family. *His* little family. And if that meant dealing with sexy…with Remy…he would.

After all, he kind of needed her.

The next morning Bo stood outside Remy's hotel room door, a bottle of mineral water in his hand. He could do with a whiskey, he thought, sucking the water down. He would be cool, calm and in control. He wouldn't allow her to goad him into an argument, and he sure as hell wouldn't allow her to distract him with her gorgeous face and slim body.

It galled him to admit that even when they'd been talking about her pregnancy yesterday, even when he'd realised that the baby was his, in the back of his mind—and in his pants—he'd known that he still wanted her. That he needed her mouth fused to his, her longs legs around his hips, needed to be inside her again.

Yeah, well, at least you wouldn't get her pregnant this time, moron, he thought sourly.

Replacing the cap on his water bottle, he frowned at the low sound coming from behind her door. Was that a cat he could hear? It was the slightest mewl, the faintest whimper. Knocking on her door, he kept his ears cocked. He didn't hear any movement from behind the door and wondered if she was sleeping. If she was, then what was that noise he'd heard?

Maybe he was letting his imagination run riot… No—there it was again.

Next he heard a faint moan that was decidedly human coming from Remy's side of the door. Without stopping to think he turned the handle—and shook his head when he realised that the door was unlocked. He pushed it open and glanced towards the bed, instantly concerned when he saw that Remy wasn't in it.

Bathroom etiquette be damned… He spun round and poked his head around the half-open door. Remy knelt on the mat in front of the toilet, clutching her stomach. She glanced up at him, her eyes wide, terrified, and awash with tears.

She groaned. 'Go away.'

'Remy? What's the matter?'

'So sick—can't keep anything down,' Remy said in a wobbly voice.

Bo walked out of the bathroom and waited until she was done. When she came staggering out of the bathroom, her hair snarled and her T-shirt barely covering her butt cheeks, he lifted his eyebrows. Her skin was literally green, and there were huge bags under her eyes. She looked gaunt.

And desperately ill.

He immediately grabbed her arm and shoved her towards a chair so that she didn't faint on him again. 'How long has it been since you've eaten? Had something to drink?'

Remy managed a small shrug. 'Not sure. A day? Two?' She lifted worried eyes to him. 'You drove me back last night. Where's my truck?'

'Still parked in the Belleaire parking area. It's safe.' Bo looked around the room, located her suitcase and headed towards it. 'You, however, are not… I think you're dehydrated.'

Remy shook her head. 'Just pregnant. Morning sickness is normal.'

'I'm fairly sure this isn't normal morning sickness!' Bo riffled through her suitcase and pulled out a pair of jeans and a hoodie. Moving back towards her, he opened the zip to the jeans and bent down in front of her to pull them up and over her ankles. 'I have to get you to a hospital.'

'I'm fine. Just let me go to bed.'

Bo tugged the jeans up her thighs. 'Don't be stupid. You're anything *but* fine.'

'But—'

Okay—she was, officially, the most stubborn woman he'd ever met. 'We are *not* arguing about this, Remy. We can do it the easy way or the hard way—your choice.'

'You are insufferably bossy,' Remy told him, dashing her hands across her wet cheeks before taking his hand to help her stand.

He yanked the jeans up and over her butt and gestured to the zip. 'Can you manage to do that?'

'I'm not *completely* useless,' Remy muttered, zipping up and doing up the button.

The jeans hung on her hips, he realised. She'd lost weight—weight she couldn't afford to lose. Yeah, there was no doubt that she needed medical attention. And he'd make sure she got it—immediately.

'Let's go. Can you walk? Or do you need me to carry you?'

Remy started to argue, but then she must have seen something on his face because she nodded.

She walked over to the bed and shoved her feet into a pair of trainers. She groaned as she bent over to tie her laces and wobbled again. Bo cursed again, and put one arm around her back and the other under her knees. He ignored her protestations and concentrated on manoeuvring his way around the bed. Stopping by the table near the door, he nodded to his car keys and cell phone and asked her to grab them.

'Only if you put me down,' Remy said, with a stubborn lift of her chin.

Bo closed his eyes, seeking patience. 'Remy, trust me—you don't want to test me right now. Now, pick up the keys.'

He'd lost her attention on 'trust me'. He could feel her muscles tense against him and felt her heave. He dropped her to her feet and looked down to see her face drain of the last two specks of colour it possessed.

Then she bolted to the bathroom and slammed the door behind her.

Bo grimaced. Nothing about this entire situation was normal, he thought as he waited for her to emerge. Nothing, he suspected, ever would be.

In the ER, a doctor who barely seemed old enough to shave, much less earn a medical degree, prodded and poked her, stuck a needle in her hand and hooked her up to a drip. Then he patted her on the shoulder and told her to wait while the nurses made arrangements to have her transferred to a room on another floor. Then, with an exhausted sigh, he rushed off to deal with the consequences of a multi-vehicle pile-up.

At the end of her bed Bo paced and spent his time speaking on his cell phone. Remy tuned him out and turned her focus inwards. For the first time she concentrated on the burgeoning life that she felt was fading away. She wasn't bleeding—not yet—but she knew that she was in serious trouble. Cradling her stomach with both hands, she started an internal conversation with her unborn child.

After having been so ambivalent before, now she begged her child to start fighting. Despite her unplanned pregnancy, she wasn't a total idiot. She knew that she'd lost a lot of fluid, that she might be dehydrated, and that it might have consequences for the baby. She was run-down and unhealthy, but she hoped—she so *desperately* hoped—that the little soul hadn't given up and decided already that she was a useless mother and was intending on bailing.

Don't let me start bleeding, she prayed.

After shaking her head at the slew of nurses wanting to flirt with Bo, and a trip to Radiology for a sonar scan, she dozed off—only to wake up feeling disorientated. *Aargh!* She was still in a hospital bed, but in a private room, still in her T-shirt, but minus her jeans. She probably looked like a train wreck. So, the past few hours *hadn't* been a horrible dream…

Forcing her tears down, she swallowed as a hawk-nosed man in his late fifties blew into the room, sat on the bed beside her and took her hand. A stern nurse of indeterminate age stood at his shoulder and Bo hovered in the background, his fists stuck in the pockets of his suit pants.

Remy frowned and yanked her hand from the man's. 'Who are *you*?'

'Henry Graham. I'm an obstetrician.'

The nurse leaned forward and Remy noticed the humorous glint in her eyes. 'Also known as God on this maternity ward.'

Dr Graham laughed. 'By everyone except *you*, Sister.'

Remy took a deep breath and forced her panic down. While Dr Graham perused her file and the nurse took her blood pressure and temperature she glared at Bo—because she needed to glare at something and he was there.

Dr Graham raised bushy eyebrows at Remy. 'You're a very lucky young woman, Ms Draycott.'

Bo stepped closer to the bed and Remy bit the corner of her lip. 'The baby…?' she asked, scared to hear his answer.

'Fine. You are severely and chronically dehydrated but the foetus is still there, heart beating strongly.' He grinned. 'Oh, sorry—that's *hearts* beating strongly.'

Remy stared at the Napa Valley's high priest of pregnancy. 'What?'

'Twins. Definitely.'

Remy shook her head, thinking that this had to be one of those jokes the medical profession played on newly pregnant women. 'I'm not having twins.'

Dr Graham tapped his folder. 'According to the sonar scan they did earlier you are.'

Remy shook her head in a series of jerky movements. 'Nuh-uh—this pregnancy is a mistake and there *cannot* be two of them.'

'Our science is pretty good these days. I promise you, it's twins.'

'I *can't* have twins! I don't know what to do with one baby—how will I manage two?' Remy wailed.

Bo took a step towards her and laid a hand on her shoulder. He looked shell-shocked and confused, but his eyes were steady. 'With my help.'

As tempted as she was, she couldn't rely on his help—couldn't rely on him for anything. She'd come here just to tell him that he was to be a father, not for anything more.

He didn't owe her—them—anything! They'd be fine... They had to be fine!

Besides, like her mother, he had a take-charge personality that instinctively raised her hackles. Yes, he looked like a male fitness model and had excellent mattress skills, but that wasn't enough to make up for his caveman personality.

She didn't need him hovering, making decisions for her, for her baby...*babies*. *She* made the decisions now—she'd never allow anyone that amount of power again.

But, a little voice deep inside her whispered, *it's kinda nice and kinda hot that he's stepping up to the plate, taking responsibility. So many men would've run at the first chance. I've given Bo a lot of chances and he's still sticking.*

Oh, shut up, voice!

Because she felt discombobulated by those unwelcome thoughts, Remy tossed her hair over her shoulder and snorted her disbelief. 'Yeah, I can just see you—changing diapers and cleaning up baby drool, doing the early-morning feed.'

Bo held her eye. 'I will if I have to.'

A part of her—the weaker side of her—wanted to believe him, wanted to curl up in his arms and rest awhile. But she'd learnt her lesson: give a strong person a little control and they'd take everything—usually because they thought they knew what was best for her. She didn't need to be looked after and propped up. She could *do* this.

Bo, and his bossy attitude could take a hike. Because the truth was that he was just the man who'd impregnated her during an admittedly fabulous one-night stand. She had to think of him that way...

'This is *my* baby,' Remy said, forcing the words out.

'Babies,' Bo enunciated, loudly and clearly, bending to speak directly in her ear. 'Double. Two. Twice. Dual. Twins.'

She *wasn't* going to lose control and slap him, Remy told herself, though her hand was itching to do so. *No hitting, Draycott, even if he deserves it!*

She sucked back her temper and tried again. 'The point is that they are *mine*—'

'Then you shouldn't have told me that I'm the father. I don't walk away from my responsibilities.' He pointed at her stomach. '*They* are my responsibility—and so are you!'

'Like hell I am!' Remy shouted.

'You became my responsibility when you fainted at my feet because you're pregnant! With *my* children!' Bo roared back.

His chest was heaving and his cheeks were stained red with temper. His eyes—his beautiful eyes—looked wild. God, he was hot, she thought. Freakin' sexy. If she wasn't attached to a drip, and if Dr Graham and the nurse weren't watching, she'd be all over him right now. Remy touched her tongue to her top lip and watched, fascinated, as the colour in his cheeks died and his eyes filled with lust.

She knew what he was thinking now because she was thinking it too. *Hot kisses, hard hands...*

Oh, dear God, the attraction between them was still as strong as it had been before. This wasn't good, Remy thought. Not good at all!

Dr Graham cleared his throat and tapped his folder against the bed. When she finally managed to drag her eyes from Bo's sexy face to his, she saw that his eyes were dark and very serious.

'You two done?' he asked.

Remy didn't bother looking at Bo. She lifted one shoulder in a tired shrug. 'For now.'

'You are very run-down, Ms Draycott. Your iron levels are ridiculously low, you're dangerously dehydrated, exhausted, and I'm assuming that you are under some stress. You need to stay on that drip for twenty-four hours and then you need to go home and rest. And you need to stop worrying.'

'You've just told me that I'm having twins,' Remy said, trying to keep her voice from wobbling. 'I think I'm entitled to worry.'

'We'll work it out,' Bo told her, his voice low.

Seeing Bo's obstinate expression, Remy decided not to protest any further. In the first place, she was exhausted, and, secondly, she suspected that he could out-stubborn her.

When she was stronger, feeling more like herself, when she could summon all her fake confidence to wage another battle, she'd explain that she didn't need his money, or his overbearing and arrogant attitude. That she didn't need him to take care of her.

She was perfectly capable of taking care of herself…

It was imperative that she kept her distance from him—emotionally and physically. She reluctantly admitted that she was as attracted to him now as she had been before, and she knew that he just needed to kiss her once, to brush that incredible mouth against hers, and she'd be in his arms and his bed again. She was that easy when it came to him, and she had to resist being swamped by lust and attraction. She wasn't going to fall into a physical relationship with the father of her babies.

Creating life together had forged a bond—she had to remain clear-thinking about this. The only reason they had reconnected was because she was carrying his children. He knew less than nothing about her. He knew her body, but nothing of her mind… And she was only useful to him because he seemed to want the children they'd made together.

She was his means to an end—yet another example of being kept around for what she did and not who she was.

She had to be careful of him. He would want to make

all the decisions and she would lose herself, go back to being who she'd been when she'd allowed her mother and her aspirations for her to dictate the course of her life.

No one would ever do that to her again. This wasn't a made-for-TV drama, it was real life—*her* real life. Bo wasn't a hero, and this story wasn't going to have a Hollywood movie ending.

There was nothing between them except some residual sexual attraction and the lives inside her. *They* had to be their focus and nothing else.

Remy shoved her hair away from her forehead and bit the inside of her lip, determined to get back to the matter in hand.

She turned back to Dr Graham and pulled up a tired smile. 'Anything else I need to know?'

'Folic acid, vitamins, lots of iron-rich food. And rest. Wait—let me repeat that: *rest*. I don't want you doing anything strenuous for a week or two. The next few weeks are pretty crucial. If you can get through the first trimester without any more problems, then I think you have a good chance of delivering two healthy babies.'

Dr Graham leaned over and picked up an injection from the tray next to her bed. She whimpered in anticipated pain. But instead of jabbing it into her flesh, as she'd expected, he placed the needle into the valve on her drip.

He tipped his head at Bo. 'No exertion, healthy food, no stress.'

Bo gave him a brief nod. 'I'll make sure that happens.'

'She'll sleep now,' Dr Graham said, nodding to the drip.

Remy wanted to protest at his talking to Bo, to remind them that she was still present…except that her tongue felt thick and her eyelids heavy.

Oh, hello, sleep...missed you so...

CHAPTER FIVE

HE NEEDED A drink, Bo decided, dropping his keys into the bowl on the hall table and his briefcase to the floor. Yanking his tie down, he flipped open the collar on his shirt and quickly rolled his sleeves up to his elbows as he walked into his kitchen and straight to the fridge.

After he'd had a glass of liquid courage he'd take a walk down the passage, knock on the door to his spare room and see if the mother of his—he swallowed his panic in two big gulps—his *children* was awake. Bo rested his unopened beer bottle against his forehead and closed his eyes. He was going to be the father of not one child but two…

Freakin' hell.

Ginny and Eli were going to roll on the floor and laugh their asses off at this latest development. He could almost hear their comments. *When you do something you go overboard!* And, *You take overachieving to a whole new level of ridiculousness.*

After spending most of the night in an uncomfortable chair next to Remy's hospital bed, he'd brought her back to his home early this morning and deposited her, still half-asleep, in the bed in his guest bedroom. Thinking that she'd be fine if he left her to rest, he'd finally made it to his office by the middle of the morning, where he'd struggled to concentrate on the work he needed to plough his way through. He'd never had a problem with focusing before, but at the most inopportune moments Remy's pale face and scared eyes had flashed onto the big screen of his mind and he'd had to resist the urge to hightail it back to his house to check on her.

He'd programmed his number into her mobile and left a sticky note attached to the phone telling her to call him if she needed anything or ran into a problem. He'd also—because he still didn't trust her not to bolt—taken the tote bag containing her car keys and purse with him to work.

He'd probably catch hell for that, but he didn't give a damn… He was *not* going to chase the mother of his twins across the country. She was going to stay put. Even if he had to tie her to the damn bed.

A knock on his kitchen counter had him jumping a foot in the air, and he whirled around to see Ginny standing on the other side of the granite worktop, looking concerned.

'God—give me a heart attack, why don't you?' he growled as his stomach fell back down his throat.

'Sorry…' Ginny slid onto a bar stool and placed her elbows on the counter, holding her face in her hands. 'Bit jumpy, aren't you?'

'No sleep,' Bo replied tersely, lifting his beer bottle in her direction. 'Want one?'

Ginny nodded. 'Listen, before I interrogate you about how you feel about becoming a daddy, I want to tell you something in case I forget…'

Bo pulled another beer out of his fridge and cracked the top on Ginny's, handing it over before opening his own. 'What's up?'

'I went for a bike ride this morning and I cycled over to Bella's Folly, thinking that I'd just check up on the house.' She shrugged and took a sip from her bottle. 'I went in via the path that comes out at the orchard at Bella's Folly and when I hit the orchard I heard voices I stopped behind the hedge and saw a couple of men standing by the back door, peering into the windows of the house.'

Bo narrowed his eyes. Okay, where was she going with this?

'Craig Cowen was there—and Glen Jance.'

'The real estate agent and the property developer…' Bo ran his hand through his hair. 'Dammit, what do *they* want with the property?'

'To bulldoze the house and put up a gated community or a mini-mall?' Ginny shuddered.

He echoed her horror but, as much as he wanted to give this news the attention it deserved, his mind was too full of Remy. She was in his house and the baby that they'd still been wrapping their heads around was now a two-instead-of-one deal.

He forced himself to concentrate. 'We need to discover what their plans might be—try to find out whether they know more about possible heirs to the estate than we do.'

'Basically, it's a race as to who gets to the heir first with a purchase offer,' Ginny mused. 'What happens if we find the heir and he refuses to sell?'

Bo shrugged. 'Let's cross that bridge when we get to it,' he suggested, glancing out through the window to see Eli striding up to the back door, looking hot and sweaty and desperately in need of a beer.

As he stepped into the kitchen Bo tossed him a beer bottle and sent an uneasy look down the passage. Shouldn't Remy be up and awake by now? How long did pregnant woman actually sleep? What if she had started to miscarry since he'd left her earlier that day? What if she'd *died*?

Can you be any more melodramatic, moron?

She was fine. The doctor had said she just needed to rest and take it easy—that she'd sleep a lot for the next couple of weeks while her body adjusted to being pregnant. But what if something had gone badly wrong in the hours since he'd last seen her?

For crying out loud in a freakin' bucket—just go and check already!

Bo slammed his beer bottle on the counter and looked at Ginny and then at Eli. 'I just need to do something and then we'll talk.'

'Well, hello to you too…' Eli said dryly to his departing back.

Remy rolled over and slowly opened her eyes, blinking at her unfamiliar surroundings. The walls to the spacious bedroom were painted in a soft green, the linen was white and luxurious, and the curtains were a deep green.

Expensive, but tasteful, Remy thought on a yawn, and not her hotel room. Knowing that she needed a minute to get all her brain cells firing at once, she sat up on her elbows and yawned again as she mentally rewound. She'd been vomiting… Bo had taken her to the hospital…twins.

Her eyes shot open. Dear Lord, she was having *twins*. Dual…duplicate…two. *Twins*. Holy hell. She was a single mother, expecting twins. *Get used to it,* she ordered herself, and shuddered in good old-fashioned panic. Sucking in air, she forced down the terror and focused on carrying *one* child. One child she could deal with, could plan for. Maybe in a week or two, when she was used to the idea of being a mommy, she could think about how she was going to be the mommy of twins.

The little she'd seen of motherhood didn't inspire her. While travelling she'd spent a *lot* of time watching people, and she'd seen frazzled mothers, tired mothers, teary mothers, irritated mothers—many with husbands and partners trying to help.

Remy swallowed. She would be alone…doing it alone. With twins. *God.* Okay, Bo had said that he'd be there, but the reality was that for the first couple of years, until they became proper little humans, able to walk and talk, the burden of their care would be on *her* shoulders.

Feeling her breath becoming rapidly more shallow, Remy decided to deal with that reality a little later and tried to make sense of the rest of the her life. She'd been dehydrated, placed on a drip for twenty-four hours, then she'd passed out. She had a vague memory of leaving the hospital, of Bo's strong arms lifting her into his low slung silver car.

And that was it… She remembered nothing more.

Remy narrowed her eyes as she sat up, feeling a lot better than she had for a week. Stronger, and more up for a fight—which was excellent news since Bo had essentially kidnapped her!

And, no, she *wasn't* being dramatic. He'd taken her from her hotel room, removed her from the hospital and brought her here—wherever *here* was!

At least he'd had the sense to kidnap her stuff as well, Remy thought as she swung her legs out of bed. Her suitcase stood in the corner and her laptop sat on the pretty desk by the window. No tote bag, though. Hmm, that was annoying. Mr Bossy had probably kept that with him to make sure she couldn't leave Bellevue.

She couldn't blame him… She might have done the same if she'd been in his position. He, like her, was obviously a strategic thinker who liked to scan the horizon for possible problems… That was something she'd have to remember when dealing with him.

Standing up, and happy to see that she'd stopped wobbling, Remy walked over to the window and pulled it open, gasping at the stunning view of vineyards and mountains in the distance.

She was at Belleaire and, if she wasn't mistaken, it was dusk. Her stomach growled and Remy looked down, surprised. How long had it been since she'd eaten? And why was she wearing a soft red T-shirt that hung off her shoulders midway to her thigh?

Remy put her hand under the shirt and touched her pantyless butt. She'd been dressed in jeans and a hoodie when she'd gone to the hospital, so who had undressed her and pulled this T-shirt over her naked body?

She prayed that it had been one of the nurses at the hospital or, at a push, Ginny. She'd just die if Bo had seen her passed out and naked. When had she last shaved her legs, under her arms? Leaning down, Remy ran a hand up her shin and let out a relieved sigh… Not too bad, she thought.

Remy lifted her hand to her hair. She could feel that it was filthy and snarled, and she knew that she needed a long, long shower.

Walking around the bed to the en-suite bathroom, she sighed in appreciation at the luxury within. The spacious room contained a spa bath, a power shower, dual basins, and a basket with a selection of soaps, shampoos, hair conditioners. Flipping on the taps to fill the bath, Remy lifted the various soaps to her nose and decided on the berry-scented range, placing everything she needed on the edge of the tub.

While she waited for the bath to fill she brushed and flossed her teeth and wondered how she was going to handle Mr Sexy-But-Bossy. Now that she'd had a decent night's sleep and was feeling remotely human she had some very hard thinking to do.

And she couldn't think of a better place to do it in that in a spa bath, up to her ears in bubbles.

Tossing in some bubble bath, Remy pulled off the T-shirt and slid into the hot water, pleasure popping along with the bubbles on her skin. An icy glass of Chardonnay would make this experience complete…

That wasn't going to happen for seven months or so—

how was she supposed to have these babies without the calming powers of the fermented grape?

Okay, thinking time. Let's deal with the twins issue...

'Are you okay?'

'Waaaaa-aaaaaaah!' Remy sat up fast and water and bubbles sloshed over the side of the tub. She gaped at Bo, who stood in the doorway to the bathroom, looking hot and tough and sexy and dishevelled. And, underneath all that, a little overwhelmed.

Remy tried to pull the remaining bubbles in the bath so that they covered her breasts—before she realised that she was stealing the cover for her groin area. Frustrated, she sank down lower into the tub and crossed her legs at the highest point they could be crossed, folding her arms over her nipples.

Bo, the jerk, just walked over to the tub and perched on the side.

'What are you *doing*?' she squawked. 'Get *out*!'

He raised an eyebrow and lifted his hands in a *what's the problem?* gesture. 'I've seen it all before.'

'That was *before*! It was different!' Remy sank so low into the bath that her chin skimmed the water. 'Go away!'

'Stop being ridiculous for a minute and talk to me,' Bo commanded in that voice that made her itch to slap him. 'How are you feeling?'

'Oooh, let's think about that. Embarrassed that I'm naked? Annoyed with you? Irritated that you have once more acted without my permission and brought me somewhere I don't want to be?'

'You're in my spare bedroom—not a cell in Alcatraz, woman,' Bo growled. 'Stop bitching at me for two seconds and tell me how you're feeling—physically.'

Remy looked into his eyes, dark and bleak, and saw that he was beyond tired. His eyes were shadowed in purple and his mouth was a thin line in his face. *She* might have had a really miserable time lately, but Bo hadn't been for a casual stroll in the park either.

'I'm feeling a lot better, thank you,' she admitted reluctantly. 'I'm a bit hungry, actually.'

Bo folded his arms across his chest and she had to give him credit for the fact that he kept his eyes firmly on her face. 'I'm not surprised, since you haven't eaten in, like, a *week*. Get out, get dressed, and I'll get some food into you.'

She opened her mouth to argue, to say that she could sort herself out, but stopped when she saw Bo cracking a huge yawn. He'd tensed in anticipation of her argument and lifted his shoulders to his ears. Exhausted and stressed and…*worried*, Remy realised. She could see it in his eyes, in the way that his hand fisted on his thigh.

'Okay, I'll get out and get dressed *and* allow you to feed me—on one condition,' Remy said, keeping her voice low.

Bo closed his eyes in dread. 'Oh, God—what *now*?'

'Can we just not argue? Just for one night can we try to be civil to each other? I don't want to fight…not tonight.'

He looked surprised at her response, and she saw the quick flash of relief on his face. *Good call, Draycott,* she applauded herself. She could argue, fight, defend her corner if she had to, but every warrior needed some downtime. Bo looked drained and exhausted and as if he just desperately needed a solid dose of 'normal'.

So did she.

Bo held her eyes. 'We wouldn't fight if you just did it *my* way.'

His words were inflammatory and she opened her mouth to take up her verbal sword. She was just about to let rip when she caught the teasing glint in his eye. He had the ability to keep his face utterly implacable, but his eyes reflected his soul. It was a good reminder to her to look before she reacted.

'Or if you saw things *my* way,' she countered gently.

Bo reached down and picked up a long strand of hair that had fallen onto her cheek. He pushed it away from her face. 'This would be a lot easier if one of us was the Chief and the other the Indian…me being the Chief, of course.'

Remy sighed as the tips of his fingers drifted across her cheek and flittered over her jawline. It was ridiculous that such a light touch could ignite a fire between her legs. She struggled to keep her brain from shutting down at the mere thought of having him touching her again, making love to her again.

'Honey,' she drawled, 'I'm pretty sure that if I was meant to be controlled I would come with a remote. Now, do me a huge favour—please?'

Bo grinned at her sass before yawning again. 'Mmm? What?'

'Get out so that *I* can get out?'

'But I've seen it—'

Remy splashed water up onto his shirt and smiled when some drops hit his face. Grandma Rosie's favourite saying popped into head and flew out of her mouth. 'Do *not* make me unleash the monkeys, Robert.'

Bo wiped his face with his hand and pulled his wet shirt away from his chest. 'So, are we calling a truce for tonight?'

'Yeah.' Remy flashed him a quick smile as he stood up. 'And as a bonus I'll try not to faint or puke on you.'

'That would be a nice change.'

While they waited for Remy to join them, Ginny told Eli what she'd seen at Bella's Folly and Bo waited for his cousin's reaction.

Shrugging his broad shoulders, Eli took a swig from his bottle of beer and put his sock-covered feet up on Bo's coffee table. 'We need to find that heir—or else we're going to end up with a shopping mall on our doorstep.'

His thoughts exactly. 'I managed to touch base with the PI I hired, but he's hitting dead ends.' Bo rubbed the back of his neck in frustration. 'The only consolation is that if *we're* having difficulties chasing down the heir, then so will anyone else.'

'And we still don't know whether anyone was actually stipulated in a will?' Eli asked.

'Nada.'

Bo caught movement out of the corner of his eye and stood up as Remy, dressed in worn jeans and a simple white T-shirt, stepped into the room. Eli lumbered his way to his feet and Remy's gaze flicked from his face to Bo's and then to Ginny's. Her expression was pleasant, but the hands rubbing her thighs told him that she was feeling a great deal more nervous than she looked.

'Hi…' she murmured.

Eli lifted his eyebrows and Ginny, as loving as always, walked across the room to pull Remy into a quick hug. 'How are you? And how's my nephew or niece? What do you think it is?'

Remy pushed her damp hair back from her face and tossed him a quick look. He read the message in her eyes. *This is your family. You get to tell them.*

He knew that Eli and Ginny were curious as to why Remy was in his house and not in the hotel in town. If he didn't explain tonight, then they would both call him later… He might as well kill two birds with one stone.

But first things first.

'Take a seat, Remy. Can I get you something to drink?'

Ginny opened her mouth, obviously to hurl a question at his head, but he quickly spoke over her.

'Remy? Wine? Beer? Something stronger?'

Remy tapped her tummy. 'Sadly, no alcohol allowed—remember? Something soft.'

So *that* was a stupid question, Bo thought as he walked to the kitchen. And stupid was how he would continue to sound if he didn't learn more than he currently knew about being pregnant, which was how to avoid making babies.

The irony of that thought was not lost on him.

If he was going to spend a lot of time with Remy—and he planned to—he was going to have to learn about pregnancy and babies and birth. He'd never had a problem with learning something new, but he'd always figured that he'd missed his chance to experience all this when Ana had died. On his way to the kitchen Bo pulled out his smart phone and tapped out a memo to remind himself to find a couple of books on gestation.

Bo grabbed a carton of juice from the fridge, poured Remy a glass and walked back into the lounge—where his three guests sat in uncomfortable silence.

Bo handed Remy her glass and shook his head. 'She's pregnant—not mute,' he muttered, taking a seat next to Remy on the couch.

'How did you fall pregnant?' Eli demanded. When he heard his own words, quickly followed by derisive looks, he rolled his eyes. 'I mean, I know *how*… What I meant to ask was how did you meet?'

Remy rested her glass on her knee. 'It was supposed to be a one-time thing. I was passing through Bellevue, we met in a bar, did the…the obvious, and that was supposed to be it.' Remy bit her lip. 'I know you guys are surprised that I'm here, in Bo's house, and to be honest so am I.'

Eli and Ginny exchanged a look and Bo thought that it was time he jumped in.

'Remy's been pretty sick. Yesterday morning I went to see her at the hotel and she was very ill. I took her to the hospital and she was severely dehydrated and anaemic. After they discharged her I brought her here…' He saw

Eli's amused expression and frowned. 'I needed to be able to check on her.'

Eli lifted up his hands. 'I didn't say anything.'

Bo scowled at him again. 'Remy needs to take it easy for a while or she runs the risk of miscarrying.'

Ginny looked worried. 'Oh, Remy, that's horrible. Of course you must take it easy, be quiet. The baby's health comes first.'

'Babies,' Bo muttered, exhausted.

'Twins,' Remy added.

There was long silence before Eli's booming laughter filled the room. Bo watched, resigned, as Eli doubled over, tears running down his face.

Remy leaned into his shoulder. 'Why is he laughing?' she asked, perplexed. 'It's really not that funny. Terrifying, yes—funny, no.'

'He's laughing at me,' Bo explained, weary. *Here they come,* he thought as Eli wiped his eyes. *The smart-ass comments. Three, two, one...*

'Overachieving again, dude?' Eli asked. 'Seriously, you don't *always* have to go the extra mile.'

'Shut up, E,' Ginny snapped, her eyes on Remy. 'Twins? Seriously? When are you due?'

Bo rolled his head against the back of the couch, realising that he was as interested in her answer as Ginny. He should *know* the date that his world would be flipped upside down.

'End of March next year. But they say that twins normally come earlier—especially on the first pregnancy.' Remy tapped her finger against her glass before pulling in a big breath.

'Well, that gives you some time to sort things out,' Ginny said prosaically. 'Are you guys getting married?'

Bo was too tired to react to the question but Remy's spine stiffened in… What? Horror? Annoyance? Panic?

She shook her head and looked at him, aghast. ‘What *is* it with you lot and the need to get married?’

Bo dredged up a smile and patted her back.

A small frown creased Ginny’s forehead. ‘So you don’t want to get married?’

Remy shuddered. ‘Hell, no!’

‘Ever? Or not just because you’re pregnant?’ Eli asked, resting his beer bottle on the arm of his chair.

‘I’m not…the type.’ She dismissed the subject with a wave of her hand. ‘Anyway, to get back to the subject, I just came to Bellevue to tell Bo that I’m pregnant and my life sort of ran away from me.’

‘Big-time,’ Ginny agreed. ‘How long are you going to be in town for now?’

Remy turned her head and her pale eyes met Bo’s. He was as interested as his sister was, so he just lifted his eyebrows and waited for her answer.

‘A couple of days. Bo and I need to talk through a couple of things and then I’ll leave.’

‘Not gonna happen,’ Bo stated, not willing to let that comment go. She didn’t know it yet, but she was staying right where she was—probably for the next eighteen years at least.

Remy turned in her seat and scowled at him. ‘What? Are you going to kidnap me again?’

‘If I have to.’ Bo shoved his hand into his hair and sighed. ‘We’re arguing—we said we weren’t going to do that tonight.’

Bo thought he heard a soft curse word before she pursed her lips. He knew that she was considering whether to carry on arguing or to let him have the last word.

She opened her mouth, closed it again, and then pouted. ‘Dammit. We *did* agree to that.’

Bo thought he’d push his luck. ‘We also agreed that I was the Chief and you were the Indian.’

Remy patted his knee, the action condescending. 'You're having delusions again…maybe they should up your medication?'

Remy curled herself into the corner of Bo's comfortable couch, feeling sleepy and full after an excellent meal delivered from the renowned restaurant on the estate. It had been a simple steak, potatoes *au gratin* and fresh garden vegetables, but beautifully cooked and presented. It had been exactly what she'd needed and wanted to eat, and for the first time in days she felt vaguely normal. Well, as normal as a highly educated, homeless pregnant vagrant could feel.

She needed a day or two of rest, good meals, some light exercise and then she felt that she'd be able to face her future and make some decisions. She'd reluctantly spend another night in Bo's spare bedroom, but then she'd move back to the hotel or into cheaper accommodation in town. She couldn't stay here…with him…

Remy looked at Bo, who was sitting at the opposite end of the couch she was on, deep in conversation with Eli. Although he still looked played out, she noticed that those broad shoulders had dropped, that his normally hard jaw had relaxed and that his eyes weren't so wary and distant.

These were his people—his rock, his north star. Over dinner she'd listened to them talk and she knew that the three shared an unbreakable bond. The Three Musketeers' motto of 'All for one, one for all' could be their rally cry.

If they had to play the characters in a movie then Bo would be the distinguished Athos—intelligent, handsome, brave but emotionally tortured. Enjoying her game, Remy looked at Eli, so blond and movie-star good-looking. He would have to be d'Artagnan—intelligent as well, but ambitious and crafty and a little…or a lot…naughty. Ginny would be the female version of Aramis, supposedly under their protection—which was an illusion she allowed her cousin and brother to have.

Ginny might be the size of a pixie, but her eyes radiated determination and a warrior spirit and she saw herself as the protector of her family. Because she was carrying Bo's babies Remy had been pulled under her mother-hen wing, and Ginny had given her the third degree about the state of her health, the babies' development, whether she was taking the vitamins and supplements she should be taking.

Bo was hard enough to deal with, but she suspected that he was an amateur compared to Ginny. Remy was surprised that she didn't feel more irritated or scratchy at Ginny's interrogation. Her mother and grandmother—independent, self-contained feminists—had been her sole female relationships in life, and it was disconcerting to realise that maybe she had missed out on something special by keeping herself to herself.

It was nice that her babies would have an aunt who was already halfway in love with them and an adult cousin in Eli who would, she presumed, like them too. If anything happened to her—God forbid—they would have a solid support base.

Did Bo realise how lucky he was to have the complete and utter support of his family? They were going to stand by him come hell, high water and twins—and had no intention of being relegated to the sidelines. The Tessiers stood together. Eli and Ginny liked her, but if she messed with Bo the gloves would come off.

The father of her babies might be a hard-ass—a hard-bodied and hard-eyed man who ran a successful enterprise—but these two people were solidly in his corner, willing to take on the world for him.

Remy shivered as a ghost walked over her grave. Nothing was going to happen to her… Women all over the world delivered healthy twins with no problems at all. Nothing would go wrong. She was just being fanciful and imaginative. But she couldn't help wrapping her arms around herself to counter the sudden drop in temperature.

Bo stopped halfway through his sentence and frowned at her. 'Are you okay?'

Remy nodded and held out her arm, showing him that her skin was covered in goosebumps. 'Just suddenly freezing cold.'

Bo immediately reached for the chenille throw behind his back. He stood up, shook it out and draped it around Remy's shoulders. Remy thanked him, and didn't miss the long, intense look Eli and Ginny shared.

Bo immediately leaned away from her. 'We need to talk about Bella's Folly.'

Ginny must have seen the confusion on Remy's face because she held up a hand to halt their conversation and fill her in. Happy to think of anything else but the rabbit hole she'd fallen into, Remy listened intently.

A strategically positioned house and land, no heir, sharks circling… Her analytical brain kicked in and she leaned forward, intrigued.

'Did she die intestate?' she asked.

Bo lifted a shoulder. 'We think so. Maybe…'

Remy sucked in her bottom lip. 'So the nearest relative inherits…?

'Except that it seems she didn't *have* any relatives. If that is proved to be true, then the state inherits, and dealing with the state is a headache of magnificent proportions,' Remy mused. 'So it would be in your best interests to find someone related to her?'

'Essentially,' Bo agreed.

Remy ran through the possibilities in her head. 'You could hire a private detective.'

'Done that, and they didn't find anyone.'

Okay, Remy thought, that was Plan A. The alphabet

still had another twenty-five letters to attach to a plan. It wasn't the end of the road.

'What about a genealogist?'

Bo and Ginny and Eli were silent for a minute before Bo spoke again. 'I didn't think of that.'

Ginny wrinkled her nose. 'What exactly do they do?'

Remy linked her hands around her bent knee. 'Essentially they trace family trees. If they have a social security number they can trace anyone. They look at birth certificates and death certificates, church records, state records, and piece together who she was, who her relatives were.' Remy looked from one interested face to another. 'I dabbled with it in college. It's mostly computer-based work.'

Of course with *her* computer skills, she could have the information for them in a day…two at the most.

Eli placed his foot on his opposite knee. 'Where would we find a genealogist?'

Should she offer her services? Should she reveal that much about herself? It would mean exposing herself and what she did—had done—and she wasn't ready to do that. Not just yet. Let *them* try the genealogist route, and if it didn't pan out then she might suggest that she have a go. Maybe…

'I know someone in Portland. He's a friend of the family and does this as hobby. Or you could find a firm that does it as a business, but they charge enormous fees if they do it for an outside party. When they look for an heir *they* usually approach the heir, and before they tell him or her what they might inherit they negotiate a percentage of the estate as their fee before they divulge any information. Either way, they take their pound of flesh.'

Bo looked at her as if she'd turned into a arachnid wearing ballet shoes. 'How do you know all this?'

The man obviously thought that because she was a traveller she didn't have a brain in her head. She tossed her head and sent him a chilly smile. 'I have a mind for trivia.'

She did. She also had a mind for maths and statistics and computers and code and science and art and cooking and literature… Being put in a box raised every hackle she had. And she was certain Robert Tessier liked his boxes; they kept his world orderly and in control.

'So you're not just a pretty face?' Bo murmured softly.

You have no idea, Remy thought, not bothering to respond to his dry comment. Bo was very used to being the smartest person in the room, she realised, but he was in for a wake-up call—because she was, without blowing her own trumpet, easily his equal.

As Ginny, Bo and Eli continued with their discussion about finding a genealogist Remy pulled back from the conversation and thought that dealing with Bo was going to be interesting. One of these days they would go head-to-head, and it would be interesting to see who would be the victor—or, if there wasn't an outright victor, who walked away with the least scars.

She could tangle with Bo on a mental level, in fact she'd relish the opportunity to do so. But if they got physical—if he touched her—she knew that she would lose any battle that took place between the sheets. He demanded control there, and she was happy to hand it over to him, knowing that he would reward her with indescribable pleasure.

She couldn't allow him that much control over her—couldn't allow him to see the chink in her armour. It would be risking too much for her to give him that much power over her, and she suspected it was a slippery slope downhill from there. If she gave the man an inch he'd end up taking everything—and there was no way she'd ever allow that to happen.

Remy rested her head against the couch and allowed the conversation to drift over her, feeling bone-deep tired again. And everyone said that pregnancy was supposed to be the *easy* part of motherhood…

She'd had the whole thing planned, Remy thought, picking at a thread on the seam of her jeans. She had genuinely believed that after she'd come back to Bellevue and told Bo she was pregnant she would be able to resume her travelling—at least for a few more months. In that time she'd find a town to settle down in, and while she grew bigger and adjusted to life in a new town she'd start making plans for a business she could start. When she'd given birth she'd have let Bo know and maybe, if he wanted, sent him a picture or two.

Instead she'd found that the father of her babies had an overdeveloped sense of responsibility and wanted to be a part of his children's lives! She had been going to raise this child—children…*eep!*—alone, and now she had to think about how she was going to accommodate Bo into that plan. She wished she could dismiss him from her life and do her own thing but she couldn't—that wouldn't be fair. He had a right to know his children and his children had a right to know him.

And even though leaving Bellevue was still part of her plan she knew that it wasn't sensible, given her health and the fact that she was experiencing a high-risk pregnancy, to leave just yet. While she felt better, she still didn't feel a hundred per cent, and her babies were at risk for the next couple of months. She had to stay put—close to medical care. It would be foolish and stupid to keep travelling; what if she threatened to miscarry and she was in a small town with inadequate medical facilities? She was a free spirit— she wasn't an idiot.

But at the very least she needed to leave his house and move back to town. Because she didn't completely trust herself not to throw herself at him and ask him for a repeat experience of that magical night six…nearly seven weeks ago. He'd kissed like a dream, Remy remembered on a huge yawn, and his big hands had been gentle but demanding. His voice, always deep, had rumbled over her skin, and in itself had been able to stoke her passion. He'd had more than a few tricks up his sleeve and she'd love to know if he had any more…

Remy felt herself sliding into sleep, and was jerked back when big hands and strong arms scooped her up and held her against a hot, broad chest. Sighing, she instinctively looped her arms around his neck and nuzzled her face into his neck, breathing in the faint notes of his aftershave. He was so big and stable and…*solid*, she thought.

'C'mon, Pocahontas, let's get you to bed.'

CHAPTER SIX

REMY WAS SITTING at the kitchen table the next morning, her tablet next to her plate. It tugged at his heart to find her hunched over a piece of dry toast, a cup of herbal tea at her elbow, looking slightly green.

Wanting a minute to catch his breath, Bo hovered outside the kitchen door, his chest heaving after his habitual early-morning run. Bellevue was looking at its best, with the oak trees that lined the long driveway turning green to gold, gold to scarlet. The grass in the fields was still green, the white pole fences had been freshly painted by Ginny's staff, and the air was crisp and clear and that particular blue that was so intense he wanted to shove his fist through it.

Remy had shoved her fist into her sternum and was taking deep breaths when Bo stepped into the room. 'Morning sickness again?'

Remy snapped her head up and managed a wan smile. 'Yeah. Not so bad as before, but still there.' She tapped the tower of three books on the table and sighed. 'These all say it should stop at three months, but—' She shrugged.

Bo resisted the urge to run his hand over her tangled curls and headed for the coffee pot instead, glancing at the books in a pile. 'They're all the same book.' He frowned. 'Why do you have three copies of the same book?'

Remy's grin hit her eyes. 'Your sister. One for you,

one for me, one for her and one for Eli. She ordered them shortly after I fainted in the bistro.'

Bo closed his eyes. 'Typical Ginny. She might give us all a quiz occasionally. Although you'd have to put a gun to Eli's had to get *him* to read it.'

'I realised that.' Remy leaned back in her chair. 'I like Ginny. She has a good...heart.'

'She really does,' Bo agreed. 'She's the best of us.' Bo gestured to the coffee machine. 'Do you want coffee?' Judging by her instinctive grimace he figured that was a no.

'Sorry. It's the smell: coffee, meat frying, onions... But don't let me stop you.'

And have her hurling all over his kitchen floor? Nah, he wouldn't take the chance. So he headed to the fridge and grabbed orange juice instead.

'It's not a problem. I probably drink too much coffee anyway. Try and eat your toast—you need something in your stomach.'

Bo reached for a glass and, dumping it on the table, poured the juice and snagged a bunch of grapes from the colourful bowl of fruit in the centre of the table.

Remy lifted her foot up onto the seat of the chair and rested her forearm on her knee.

Bo pulled out a chair, flipped it back to front and rested his arms on the top strut. 'So, do you want to chat?'

Remy looked at the huge clock on the wall. 'Aren't you in a hurry to get to work?'

He looked at the huge simple clock. Seven-forty. 'I can be late. It's one of the perks of being the boss.'

'Okay...shall I start?'

Bo nodded, and watched as Remy stared down at the table, obviously gathering her thoughts. Eventually she lifted her face up to look at him. Her amazing eyes looked troubled and a little scared.

'I'm still taking all this in, Bo. I thought I would come here, tell you that I was pregnant and then keep travelling.'

'That's not going to happen,' Bo growled, and then he lifted his hand. 'Sorry…sorry. Carry on.'

Remy pursed her sexy mouth and his pants suddenly got tighter. Inexplicably, his excitement just increased when she flashed him the evil eye. But instead of escalating the fight she just sighed and carried on speaking in a normal voice.

'I didn't expect to get so sick, or for you to be so interested in being part of the babies' lives. So I'm really struggling to figure out what to do.'

'Stay here.'

'You make it sound so easy.'

'It is.' Bo popped a grape into his mouth.

'Define "here". Here, as in at your house—or here as in Bellevue?'

'Either. Both.' Bo ran a frustrated hand through his hair.

'For the pregnancy or for the rest of my life?'

Bo knew that if he told her she wouldn't be going anywhere soon he'd lose her, and that they'd end up having a huge shouting match that would solve nothing. No…as much as he wanted to be a control freak dictator, he knew that he'd be making this process so much harder than it needed to be. He had to be smart and strategize his way through this… Remy, unlike Ana, was a woman who made her own decisions.

And that wasn't meant in any way to malign either woman. They were just so damn *different*. Despite Ana's recklessness and always confident if slightly bohemian attitude, underneath she'd been so very insecure and had always looked to him for answers. Looking back, it had sometimes irritated the hell out of him. Sometimes, especially when he'd been stressed and busy, he'd wished that she'd just take the initiative and make the decision—

whether it was a weekend away or new curtains for their bedroom. But she'd always craved his approval and a part of him wondered if her antipathy towards children had been rooted in the fact that she hadn't wanted to share his attention with them. *Unfair, Tessier, cut it out.*

Remy, on the other hand, needed nobody's permission to do anything. She was strong and independent and a little wild… And he knew that her inability to consult would irritate him—*did* irritate him.

He just couldn't win.

But right now he had to win this battle—not the whole war.

Bo sipped his juice and kept his expression pleasant. 'Why don't we take it…? What's the word for parts of a pregnancy?' He looked at the pile of books and snapped his fingers. 'Terms…?'

'Trimesters?'

'That's it. Why don't we take it trimester by trimester?' Bo rested his chin on his fist. 'The doc said that this trimester is dangerous, that you should be careful. You're—what?—eight weeks now?'

'Seven and a bit,' Remy agreed.

'So, I *suggest*—' he emphasised the word 'suggest' '—that you stay with me, here, for the next four or five weeks, until the danger period passes. I can keep an eye on you and be around if you run into problems.'

Remy cocked her head, deep in thought. 'And after that?'

Bo shrugged. 'We have another conversation and see where we are.'

Remy tapped her finger against her cheek. 'What if I can't see myself staying here, Bo? What if this isn't my town? My spot? What then?'

He wanted to shout that it *was*—wanted to tell her that there was no way in hell he could comprehend any arrangement that wouldn't have him seeing her—correction—seeing *his children* every day of his life. But he held back, knowing that if he uttered any of the above he would lose all the ground he'd gained.

It took a massive amount of willpower for him to look casual, to put a reassuring look on his face. 'Trimester by trimester, Remy. We'll cross that bridge when we come to it.'

He'd blow the freaking bridge up if he had to. But she didn't need to know that.

'Concentrate on the next couple of weeks and then we'll chat again. What do you say?'

Remy looked out of the kitchen door and down the passage. 'I don't know if me living with you is a good idea. I think I should move back to town.'

'Why?'

A blush stained Remy's cheekbones. 'I don't want to… to inhibit your…um…social life.'

Social life? What was she going on about? He didn't *have* a social life—hadn't had a sex life since she'd whirled into and out of his life nearly two months ago… Oh, so *that* was what she was asking: whether he had someone who would be upset that she had moved in.

'I'm not seeing anyone, Remy. Haven't seen anyone since you.'

Was that pleasure and a feminine self-satisfaction he saw flashing in her eyes? Nah, it couldn't be. Being pregnant with twins and her resultant sickness had probably wiped the hectic sexual chemistry between them from her mind. Pity… Because, pregnant or not, she was still the only woman he could imagine in his bed.

And that would be the worst idea in the world…

He couldn't complicate this indescribably complicated situation any more by throwing sex into the mix. But he suspected that was a great deal more easily said than done, since she just had to breathe to start the celebration in his pants.

God, this was going to be torture…

Remy chewed her last piece of toast, swallowed, and picked up her tea cup. When she blew out a long breath he knew that he had her.

'Okay, we'll do it your way for the next few weeks and then we'll re-evaluate. But I have a couple of conditions….'

Of *course* she did. *What* a surprise. 'Uh-huh? And what would they be?'

'Have you hired someone for the bistro yet?'

Her left-field subject-change had him scrambling to catch up. He frowned. 'It's on my long list of things to do. Why are you asking?'

'I'll go mad with nothing to do for the next month or so, and I did tell Ginny and Eli that I would help you guys decide on a menu for the bistro.'

Okay, her words were in English but she wasn't making any sense. 'Whoa—back up…explain. You're a *chef*?'

Remy explained how she had met Eli and Ginny in the diner and their discussion about the type of food they wanted to serve. Bo recalled Ginny mentioning having met someone who would be perfect for the position but he'd never considered that it could be Remy. Why *would* he? It was just another reminder of how little he knew of the mother of his children.

He really needed to do an internet search on her, to find out as much as he could, because he knew that he didn't have the patience to wait for Remy to dole out bits of information.

'No, I just know a lot about food. I blog about it and I love to cook. I told them that I would cook some sample dishes, help you guys decide on a menu…maybe design some menus for you.'

Remy gnawed on her bottom lip and he wanted to soothe it with his tongue. *Concentrate, Tessier.*

'I don't expect an answer now—think about it. If you say no I'll find something else. If you don't want me involved with Belleaire business maybe I'll do some waitressing.'

'You told me that you are a shocking waitress.'

'I'm not that bad. I was flirting with you.'

Bo smiled at her, remembering the sassy girl in the bar who'd literally stolen his breath away. 'You did that really well.' He shook off the memories and mentally pulled back. 'I'm not crazy about you working—not after what Dr Graham had to say. Especially waitressing…being on your feet all day. You just need to rest—and that includes not worrying about money. If you give me your banking details I'll transfer some money into your account as soon as I get to work.'

Remy looked at him as if she'd just found out he had a penchant for wearing red lacy underwear. 'You're joking, right?'

Bo held her eye.

'I don't need money—I need to *do* something. If I stay here then I need to do something to repay you for my food and board. I'm not staying here for free.'

'You're having my children, getting ill for them, it's not a problem and it's the least I can do.'

Remy lifted that stubborn chin. 'It is a problem for me. I don't take charity.' She stood up and pushed her chair back. 'I think it's better that I just go back to town, find a place to rent.'

Bo sat up and looked at her straight back, saw the tension in her neck, in her shoulders. She didn't know how to fight, he thought on a moment of clarity. Her default course of action was to remove herself from the argument and go it alone, to do her own thing. Yeah, well, *that* had to change.

'Remy, we are going to have children together. We're going to have to start learning to deal with each other to work things out. We've got at least twenty years ahead of us doing that, and nothing will be accomplished if we walk away from a discussion when it gets tough.'

She'd kept her back to him, but he could tell by the tilt of her head that she was listening.

'Come back, sit down, and let's work this out.'

She kept on staring out of the window but after a long, long time turned around and folded her arms across her chest. 'You're the father of my children, Bo, but your responsibility doesn't extend to me. I will take care of myself in every way that counts. And there is no way in *hell* that I am going to live in your house, eat your food and use your utilities without paying for them or at the very least earning my way. I will *not* sacrifice my independence—financial, emotional and mental—for anybody or anything!'

Whoa! Okay, then, Bo thought, astounded by her vehemence. Someone had done a number on her head. 'It's just money, Remy. I'll make more tomorrow.'

'It's *your* money, Bo, and I won't take it. I wish you would realise—accept—that you are *not* responsible for me.'

He could be—would be happy to be, if she'd let him. He was thirty-five years old. Wasn't it time he started being responsible for someone? Why not Remy?

'But I *am* responsible for those lives you're carrying, and because of that I want to make your life as easy as possible. I have the money to do that, but you have more pride than Lucifer himself.'

Bo stood up, walked across the kitchen and threw the grape stalks into the bin. Money was a tool, he thought, frustrated. What was the point in having the stuff if he couldn't make life easier for those he cared about? He could spend it all, lose it all, and he'd shrug his shoulders, put his shoulder to the wheel and make some more. Being poor didn't scare him, and being rich didn't define him—so why wouldn't she let him use it to make a difference? She was carrying *his* family, which should count for something.

He turned to look at her and held her hot gaze. 'I intend to pay for everything you need.' He saw her face tighten and cursed his choice of words. 'I would *like to* pay for everything—' he amended '—for you and for the kids.'

Remy bit her bottom lip and shook her head. 'I can't let that happen.'

Yeah, *that* was a surprise. Bo threw up his hands. Why not? He had the space, the money, the ability to help her. Why was she being so stupidly proud? And why was he feeling so stupidly annoyed? Horny, frustrated, annoyed… and horny. *God.*

Remy looked at him, her pale eyes steadfast. 'Getting back to our original discussion: I need to do something apart from thinking of these babies. If I don't I'll go mad.'

When she looked at him like that, vulnerable and a little fragile, he'd give her the whole damn world if she asked for it. What the hell…? He needed someone at the bistro and she was here.

'Okay—sure. Do some sample menus for us. I'll pay you an hourly rate.'

'I'm staying here, and if you feed me I'll do it for free.'

Aaargh! Stubborn! He needed a shower. A cold, hard shower. And possibly also a frontal lobotomy to remove the indefinable, churning, volatile emotions he felt whenever he got within twenty metres of this ruddy woman.

Way past time to change the subject—especially since he wasn't winning the argument. He'd have to find another way around her pride.

'There was a message on my machine from the obstetrician's office: you have a follow-up appointment tomorrow at ten.'

Remy grimaced before nodding. 'Okay.'

'I'm coming with you. I want to look at my boys.'

She opened her mouth, no doubt to argue with him, but abruptly changed her mind. 'There might be a daughter in there somewhere,' Remy pointed out, her hand spread across her lower stomach in a protective gesture that rocked his stomach. Her eyes flashed with humour. 'There might be *two* girls in there.'

Good God, he didn't know if he could handle that. 'Girls are complicated…and emotional, irrational. Difficult. I need *boys*, Remy.'

Remy grinned. 'Pigtails, tears, hugs, make-up, PMS, boyfriends, weddings…'

Bo sighed and closed his eyes. Walking over to her, he bent his head to speak into her stomach. 'Take pity on me, guys. Your mother is enough of a handful all on her own.'

'Ha-ha—funny,' Remy said as he stood up.

Bo ran a finger down her cheek, resisting the urge to pull her into his arms, to push his chest into her soft breasts, to slide his thigh between her bare legs, to taste that amazing mouth again, to see her eyes fog over from the pleasure he could give her.

Complicated, he reminded himself.

'I thought so.' He couldn't resist drifting his thumb across her full bottom lip. 'If I tell you to get some more rest, will you argue with me?

'Not today—and not about that,' Remy murmured.

Miracles, Bo thought as he walked away, actually did happen.

Bo and Remy sat in front of Dr Graham's desk and sent nervous looks at the plastic model standing on the corner of his desk. Judging from the box leaning against the wall, Remy knew that it was a called a 4D Pregnancy Pelvis, complete with a baby nestled into the sawn-off uterus. It was fascinating…and slightly gross.

Bo leaned forward and tapped the plastic baby, which promptly rolled out and hit the desk with a loud thump.

Remy giggled. 'You just dropped it on its head.'

Bo picked up the plastic model, looked at it, and slotted the infant back into its cradle. 'It's a puzzle for doctors.' He cocked his head. 'It looks a bit crowded in there—where would the other one go?'

Remy looked down at her still flat stomach and back to the model. 'I don't have a clue.'

Bo leaned back in his chair and placed his ankle on his opposite knee. 'I don't have twins in my family. You?'

Remy thought for a minute. 'I think a great-aunt of mine had twins.'

Bo half smiled. 'So you falling pregnant with twins is *your* fault?'

Remy bumped her elbow into his side. 'I'll cop to the twins if you cop to the fact that you took your time putting on a condom!'

'I don't recall you stopping to remind me,' Bo shot back.

True… She'd been so utterly lost in what they were doing, lost in *him*, that she hadn't noticed. And he had been the thinking one—he'd been the one to remember to cover himself. If it had been up to her… Remy released a long, hot sigh. She would be pregnant. Oh, wait—she *was* pregnant! With twins!

She slapped her hands across his chest. 'If you hadn't leaked…'

'If you hadn't wiggled…'

Bo's eyes were hot on hers. They looked like heated aluminium when he was turned on, she thought, and seeing the passion in his eyes, seeing his desire for her—despite their current craziness—sent heat to her womb and caused her to clench her legs together. She knew that her nipples were on display, and she could feel a hot flush cross her chest, slide up her neck.

She could jump him right here and right now.

And she knew that he would let her.

Her pregnancy had done nothing to dampen the electric attraction between them.

Dammit.

'We can't.' Remy forced the words out, leaning backwards to keep herself from slapping her mouth on his. 'Too, too complicated for words. We have to be sensible about this, Bo.'

Bo tightened his jaw but his eyes didn't leave hers. 'I know...' he growled.

He dropped his leg and leaned forward and Remy got a quick view of the steel-hard erection tenting his pants.

'We're going to be parents together, we're currently living together, yet we're practically strangers.'

'We *are* strangers,' Remy insisted.

'You and I, in any combination, are an accident waiting to happen.'

He sounded as if he was trying to convince himself as well as her, Remy thought. He wasn't doing a particularly good job either.

'And we have the proof.' Remy patted her stomach. 'Which is all *your* fault.'

She added the last comment deliberately, knowing that her accusation would lighten the mood and hopefully break the sexual tension between them. If he kept looking at her like that—as if he wanted to lick her from top to toe and back up again—she was going to accost him in front of the plastic baby.

'You. Wiggled.' Bo enunciated the words clearly.

'I see that you two are still at it?'

Remy snapped her head round and saw Henry Graham standing in the doorway, his shoulder leaning into the door frame and an amused smile on his face.

'How long have you been standing there?' she demanded.

'Long enough.' He strode into his room, slapped a folder onto his desk and frowned at the plastic model. 'Have you two been playing with my pelvis?'

Remy giggled. 'Bo dropped the baby on its head, Dr Graham.'

'Snitch…' Bo muttered.

'Call me Henry—and let's hope he does better with the real thing.' Henry jerked his head to the bed in the corner. 'Talking of the real thing, let's go have a look.'

That evening, while Remy whipped up a quick Thai curry, Bo showed Ginny and Eli his fuzzy photograph of the babies. She had her own photograph, tucked into the back pocket of her jeans, but she couldn't make out much. Bo could point out the heads and the hearts.

Yep, he'd definitely been the one paying attention in class.

'Was it amazing, seeing them, Bo?' Ginny asked, her eyes shining with excitement.

Bo took a moment to reply. He flicked her a glance and their eyes collided. 'Yeah,' he replied gruffly, and she could hear the emotion in his voice.

Amazing, Remy thought, testing the word. Why didn't she feel that? It was weird that everyone, even Eli, was so much more excited than her. What was wrong with her that she couldn't yet feel love or excitement or joy? Was she that emotionally retarded? That selfish?

Maybe it was because she'd never been particularly maternal—had never spent much time around kids or thinking about being a mom. In fact the thought of having children scared her—a lot. What if she was as driven, as demanding as *her* mother? She didn't want to be a pushy mom, but that was what she'd known, what she'd been taught.

She still couldn't get her head around twins. And if she couldn't wrap her head around how she was going to cope with *one* baby, the thought of two had her breaking out in a cold sweat. Two would mean double everything: from diapers to formula, childcare fees, clothes, transport—everything. Two would cost more both financially and emotionally. Two would be double the work, double the struggle, double… Damn, double *everything.*

She couldn't do this. She really couldn't.

She shut off the gas, dropped the spatula and escaped through the open kitchen door and into the cool night. Wrapping her arms around her stomach, she skirted the house and headed for the guest house. Slipping up the dark steps, she sat on the swing bench in the far corner and looked out over the land.

Her life was utterly out of control.

She was staying in Bo's house, cooking for Bo's family and having Bo's babies. She was even about to start working for Bo. She felt as if there were a million ropes tying her to Bellevue and to Belleaire, and obviously to Bo. She didn't like it. She hadn't been tied to anything or anybody for so long.

Remy pulled the band out of her hair in an effort to ease the headache pounding the back of her skull. There was no getting away from it. She was going to be tied to Belleaire and Bellevue and the Tessiers—especially Bo—for a hell of a long time.

Remy felt her heart pound and realised that she wasn't inhaling enough air. She hadn't had a panic attack for years, but if she didn't calm down and get a grip she was going to lose that battle—and soon. She had to regulate her breathing…and her thoughts.

'Let's take it trimester by trimester,' Bo had said.

She had to do that, she realised. She couldn't think further than the next three months. If she did she'd be a basket case before the kids were even born.

You're pregnant—just think about that for now, she told herself.

Remy pursed her lips and recounted what she knew and had read of pregnancy. Weight gain, stretch marks, possible incontinence, blotchy skin, droopy boobs. Hers weren't too bad at the moment—still perky and definitely fuller—but after breastfeeding twins—the better option, according to Ginny's pregnancy book—she was bound to have long, thin, desperately droopy boobs that reached halfway to her crotch.

She'd never get laid again. Even if she had time after the birth she doubted she'd have the energy. And, realistically, what man—Bo—would be attracted to a thin, worn-out, irritable woman with stretch marks, yellow-tinged skin and boobs that functioned as a dairy? Even if she did get a man—Bo—into her bed by force, drugs or bribery, she'd have to interrupt proceedings halfway through to go and pee!

There was no other solution. She'd have to have a hot and torrid affair before she became too gross and too… *mumsy.* Which meant, realistically—since she had the equivalent of two voracious locusts growing inside her—some time in the next month or two. Hmm… Who could she consider? *Ooh, big surprise,* she thought sarcastically, *what about Bo? He's only been constantly on your mind since you met him.*

Except that she really believed what she'd told him the other night: sleeping with Bo would be a colossal mistake. He was going to be part of her life for the *rest* of her life. It would be a lot simpler, a lot smarter, to keep their sexual escapades to one night.

'You okay?'

That would be a *no*, Remy thought, and blinked as her eyes focused on his face. He looked big and tough, but his remoteness was softened by the concern in his eyes. It killed her. She could cope with his sarcasm and his irritation and his brusque attitude, but when this taciturn man displayed his softer side she wanted to fall into his arms and allow his strength—mental as well as physical—to hold her up.

Bo placed his hands in the back pockets of his worn jeans. 'What on earth were you thinking about? You were miles away.'

'Sex,' Remy said, her eyes filling with tears.

If she hadn't felt so wretched she would have been amused by the shock on his face.

'What the hell…?'

'I was thinking about sex, Bo. And that my boobs will drop and my…you know…will stretch, that I'll have ugly stretch marks from the weight gain and that nobody will ever fancy me again!'

I want you so much but I can't have you again. I want to feel sexy and pretty and have you look at me like you did before, with lust and passion and heat. Now I'm just an incubator for your chicks.

Tears that she hated but couldn't stop rolled down her face.

Bo looked at her, utterly perplexed by her sniffles and sobs. He blinked. 'I have no idea what to say except that you're being ridiculous!'

Remy's sobs grew louder, and the more she tried to stop crying, the more her tears fell. 'I'm not being ridiculous—it's true! I'm going to be ugly and tired and horrible, with long, lank hair and raccoon eyes, and nobody will *ever* want to have sex with me again!'

Bo pulled her forward so that she sat on the edge of the

bench and stepped between her knees. He cradled her face in his big hands and kissed the tip of her wet nose.

His voice was very soft and gentle when he spoke again. 'You are utterly gorgeous and…' through her tear-soaked eyes she saw his Adam's apple bob in his throat '…and men will flock to make love to you.'

'I'll have *twins*!' Remy howled. 'I'll be constantly exhausted and stressed and I will probably end up being an abusive mother!'

Bo tucked her head into his neck and gently rocked her. 'You won't. You'll be a wonderful mother. And I'll always look after you, Remy.'

Tears dripped from her neck onto the collar of his shirt. 'You can't *say* that. I'm not your responsibility, your problem. I have to do it myself. They are *my* babies.'

'You are strong enough to do this, Remy,' Bo said as she lifted her head to look at him. His thumbs swiped at the wetness under her lower lashes. 'You can *do* this—I promise.'

Remy dropped her eyes, wishing it were true. But this was her life, not a fairy tale. Bo was not going to rescue her. She'd have to do that herself.

'And I can give you a *very* good indication of how sexy you are,' Bo added, still standing between her spread legs, his broad hands on her knees.

Remy looked up at him, rapidly blinking her eyes. 'What's that?'

'Look down, Remy.'

Remy dropped her eyes to look at his chest.

'No, further.'

Remy's tears dried up when she saw the long length of him tenting his pants. She stared at his crotch for a moment, before lifting her eyes back up to his.

'Yeah… I don't even need to touch you to get turned on. You might be pregnant, but you're still all woman, still sexy, still someone I'd like to taste again, tease again… someone whose breathy cries I want to hear as she falls apart in my arms.'

Bo dropped to his haunches and his hands gripped her knees.

'I remember your taste, your smell, how fabulous we were together. And, trust me, I'd love to be in your bed again, inside *you* again.'

Remy licked her lips and placed her hands on his thick wrists, loving the feel of his skin, of the crisp fabric of his turned-back cuffs brushing her skin. 'I want that too…'

'But?'

'Complicated. *So* complicated.'

Remy dropped her head and rested it on his collarbone. She sighed when his hand came up to grasp the back of her neck, holding her head in place. Warm, strong, safe.

'Promise me something?' he said.

'Yeah?'

'If you get the urge to have one last sexual fling before you get big and bulky come to me, okay?'

Since he was the only contender, that was an easy enough promise to make. 'If I decide to complicate our lives further, it's a deal.'

Bo just held her head, and she felt his lips in her hair. 'Would it be so bad, Remy? You and I sleeping together?'

Remy turned her face so that she was facing the wall, knowing she should pull away but not able to do so just yet. 'I'm not relationship material, Bo. I have far too many issues about marriage and control to be successful at one.'

'I don't want a relationship either.'

'So what were you thinking? Benefits with your baby mama?'

'The hell if I know.' Bo shrugged. 'All I know is that you frustrate the hell out of me, mentally and sexually, and you're going to drive me insane.' He cradled the side of her face in his big hand. 'I want you—don't doubt that.'

'I want you too. But I'm a big believer in keeping things simple and prioritising what's important. Sex isn't. Building a relationship on friendship and respect because we're having children together is. Having sex will always complicate that—taint that.'

Remy looked up at the ceiling and let out a long stream of air.

'I don't want to con myself, Bo, but I'm also human. I don't want to sleep with you and get so caught up in the fantasy of having my hot lover's babies, starting to play happy families, to find that once the bloom and the excitement wears off we're only together because of a one-night stand that carried on way past its sell-by date. I don't want to be stuck in a situation that I can't get out of, that is messy. I don't *do* messy.'

Bo dropped his hand and stepped away. 'You don't pull any punches either.'

'But am I wrong?'

Bo rubbed the back of his neck in agitation. 'I suppose not. I'm not ever going to remarry, fall in love again, so maybe it is better to keep our distance…sexually.'

And didn't *that* statement feel like a hot poker rammed into her chest?

'Did you love her that much?'

Bo lifted his head and looked her in the eye, his eyes deep and dark. 'I *still* love her that much.'

There was absolutely nothing she could say in response to that.

CHAPTER SEVEN

After supper Bo returned to his office in the administration block, and instead of working, as he'd intended to do, he sat on his desk and allowed himself to look back on the day, to remember standing in that dark room with Remy, watching the synchronised beating of his twins' hearts.

Standing up, he went to the credenza on the far wall, hauled out a bottle of whiskey and a glass and poured himself a healthy shot. In between sips he pulled his tie off, threw it onto the antique coffee table in the lounge area and walked over to the floor-to-ceiling windows to watch the moonlight glint off the vines, which were heavy with grapes.

Seeing those smudges on the monitor had moved him far more than he'd expected. Before that he'd accepted Remy's pregnancy on a cerebral level, but seeing the living proof of their twins had smacked him in his emotional solar plexus. He was thankful that the room had been darkened. It had effectively hidden his watery eyes. It had been the first time in five years that he'd felt any true, visceral emotion apart from grief…

He'd been intrigued, amazed, nervous and utterly overwhelmed. It had taken all his concentration and willpower to listen to Dr Graham, to hear what he had to say…to fight against the powerful urge to take Remy in his arms. He could have spent a very long time just holding Remy and watching those two heart beats flutter in the kidney shapes on that small monitor.

He'd felt happy, he realised. And excited, grateful—amongst other feelings that he'd been a stranger to for a long, long time.

Bo turned his back on the moonlight drenched vines and, as per normal, looked across the room to the portrait of Ana. He let his eyes drift over her features, reminding himself of the curve of her cheek, the slant of her eyes. Since Remy had catapulted back into his life he'd hardly had time to think about Ana. He didn't want her to fade from his mind, to be relegated to a dark and dusty corner. She was still his wife…

But he'd soon be the father of another woman's children and Ana was *dead. They should've been our kids, honey, I would've changed your mind eventually,* he told her silently. But for the first time he couldn't imagine Ana having his children. When he tried to put her onto that couch in that room with the sonar scan, Remy's face and body appeared.

I promised I'd love Ana for ever. I told Remy that I still loved her... That was the truth.

Wasn't it?

Bo tossed his whiskey back, felt the burn of the liquor in the back of his throat and rested the cool glass against his forehead. Everything had changed, he thought, feeling his throat tighten. Over the past few years the one constant he'd had, the only truth he'd held on to, was the fact that his hopes and dreams of having a family, of being a lover, a husband and father, had been died with Ana on the side of the road.

One night with Remy had crumbled the foundations of that belief.

He was going to be a father—that was cast in stone. He

also wanted to be a lover—Remy's lover—and had even suggested it to Remy earlier. Where did that leave Ana?

Dead, his inner voice of reason answered prosaically.

But he still loved Ana—still wished that she was here, still missed her. How could he still be grieving for her and yet wanting Remy with his next breath? How could he reconcile the two? It didn't make sense…the two emotions should be incompatible.

He loved his wife…he'd promised to love her for ever…

But Remy was here: gorgeous, sexy, trying so hard to tough her way through a difficult situation. She was braver than he'd thought and more vulnerable than she portrayed herself as being. She had hidden depths, and he knew that there was a lot more to her than her being a traveller-cum-cook. She fascinated him in ways that Ana never had…

Not fair, he chastised himself. Ana had been an open book and Remy was…not. He knew next to nothing about her.

Bo glanced at his computer and thought about doing an internet search on her. Or he could pick up the phone and ask his private investigator friend to do a background check on her. He should know who he was having children with—what her background was, what he was getting into.

Or, that annoying inner voice suggested, *you can just ask her. Besides, it isn't like you can ask her to send the twins back if you don't like what you find out...*

Bo ran his hand over his jaw and held his chin. The problem was that he already liked her a bit too much, and he didn't know if finding out anything negative about her would change that.

He wanted her. It was that easy and that difficult.

Bo walked over to the credenza and for the first time in five years picked up the photograph of his wife and placed it face down on the wooden surface. Feeling disloyal, he immediately picked it up again and put it back in its proper place.

His jaw firmed and his back straightened. Ana would stay exactly where she was…in his heart and in his thoughts. It would take more than a gorgeous, sexy, funny woman to dislodge her from his life—even if she *was* carrying his twins.

Bo looked up at the sharp rap on his door and saw his cousin leaning his shoulder into the door frame, his hands in the front pockets of a pair of dirty worn jeans. He was wearing a massive grin that had Bo straightening.

'We're ready to rock and roll?' he asked, his excitement over what that smile meant kicking his sombre mood into touch.

'Harvest time.' Eli nodded. 'The Pinot Noir is ready to harvest. Ready to get your hands dirty, pretty boy?'

Six weeks had passed on Belleaire. It was mid-October and the harvest was finally over, Remy thought, staring out of the kitchen window of Bo's house. All the varieties of grapes had been picked, starting with the delicate Pinot Noir and the Syrah, which had been hand-picked. The Cabernet Sauvignon had been the last variety to be harvested and now everyone—especially the three owners of Belleaire—could take a deep breath and congratulate themselves on a good haul.

Or they could if they slowed down for ten seconds to do that.

Remy took a sip of her tea and pulled a face at her reflection in the glass. Bo had been up at daybreak for weeks, and she knew that he'd spent time in the vineyards, harvesting grapes himself, before rushing back to his house to shower and change for meetings. Then he'd return to the fields to help Eli, and after the sun went down he'd either go back to his office to catch up on his work or hit the desk in his study down the passage.

In between planning the menus for the bistro and testing the recipes she'd done some consultancy work for a Silicon Valley tech company, which had paid well but bored her to tears. She'd also taken to making meals for Bo, Ginny and Eli… Breakfast wraps, club sandwiches for lunch, dinners that they could quickly reheat before falling, exhausted, into bed.

Remy couldn't believe that the weeks had passed so quickly. At thirteen weeks her stomach was slightly rounder, her breasts considerably bigger, and the babies were, for the most part, out of the woods. She'd picked up the weight she'd lost when she'd been so ill, but she still was thinner than she should be.

On the plus side, the debilitating tiredness and the nausea had gone. She felt…well, wonderful. Strong, and healthy, and very strangely sexy.

Sexy... Hmm, that was a tame word for horny as hell.

Remy saw some movement in the vineyards and sighed when she saw Bo and Eli walking down the row of vines. Blond and dark…tall and built and so, *so* hot. If Bo had been alone she doubted whether she'd have had the willpower to keep from walking to him and plastering her mouth to his, to keep from running her hands up and under that sweatshirt, from unbuttoning the snap of his jeans.

'Good-looking devils, aren't they?' Ginny asked from her seat at the table, a bottle of beer on the table in front of her.

God, she'd kill for a glass of wine, thought Remy.

'Mmm…' she replied, trying to sound as non-committal as possible.

Ginny didn't need to know that many times over the past weeks she'd contemplated having a quick affair with Bo, but each and every time had nixed the idea. On a purely sexual level, to have Bo and then be denied the pleasure of his lovemaking would be hell, and she'd be even more frustrated than she currently was. How would she cope with the additional memories in the years to come? Honestly, reliving one night of mind-blowing passion was hard enough; remembering a couple of *months* of passion would be the equivalent of Chinese water torture—not that she knew exactly what that was, but it sounded horrible.

She blew air from her cheeks. They'd agreed to keep things simple, she reminded herself. Sex equalled complicated.

'I've never seen Bo spark off someone as he does with you,' Ginny stated, pushing back her messy blonde hair. Like her partners, she'd been working non-stop and she looked exhausted.

Remy turned away from the window and looked at Bo's sister. 'Surely he and Ana…?'

Ginny tipped her head. 'Ana was… Ana—someone we grew up with. She had no secrets.'

'And I do?'

Ginny lifted her eyebrows. 'Honey, we still know next to nothing about you. '

'Nobody has asked,' Remy pointed out. Her past wasn't a secret, but neither did she go around announcing that she was MENSA member with mommy issues.

And, talking about mommies, maybe she should tell her own mother that she was going to be a grandmother and that her new baby was going to be an uncle. Oh, boy…

'Bad timing…the past few weeks have been crazy. Harvest always is.' Ginny took a sip of beer. 'So, what's going on between you and Bo?'

'We're having twins together.'

Ginny rolled her eyes at this statement of the obvious. 'I meant…romantically.'

Remy was quick to shake her head. 'Nothing.' She saw

the look of disbelief and hastened to reassure her. 'Really—nothing! I'm not good at relationships, I don't believe in happy-ever-after, and Bo had and lost his. So we're just going to try and be friends, so that we can be the best parents we can to these two.' Remy touched her stomach.

Ginny stared at her for a long moment. 'That is the biggest load of rubbish I've ever heard! You two are doing a wonderful job of conning each other *and* yourselves.'

Remy found it hard to keep eye contact. 'I'm not sure what you mean.'

Ginny snorted. 'You know exactly what I mean. There is *nothing* friendly between you. Hot, lusty passion, maybe—but friendship? You're dreaming if you believe that.'

'We're going to be in each other's lives for long time, Ginny. It's not clever to start something that will end badly.'

'Who says it has to end?'

'Now who's dreaming?' Remy scoffed. 'It always ends, Ginny—always. Usually when I mess it up…' She held up her hand. 'This isn't just about us, Ginny, we have two other people to consider as well.'

Ginny pushed her chair back as she stood up. Walking over to Remy, she placed her hands on Remy's shoulders and squeezed. 'Bo wants a family. He operates best in a secure relationship and he likes you. You look like you need a place to land, and you won't find a better man. And you want to rip each other's clothes off… Both of you should stop thinking for five minutes and start *feeling*.'

Uncomfortable with Ginny's intensity and, worse, with the longing Ginny's words made her felt, Remy thought that it was best to change the subject.

She folded her arms across her chest and caught Ginny's eye. 'So, how's *your* love life, Ginny?'

'Shocking!' Ginny replied cheerfully. 'I haven't had sex in for *ever* and am convinced that I'm going to die an old maid!'

'*Are* you?'

Ginny shrugged. 'I'm not opposed to the idea. I like being on my own… I enjoy my own company. I feel… *smothered*…when I'm in a relationship. I don't need to talk to someone, see someone every day. And I always seem to hook up with men who want the package: marriage, double beds, kids…being entangled day after day, night after night.' She shuddered dramatically. 'Ugh.'

'Yet you're happy to push Bo and I into that?' Remy said, her tone dry.

Ginny flashed her huge smile. 'Because *you* both have a picket fence tattooed on your butt.' Ginny leaned forward and kissed her cheek. 'I'm going to go home, take a shower and fall face down into bed—blissfully alone.'

Ginny looked at her expectantly, her head cocked.

Remy angled her head towards the fridge. 'Lasagne—your portion is on top.'

Ginny headed straight to the fridge. 'Even if you weren't incubating my nephews…'

What *was* it with the Tessiers and the idea that she was carrying boys? There was a fifty-fifty chance that there were girls in there too!

'…I'd keep you around just for your cooking skills.' Ginny told her as she sauntered out through the door. Poking her head back into the room, she waggled her eyebrows. 'I'm still convinced that you would be a fabulous sister-in-law.'

Remy picked up an apple from the fruit bowl on the table and threw it at her.

Ginny snatched it out of the air and took a bite, before ambling off, leaving her scent and her laughter behind.

A few nights later Bo and Remy stood on his porch, watching Ginny and Eli walking off to their respective houses. It was the first meal they'd all shared together since before the harvest had started and Remy had cooked, using the opportunity to run some of her ideas for the bistro past the three of them. They'd had pulled pork, scallops, yellowtail and Thai green curry. They were all full to bursting, but Bo had known from the first bite that they'd found their permanent chef/manager for the Blue View.

Bo rubbed the back of his neck. like their plans for Bella's Folly, the Blue View Bistro had been neglected these past weeks. Now that the grapes were in he could get stuck in and make some decisions, and he was more than happy to cross finding a chef for the bistro off his long list of things to do.

That was if Remy would consider taking the job… He had no idea what she was thinking from one moment to the next.

Bo slid his arm around Remy's waist and gave her a quick squeeze. He could feel the thickening of her waist, had long ago noticed her swelling breasts. She'd always been on the scrawny side, and the small amount of weight she'd picked up suited her. He'd never found her more sexy.

Bo moved his hand from her waist to between her shoulder blades and steered her inside. Immediately she started to clear up the debris from dinner. He stepped forward and, gripping her by the tops of her arms, shoved her onto the couch.

'Hey!'

'Hey, back at you. It's after midnight, you've spent most of the day cooking, you're exhausted and nobody but me and you is going to know that you didn't clear up tonight. And since it's my house, and I don't care, neither should you.'

'I can't go to bed and leave a mess. I'll never sleep.'

'Then *I'll* do it.'

Remy shook her head, and Bo felt his teeth grinding together as her eyes drooped closed. He felt like thumping his head against the nearest wall. *Why* wouldn't she let him look after her? He found it deeply ironic that for the last five years he'd had to fight off women wanting him to take care of them and the one he wanted to take care of wouldn't let him.

Screw irony—it sucked.

Bo held out his hand. 'Let's go to bed.'

That woke her up. Remy's eyes widened and he saw the panic in them. He took her hand, and before he could react she stepped closer to his chest. He felt her bump against his stomach, those fabulous breasts against his chest, and couldn't believe how turned on he was.

'Together?' Remy suggested, with far too much sex in her voice.

Bo closed his eyes and inhaled her perfume. For a brief moment he could believe that she wasn't pregnant, wasn't his responsibility. She was just a woman to whom he was absolutely, inexplicably attracted.

He lifted his hand and ran his thumb across her exposed collarbone. Her skin was luminous and creamy and she smelled of those mysterious scents that made a man's nose quiver. Lilies, powder, woman… He looked down at her chest, his eyes tracing the blue veins that ran along the tops of her breasts. He followed one with his finger, halting when he came to the barrier of her T-shirt. He heard her swift intake of breath, felt her hand clutching the fabric of his shirt. Glancing down, he noticed that she was gnawing her bottom lip, her eyes on the floor. Lifting her chin with his finger, he connected with her deep eyes and, like before, fell into temptation.

He finally slid his lips over hers, as he'd wanted to do for so many weeks. They were smooth and luscious. Her hands had flattened against his chest. He was as aware of her fingertips digging into his skin as he was of her softening mouth. She was more than he'd imagined—more intoxicating, more womanly, more exciting.

Simply *more.*

This was what he'd been waiting for. This kick of his heart…this buzz in his head. How had he lived so long without touching her? *Had* he lived?

Wrapping his hand tighter around her waist, he pulled her closer and, clasping her face in his hand, deepened the kiss, falling into her mouth. Surely he was allowed this momentary pleasure? This brief respite from constantly wanting her?

Needing to explore, Bo ran his hands down her back, over her hip and up the sides of her ribcage. He ignored Remy's soundless plea to touch her breasts…if he did he wouldn't be able to stop. He tasted her, savouring her for one last time, before reluctantly dropping his hands and running his hand over his face, around the back of his neck.

Remy sat down on the couch and placed her hand on her stomach. *Oh, that's right... There's the other reason why I can't screw her senseless...the twins.*

Remy read his mind. 'Dr Graham said that if we didn't swing from the chandeliers sex should be fine.'

Bo's mouth fell open. 'You've discussed this with him?'

'He *is* my ob-gyn.' Remy placed a hand on the cushion behind her and stretched. 'And he brought it up…as did Ginny earlier.'

She'd lost him. 'What?'

'Apparently we have something cooking, Bo—some hectic electricity that people are noticing. Are we going to carry on ignoring it? Or are we going to give in and do what we both want to do?'

'God, I really want to,' Bo admitted quietly, sitting down next to her and placing a hand on her slim thigh. 'I don't know how much longer I can resist you. The memories of that night ambush me all the time.'

Remy linked her fingers in his. 'Me too.' She closed her eyes. 'It'll end badly, and we might end up hating each other—where will that leave us?'

Bo's breath skimmed across her hair. 'I know, Rem. My body just doesn't want to listen to my head. And I have a feeling that this…this need for each other is stronger than our intellect.'

Remy pulled her feet up onto the couch and snuggled down, so that her head was lying on his strong thigh. 'That's never happened to me before…my intellect has always been up-front and centre.'

Bo pulled a strand of hair off her cheek and allowed his fingers to drift lightly across her jaw. 'What do you mean?'

'We really don't know that much about each other, do we?'

Remy sighed and rolled onto her back so that she was staring up at him. He placed his hand on her stomach, feeling the rounded proof of his children.

'Harvest time is always chaos, and there isn't much time for chatting,' Bo replied, trying to keep down his rising excitement at finally being allowed to peek under the surface. 'I'm here now, and listening. Talk.'

Remy thought for a moment. 'Well, I guess the first thing you should know about me is that I'm smart.'

'I know that.' This wasn't news, Bo thought, disappointed.

'You don't understand. I'm pretty much always the smartest person in the room.' There was no false pride in her voice—she sounded as if she was ordering a pizza. 'I have a PhD in computer science and I received it a couple of months after my twentieth birthday.'

Ok, that *was* smart. That was *stupid* smart. Bo tried to connect the dots. 'So how does a woman with a PhD in computer science end up travelling and picking up strange men in bars?'

'What? Aren't smart girls allowed to want sex?' Remy narrowed her amazing eyes at him.

'I'm all for women wanting sex—especially if they're beautiful and smart and want to have it with me.' Bo smiled at her, pushing away the thought of how often she'd picked up other guys in bars. *Not going there,* he told himself.

Not. Going. There.

Remy sat up, turned to face him, and sat cross-legged on the couch next to him. Her elbow was pushed into the side of her knee and her chin rested on her fist. 'I graduated and landed a job at Tiscot's in their IT department. I got rapidly promoted and four years later was appointed as their CIO.'

Bo made some swift calculations. 'You only held the position for a year?'

'And a bit. It was long enough to put me into hospital with a perforated ulcer.' Remy lifted a shoulder. 'I was pretty sick…and depressed and unhappy. So I gave it all up and walked away to travel.'

Easily said, Bo thought, but not easily done. 'That's a hell of a decision.'

Remy leaned back and folded her arms. 'I heard all the arguments about why I shouldn't from my mother—there's nothing you can say that I haven't heard before. I know that I'm wasting my brain, wasting opportunities, not reaching my potential. I *know*…okay?'

Bo wanted to tell her that she was pushing her own buttons, but checked the words at his teeth. Instead he gripped her foot in his hand and squeezed. 'Was it the right decision for you? Did leaving make you happier?'

Remy's eyes filled with confusion at his questions. 'Absolutely.'

'Then why would I judge that?' Bo asked her, keeping his tone mild. He waited for a minute before probing some more. 'I take it that your mother wasn't supportive?'

'My mother is only supportive when I'm marching to the beat of her drum—when I'm making her look good, doing what I should,' Remy stated bitterly. Frustrated, she ran a hand over her face. 'Ignore that… I'm just tired. My mother and I have…issues. She's very smart, very driven, very ambitious, and she hates the fact that I'm not achieving as she'd like me to.'

Remy fiddled with the silver beaded bracelet on her wrist.

'She's just had her second baby and I'm hoping that he's not…not so smart.'

'Whoa…back up! Your mother has just had a *baby*? But—'

Remy smiled. 'She's only forty-four. She had me when she was seventeen. Can you imagine being seventeen and raising a gifted child? I taught myself to read when I was three…'

Bo shook his head in disbelief. 'How does your mom feel about having grandchildren who will be less than a year younger than her own child?'

Remy couldn't meet his eyes. 'Ah…that… Well, I haven't told her yet.'

Ah, hell. 'Are you planning on telling her? Or are you going to spring it on her when you go into labour?'

'The idea has its merits…' Remy muttered. 'You don't understand, Bo, she'll go nuts. You have no idea how crazy my mother can be when she loses it. And she *will* lose it. This is not in her plan for me. She's still trying to persuade me to go back to the corporate world or return to academia—go back into researching and working on AI.'

'AI?'

'Artificial intelligence.' Remy waved her hand as if to dismiss the subject—as if developing artificial intelligence was *nothing.* 'I don't want to disappoint her again… She tends to…'

Bo lifted his eyebrows, waiting for her to finish.

'To withdraw, to hold back…to whip back her approval.'

And you're still looking for it—probably looking for her love too. Complicated girl, Bo thought. Very smart and very complicated.

So, nothing new about this situation, then.

'Are you going to ask her to support you? For money? For help with the twins?' Bo asked.

'No.'

'Then she doesn't have a right to pass comment on anything you do. You're an adult, Remy—possibly a bit too smart for your own good, but still an adult. Tell her you're pregnant, tell her to deal with it and move on.'

Remy looked at her hands. 'You make it sound so easy.'

'It *is* easy,' Bo replied, his hand stroking her thigh. 'What *isn't* easy is wanting you and having you in the room next door, knowing that you're off-limits. Is there any way around that?'

Bo held his breath as he waited for her answer. 'We should be talking about the future…about the twins, our situation. The danger period has passed and I should be thinking of moving out, finding my own place. I should be making plans for the future.'

He'd heard a lot of 'shoulds' in there, so just waited for her to continue.

'I'm thirteen weeks pregnant, Bo.'

What did *that* have to do with the price of eggs? 'Yeah…so…?'

'I'm thirteen weeks pregnant and I have maybe eleven or twelve weeks to go before I get very big and bulky and sex becomes…challenging. After I give birth I am going to be the mommy of twins, and doing it single-handed is going to exhaust me.'

'I told you I would help—'

Remy held up her hand to interrupt him. 'I appreciate

that, but you won't be able to get up at night and breastfeed them, Bo.'

Good point.

'Anyway, the point I'm trying to make is that it will be a while before I'll be in a position to have a love life and I enjoy sex—especially with someone who knows what he's doing.'

Bo's ego puffed out its chest.

'So maybe we can do it for the next little while, and then when I get too big we can stop and use that time to transition into being friends who are co-parenting.'

If only she'd give him a chance to show her how good he could really be… Wait—hold on…*what*? Had she just said *yes*?

Bo frowned. 'Run that by me again?'

Remy lifted one eyebrow. 'Would you like me to draw you a picture? Would that help?'

Bo swiftly turned, lifted his hand to cradle her face. His eyes laughed into hers. 'You are *such* a smart-ass.'

Remy nodded, her eyes on his mouth. 'The tests *did* tell me that.'

He grinned as he ducked his head to kiss her, intending to be soft and gentle. But as soon as his lips met hers all his good intentions flew out of the window. He'd been lusting after her for days, weeks, constantly entranced by her sparkling eyes and her sharp mind. At that moment he could no more have stopped himself from kissing her than he could stop the sun from shining.

She tasted of Thai food they'd eaten earlier, hot and spicy, and her mouth was warm as her lips opened to receive his probing tongue. In typical Remy fashion she held nothing back, her passion rising with his as their kisses became deeper and longer. With his help she twisted so that she was nestled in his lap. His erection swelled his jeans and probed her thigh. Her one hand fisted in his hair and her other hand rested inside the collar of his shirt, tracing circles on his skin.

Bo skimmed his hand up her side, over the thin long-sleeved T-shirt she wore. She tensed as he caressed her thickened waist, and through his kisses he murmured words of reassurance. She'd never been so beautiful, blossoming with life. Scooting his hand under her shirt, he caressed her stretched stomach, feeling the wonder of soft skin over her hard belly. Moving higher, he cupped her enlarged breast, instinctively seeking her nipple, which instantly bloomed in his hand—a sharp, spiky response to his thumb gliding across its nubby surface.

Remy gasped and wrenched her mouth away from his, arching her back as she buried her face in his neck and swiped her tongue across his skin. *This* was what he remembered: this intensity, this flood of lust and emotion that he hadn't experienced since.

Bo groaned as his hands met at her back and unsnapped her bra, pulling it away to let her breasts fall naturally into the cup of his hands. Laying her across his lap, resting her back on the arm of the couch, he drew her shirt over her head and took in the wonder of her bare torso. Her jeans were tucked under her tummy, beautifully rounded with pregnancy. Her nipples were darker than he remembered, but her breasts were just as firm and tasted just as sweet.

Somewhere in the distance he heard her moan, felt her fingers under his shirt as they danced across his belly. His concentration was fierce as he took his time, alternately sucking and licking her magnificent breasts. Even as she squirmed, silently arching her hips for more, he carried on, not quite done with his physical adoration.

Bo sensed Remy's frustration and responded with a silent chuckle. She wasn't the only one who craved more; his penis was as hard as stone and desperate to escape the confinement of his jeans. But this wasn't about him.

Tonight was about Remy and the pleasure he could give her—better and bolder than the pleasure she'd experienced when he'd last held her naked in his arms.

'Lift your hips, sweetheart,' he murmured against her mouth, and Remy, eyes glazed with passion, obliged.

Bo pulled down her jeans with one hand, his eyes locked on her face as he fumbled with her shoes, eventually tossing the annoying articles to the floor. Her jeans followed and she lay across him, her femininity hidden by a tiny triangle of soft rose cotton. Her thighs were slim and baby-smooth; he could feel her hip bone next to the place where her stomach ballooned.

Bo kissed her shoulder as he whispered, 'You're so incredibly beautiful.'

Remy hiccupped her laugh. 'Beautifully *fat*.'

'Beautifully gorgeous,' Bo insisted, before capturing her mouth again and only breaking the kiss to help her pull his shirt over his head.

Then her hands were all over his chest, his shoulders, sneaking towards his belt buckle. She managed to undo his belt, unsnap his jeans button, but before he lost control he held her wrists together with one hand.

'Let me pleasure you?' Bo asked, and saw the soft reply in her eyes, tasted it in her lifted lips.

She became compliant beneath him, her trust that he would take care of her blindingly obvious.

While kissing her—he couldn't get enough of her luscious mouth—Bo moved his hands to her slender ankles, tracing his way up her calves to her thighs, lingering to knead her bottom. His long fingers slid under her bottom, probing to stroke lightly between her legs. Unconsciously, Remy let her thighs fall open, and Bo could see the sudden dampness of her panties.

He ignored Remy's whimper as he removed his fingers, felt her subsequent intake of breath as he trailed his hand over her pubic mound, bending his head to suck her breasts as he drew circles across the fabric, feeling her soft curls beneath his fingertips. Needing to feel her, he ripped the fabric away, and neither of them noticed nor cared that the flimsy fabric ripped at her hips, allowing him quicker access to her warm, secret places.

His fingers—urgent now—slid over and into her furrows, automatically finding her clitoris, causing her to lift her hips, thrusting into his hand. Astounded at her passionate reaction, by the tension he could feel in her, Bo felt immensely powerful, intensely male. At that moment he absolutely believed that he had been put on this earth to give Remy pleasure, and he proceeded to do exactly that.

Fingers probed and entered her, his thumbs caressing that centre of pleasure until she was whimpering into his neck, begging for release. When he felt that she was close he removed his fingers and, ignoring her protestations and his own demand for sexual release, slowed the process down by kissing her mouth, and her breasts, before taking his mouth south and kissing her intimately—until she crested and flew, before sinking back to earth murmuring his name.

Pulling him up, Remy cradled his head into her neck, half sobbing from the pleasure of the experience. Bo felt her yawn and smiled as he tried to move, with Remy clinging like a limpet to his neck. Scooping her up, he held her close against his chest as he walked to her bedroom, pulling back the covers with one hand before placing her on the clean fresh sheets.

Kissing her lightly on the lips, he smoothed a hand over her tumbled hair as her hands dropped to her sides. 'Where are you going?' she asked sleepily.

'Bathroom. Be right back,' he replied.

'Mmm…okay.'

Bo stepped away from the bed and stood in the doorway that led to the en-suite bathroom. Remy yawned again, tucked her hands under her head and fell asleep. As he had known she would.

When he was sure she was fast asleep Bo moved from his position, pulled the bedcovers over her and kissed her forehead. 'Sweet dreams, Rem.'

And it was back to the shower for him…

CHAPTER EIGHT

REMY BOLTED UPRIGHT, saw that she was in her own bed and that it was empty. She slapped her hand against her mouth. She'd happily taken the orgasm Bo had given her and promptly passed out. He must think she was the biggest tease in creation…

On the plus side, it had been the best sleep she'd had in ages…

Remy shoved her hands into her hair and pushed it away from her face. How should she handle this? Handle him? Should she joke her way through it? Apologise? Beg him to come back to bed so that they could do it properly? She'd propositioned him once before—why was it so difficult to do it now?

The last time it had been about sex with a stranger… Bo wasn't a stranger any more. She knew him. Not well, admittedly, but better than she had before. She knew that he worked like a demon, hated peanut butter, and that he drank beer when he was relaxed and Irish whiskey when he was stressed.

She knew that he wanted her—but not enough to take her to his bed, to show her the room he'd shared with his wife. It hadn't escaped her notice that Bo had brought her back to *her* room; she instinctively knew that if they were about to embark on a sexual affair, then it would be in this room. His room was, and would always be, off-limits.

His wife still occupied that space…

Aaargh! She had no right to be even vaguely perturbed, even a smidgeon upset by that thought. She and Bo had agreed to an affair, to sex, and where they did it shouldn't worry her. She was *not* going to get emotionally attached—she couldn't and wouldn't.

This was sex—pure and simple. Sex with a little liking thrown in, but nothing more.

You're starting off on a very bad foot, Draycott, she warned herself. *Pull yourself together immediately!*

'Was it that bad?'

Remy jumped at Bo's voice and snapped her head up, her mouth and eyes softening as they landed on him. He stood in the doorway to the bedroom, his hands gripping the door frame above him head, dressed only in a pair on unsnapped jeans. The muscles in his chest moved and his stomach muscles rippled. With his mussed hair and stubble he looked a little wicked and a lot disreputable. Hot. Sexy. Dangerous. How could she resist?

'I fell asleep.' She licked her lips as her eyes travelled down, and up over his body again.

'I noticed,' Bo replied dryly.

Remy, deciding that faint heart never won fair man, pulled off her shirt and leaned back against the pillows, fighting the urge to cover up her naked body. Bo's eyes glazed and his grip tightened as he examined her body, his eyes eventually landing on her rounded stomach. He stalked over to her, sat on the bed beside her. His hand was both hesitant and warm as he touched her bump.

'It's so beautiful. *You're* so beautiful.'

'Ever done it with a pregnant woman before?' Remy teased.

'Uh…no.'

'Well, I've never been pregnant before—so we're both virgins, in a strange way.' Remy placed her hand on the hot skin of his hip and slid it down so that she was gripping his hip bone under his loose jeans. 'I'll be gentle with you.'

'I appreciate your consideration…' Bo murmured as his dropped his mouth to hers.

They had much to discuss, Bo thought as he handed Ginny a cup of coffee. They were waiting for Eli to arrive at the first post-harvest meeting they'd managed to schedule and, frankly, it was a miracle that he'd managed to make it there at all.

Leaving a naked Remy, sleepy and sexy, had been a task of Herculean proportions.

Their one-night stand hadn't been a fluke. After they'd been sleeping together for a week, the sex kept getting better and better. She was a creative lover and she seemed to be as into him—sexually—as he was into her.

Two or three months, he reminded himself. That was all they had before she got too big and uncomfortable—before they had to make the transition to being friends and about-to-be co-parents.

He intended to make every moment count.

'Have you spoken to Remy about managing the bistro?' Ginny asked him, yanking him out of the bedroom.

'Uh…no, not really. Nothing formal has been decided,' Bo replied, pouring himself a cup of coffee and swallowing his yawn. If he was tired from being up all night, then Remy would be exhausted. He'd turned to her time and time again.

How much sex was too much? Was there a limit?

'Maybe we *should* formalise that.' Ginny frowned. 'I don't like the idea of her working for nothing.'

'I don't either, but she's so damn independent.' Bo sat on the edge of his desk and stretched out his legs. 'You two seem to have hit it off.'

Ginny tipped her head. 'I like her. She's smart. But

there's something about her that makes me want to protect her…'

'That's because you are a mother hen,' Bo teased. If Ginny could, she'd shoo everyone under her wing to keep them from bumping their heads or their hearts.

Ginny didn't bother arguing. 'So, has Ginny found somewhere else to live?'

Bo lowered his coffee mug to look at his sister. 'She's living with me.'

'But she doesn't want to stay there for ever. She's approached a couple of real estate agents, looking for a small cottage to rent.'

But now that they were sleeping together why would she want to move out? What the hell was happening?

He waved his mug in the air and the coffee threatened to spill over the sides. 'She's not earning a salary from us—how can she afford the rent?'

Ginny stood up and took the mug from his hands, placing it on the desk behind him. 'Honey, haven't you realised yet that the last thing Remy needs from you is money? Don't you two talk at *all*?'

Not much, no.

'According to one of my friends, who is an estate agent, Remy has has decided that she can't live with you—that she needs her own place…a place to bring her babies to that's a home. *Her* home.'

Bo couldn't identify the emotions boiling in his gut. Frustration, hurt, panic… 'My place can be her home.'

Ginny sighed in sympathy. 'No, darling, it can't. It was Ana's home. And, as welcome as you make her feel…' Ginny's face suggested that she knew they were sharing sheet time '…it's not a place where she can nest.'

'What does *that* mean?' Bo demanded, aggravated.

'Remy will want a nursery she can decorate. She needs

a place where she can put up photographs—paint the walls bright pink if that's what she wants to do.'

Bo blew out his breath and silently counted to ten. And then to twenty. 'I don't like the idea of her being on her own.'

'Me neither. I'd let her move in with me, but I don't think I want my walls painted pink.'

'*And* you like your space too much.'

Ginny folded her arms beneath her breasts, clutching at the fabric of her pink top. 'I do have an idea for what to do about Remy.'

Bo was happy to listen. His sister, as he'd discovered a lifetime ago, wasn't a fool.

Ginny stepped back and resumed her seat. 'Why don't you let her stay in the guest house? It's empty more often than not and it's just sitting there.'

He would—except for one little problem…he didn't want her to leave *his* house. His bed. The bed in the guest room, he clarified.

Ginny continued, swept away by enthusiasm, 'And Remy could pay you rent—which would make her happy.'

'But it doesn't make *me* happy,' Bo grumbled, walking around the desk and sinking into his chair.

'You know it's a good solution, Bo. She'll be close by if there's a problem, and once the twins are born you'll have easy access to them.' Ginny linked her hands around her knee. 'She needs to keep her independence, Bo—some pride. Let her find her feet, some solid ground. She needs that more than she needs you swooping in and dictating how her life should be.'

'Remy wouldn't listen to me anyway.'

Ginny smiled. 'Another reason I like her: she's won't roll over and let you scratch her tummy like—'

Ginny quickly looked away, but Bo knew what she had been about to say. *Like Ana did.*

'Ana was a totally different personality. She didn't *need* to make everything into a battle,' Bo muttered. Actually, before they married they never fought about anything and afterwards they stopped talking unless it was to argue about having kids. Their motorbike ride the morning of her death had been an attempt to reconnect, to rediscover the magic.

'Ana never argued about *anything*. Her favourite words were, "Yes, Bo."' Ginny lifted up her hand to stop the discussion. 'I loved Ana—you know that—but Remy…? Well, I love her too. Better than that, I *like* her. A lot.'

Ginny and Ana had been friends…sort of, Bo conceded. But she and Remy were already *close* friends—something she'd never managed to be with Ana. Should that mean something? And if it did, what?

He'd forgotten how damn complicated women could be.

'Sorry I'm late,' Eli said, walking into the office and tossing his ball cap onto the coffee table. 'Coffee—I need coffee.'

Eli poured himself a cup, sat on the edge of the couch and sipped. After a minute the caffeine hit his bloodstream and he looked up, his eyes bright and bold. 'I have news.'

'Good, I hope?' Bo replied, looking at the pile of folders on his desk.

'Do you remember I contacted that genealogy expert to find out who Bella's nearest heir was?' Eli asked as he placed his ankle on his knee.

Bo winced. That was another thing he'd meant to do but had forgotten while he'd been dealing with Hurricane Remy. 'I dropped that ball,' he admitted ruefully. 'Thanks for picking it up.'

Eli waved his gratitude away. 'Hearing that you're about to have twins with a one-night stand you're still lusting after would confuse any guy.'

Bo glared at him. 'Don't go there. What's the news?'

'Well, the genealogy tracers found somebody who will inherit.' Eli looked smug.

Ginny leaned forward. 'Who is the heir? And when can we contact him?'

'Well, turns out it's none other than the bad boy of rock Digby West! Who, according to his agent, has no interest in doing anything productive with the land other than making as much money from it as possible. '

'Wow! Okay, I didn't see that one coming!' quipped Bo. 'Does that mean he's receptive to an offer?' he demanded.

Eli shrugged and grinned again. 'According to his manager, he is.'

'Seriously?' Bo said, his excitement rising.

'Getting the genealogist involved was a genius move and one which no other interested party had thought of. Thanks to Remy's suggestion it meant I was first in line to get in touch with Mr West's business manager to make an offer. So there is a solid chance that Bella's Folly will soon be ours!'

Bo leaned back in his chair and twisted his lips. 'Eli—you are a legend!'

Ginny dropped her head into her hands and laughed loudly. 'Only *Bella's* closest heir would be a spoilt, materialistic, entitled pig of a celebrity. Lucky for us he's only interested in the money!

Bo nodded his agreement. Only Bella.

It turned out that hearing she was going to become a grandmother, and that her new son was to be an uncle before her first birthday, did not thrill her mother.

What a surprise, Remy thought.

She'd elected to tell her mother and grandmother face-to-face—she felt that she owed them that—so she made the long trip to Portland and their reactions—horrified—Jan—and surprised—Rosie—were what she'd expected.

What she hadn't expect was her mother resting her head into the crook of her arms and sobbing over her sleek kitchen table. Her mother never cried—*never*. Remy sent her grandmother a *Has she lost it?* look, and Rosie responded by lifting her shoulders in a helpless shrug.

'Mom? Is it such a tragedy that I'm pregnant?'

Jan lifted her tear-stained face and shook her head, obviously and utterly miserable. '*Anyone* can have babies,' she stated fiercely, 'but that mind—*your mind*—comes along once in a generation. And what are you doing with it? Nothing! Playing with menus and setting up a restaurant. You could be changing the world.'

'I don't want to change the world,' Remy protested.

'It doesn't matter what you want—it's your responsibility!' Jan stated, her skin blotchy with temper.

'I have a responsibility to these children too, and to myself,' Remy replied. 'I'm sorry that my choosing a…a gentler way of life and stepping away from the IT world upsets you so much, but I don't want what you want for me. I want a family. I want these children. I want to be… normal.'

'The problem is that you are *not* normal.'

Jan spat the words out and Remy recoiled; her mother's words were the emotional equivalent of hard steel stars striking her heart. She wasn't normal…but *damn* she wanted to be.

Rosie, ever the peacemaker between the two of them, stepped into the conversation. 'Tell us about the father.'

Glad to step off the subject of her normality—or lack thereof—Remy briefly explained that Bo was widowed and how excited he was about the children, how much he wanted a family.

'So you're basically his brood mare?' Jan commented, her eyes miserable.

'Are you *Hank's* brood mare?' Remy asked, irritated

with her negativity. Before her mother could answer Remy turned to Rosie and continued. 'We're going to co-parent these children—raise them together. Separate houses, separate lives, but sharing the twins.'

'You have *got* to be kidding me,' Jan muttered, leaning back and folding her arms. 'Does that mean that you're staying in Belle…whatever that town is called?'

'Bellevue,' Remy corrected her, and nodded reluctantly.

She'd never made a conscious decision to stay, but she knew that it was the logical, sensible choice. If she wanted her children to have a dad—and who wouldn't?—this was the way it had to happen. And Bellevue was an arty, sophisticated, vibey town—she'd liked the place from the moment she landed there.

And Bellevue held Belleaire, and Belleaire held Bo—who was becoming far more important to her than she'd ever imagined. And not only as the father of her babies.

Remy traced her thumbnail across the seam of the tablecloth and nibbled on her bottom lip. She couldn't imagine a life without Bo in it, and she was already dreading the moment when she would have to step back and away—when they'd change their status from temporary lovers to co-parents.

God, it was going to be horrible!

'Tell me about him,' Rosie demanded, running her spotted hand over Remy's head as she passed her on the way to the coffee pot.

Remy thought she'd keep it simple. 'He's successful, good-looking and smart.' She couldn't help the sour look she sent Jan. 'He's big into his family and has a protective streak a mile wide.'

Jan's eyes narrowed. 'Ah…*now* I get it.'

What crazy rabbit had her mother pulled out of her hat now? 'Get what?'

'Why you're doing this—why you're staying in that small town, attempting this co-parenting lark.'

'You and Hank are co-parenting—you're raising a child together. I don't understand your logic…you're acting crazy.' Remy shoved her hands into her hair and pulled. By the end of her visit she was convinced that she'd be pool-ball-bald.

'You just want a man to protect you and to support you—you've always wanted that. As a little girl you always asked for a daddy for Christmases and birthdays—that was your constant request.'

'Isn't that normal?' Remy demanded. Of course she'd wanted a father—preferably one who'd provide a balance to her mother's constant demands to work harder, be smarter, achieve more. Someone who'd love her for just being Remy.

'You should be *above* wanting what is normal! You're too smart for that!'

Remy's mouth dropped open and Rosie gasped her dismay.

'Mom, I am *not* a freaking robot! I am a human being with feelings and emotions and wants and needs. Just because I'm smart it doesn't mean that I don't deserve a family, or children, or a man standing in my corner.'

'When you receive such a blessing as your intellect you should be grateful and concentrate on that.'

Remy stared her down. 'Are you nuts? Where is this coming from?'

Jan stood up and placed her hands on the table, her eyes wild. 'You had everything, Remy! *Everything!* You could've had the world at your feet, money in the bank, accolades and recognition. You could've been *somebody*!'

This wasn't about her, Remy suddenly realised as understanding swept through her. This had nothing to do with her and everything to do with her mother's lost hopes and dreams. This was about the seventeen-year-old girl who'd fallen pregnant, who'd had to give up her scholarship to raise a child, who'd had to get her degree the hard way. This was about the young, brilliant scholar who'd felt hampered and hindered by her child, and about the mother who was still vicariously living through her daughter.

'Now you're going to be some man's convenience—this man's means of providing the family he so desperately wants! You've always complained about people—*me*—loving you, wanting you for the things you do and not for who you are. I find it so damn ironic that you're doing the same thing with this man.' Jan wiped her eyes with the tips of her fingers.

'That's *enough*, Jan!' Rosie snapped, placing her hand on Remy's shaking shoulder. 'That's more than enough!'

Jan looked up at her mother with wet, anxious eyes. 'She's wasting her life...wasting her brain. Wasting...*everything*.'

'That's your perception. And even if I agreed with you—and I don't—I would still say that it's her life to waste,' Rosie stated, her tone brooking no disagreement.

Remy, deciding that she'd had more than enough, pushed her chair back and quickly stood up. 'I'm sorry you feel this way, Mom, and I hope that someday we'll be able to move beyond this conversation and get to a place where you can think that I'm enough just because I'm Remy.'

She looked across the room to where Callum was asleep in his pram.

'All I ask of you is to not put the same crazy pressure on him that you did on me—no matter how smart he is. Tell him that he's worthwhile, that he's a blessing just because he's standing on this earth and breathing. That he doesn't need to be or do anything to feel worthwhile—that he's enough just as he is.'

Remy picked up her bag, slung it over her shoulder

and walked to the back door. Rosie followed her out and at her truck placed her hand against the side of her cheek. 'I think *you* are wonderful,' she said softly, 'just because you're standing here and breathing.'

Remy held her grandmother's hand against her face, relishing the familiarity of her touch, the comfort it always gave. 'I know you do.'

Rosie sent her a sad smile. 'For all your fancy words and your protestations, I just wish you believed it too.'

On the stage, bright-eyed couples stood around self-consciously, some of the women exchanging small talk while the men looked at the floor, the ceiling, or out of the window. Bo realised why they weren't making eye contact with the midwife, or each other, when he and Remy reached the group. On the free-standing board she'd pinned pictures of a sweating, screaming woman giving birth, her face contorted and her legs wide open.

Bo felt his stomach lurch. How quickly could he reach the door? Ten seconds? Twenty?

Earlier he'd been convinced that it was vitally important that he accompany Remy to antenatal classes. Suddenly he wasn't nearly so convinced.

He heard Remy's introduce him to the midwife, and when she pinched his side he wrenched his eyes from the board and focused them on a petite brunette with a wide smile and sparkling brown eyes. She barely seemed old enough to have sex, let alone lecture on childbirth.

After shaking his hand, Tarryn rapped her fist on the tabletop and the eager parents-to-be dropped into their chairs and gave her their full attention. Bo guided Remy to the last available chairs—smack in the middle of the front row and directly in front of the gruesome photos.

Tarryn started to speak, but Bo couldn't concentrate on a damn thing. Not when he was being constantly slapped in the face by the sight of the screaming woman trying to force a watermelon-sized baby through a hole made for a pea.

Bo lifted his hand, and when Tarryn acknowledged him he spoke. 'I'm sorry, but if I'm going to be here for the next ninety minutes can you turn that board around?'

Tarryn frowned, slightly confused, before following his pointed finger. Seeing the board, she laughed. 'Oh, good grief! I'd forgotten that was up. I use it as a deterrent when I talk to teenagers about safe sex.'

'Guess we're all past that,' Bo said dryly.

Tarryn rolled the board around and Bo relaxed when he saw serene pictures of rolling landscapes and calm seas. Right, he was now ready to be bored out of his skull. He'd read some baby magazines, and a couple of books, and felt he knew enough about pregnancy and childbirth to get through the process. He was here to support Remy. While the group discussed childbirth options and pregnancy symptoms he'd work through a couple of issues that were currently plaguing him.

He needed to think about his scheduled trip to the UK and France—he wasn't leaving Remy on her own so Eli would have to go in his place—and he wanted to work on the plans relating to how best to use Bella's Folly when Digby West finally got around to signing the papers. And then there was Remy, whom he was never *not* thinking about.

She'd been quiet since she returned from Portland two days ago, and Bo felt bad that he hadn't had time to ask how her mother and grandmother had taken the news about the pregnancy. She was growing bigger, Bo realised, eyeing her stomach. Their hectic, adventurous, utterly amazing sex-life was soon going to come to an end… Not even he would risk hurting the twins.

'Today we're going to talk about sex!' Tarryn chirruped.

Oh, my God, please don't, Bo muttered silently, and squirmed in his chair along with the rest of his sex. He'd spent far too much time thinking about sex and imagining what he intended to do to Remy that he had no desire to talk about it.

Besides, how could he listen to Tarryn lecture about sex when she looked as if she'd lost her virginity last week?

'So let's get this straight: you can make love even when you feel as big as a house and as sexy as a limp washcloth. But we *do* need to talk about positions—because I don't recommend the missionary position from about sixteen weeks' gestation,' Tarryn continued, either ignoring or blithely unaware of the flushed male faces.

Well, huh… On the plus side, maybe he and Remy could extend their agreement. But on the negative side they were talking about *sex*…with *pregnant women*. Discussing it went against every law of nature, and Bo felt as if he should hand in his man card. Why couldn't Tarryn just talk to the women about this and then they could pass the information along?

Bo forced himself to slouch in his chair, to paste a look of boredom on his face, but his eyes kept darting towards the open door. Tarryn stood up and lifted a pack of papers from the desk and Bo groaned internally as he caught a glimpse of the illustrations. The *Kama Sutra* for pregnant couples? God, please shoot him now.

He could feel Remy's shoulder shaking against his and risked a glance at her face. She had her bottom lip firmly between her teeth and she was staring intently at the floor, fighting laughter.

'This is *so* not funny!' Bo hissed in her ear.

Remy gurgled. 'You insisted on coming with me.'

Bo glared at her as he accepted a set of Tarryn's papers, carefully placing it face down on his knees.

Bo squirmed through descriptions of 'woman on top',

spooning, hands and knees, and side-lying. He heard about shallow penetrations and stimulating the clitoris and the need to be creative…

Tarryn took a sip of water and Bo silently begged her to shut up. He wasn't sure how much more he could take. Listening to her was like watching a particularly steamy sex scene at the movies. Enough to titillate but stopping just short of tipping into porn. Either way, he was horribly uncomfortable.

'Okay, so let's talk about orgasms,' Tarryn suggested.

Did she expect them to answer? Bo wanted to put up his hand and say that he'd like another one in the very near future, if that could be arranged, just to see her reaction.

'So, orgasms can be different during pregnancy—and some woman only orgasm during pregnancy when they never could before.'

'Not something *you* suffer from,' Bo muttered, his head tipped towards Remy.

Remy shoved her elbow into his ribs. 'Shut up!'

Bo heard a low groan from the back of the room, and he sympathised. He'd give up his credit line to be anywhere else but here…preferably in a bed with Remy.

'So, orgasms are really good for you *and* your baby. The baby experiences the same euphoric hormone rush that you do—'

So, hell, even the twins got in on the action? That sounded a bit creepy…

'Now, let's go on to sex after birth,' Tarryn suggested—as if they actually had an option. Which they didn't. 'Many women aren't very interested in sex for at least three months after the birth and some take a lot longer. You might battle, Remy, being run off your feet with two babies to look after.'

'I'll hire you an army of nurses if it means you'll find your libido faster,' Bo suggested, *sotto voce*. The couples on either side of them picked up his muted words and laughed. Remy aimed another elbow into his ribs.

'We won't be having sex then, remember? We'll just be friends.'

Oh, right. Damn.

Tarryn grinned. 'I see a couple of men ready to bolt, so we'll change the subject. But before I forget you'll need to bring a mat to next week's class,' Tarryn told them.

Bo's eyes widened. His heart sank to his toes. *What the hell for?*

He decided he'd just rather not know.

CHAPTER NINE

REMY WAS WALKING past Bo's bedroom when she saw movement behind his partially open door. Stopping, she stuck her foot out and—whoops, look at that!—the door opened. Leaning her shoulder into the door frame, she watched Bo pull on his trainers, then snap the band to his heart-rate monitor around his broad chest, completely unaware that she was watching him. Beautiful man, she thought, as she always did.

His room… Ana's room… Up until this point she'd absolutely and resolutely respected his wish to keep her out and, as hard as it had been to keep her curiosity in check, she'd never once opened this door. Not even to take a quick peek.

Thinking that he had a right to know that she was there, she cleared her throat and he looked up, his eyes wary. When he didn't shoo her away Remy took half a step across the threshold and stood next to the tall credenza at the entrance of the room.

It was lovely, Remy admitted, looking around in frank curiosity. The walls were a pale shade of aqua, except for the one behind the huge leather headboard, which had been painted a deep rich brown, and pen and ink sketches of his family, of Belleaire, Bellevue and the surrounding areas, were grouped on the walls.

There were no photographs except for the massive

portrait above his bed. It could only be Ana, gorgeously mussed, sleepy and sexy, and obviously naked beneath the sheer sheet that was draped over her curvaceous body.

Okay, so that explained why he'd never feel comfortable sleeping with her in his own bed. There was no way they could share such uninhibited, joyful, stupendous sex with her looking down at them.

Bo saw her looking at the portrait and the steel shutters in his eyes dropped. Remy shook her head and held up her hand. 'Don't do that,' she chided softly.

'Do what?' Bo challenged.

'Retreat…close yourself off.' Remy gestured to the photograph. 'She was your wife; you obviously loved her—'

Remy saw Bo's jaw tighten. 'I don't talk about Ana. Ever.'

'Why not? Doesn't she deserve to be spoken about?' Remy asked gently. 'Doesn't she deserve to be remembered?'

'Of course she does,' Bo said through gritted teeth.

'I understand why you won't discuss her with just anyone, but what I *don't* understand is why you won't discuss her *at all*. Not even with Ginny and Eli. If she deserves to be remembered, why don't you talk about her?' Remy asked, walking across the room to sit on the corner of his king-sized bed.

This was a conversation that they needed to have, she realised—that *he* needed to have.

Bo fiddled with his heart-rate monitor and ignored her question. Since he'd yet to kick her out of his room, or tell her to be quiet, she thought she'd push a little more. 'Is it because it hurts too damn much?'

She saw the answer in his quick shrug, in his bleak eyes. Yeah, it still hurt like crazy. Remy sent an envious glance up to the blue-eyed blonde. *Lucky girl,* she told her silently, *being loved by this utterly spectacular man.*

'Tell me something about her.'

Bo stared at the carpet between his feet and shook his head.

'It doesn't have to be something big,' Remy told him. 'Tell me something you remember…something funny…'

'Why?' Bo croaked. 'What's the point?'

The point is that nearly five years is far too long to keep all this emotion bottled up inside you.

'One thing, Bo,' Remy whispered, hoping that he'd take that tiny step. He needed to offload on someone, and besides, she was very curious about what it was about her that made Bo love her so intensely.

Bo took so long to speak that she didn't think that he'd engage with her, and Remy was surprised when he actually did.

He gestured to the photograph. 'She looks so relaxed, so sexy in that photograph, but she was actually seriously tipsy. It was the only way I could get her to take her clothes off—to pose like that.'

'*You* took that photograph?' Remy lifted her eyebrows, astounded. 'The colours and contrast are amazing—and so artistic. I thought it must have been done by a professional.'

Bo shook his head. 'Everyone thought that she was this hippy, free-spirited woman but that was the front she showed the world. Actually, she was pretty insecure and quite a prude. I had to get her half-wasted before she lost her inhibitions and allowed me to shoot her. I took that photo about a year before she died.'

'It's stunning.' Remy dropped her hand and stretched out on the comforter, resting her head in her hand. 'Who did the sketches?'

'Me again. In the early days, when I had more time, we used to pack a picnic basket and she'd take her book and I'd take my sketch pad and we'd spend the day outdoors.'

'Do you still miss her?'

Bo ran a hand through his hair. 'I did… I *do.* Not as much as I did,' he added reluctantly.

Remy bit the corner of her mouth and wondered whether she was brave enough to ask the question she most wanted the answer to. Gathering her courage, she traced the diamond stitching in the comforter with her fingernail.

'You obviously loved her very much, and everyone says that you had a brilliant relationship, so knowing that—having had that—why wouldn't you want to try and find it again? With someone else?'

Bo didn't hesitate to reply. 'Because I don't know if I can love someone else as much as I did her—and how do I enter a relationship knowing that? Knowing that Ana will always have the bigger piece of my heart? It won't be the same as what I had with Ana and I'll feel cheated. Worse, I'll cheat the woman I enter that relationship *with.*'

'Does it have to be the same?' Remy asked, her heart pounding in her chest. 'Why can't it be as good but different?'

Bo shook his head. 'I really don't think that's possible. Besides, I made a promise to Ana that I have to keep.'

'What promise?' Remy asked, knowing that he probably wouldn't tell her.

'I promised to love her.' Bo's words were tinged with desperation.

Okay…that wasn't a surprise. She knew that love didn't die with death—that it lived on regardless.

'You can love her and still have a relationship with someone else, Bo,' Remy replied. Why did he think that one excluded the other? Where did such a rigid idea of love come from?

'With who, Remy? *You?*' Bo slapped his hands on his hips and his face tightened. 'What are you getting at?'

'I'm just trying to understand you.'

Those eyes darkened, hardened, as he mentally retreated. 'You don't *need* to understand me. We're only sleeping together, and soon we'll stop doing that so there's no point. We're friends having a few months of sex—that was the deal, remember?'

She hadn't forgotten what they were doing—not for one second—but his words still stung like icy bullets. 'Jeez, calm down, Bo. It was just a random conversation.'

Bo's expression turned sarcastic. 'Sure it was.'

'Excuse me?'

'There's always a subtext to these conversations. I've had enough of them over the past five years,' Bo said, his expression grim.

Okay, now he was making her mad. 'Are you suggesting that I'm trying to figure out whether or not I have a chance with you?'

His indolent shrug and lifted eyebrow screamed, *Aren't you?*

'I am *not* advocating for a continuation of this relationship and I am *certainly* not pushing for more!' Remy shot to her feet, her eyes blazing.

'Then what was the point of talking about my dead wife?'

God save me from moronic males, Remy thought. 'I had a crazy thought that we were friends and that friends discuss things. It just goes to show how stupid I can be on occasion.'

Remy flounced over to the open door, but before she could leave his room Bo's hand on her elbow had her spinning around and she thumped into his chest. As per usual, her blood started to hum and her skin prickled. She could be dead and he would still turn her on, Remy admitted reluctantly. It was supremely annoying.

'This is why I don't like talking about Ana.' Bo said his eyes hot and frustrated. 'It always leads to an argument.'

Remy jerked her arm out of his grip. 'No, it leads to an

argument because you're an idiot. I just wanted to know a little about your past. I might not be the most experienced person when it comes to interpersonal relationships, but even I know that talking, sharing, becoming friends, involves a little bit of back and forth, a little bit of risk… But you don't like risk.'

Bo's chin jutted out. 'I can do risk.'

Remy snorted. 'In business—sure. Emotionally, you're a chicken.' She made herself smile at him, made herself pat his cheek even though her heart ached. 'A total wuss. And I suggest you deal with that—because I'd like the father of my children to teach them that life begins at the end of your comfort zone.'

Bo's eyes narrowed. 'I cannot *believe* that you have the gall to stand there and pass judgement on my choices, my life—especially since you're not exactly an expert in love and relationships. How many times have *you* been married? How many long-term relationships have *you* been in, huh?'

Such a valid point, Remy conceded, her heart aching.

'You can't just apply your big brain to matters of the heart, Remy! It doesn't work like that. We normal people don't operate like that…'

'"We normal people..."' Remy repeated his phrase. 'Like I haven't heard *that* all my life.'

She wanted to argue, but she knew that she couldn't.

'You're right—I have no idea what it feels like to love so intensely…' She hesitated, thinking that she, if she allowed herself, could fall into love like that. With him. *If* she allowed herself. Which she wouldn't. 'I don't know what it feels like to lose that kind of love, so I apologise. I was talking out of my hat.'

'Remy—'

Remy shook her head and darted out of the door. She couldn't be around him, keep talking to him, knowing that he thought she was a little strange…a lot exasperating. He might love her body, and he was already in love with his children, but he wasn't attracted to her mind.

Because he was 'normal' and she wasn't.

Thanks, life, for that latest reminder. FYI, it's not a lesson that I've ever been allowed to forget.

Bo took his shirt from the back of his athletic shorts and wiped the sweat off his face as he pounded down the road towards his house. When he'd slipped out the sun had been just dipping behind the horizon and pink shadows had slid across the vines. It was now nearly dark, and the evening air he was sucking in after a gruelling six miles was on the cold side of cool.

This was *his* time, his thinking time, but he couldn't get past the argument he'd just had with Remy. He'd hurt her with his 'normal people' comment and he regretted that. It had been said in the heat of temper but it was no excuse. His words had cut a lot deeper than he'd expected. And, recalling her telling him about her demanding mother, he supposed he could understand why. She'd never been allowed to be normal—she'd always been pushed to do more, *be* more.

'Normal' was what she'd been striving towards for years, and he'd slapped her down because she'd come a little too close to verbalising truths he'd prefer not to hear.

But was she right? *Was* he an emotional coward because he didn't want to risk loving someone, losing someone, again? Was that a bad thing? Wasn't he allowed to protect his heart, his soul, his emotions? He didn't want to go through the pain he'd experienced again—especially the pain of losing his wife.

Over the past few months he'd also started to realise that he couldn't ignore the last six months he spent with Ana and that he had to accept that his relationship with her hadn't been as perfect as he remembered it being. At the end some pretty serious cracks had developed, cracks he wasn't sure they would've been able to repair. Was he also scared of taking the risk of loving again and then it going wrong? Maybe. Probably. He had a right to avoid it. And if that meant being labelled a chicken, then he'd deal with it. Except that he didn't want his children living a half-existence, growing up to believe that love was scary, that it was painful. He wanted them to experience the joy of love and the profound happiness it brought them. Because he had felt that with Ana, ok, maybe not at the end but before that he'd been ecstatically happy. But how could he teach them that and still manage to protect himself?

On that point, was he as well protected as he thought he was? Remy had sneaked into the empty and guarded places of his heart and if something happened to her he would be devastated. He enjoyed her, cared for her, was constantly lusting over her, but that didn't necessarily mean that he was feeling more for her than he should. He couldn't be—*shouldn't* be. Falling for Remy would be stupid, crazy, terrifying. She was wilful and strong…but so vulnerable, and more in need of love than anyone he'd ever met.

Bo shook his head as he ran past Ginny's house. He had too much on his plate already, he thought, panicking. The business demanded so much from him and he was going to be a father in a couple of months. He couldn't afford to let this become any more complicated than it needed to be.

Remy was the mother of his kids and his temporary lover—his amazing but temporary lover. He had to keep it that simple. Because making it complicated by contemplating more was just asking life to bite him on the ass again.

It was late on Friday afternoon and Remy stood in the middle of the heaving supermarket, white fingers clutching the handle of her basket and quietly cursing. She knew she'd braved the madness of Friday afternoon shopping for a reason, but as soon as she'd stepped into the insanity her mind had gone absolutely, positively blank. Stamping her foot, Remy stared at the magnificent cheese display and tried to recall what could possibly have motivated her to be in this hellhole.

Her short-term memory loss—or baby brain—was worsening daily, Remy admitted wearily. Two days ago she'd asked Bo the same question twice, ten minutes apart, and he'd bluntly told her that she was losing it. She freely admitted that it was a very real possibility. She routinely lost the keys to the car, she'd found her hand cream in the fridge, and had quickly learnt to write down anything that was marginally important.

Twenty-four weeks down, sixteen to go—but because it was twins she'd probably only make twelve weeks before she went into labour. Her babies weren't just taking over her body: they were also affecting her mind. The father of her babies wasn't helping either. No, that wasn't fair, Remy admitted, staring at a pile of firebox-red peppers. Bo hadn't changed. He was still the same in-love-with-his-dead-wife man she'd met months ago—it was *her* feelings that had shifted, evolved.

Despite her best intentions she was falling in love with him; despite knowing that love was a crazy emotion that she wanted nothing to do with she was tumbling into that madness. And the more she tried to fight it, the deeper she fell. He was a spectacular human being: funny, smart, hot as hell. Loyal and passionate. She couldn't have chosen a better man to be the father of her children…

But while he was going to be in her life for a long, long time he would only ever be her temporary lover—and then they'd be, at best, friends and co-parents. As the mother of his children she would always have a place in his life, but it wasn't the one she most wanted—the one her restless and unhappy heart ached for.

She wanted to be his partner, his lover, the love of his life—but how could she compete with his dead wife? With a marriage that by all accounts had been made in the stars? Even if some miracle occurred and Bo decided that they *could* be more—have more, be a family—she knew that she would always be second-best, his second choice, the substitute mother and wife.

She'd always been the best, had always strived to be number one, and now she'd realised that most of her achievements, all the accolades for finishing first, meant nothing. But this race, for Bo's love, meant *everything*! And it was a race she could never win…not when her competition was a ghost.

Even if for some reason a miracle happened—which was highly unlikely—she'd always doubt his love, doubt that he loved her, wonder how much of his love was determined by the fact that she'd given him the family he'd always wanted. She'd always, always fall short of the mark…

She was an all or nothing type of girl…always had been.

She had to stop sleeping with him—had to find some distance from him. She had to retreat and shore up her defences, rebuild her walls. She was too close to falling over the edge…too close to handing over her heart and suggesting that he stamp on it. If she could remove herself from his orbit, put some space between them, then she could start working on how to manoeuvre him out of her heart and her head.

If she could fall in love with him, then with a little work and grace, and prayer, she could fall *out* of love with him too. Every action had an equal and opposite reaction. That was a universal law of science. Surely it could be applied to the human mind as well? Well, she was going to test the theory, and the first thing she needed to do was to move out of his house, find her own place. She'd been trying to find somewhere, but cottages and flats to rent were non-existent. She'd just have to try harder—maybe look to areas away from Bellevue.

Good plan, Remy thought as she headed for the exit, tossing her basket into the pile on the way out.

As Remy passed the tables outside a busy coffee shop a couple stood up from a table on the fringes and Remy impulsively slid into a chair at the table, still warm from the ample feminine bottom that was now waddling towards the parking lot.

Remy folded her arms on the table and pushed aside the dirty coffee cups, sending the waitress a brief smile as she hurried to remove the used crockery. After ordering a milkshake, she pulled a notebook out of her bag and started to plan her retreat from Bo.

It would hurt, but not as much as allowing him to break her heart over and over again if she was idiot enough to hand it to him.

'Remy!'

Remy glanced up and smiled as Ginny weaved her way through the tables towards her. Oh, this was wonderful! She could do with Ginny's irreverent sense of humour, her no-nonsense approach to life and her boundless support. She could tell Ginny her memory-loss tales and know that Ginny was laughing *with* her and not at her. Well, maybe she'd laugh at her—but very kindly.

'Oh, you clever thing! Well done for getting a table—and it's so *busy*! I thought we'd have to wait for ages.'

Remy accepted the kiss on her cheek and a quick hug. Tucking her dress under her, she sighed internally at Ginny's slim-fit jeans and skimpy top. *She* wanted to wear sexy jeans and skimpy tops. *She* wanted an even complexion and bouncy hair—

Ginny turned to the side and draped one long leg over

her knee. She tapped an unvarnished nail on the small wooden table. 'What's the matter?'

Remy shrugged, embarrassed. 'I shot down here to buy something but I can't remember what. I stepped out of the car and—whoosh! Gone!'

'Hmm. So, do you think there's any chance that you might have come down here to meet *me*?' Ginny teased.

Remy groaned. 'When did we make this arrangement?'

'Three days ago.'

'I'm losing it. Seriously, Ginny, I need a brain transplant.'

'Well…' Ginny said, and then, seeing Remy's earnest worried face, she patted her hand. 'Everyone forgets things—especially in pregnancy.'

'You're being way too kind.'

'Your brain is just being stretched—and, God help you, you're living with my brother!' Ginny said gaily, and ordered two glasses of light wine and a massive slice of chocolate cake from a passing waiter. Seeing Remy's dubious expression, she snorted. 'It's a glass of low-alcohol wine—not one hundred per cent proof moonshine.'

'And the cake?'

'Scientifically proven to raise memory levels. And to raise serotonin levels—the happy hormone.'

'I have enough hormones in my system without adding another to the mix. Happy or not.' Remy propped her chin in her hand and fiddled with a small vase holding a perfect yellow daisy. 'I feel—I feel like I don't recognise myself. My driving sucks, your brother thinks I'm nuts, and I can't remember arrangements I make.'

And I'm determined to fall out of love with your brother because that was never part of the plan!

Remy felt her eyes well and frantically blinked away tears. She felt enough of a fool—she didn't need to be a blubbering one on top of it. She tossed her hair and managed a weak smile.

Ginny covered her hand with hers. 'What's going on, Rem?'

'I'm tired and weepy and emotional. Can we change the subject—' she looked up as the waitress placed the cake between them '—before I sob all over the cake?'

Ginny leaned forward and speared Remy with her amber eyes. 'No. I repeat: what's bugging you?'

'I'm fine.' Remy saw Ginny's eyes narrow and sulkily picked up her cake fork and stabbed the moist cake. 'Okay, I'm *not* fine. I'm living in Bo's house, off Bo's generosity.'

'He doesn't mind—'

'*I* mind, dammit! I don't *want* Bo's money!'

'Please, *please* don't tell me you want his love,' Ginny said equably, and daintily chewed a mouthful of rich, dark cake. Ginny scowled when Remy failed to deny her accusation. 'Dammit! I was worried this was going to happen.'

'I have just decided that I need to fall *out* of the little love I'm *in*,' Remy admitted reluctantly.

Ginny stared down at the table, and when she spoke again her voice was filled with regret. 'I think that's a great idea, Remy—not because I don't think that you're good for him, or because you don't deserve his love, but because I'm terrified that he buried all that with Ana and that he has none to give you. Or at least not what you deserve.' Ginny bit her bottom lip. 'He adored her, Remy—was besotted with her. I want that for *you* but I'm not sure he can love like that again…that he'll allow himself to love like that again. It's too big a risk for him.'

Yeah. She got that. God, what a mess.

'So you're saying that I should pull back emotionally?'

Ginny looked sad, but resolute. 'Yeah, I really do. Because I like you—hell, I *really* like you. And I want you to be happy. And being in love with a guy who can't love you the way you deserve to be loved is not fair on you.'

Ginny pushed her hair behind her ears and her expression turned hopeful.

'Maybe you aren't really in love with him? Maybe, for all your declarations of independence, you're doing what women throughout millennia do when they find themselves in a fix. They look for a mate. For a protector and a provider.'

Remy tipped her head and listened to Ginny's theory, ignoring the voice that insisted she was clutching at straws.

'Bo is for all intents and purposes what most women would consider a good catch. He's reasonably handsome—'

'Freaking hot…' Remy muttered.

Ginny grinned. 'He's financially fluid…has all his own teeth and hair. He's a perfect specimen and he's also the natural father of your babies.'

Remy let out a long sigh. She wished that Ginny was right—that the reason she felt warm and fuzzy every time Bo walked into the room was because she was terrified of walking this road alone. That because Bo refused to let her do that she was confusing her gratitude with love.

Oh, she wished it could be that easy.

But Ginny was looking so hopeful, so excited that she'd found an explanation for her craziness, that Remy couldn't disappoint her. 'Yeah, maybe that's it.'

Ginny smiled her relief but didn't get the chance to respond. Someone called out Ginny's name, and they both lifted their heads as a sleek blonde walked over to their table.

'Carina—hello. I didn't see you standing there! Carina, this is Remy, an old friend. Remy—Carina Westwood. She's an estate agent.'

Remy's ears pricked up. She liked meeting estate agents, and although it seemed as if she'd spoken to all the agents in the town, she hadn't got as far as Westwood's in the phone book to ask them whether they had any cottages to rent. None of the estate agents she had contacted so far had been able to find her a suitable two-bedroomed flat or cottage. It was deeply frustrating—

'How's business?' Ginny asked.

Carina readjusted the designer shoulder bag over her shoulder. 'Good. Rentals are a bit slow. I've got quite a few properties on my books—'

'Cottages?' Remy asked hopefully.

'One or two.' Carina's eyes widened as they fell on Remy's stomach and she grimaced. 'Oh, no—this is not happening.'

Remy laughed at her horrified face. 'It's not that bad. I'm just pregnant, and it's not contagious. Tell me, do you have any two-bedroomed properties?'

Carina's hand fluttered against her chest in agitation. 'Uh, no, I don't think so. Nothing that would suit you.'

Huh? What was going on? Remy clamped her tongue between her teeth before speaking, her tone very even. 'How would you know what might suit me?'

'Um…'

Remy narrowed her eyes. 'Why are you back-pedalling? You just said that rentals are slow, that you have properties to rent, and I'm in the market. Sounds like a match made in heaven.'

'This can't be happening to me…' Carina muttered.

Something weird was going on here, Remy thought, pushing herself to her feet. 'I haven't been able to get a viewing on a single property to rent from any estate agents in the area in weeks. That sounds a bit screwy to me, since you have just confirmed that there *are* properties to rent. Now, would you like to tell me why you won't rent to me?'

'God, no!' Carina fluttered her hands in the air.

'Fine—I'll just report you to the estate agents board for

prejudicial behaviour. Maybe I'll write a letter to the local paper, stating the same complaint.'

A frown pulled Carina's super-thin eyebrows together. She shifted from foot to foot, uncertainty all over her face.

Remy held her stare, and Carina eventually let out a big sigh. 'Somebody from Bo Tessier's office called and strongly suggested that we don't rent to you.'

'What?' Remy kept her voice pitched low, but Carina was left in no doubt that her cup of anger was about to run over.

'Oh, dear…' Ginny murmured.

Carina threw up her hands. 'Okay, it was Bo's assistant. She said that if we ever wanted a chance to move any of the many properties the Belleaire Group owns, she suggested that we don't try too hard to find you a place to rent. No agent would risk losing out on a Belleaire sale for a small rental.' Carina's face fell. 'And since I've let the cat out of the bag, now I'll never get the chance to move *anything*.'

Ginny stood up and patted Carina on the shoulder. 'Relax—Bo is an idiot, but he's not unfair.'

'The sneaky, slimy, devious jerk!' Remy grabbed her bag off the corner of her chair and poked her finger into Carina's arm. Carina stepped back, her eyes widening, as Remy sent her her favourite corporate shark smile. 'You will set up a series of appointments for me to see *all* the cottages for rental in the area tomorrow. Are we clear?'

Carina swallowed and looked at Ginny for direction.

Ginny grinned widely. 'She's a lot scarier than Bo *and* she's pregnant. I'd listen, if I were you.'

Carina swallowed again, and together she and Ginny watched Remy waddle away. 'I am *so* screwed,' Carina wailed.

Ginny opened her wallet and withdrew some bills, tossing them onto the table with a flourish. 'Don't worry about it. *Bo*, however—' Ginny's eyes danced with glee '—stands to lose some *very* important parts of his anatomy. Feel sorry for *him*. He's toast.'

CHAPTER TEN

At Belleaire, Remy parked her truck in the visitors' parking area in the staff car parking and stomped her way up the path to the administration block of the Belleaire Group, which was screened from the tourist end of Belleaire by a thick copse of trees. This was her first visit to the office, and she followed the path to the tinted front door and yanked it open with such force that the pretty young receptionist jerked her head up.

'Ma'am, we're closed for the day,' she said, her high-pitched voice grating like nails on a chalkboard.

'Is Bo here?'

Pretty Young Thing found her gumption and lifted her nose in the air. 'Is he expecting you?'

'No—'

'Then I'm sorry. I cannot let you in without an appointment. His PA has already left for the day… Maybe you could call her and make an arrangement to see Mr Tessier?'

Remy slapped her hands on her hips and cocked her head. 'Call him and tell him that Remy is here.'

'No. As I said—'

To hell with this, Remy thought. She skirted the wide reception desk and headed straight for the door that led to the offices beyond.

'Hey, you can't go back there!'

'Just did.'

Remy lifted her hand in dismissal as she looked down the long passage. The area to her right seemed to hold a conference room, a kitchen and washroom facilities, so she headed down the passage, grateful for the nameplates on the doors. When she saw the sign for the CFO's office she knew she was getting closer. Then she ran out of passage, but directly in front of her was a door labelled 'PA to the CEO'.

Remy pushed it open and saw the door to Bo's office was open. Bo stood in front of the floor-to-ceiling windows, but instead of looking out at the view of the vineyards, and behind them the mountains, he was holding a large silver-framed photograph.

It could only be a picture of his wife—of Ana.

Perfect. Freaking perfect.

And wasn't that just another reason why she couldn't allow herself to feel anything more for this man than friendly detachment? Why she had to keep her emotional distance? She couldn't allow herself to think of him in any terms other than friendship because he certainly wasn't thinking of *her* in any other way.

He was still in love with his wife—he'd always be in love with his wife. She'd never be her, *couldn't* be her, and there was no way that she'd ever allow herself to feel as if she didn't quite live up to expectations.

She'd spent her entire life doing that, and she'd spent the last three years breaking that habit of a lifetime.

She wasn't going back there…not even for him.

Besides, maybe Ginny was right. Maybe she *was* just having a momentary loss of focus. Maybe she was letting her hormones rule, making her think that she needed a man to help and protect her. She could raise these children on her own if she had to. She didn't need Bo and she certainly didn't need Bo to love her to do it.

Love, she reminded herself, was a stupid, fickle emotion anyway.

Good talk, Remy, she said silently as she lightly rapped on the door.

Without waiting for him to tell her to come in, she walked into the room and slapped her hands on her hips.

'Did you genuinely think that you would get away with it?' she demanded, her eyes flashing gold fire.

Bo took his time replacing the frame on his credenza and Remy's eyes darted to the photo: blonde hair, blue eyes, unfairly gorgeous. *Enough of that,* she thought, and straightened her spine.

Bo placed his bottom on the corner of his desk and pulled down his tie. 'What are you talking about?'

'You put out a warning to the estate agents in the area "suggesting"—' Remy put air quotes around the word '—that they not rent a cottage to me.'

Bo's expression of cool assurance didn't change. 'So?'

'You had no right to do that!' Remy snapped as her temper started to bubble.

Bo lifted one powerful shoulder. 'I don't want you moving out of my place, and I especially don't want you living in town.'

Remy's fingers dug into her hips. 'I can't live with you for ever! At some point I am going to need my own place.'

Bo held the edges of his desk with a tight grip. 'I know that. I have a place for you to stay. The guest cottage—the house behind Eli's—is vacant. You can move in there when…' he looked down at her stomach '…when it's time.'

He had it all figured out, she thought, shaking her head at his take-control-and-do-it-my-way attitude. She doubted that the guest cottage would come with any type of rent or utility bills. Remy shook her head and strengthened her resolve. She'd been living with Bo for a couple of months now, but it was time to move on, to make him see that while she was, to an extent, willing for him to contribute financially and emotionally to raising their children, he was not responsible for her well-being.

Just rip the sticky plaster off, Remy. Quick and hard.

'That's not going to work for me,' she stated.

Bo straightened and his eyes deepened in colour—a sure sign that he wasn't happy. 'Excuse me?'

'Not going to work for me.' Remy repeated the words very slowly, as if she were talking to a deaf person.

As she'd expected, Bo's eyes deepened to the colour of wet slate. A muscle jumped in his jaw and Remy knew that, if she were clever, she'd back off…all the way off.

But that was what she'd done with her mother. She'd failed to stand up for herself. Never again. And if that meant taking on the devil, or Bo, then she'd do it.

'You don't get to make decisions for me, Bo. Ever. If I want to move into a cottage in town, or if I want to move to freaking Timbuktu, you can't and won't stop me.'

'I damn well *will*!' Bo growled. He was still in exactly the same position, but his entire body was vibrating with energy.

'I am not your wife—nor your girlfriend'

'You are the mother of my children!' Bo roared, running his hand through his hair.

'They are still inside *me*!' Remy shouted back. 'I am here—they are not! This is about me—not them.'

'This is about you being the most stubborn woman ever freaking created! Why are we fighting about this? I have a house—you need a house!'

'We're fighting about this because you didn't talk to me about moving to the guest house—you just decided that was what I should do!' Remy retaliated. She looked at the photograph and shook her head. 'Please tell me that your wife tolerated this macho alpha attitude!'

Remy knew that she'd crossed the line when his face

tightened and his eyes went from the heat of temper to the ice of pure anger.

'Leave Ana out of this. What we had together has *nothing* to do with you.'

'Of course it doesn't,' Remy mocked, pushing down the wave of hurt that had smacked her left of centre. 'You just wish that these were *her* kids, that she was here and I wasn't. I get it.'

Remy held up her hand as she saw him open his mouth to speak and shook her head.

'The problem is that I *am* here, these are my children, and you have to deal with it. And I'm not going to play the acquiescent woman, happy for you to orchestrate my life. Not going to happen. And the sooner you get used to that idea the easier this…this *situation* will be.'

Bo looked as if he had a lot to say, but Remy couldn't afford to listen. The tears were too close to the surface and any minute now the dam would break.

'I am *not* Ana. I will never be her. I will *not* be pushed around. I don't *need* you, Bo—do you understand that? I don't need your money. I can do this on my own! I don't need *anybody*!'

Bo cocked his head. 'Is that a threat?'

Yes...no—maybe. Probably. 'It's a statement.'

'Sounded like a threat to me.'

Bo stood up and walked across the room until he was standing so close to her that the tips of her breasts rubbed against his shirt front. Remy swallowed but refused to drop her eyes from his, not prepared to let him see that she was intimidated.

Because she was…just a little bit.

'Never,' Bo growled, his voice coated in ice, 'threaten to take my children away from me again. If we have a problem we sort it out—we yell and scream until we come to

a compromise—but we don't threaten. Ever. Don't do it again.'

Remy, feeling humiliated that her temper had pushed her into saying things she didn't actually mean, just looked mutinous.

Bo gripped her chin and squeezed. 'Are we clear?'

Remy narrowed her eyes. 'Only if you agree not to meddle in my business.'

Bo shook his head. 'When are you going to realise that you *are* my business? Now, get the hell out of my office. I have work to do.'

Remy shook her head. She wouldn't be so easily dismissed, wouldn't allow him to dictate her life, her actions, her future. *Just do it,* she told herself. *Take a deep breath and end it now...*

Remy put some steel into her spine and forced the words out. 'I'm calling it quits.'

Bo sent her a hot glare. 'What?'

Remy pointed her finger at his chest before pulling it back to herself. 'You and me. The affair… I'm ending it.'

'Why? Because I want you to live close to me?'

Remy wrapped her arms around her chest, suddenly feeling icy cold. Oh, God, this was going to be hard. Possibly the hardest thing she'd ever done. Maybe she was doing the wrong thing, going cold turkey; maybe there was another option…a middle ground. Maybe she *could* be part of his life, more than just the mother of his twins and his temporary lover. Maybe…

You're being a romantic fool, Remy told herself. *You're nothing more to him than an incubator and a willing body... This isn't a freakin' fairy tale. It's your life. So start dealing in what is!*

'You and I should never have complicated our lives by sleeping together. Sometimes I think that it would've been a lot easier if I'd left you out of this equation all together.'

Bo's face drained of colour. 'Do you really believe that?' he demanded, his voice low and taut.

Remy lifted a shoulder in a half-shrug. 'Yeah, I do. I wouldn't be second-guessing myself, having all these crazy feelings—wouldn't be constantly questioning my decisions. I wouldn't be competing with a gorgeous ghost. I wouldn't be feeling so…lost. Confused. Scared. I should've kept running.'

'I can't believe what you're saying.' Bo ground the words out. 'And, goddammit, if you think you're going to run now, I swear I'll hunt you down and bring you back. My children will be raised at Belleaire!'

Remy felt the bullet-like impact of his words and it took all her strength to keep her knees from buckling. It was one thing to suspect how he felt, but it hurt far more to have those fears confirmed. She *was* only of use to him as a willing body and an incubator. Whatever she'd thought he felt for her, any affection he had for her was only because she was useful to him. It was just another example of being appreciated for what she did and not for what she was…

But she'd never imagined that it would hurt this much. Maybe she was more deeply in love with him than she'd thought, than she was prepared to admit. His words had just ripped away all her obfuscation, the emotional smoke screen that she'd created between her feelings and the reality of her situation.

She was in love with him. But he saw her as a tool, as a way to achieve his objective. Any woman would have done—she wasn't anything special.

'God, I'm such a fool.' Remy looked at him with wide, helpless eyes. 'For someone who has an enormous brain, I am utterly stupid when it comes to men. Fantastically moronic when it comes to *you*.'

Bo frowned and pushed his hand through his hair. 'What the hell are you going on about?'

Remy released a little trill of pain-laced laughter. 'Oh, nothing serious! Just the fact that I feel so much more for you than you feel for me—that you see me as a plaything and an incubator for your chicks. Just that my heart is breaking because there is a walking, breathing woman in front of you who wants nothing more than to love you but you prefer to live in the past, where it's safe and secure, where you can't be hurt again. God, can I pick them or what? First my mother—then you. Why can't the people I love just love me back for what I am and not what I do?'

Bo just stared at her, looking as if he was trying to make sense of her words. 'I— What? You're in love with me?'

Idiot—of course she was.

She waved his comment away. 'That doesn't matter. What matters is that I'm walking away from this stupid situation. From Belleaire, from the bistro, from *you*. When the babies are born you can have visitation rights—supervised until I decide otherwise. You can pay child support—a reasonable sum—and I will take care of all the other bills. Other than that, I don't think we need to have much to do with each other.'

'I don't know what the hell is happening here!' Bo roared, temper flashing in his eyes.

Remy sent him a sad smile. 'Well, I'm leaving. So that'll give you some time to work it all out.'

Bo lifted his hand in entreaty. 'Remy—don't,' he said, his voice suddenly hoarse. 'Don't run away again. We can work this out.'

Remy walked over to the credenza, lifted the silver photo frame that contained Ana's picture and handed it to him. She lightly tapped the frame with her index finger and shook her head. 'No, Bo, we really can't.'

In the still, cold morning light, his hand fisted around the stems of a bunch of freesias, Bo started jogging up the path to the highest hill on the estate, to the small cemetery that held the ashes of all his family: his parents, his grandfather, Eli's mum. And Ana.

They were a couple of weeks off the fifth anniversary of her death, but Bo felt compelled to put some flowers on her grave, to try and connect with the memory of her.

He needed to spend some time with his best friend, his wife…

Except that there were a couple of problems with that statement. The biggest one being that it wasn't the truth any more. How could she still be his best friend and wife if she wasn't here? And for the last six months of her life they'd been at odds and he was no longer convinced that they would've survived her no-babies decree.

Remy was—had been, dammit—the one who'd listened to him talk after work, the one he'd held in his arms, the one he'd made love to at night and the one he'd be sharing a future with. Even if that future was only as the twins' father, as she'd insisted three weeks ago.

The longest three weeks of his life…

Bo jogged his way to the top of the path, and as he rounded the corner he saw the wooden bench he'd placed there years ago, overlooking Ana's memorial stone. Seeing the bench made his heart jump, and he dropped onto the wooden slats with a long sigh. Below him were the eastern situated vines and a series of tunnels growing organic fruit. Tall oak trees kept the cemetery in shade. Ana had once said it was the most peaceful spot on the estate, so he presumed she would have approved having her memorial stone right here.

Ana Hope Tessier
Death leaves a heartache no one can heal,
Love leaves a memory no one can steal.

'I still like the inscription.'

It was a measure of his tiredness that he didn't even flinch at the sound of Ana's voice inside his head.

'Ana, you're not real,' he muttered back.

'I thought you wanted to talk to me.'

Bo heard the amusement in Ana's ghostly voice and closed his eyes. He was going nuts. It was the only explanation.

'I need to talk—not to hear *you* talk.' Bo waited a beat. 'That's a lie. I do miss you.' He was partaking in this conversation…he definitely needed medical attention. But a part of him did still miss the marvellous relationship they'd shared for most of their time together.

'I know, but now you miss her too. So why are you here talking to me when you should be talking to her?'

He felt fingertips touch his shoulder and hurtled upwards, spinning in his seat. His heart slammed against his ribcage and he slumped into the corner of the bench. When he'd recovered his breath he scowled up at Ginny. 'You nearly gave me a freakin' heart attack!'

Ginny sat down next to him and pulled her feet up onto the bench. She smiled at him. 'Did you think I was a ghost?'

Bo wasn't going to dignify that with an answer—especially since it was partly true. 'Why are you here?' he demanded.

'Someone has to pull your head out of your ass,' Ginny replied, equable as ever. 'Why are you up here talking to Ana when you could be talking to Remy?'

'Not going there,' Bo warned her.

'You're sulking because, unlike Ana, she won't dance to your tune.'

Yeah; Ana had been easy-going except when it came to what was so incredibly important to him. He glanced at her stone and sighed. *Sorry, honey, but you know that's true.*

Bo brushed a hand across his forehead and scowled. 'Not. Going. There.'

'We so *are*,' Ginny assured him. 'Why won't you let yourself move on, Bo? You love Remy—any fool can see that.'

'I loved Ana,' he stated, a little desperately and knew his statement lacked the conviction he'd had half a year ago. 'I still love her.'

'Yeah? So? Why can't you love Remy too?'

That was what he was trying to work out.

Ginny expelled a frustrated sigh. 'You make everything so damn complicated, brother dear. You are *allowed* to love Remy too. You are man enough—have enough love—to do both. Ana is gone. Remy is here and I want you to be happy. She makes you so damn happy.'

'She does,' Bo admitted.

'Love her. Be happy. Think of Ana sometimes, but for God's sake live your life! You are using Ana as an excuse not to be with Remy, to not take a chance on love again, and she would *hate* that!'

Bo stared at the stone. Was that what he was doing? Was he clinging to Ana as an excuse so that he didn't have to risk feeling love? Being in love again? God, this felt weird, but it also felt like the truth. Maybe he *could* love Remy and still keep his promise to Ana. He was allowed to think of Ana, to miss her, but he could still laugh and love with Remy, could build a life with her.

With Remy… Even if she wasn't carrying his children…

The feelings he had for her were not tied up with the twins. They were distinctly separate. Yes, she was completely different from Ana—and that was okay. She was smart and stubborn and so damn vulnerable, thinking that she couldn't be loved for who she was. She was perfect, pregnant or not. Perfect for *him*…

'Be happy, darling.'

Bo felt a shimmer move through his hair. Was it Ana? Or was it just being so close to this place where he'd left her that made him imagine her voice? But if it was just his imagination why did he feel such peace? Why did he suddenly know exactly what to do and how to do it?

Bo slung his arm around Ginny's shoulders and kissed her head, before lifting his face to the weak autumn sunlight. 'Thanks, Gin.'

Thanks, Ana.

Remy gently pulled down the interior designer's rendition of what the Blue View Bistro would look like when it was completed and stared down at the paper in her hands. The walls were now painted those vibrant colours and the tables were mismatched, as was the crockery. There was exciting art on the walls and the terracotta floor sparkled. The kitchen had every appliance known to man and, more importantly, she'd trained the chefs to cook all the dishes on the menu she'd designed to perfection.

The staff the bistro needed had been hired and she could leave…she *should* leave. She had to leave because she was no longer *living.* She was only existing, Remy thought, folding up the piece of paper and tucking it into the back pocket of her jeans.

She walked out of her restaurant and quickly reminded herself that the restaurant wasn't hers. Nothing was, she thought as she pulled the door closed behind her.

She was now simply the woman who made the ten-minute drive from her rented cottage in town to Belleaire every day to her job as manager of the bistro, complete with a generous salary package. Oh, she was Ginny's friend, and Eli frequently arrived at midday to mooch lunch off her, but she hadn't had any real contact with Bo for more than twenty days.

The twice daily, early-morning and late at night 'Are you okay?' messages didn't really count.

As she walked towards her truck to go back to her empty cottage Remy reminded herself that he wasn't asking how she was—he was enquiring about the welfare of the twins… She knew that they were his top priority.

She still missed him, Remy thought as she drove back to her lonely little cottage on the outskirts of Bellevue. She missed his strong arms wrapped around her at night, his deep voice, missed feeling as if she was stronger and bolder and better when she was with him.

Remy used the back of her hand to wipe away the tear that clung to the tip of her nose and wondered when she'd stop crying over him.

She'd sent him an email earlier in the day, resigning as the manager-slash-chef of the Blue View. She couldn't work there any more. She couldn't cope with being so physically close to him, to seeing him in the distance but not being able to talk to him, laugh with him, love him. Besides, she was rapidly expanding, and the long days on her feet were taking a toll on her. She was mentally and physically whipped.

Until the babies were born she would sit at her desk in the cottage and take on the many consulting jobs that kept dropping into her inbox. They were brain-numbingly boring but they'd help pass the time. She wanted to meet her babies. She wanted to be so busy loving them, looking after them, that she forgot about the grey-eyed man who'd created them with her. They were the only thing she could imagine that might dislodge thoughts of him from her head.

Her mobile rang on the seat next to her and Remy glanced down at it before steering her truck to the side of the road and stopping. She scooped the phone up, sliding her thumb across the screen to answer the call. She didn't bother to hope that it would be Bo—he hadn't bothered to see her in weeks and she knew that he wouldn't. Bo was still in love with his wife and always would be…

'Remy, are you there?'

Remy sighed at her mother's voice in her ear and wished she'd checked to see who was calling before she'd answered. She really didn't feel like dealing with her mother's disappointment today.

'Hi.'

'You're still angry with me,' Jan stated, and Remy was surprised at her insight. Usually Jan didn't give much thought to what other people were thinking or feeling.

Remy started to deny her statement, then shrugged her shoulders and admitted the truth. 'Yeah, I am. I wasn't expecting you to support me, but I didn't expect such a violent reaction to the news that I am pregnant.'

'You took so long to tell me.'

'Why are you surprised by that? I knew that you wouldn't be happy,' Remy replied. 'Look, Mum, I'm tired and stressed, and I really don't want to fight with you. Can we postpone this argument?'

Jan didn't reply for the longest time, and after a tense few minutes Remy blew out her breath.

'Okay, well…good talking to you, Mum,' she said sarcastically. 'Bye—'

Remy tossed the phone onto the seat next to her and resumed driving. As she swung into the driveway in front of her tiny cottage her mobile rang again. God, how she wished she was back at Belleaire. But she didn't belong there any more. She didn't belong anywhere…

'What Mum?' Remy demanded.

'I was wrong,' Jan stated softly. 'About so much, and for far too long. You are so much more than your mind, Remy.'

Huh? What? This couldn't be her mother trying to apologise. Could it? 'Sorry?'

'I had no right to project my hopes and dreams on you, to try and live my life and unfulfilled ambitions through you,' Jan said firmly. 'And I never regretted having you—not once.'

Really? Remy climbed out of her truck and waddled towards her front door. Well, hell… What was she supposed to say to that? 'Um…okay?'

'I hope you can forgive me, and I promise never to mention computers again.'

That was a stretch. The corner of Remy's mouth kicked up. 'Never is long time, Mum.'

Jan's laugh was soft. 'Okay, I promise to try and not nag you. I'm just…really sorry, darling. I really am.'

Remy had never heard her mother apologise, so she knew that this was a watershed moment. She could either hold on to her resentment towards Jan or she could let it go. And, quite frankly, she had enough on her plate with a broken heart and rapidly approaching motherhood without borrowing more trouble.

'It's over, Mum,' Remy said, putting her key into the lock and twisting open her front door. 'We'll be fine.'

She heard Jan's sigh of relief as she stepped inside. She dropped her keys onto the hall table and frowned when her keys hit the tiled floor. Where was her table?

'What on earth…?' she murmured, looking around. Her cottage was empty—completely and utterly bare.

'What's the matter?' Jan demanded in her ear.

Remy was about to reply that she'd been robbed when she saw a sheet of paper in the middle of the floor of the empty living room. Even from a distance she could see the strong lines of Bo's handwriting and her heartbeat accelerated.

'I'll call you later, Mum.'

She shoved her mobile into her pocket and walked

across the room. She stood over the piece of paper and read the words written below.

Your stuff has been kidnapped. The ransom is dinner, my place, tonight, six o'clock. We'll discuss whether you get it back then.

Remy, furious, yanked her mobile out of her pocket and angrily punched in his number. He answered immediately.

'Robert Tessier, what the *hell* have you done with my things?'

'What did my note say?' he replied genially.

She glanced down. 'That the price of getting my stuff back is dinner tonight. Your place at six.'

'Well, don't be late.'

'You *stole* the furniture, Tessier. It's not mine! I rented this place furnished! You could be arrested, you know! In fact, I think I'm going to report that I've been burgled.'

'Don't bother,' Bo said lazily. 'I got the owner's permission to temporarily abscond with his furniture.'

'This is nuts. *You* are nuts.'

'Tick-tock, babe.'

Remy hurried across the cottage, stormed into her bedroom and, despite knowing that they would be empty, yanked open the cupboard doors. 'I'm filthy and tired and I want to shower and change. You also stole all my clothes!'

'So come naked. Trust me, I won't complain.'

The grin she heard in his voice locked her jaw.

'You are the most arrogant, managing, annoying—'

Bo broke into her rant. 'Be here at six or you'll never see your stuff again.'

Remy stared at her dead phone. Seriously?

She knocked on his front door a half-hour late, just as he'd expected her to, and he knew that she'd used that time to stoke her temper. She looked like a fluffed up bantam hen—annoyed and flustered.

He'd never loved her more.

Remy stepped inside his house and tapped her foot in aggravation. 'So, what's this about?'

'Lots of things,' Bo replied, pulling her into his house and closing the door behind her.

It had started to drizzle outside and the thought of her driving on a wet road made his heart clench. She wasn't Ana, he reminded himself. Nothing was going to happen to her.

He pulled in a deep breath and resisted the urge to pull her into his arms. If he did, he'd lose her before he even started. Remy, unfortunately, would not be placated by a couple of hot kisses.

Pity, because it would be so much easier than eating crow.

'Do you want some wine?' he asked. 'Maybe a half-glass?' He gestured to an open bottle of fifteen-year-old Merlot standing next to two glasses on the coffee table in his lounge.

'No. I'd like my stuff back—and maybe an explanation for your craziness,' Remy stated, her gold eyes flashing fire. 'You haven't spoken to me for three weeks and then you do *this*? What the hell are you thinking?'

'I did text you. I was worried about you.'

'*Pfft.* You were worried about the twins—not me,' Remy replied quickly, and he saw the pain in her eyes before she whirled away to stomp over to the window to stare out into the darkness.

He'd really messed this up, Bo thought, angry at himself. She really believed that her only worth to him was the fact that she was carrying his children. He'd hurt her, and by not contacting her he'd allowed her to keep believing that. He rubbed his hand over his rough jaw and felt thoroughly ashamed of himself.

Bo walked up to her and stood behind her, as close as he could without touching her. He felt her tense and lightly rested his hand on her hip. 'No, don't move…just listen,' he said when she started to move away. 'When I texted you I was asking about *you*—how *you* were. I've spent every minute of the past few weeks worrying about you.'

'Yeah, right…' Remy muttered.

Okay, he didn't blame her for not believing him, but he could show her. He intended to—soon.

Remy dropped her head to stare at the floor. 'Just give me my stuff back and let me go, Bo. This isn't helping.'

Bo turned her around and lifted her chin to make her look at him. His heart clenched at the tears brimming in her eyes. 'This is about your stuff being in the right place and getting you to follow.'

'You're not making any sense,' Remy complained. 'And you have a very peculiar expression on your face.'

Bo shrugged, slightly embarrassed. 'I'm trying to tell you that I love you. For the past few months I've loved you in different ways at different times, but today I realised that I just *love* you. In every way possible.'

He saw hope flare in her eyes, but then it died just as rapidly as it had appeared.

'You don't love me—and even if you do, it's just rubbing off because you love our children so damn much.'

A tear fell and his heart broke just a little.

'You don't love me anything like you love Ana.'

Bo stroked her bottom lip with his thumb. 'And you call *me* stubborn?' He shook his head and picked up her hand. 'Come with me.'

He loved her? Was that really what he'd said? *What?* For the first time in her life Remy couldn't think straight, couldn't think of anything but what he'd said…

'I just love you. In every way possible.'

Oh, how she wanted to believe him.

His hand was tight around hers, but when Remy saw where he was taking her she planted her feet and shook her head. She was *not* going into Ana's room—not again. She was not going to compete with a ghost and lose to a ghost… *Been there, hated that.*

She tried to tug her hand from Bo's grip but he held her tight. 'Let me go, Bo, please. I can't do this.'

'Yeah, you can. I need you to come inside with me. Trust me, Rem—please?' Bo said calmly. 'Give me a chance to explain, to put this behind us.'

She wanted to walk away, to keep her heart protected, but she couldn't resist the entreaty on his face. His eyes were steady and she hadn't seen those shutters fall once.

Bo used his other hand to open the door and Remy looked past him into the bedroom. The first thing she noticed was that the massive portrait of Ana was gone from above his bed…along with the bed and all the other furniture. Even the curtains were gone.

Remy stepped into the room and lifted her hands in confusion. 'What is it with you and bare rooms today?'

'I'm trying to make a point.' Bo leaned his shoulder into the door frame and lifted his mouth into a semi-smile. 'Ana and I only moved into this house a month before she died—did you know that?'

How would she know that since he never spoke about her?' 'No.'

'So, in reality, this isn't really her house. It's mine.'

Remy really didn't know where he was going with this. 'I'm not following you.'

'I love this house, and I'd like to carry on living here—with you. I want to share this room with you, so I stripped it.'

Remy blinked, trying to assimilate everything he was saying.

'And if you think that you might be able to live here with me, I want you to choose what goes back in this bedroom. I want this room to be our room, this house to be our home, the twins' home.'

'Uh…'

Bo ran a frustrated hand over his face. 'I'll strip the whole damn house, if that's what you need. I'll build another house, if that's what makes you feel comfortable. Hell, I'll even move into that stupid rabbit hutch you've been living in lately if that makes you happy. I just want to be with you.'

Remy looked at his emotion-filled eyes and bit her bottom lip. It would be so easy to throw herself into his arms, to surrender to the happiness that wanted to consume her, but she couldn't—not just yet. She had to be sensible…

So she stepped away from him and paced to the windows and back, wringing her hands. 'Look, Bo, I appreciate the sentiment and the gesture…'

'But…?'

'But I know that you are an intensely loyal person and that you have loved Ana for a long, long time. You say you love me now, but I don't know if you are going to change your mind again. I don't know if you love me because you want a family and this is your way to get one. I need to know that you love me for *me*. I don't want to compete with a ghost and I don't want to get hurt again. I don't know if my…' She stuttered to a stop and then forced the words out. 'If my heart can stand it.'

Bo looked at her and folded his arms. He nodded once and cocked his head. After a long silence he started to speak. 'I can't make you believe me, Rem. All I can do is tell you that I love you and that my love for you is completely and utterly separate from my love for our children. I would be begging you to love me, be with me, even if you weren't round and lovely and carrying my sons.'

'Daughters.' Remy automatically contradicted him.

Bo smiled as he walked over to her and cupped her face in his big hands. 'I loved Ana deeply, Rem. I'm not going to deny that. But I loved her when she alive and I was a different man. I've moved on, and you're here, and it's *you* that I'm utterly crazy about. You are the first thought in my head when I wake up and the last thing on my mind when I go to sleep…*you*, Remy. I love you—please believe me. Give me another chance to prove it to you.'

Remy blinked her astonishment. She was standing in an empty room, her face and her heart in the hands of this amazing man, and she was *hesitating*? What was wrong with her? She had a second chance to be happy and by God she was taking it!

She leaned back and smiled at him, suddenly totally at peace. This was how it should be, she thought. All she'd needed was this simple, sincere declaration from him and her world made complete sense.

Bo's love didn't need fanfare and parades: it was quietly deep. His love was reflected in his actions and Remy had absolutely no doubt that she would always come first in his life.

She took a deep breath and blurted out her next words. 'So when do you want to get married?'

To his credit, Bo didn't even flinch. He just brushed his lips across hers and smiled. 'Oh, so *now* you want to get married?'

Remy sent him a teasing look. 'The twins might not appreciate being illegitimate.'

Strong arms pulled her towards him. 'Not a good enough reason to get married. Give me another one,' he commanded.

Remy lifted her hand to touch his cheek. 'I love you. I want to be your wife. Is that okay?'

Bo's eyes went soft. 'That's very okay.'

Bo's mouth touched hers and Remy sighed. This was where she belonged, she thought. This was what she'd been looking for: this man, this place, this life. Standing there, in his empty bedroom, she kissed him as her hands travelled up and down his body, so grateful that she was back in his arms and back in his life.

After long, love-soaked minutes she lifted her mouth from his and placed her hands on his chest. His hands were down the back of her panties and warm on her bare flesh.

'Please tell me that the guest bedroom still has a bed?' she asked with a cocked eyebrow.

Bo bent down and scooped her off her feet, held her against his chest. 'It most definitely does. Let me show you.' Then he stopped and looked down at her, love and happiness making him look younger. 'Just promise me that you won't fall asleep midway through, okay?'

Remy grinned. 'Make it good, then.'

'Oh, I intend to. Every day for the rest of our lives, Rem.'

Now, *there* was a promise she could believe in, Remy thought as he carried her off to start the rest of their lives.

EPILOGUE

Two years later

A NEW 4D model sat on Dr Graham's desk and Bo couldn't help noticing that his wife refused to look at it. She'd refused to look at anything since she'd found out that he'd made an appointment with Henry and insisted that she have a physical.

It was all her fault for being so stubborn and refusing to consider the obvious.

'I am *not* pregnant,' she told him for the hundredth time, and he just smiled at her.

God, he loved her. He reached across, took her hand and pulled it across so that it rested on his thigh. 'So you keep telling me. But if you'd been prepared to do a test, like I asked, you wouldn't be here.'

'I am *not* pregnant,' Remy insisted, her eyes huge in her face.

She was. Of course she was. He could tell—he knew her that well. 'Would it be such a bad thing if you were, Rem?' he asked gently.

Remy rested her head on his shoulder and closed her eyes. 'Of course not… But I don't have time to be pregnant, Bo! We're expanding the Little Blue and opening the new restaurant in Calistoga. The online deli and wine shop is so *busy* and our boys run me ragged. And I sort of thought that two was it…?'

Bo just shrugged. He'd have a football team if she'd co-operate.

'Besides, I'm on the pill. There has to be another reason I'm late.'

Remy tried to glare at him but, as always, he saw the love in her eyes.

'And if I am, then it's you and your super-sperms' fault.'

Bo smiled at her machine-gun conversation. A nervous Remy was a voluble Remy, and she had yet to shut up this morning.

'Can I phone the twins?' Remy pleaded, tugging on his hand.

'No. You spoke to them fifteen minutes ago and they're fine. Ginny is spoiling them rotten on their first sleepover.'

'They're only fifteen months old!' Remy protested. 'Too young to be sleeping out of their own beds.'

She might think so, but their sons had been born hell-raisers and Bo had no doubt that they had Ginny sussed already. They were pure, undiluted energy without an off switch, bright, funny and insatiably curious, and Bo knew that they were going to keep them on their toes.

Bring it on, he thought on a grin. He couldn't wait.

He had these two wonderful boys in his life because of this amazing woman, whom he loved with every strand of DNA he had. She was his everything….

Henry Graham stepped into the room and after shaking hands with them both placed his hands on his hips. 'So…pregnant again?'

'I don't think so—he does,' Remy stated, jerking a thumb in his direction.

Henry smiled and nodded his head towards the sonar machine. 'Well, we can either do a quick pregnancy test or a quick scan. If the test shows up positive, then I'll do a scan anyway, so why don't we skip that step and you hop onto the bed and let me take a look?'

Bo felt his heartbeat accelerate as Remy lay down on the bed and unzipped her linen trousers to expose her tummy. Her body was slim and long and he loved it, but he couldn't help feel excited at thought of her blooming with life again.

Henry squirted gel onto her stomach, then placed the probe and started moving it around. Bo felt her hand sneak into his and dropped a quick kiss on her lips.

'Love you,' he stated quietly.

'Love you back,' Remy whispered, and looked towards the screen.

'Well, Bo is right, Remy—you are definitely pregnant. There's the amniotic sac and there's the heartbeat… No, wait…there's *two* heartbeats!' Henry said, laughter in his voice.

Bo sent him a quick look and Henry shook his head. He watched Remy as the words sank in. Her eyes looked shocked.

'Uh…*gumf…whaaat*? I'm actually *pregnant*? With *more twins*?'

Over her head, he and Henry exchanged conspiratorial grins. Then they heard Remy's shallow breathing.

'She's looking rather white and like she might faint. Maybe you should put her out of her misery, Bo?' Henry suggested.

Bo leaned over her and cupped her face in his hands. 'Breathe, darling. That's a joke—we're not having twins,' he told her.

She almost looked disappointed and he could relate to that.

'We're *not*?'

'But, like I repeatedly told you, we *are* having another baby.'

Remy looked at the screen and back at him, and he held his breath, waiting for her reaction. His heart resumed beating when she smiled.

'This time it had better be a girl,' she told him, her eyes finally filling with excitement. 'There's far too much testosterone in our house as it is!'

Bo rested his forehead against hers. 'And we all love you wildly.'

Remy smiled and touched his lips with hers. 'You really do.' She whispered against his mouth. 'I'm a very lucky girl.'

* * * * *

PROOF OF THEIR ONE-NIGHT PASSION

LOUISE FULLER

To Georgia.

For endlessly listening to my rants and for sending me cheering photos of chickens and rabbits.

All my love. X

CHAPTER ONE

Rubbing her eyes, Lottie Dawson drew the curtain back and gazed out of her bedroom window. The garden was in darkness, but she could hear the steady patter of the rain, and in the glow of the night light the glass was speckled with fat blobs of water.

Yawning, she glanced over at the clock beside her bed. It was only five-thirty a.m., an unpleasant hour at most times of the year, but particularly so on a cold, wet November day in rural Suffolk. But for once her eleven-month-old daughter's early-morning routine was an advantage. Today they were going to London, and she actually needed to get up.

Turning round, she glanced over to where Sóley was standing in her cot, her blonde curls flattened against her head, her mouth clamped around the edge of her teddy bear.

As Lottie walked towards her she held up her fat little arms and began dancing on the spot.

'Hi.' Leaning forward, she lifted her daughter up, pressing her body close.

Her heart swelled. She was so beautiful, so perfect. Born in December, on the shortest day of the year, she had been as golden and welcome as the unseasonal sun that had come out to celebrate her birth and inadvertently suggested her name.

'Let's go get you some milk,' she murmured, inhaling the clean, sweet smell of her daughter's skin.

Downstairs, she switched the light on in the kitchen and frowned. A frying pan sat in the sink and the remains of a bacon sandwich were congealing on a plate on the crumb-strewn table. Beside it stood an open tool box and a tattoo gun.

Lottie gritted her teeth. She loved living with her brother Lucas, and he was brilliant with Sóley, but he was six foot four, and it sometimes felt that their tiny cottage wasn't big enough for him—especially as his idea of domesticity was taking his boots off to sleep.

Tutting under her breath, she shifted Sóley's weight to her hip. 'Look at all this mess Uncle Lucas has made,' she said softly, gazing down into her daughter's wide blue eyes.

There was no time to deal with it now. Not if she was going to get herself and Sóley dressed and up to London by eleven o'clock. As she filled the kettle her pulse skipped forward. The gallery in Islington was tiny, but it was hosting her first solo show since giving birth.

Incredibly, some of the pieces had already sold and it was great to know that her work had an audience but, more importantly, the Barker Foundation wanted to talk to her about a commission. Getting funding was a huge step up. Not only would it allow her to continue working without having to teach in the evenings, but she might also be able to extend her workshop.

Glancing into the living room at the dark shape on her sofa, she imagined her brother's eye-rolling reaction to her pragmatism.

Ever since she'd bought the cottage he'd been teasing her about selling out, joking that getting a mortgage was the first step towards the dark side. As far as he and their mother Izzy knew the money had come from a private commission, and Lucas had a very dim view of private clients believing they were only interested in buying art as an investment rather than out of aesthetic appreciation.

She bit her lip. She hated lying to them, but telling the truth—that the deposit for the cottage had been given to her by her biological father, a man who up until two years ago hadn't even known she existed—was just not an option.

Having tested the milk on her tongue, she handed the bottle to Sóley and they both retreated upstairs. Pulling open drawers, she thought back to the moment when she had finally met Alistair Bannon in a motorway service station.

Her stomach clenched. She'd spent so many hours as a child staring into a mirror, trying to work out which of her features came from that man, but even before he had opened his mouth it had been obvious that he was not looking to reconnect with a fully-grown daughter. It wasn't that he didn't accept her as his child—just that he felt no urgency to know her, and their meeting had been strange and strained and short.

From downstairs, she heard the clump of boots hitting the floor. Lucas was up.

She wondered how her brother would react if she showed him the letter her father had sent afterwards. It was polite, carefully worded to offer no obvious rejection but no hope either, basically saying she was a remarkable young woman and he wished her well. Enclosed with the letter had been a cheque for an amount that he hoped would cover his financial contributions for the years he had missed.

Staring at his signature on the cheque, she had felt sick, stunned that she could be reduced to a four-digit sum, and she'd been tempted to tear it up. Only then she'd got pregnant.

Stripping off, she gazed down at her naked body, at the silvery stretch marks that were still faintly visible on her stomach.

Becoming a mother had been so far away in her future plans that she hadn't even suspected she was pregnant but, having been unable to shift a persistent stomach upset she had gone to the doctor, and three days and one urine sample later she had officially been having a baby.

A baby who, like her, was going to grow up never knowing her father. She still wasn't entirely sure how it had happened. They had used protection, but that first time had been so frantic, so urgent, somehow it must have failed.

Shivering, she pulled on her clothes, trying to ignore the sudden thumping of her heart.

She could still remember the night her daughter was conceived. She doubted she would ever forget it. It was like a fever in her blood. The heat and the frenzy had faded, but the memory remained in her bones and on her skin, so that sometimes she'd catch sight of the back of a blond head and a pair of wide shoulders and would have to stop and close her eyes against the urgency of wanting him.

Ragnar Steinn.

She would never forget him either.

It would be impossible.

It would be like trying to forget the sun.

But, despite having the muscular body and clean-cut profile of a Norse god, he had shown himself to be depressingly human in his behaviour. Not only had he lied about where he was staying, and about wanting to spend the day with her, he'd sneaked off before she'd woken up.

And yet together they had made Sóley, and no amount of lies or hardship or loneliness would ever make her regret her beautiful daughter.

'Looks like we've got snow coming,' Lucas said as she walked into the tiny sitting room, holding Sóley on her hip and munching a piece of toast.

He had switched on the ancient television and was wolfing down the remains of his bacon sandwich.

Catching sight of her expression, he grinned sheepishly. 'Sorry about the mess. Look, I'll tidy up, I promise, and I'll chop that wood today. Get it all stacked before the temperatures drop. Do you want me to have little Miss Sunshine?'

She shook her head. 'No, but you could give us a lift to the station.'

'Okay—but only if I get a cuddle.'

He held up his hands and Sóley leaned towards him, grabbing at his shirt collar. Watching her brother's face soften Lottie felt her anger and resentment fade as he pulled the little girl into his arms, wincing as she reached for his hair and grabbed it tightly in her fist.

Unpeeling her fingers, he handed his niece a piece of banana and glanced up at his sister. 'You couldn't put the kettle on as you're up—?'

Glancing at the clock on the wall, Lottie did a quick calculation in her head. There was time before she had to leave. She sighed. 'I'll make some tea.'

Rinsing out the teapot, she put the kettle on the stove.

'You know, I think Sóley is a lot more with it than most kids her age,' she heard Lucas say.

'You do?' Smiling, she poured water into the pot. For someone so laid-back, her brother was extremely partisan and competitive when it came to his niece.

'Yeah—I mean, she's watching the news like she knows what's going on.'

'Good. That means we can outvote you when the football's on.'

'No, seriously, she's completely transfixed by this guy—Lottie, come and look.'

'Okay, I'm coming.'

Walking back into the sitting room, she looked over to where her daughter had pulled herself up in front of the television.

Lucas was right, Sóley did seem to be fascinated. Pulling her gaze away from her daughter's plump cheeks, Lottie glanced at the screen.

The interviewer—a woman—was gazing at the man opposite her with the same fascination as her daughter, so that for a moment Lottie only registered his blond hair and eyes that were the cool, clear blue of a glacier. Then slowly his features came into focus and she felt her mouth slide open.

It was him.

It was Ragnar.

She had wanted to find him after she'd found out she was pregnant, and then again when their daughter was born. But both of them had shut down their profiles on the dating app they'd used to meet up, and there had been no trace of any Ragnar Steinn—or at least none that looked like him—on any internet search.

Her jaw tensed. Not that it would have changed anything if she had managed to get in touch. His clumsy lies had made it clear enough that he'd only been interested in her for one night only, so he was hardly going to jump at the news that he'd fathered a child with her.

She watched mutely, ice working its way up her spine, as Sóley began patting the screen. Her heart was jumping in her chest.

'Who is he?' she asked. 'I mean, why is he on TV?'

She had been aiming for offhand, but her voice sounded thin and breathless.

Thankfully, though, Lucas was too distracted to notice.

'Ragnar Stone. He owns that dating app. Apparently he's launching a VIP version.'

'Dating app?' she said woodenly. It felt as if she had stopped breathing.

She was about to ask which one, but there was no point. She already knew the answer. Only she'd thought he was like her—someone using the app to meet people. She hadn't known that he owned it—in fact, thinking about it, she was certain that he hadn't mentioned that to her.

'You know—*ice/breakr*?'

Lucas glanced up at her, and she watched his face still as his brain caught up with his mouth.

'Course you do…' he said quietly.

It had been Lucas who had signed her up to the app. Lucas who had coaxed her into replying to the 'ice breaker' question. It could be on any topic from politics to holidays. Not all of the questions were profound, but they were designed to spark an instinctive response that apparently helped match couples more accurately than a photo and a list of likes and dislikes. She knew he felt responsible for everything that had happened, but she was too stunned and angry to dismiss his obvious guilt.

Ragnar *Stone*!

So he'd even lied about his name.

And he hadn't just been using the app—*he owned it.*

She breathed out unsteadily, trying to absorb this new version of the facts as she'd known them, grateful that her brother's attention was still fixed on the TV and not on her face. Grateful, too, that she hadn't shown him Ragnar's profile at the time.

Her skin was trembling.

'Is he in London?' she asked.

'Yeah, for the launch. He's got an office here.' Lucas wiped Sóley's mouth with the hem of his shirt and met her gaze. 'One of those converted warehouses in Docklands. You know Nick?'

She nodded. Nick was one of Lucas's cohorts. He played drums in their band, but in his day job he was a graffiti artist.

'He did this huge old-school design the whole length of Ragnar Stone's building. He showed me some pictures and it looks really sick.' He nodded his head approvingly.

Lottie cleared her throat. 'Did he meet him?'

Lucas frowned. 'Nah. Best you can hope with a guy like Stone is that you catch a ride on his slipstream.'

She blinked. Yes, she supposed it was. That was basically what had happened twenty months ago in her hotel room. If she hadn't understood that before, her brother's words made it clear now that she and Sóley were not permanent features of that ride.

'So what time do you want me to drop you off?'

Taking a shallow breath, she looked over at her brother, but her eyes never reached his face. Instead she felt her gaze stretch past him to the TV screen, like a compass point seeking the magnetic north. She stared at Ragnar's face, the artist in her responding to the clean symmetry of his features and the woman in her remembering the pressure of his mouth. He was so beautiful, and so very like his blonde, blue-eyed daughter in every way—except the dimples in her cheeks, which were entirely her own.

She felt something twist inside her. What if it was more than just looks? Growing up not knowing where half her DNA came from had been hard when her mother and brother were so alike in character. It had made her feel incomplete and unfinished, and even finally meeting her father hadn't changed that. It had been too late for them to form a bond and get to know one another.

But would it have been different if he'd found out about her when she was a baby? And, more importantly, could she consciously deny her own child the chance of having what she had so desperately wanted for herself?

The seconds ticked by as she wondered what to do. He would have a PA for sure—only she couldn't tell them why she was ringing. But would they put her through to him without a reason? She bit her lip. More importantly, could she honestly go through with it? Tell him over the phone that he was a father?

She cleared her throat. 'Actually, Lucas, could you have Sóley for me after all?' she said, glancing over at her daughter. 'There's something I need to do. In person.'

* * *

Being interviewed was probably his least favourite part of being a CEO, Ragnar Stone decided, as he stood up and shook hands with the earnest-faced young man in front of him. It was so repetitive, and most of the answers could easily have been given by even the most junior member of his PR department. But, as his head of media Madeline Thomas had told him that morning, people were 'in thrall to the personality behind the brand', so he had dutifully worked his way through twenty-two interviews with just a half-hour break for lunch.

And now he was done.

Shrugging off his jacket, he loosened his tie and pulled a black hoodie over his head as his PA Adam came into the room.

'What time is the car coming to pick me up in the morning?' he asked, reaching down to pick up a slim laptop from his desk.

'Six-thirty. You have a meeting with James Milner at seven, you're seeing the graphics team at eight, and then breakfast with Caroline Woodward.'

'I'll see you tomorrow.' Ragnar smiled briefly at his PA. 'And thanks for keeping it moving today, Adam.'

Stepping into the lift, he ran his hand over his face. Only one more week and then, once this final round of publicity was over and the new app went live, he was going to take some time away from all this.

He knew he'd left it too long. His annual two-week recharge ritual had dwindled to a couple of snatched days, but since launching *ice/breakr* two years ago life had been insane.

Working long hours, eating and sleeping on the move in a series of hotel rooms, and of course in the background his gorgeous, crazy, messy family, acting out their own modern-day Norse saga of betrayal and blackmail.

Glancing down at his phone, he grimaced. Three missed calls from his half-sister Marta, four from his mother, six texts from his stepmother Anna, and twelve from his step-brother Gunnar.

Stretching his neck and shoulders, he slipped his phone into the pocket of his hoodie. None of it would be urgent. It never was. But, like all drama queens, his family loved an audience.

For once they could wait. Right now he wanted to hit the gym and then crash out.

The lift doors opened and he flipped his hood up over his head, nodding at the receptionists as he walked past their desk and out into the dark night air.

He didn't hear their polite murmurs of goodnight, but he heard the woman's voice so clearly that it seemed to come from inside his head.

'Ragnar.'

In the moment that followed he realised two things. One, he recognised the voice, and two, his heart was beating hard and fast like a hailstorm against his ribs.

As he turned he got an impression of slightness, coupled with tension, and then his eyes focused on the woman standing in front of him.

Her light brown hair was longer, her pale face more wary, but she looked just as she had twenty-odd months ago. And yet she seemed different in a way he couldn't pin down. Younger, maybe? Or perhaps she just looked younger because most of the women in his circles routinely wore make-up, whereas she was bare-faced.

'I was just passing. I've got an exhibition up the road…' She waved vaguely towards the window. 'I saw you coming out.' She hesitated. 'I don't know if you remember me…?'

'I remember.'

He cut across her, but only because hearing her voice was messing with his head. It was a voice he had never forgotten—a voice that had called out his name under very different circumstances in a hotel room less than a mile away from where they were standing.

He watched her pupils dilate, and knew that she was thinking the same thing.

For a second they stared at one another, the memory of the night they shared quivering between them, and then, leaning forward, he gave her a quick, neutral hug.

Or it was meant to be neutral, but as his cheek brushed against hers the warm, floral scent of her skin made his whole body hum like a power cable.

Stepping back, he gave her a small, taut smile and something pulsed between them, a flicker of corresponding heat that made his skin grow tight.

'Of course I remember. It's Lottie—Lottie Dawson.'

'Yes, that's *my* name.'

Seeing the accusation in her eyes, he felt his chest tighten, remembering the lies he'd told her. It wasn't hard to remember. Growing up in the truth-shifting environment of his family had left him averse to lying, but that night had been an exception—a necessary and understandable exception. He'd met her through a dating app, but as the app's creator and owner, anonymity had seemed like a sensible precaution.

But his lies hadn't all been about concealing his identity. His family's chaotic and theatrical affairs had left him wary of even the hint of a relationship, so when he'd woken to find himself planning the day ahead with Lottie he'd got up quietly and left—because planning a day with a woman was not on his agenda.

Ever.

His life was already complicated enough. He had parents and step-parents, and seven whole and half-and step siblings scattered around the world, and not one of them had made a relationship last for any length of time. Not only that, their frequent and overlapping affairs and break-ups, and the inevitable pain and misery they caused, seemed to be an unavoidable accompaniment to any kind of commitment.

He liked life to be straightforward. Simple. Honest. It was why he'd created *ice/breakr* in the first place. Why make dating so needlessly confusing? When by asking and answering one carefully curated question people could match their expectations and so avoid any unnecessary emotional trauma.

Or that was the theory.

Only clearly there been some kind of glitch—a ghost in the machine, maybe?

'So it's not Steinn, then?'

His eyes met hers. She was not classically beautiful, but she was intriguing. Both ordinary and extraordinary at once. Mousy hair, light brown eyes… And yet her face had a capacity for expression that was mesmerising.

And then there was her voice.

It wasn't just the huskiness that made his skin tingle, but the way she lingered over the syllables of certain words, like a blues singer. Had he judged her simply on her voice, he might have assumed she had a lifestyle to match—too many late nights and a history of heartache, but their night together had revealed a lack of confidence and a clumsiness that suggested the opposite. Not that he'd asked or minded. In fact it had only made her feverish response to him even more arousing.

Feeling his body respond to the memory of her flowering desire, he blocked his thoughts and shrugged. 'In a way it is. Steinn is Icelandic for Stone. It was just a play on words.'

Her eyes held his. 'Oh, you mean like calling your dating app *ice/breakr*?'

So she knew about the app. 'I wanted to try it out for myself. A dummy run, if you like.'

She flinched and he felt his shoulders tense.

'I didn't intend to deceive you.'

'About that? Or about wanting to spend the day with me?' She frowned. 'Wouldn't it have been fairer and more honest if you'd just said you didn't want to spend any more time with me?'

Ragnar stared at her in silence, gritting his teeth against the sting of her words. Yes, it would. But that would have been a different kind of lie.

Lying didn't come naturally to him—his whole family played fast and loose with the facts and even as a child he'd found it exhausting and stressful. But that night he'd acted out of character, starting from the moment he'd played games with his American father's name and booked a table as Mr Steinn.

And then, the morning after, confronted by his body's fierce reaction to hers, and that uncharacteristic and unsettling need he'd felt to prolong their time together, the lies had kept coming.

'I didn't—'

'It doesn't matter.' She swiped his answer away with a swift jerk of her hand. 'That's not why I'm here.' She glanced past him into the street. 'There's a café open down the road…'

He knew it. It was one of those brightly lit artisan coffee shops with bearded baristas and clean wooden counters. Nothing like the shadowy, discreet bar where they'd met before.

His heartbeat stalled. He could still remember her walking in. It had been one of those sharply cold March evenings that reminded him of home, and there had been a crush of people at the bar, escaping the wind's chill.

He'd been on the verge of leaving.

A combination of work and family histrionics had shrunk his private life to early-morning sessions with his trainer and the occasional dinner with an investor when, finally, it had dawned on him that his app had been launched for nearly three months.

On a whim, he'd decided to try it out.

But, watching the couples dotted about the bar, he had felt a familiar unease clutch at his stomach.

Out of habit, he'd got there early. It was a discipline he embraced—perhaps because since childhood any chance to assemble his thoughts in peace had always been such a rarity. But when Lottie had walked through the door rational thought had been swept away. Her cheeks had been flushed, and she'd appeared to be wearing nothing but a pair of slim-heeled boots and a short black trench coat.

Sadly she'd been clothed underneath but he'd stayed sitting down. If using his own dating app had been impulsive, then not leaving by another door had been the first time he'd done something so utterly unconsidered.

'And you want me to join you there?'

Her eyes met his and there was a beat of silence before she nodded.

His pulse accelerated.

It was nearly two years since that night.

He was exhausted.

His head of security would be appalled.

And yet—

His eyes rested on the soft cushion of her mouth.

The coffee shop was still busy enough that they had to queue for their drinks, but they managed to find a table.

'Thank you.' He gestured towards his *espresso.*

His wallet had been in his hand, but she had sidestepped neatly in front of him, her soft brown eyes defying him to argue with her. Now, though, those same brown eyes were busily avoiding his, and for the first time since she'd called out his name he wondered why she had tracked him down.

He drank his coffee, relishing the heat and the way the caffeine started to block the tension in his back.

'So, I'm all yours,' he said quietly.

She stiffened. 'Hardly.'

He sighed. 'Is that what this is about? Me giving you the wrong name.'

Her eyes narrowed. 'No, of course not. I'm not—' She stopped, frowning. 'Actually, I wasn't just passing, and I'm not here for myself.' She took a breath. 'I'm here for Sóley.'

Her face softened into a smile and he felt a sudden urge to reach out and caress the curve of her lip, to trigger such a smile for himself.

'It's a pretty name.'

She nodded, her smile freezing.

It *was* a pretty name—one he'd always liked. One you didn't hear much outside of Iceland. Only what had it got to do with him?

Watching her fingers tremble against her cup, he felt his ribs tighten. 'Who's Sóley?'

She was quiet for less than a minute, only it felt much longer—long enough for his brain to click through all the possible answers to the impossible one.

He watched her posture change from defensive to resolute.

'She's your daughter. Our daughter.'

He stared at her in silence, but a cacophony of questions was ricocheting inside his head.

Not the how or the when or the where, but the *why*. Of course he'd used condoms but that first time he'd been rushing. And he'd known that. So why hadn't he checked everything was okay? Why had he allowed the heat of their encounter to blot out common sense?

But the answers to those questions would have to wait.

'Okay…'

Shifting in her seat, she frowned. '"Okay"?' she repeated. 'Do you understand what I just said?'

'Yes.' He nodded. 'You're saying I got you pregnant.'

'You don't seem surprised,' she said slowly.

He shrugged. 'These things happen.'

To his siblings and half-siblings, even to his mother. But not to him. Never to him.

Until now.

'And you believe me?' She seemed confused, surprised?

Tilting his head, he held her gaze. 'Honest answer?'

He was going to ask her what she would gain by lying. But before he could open his mouth her lip curled.

'On past performance I'm not sure I can expect that. I mean, you lied about your name. And the hotel you were staying at. And you lied about wanting to spend the day with me.'

'I didn't plan on lying to you,' he said quietly.

Her mouth thinned. 'No, I'm sure it comes very naturally to you.'

'You're twisting my words.'

She shook her head. 'You mean like saying Steinn instead of Stone?'

Pressing his spine into the wall behind him, he felt a tick of anger begin to pulse beneath his skin.

'Okay, I was wrong to lie to you—but if you care about the truth so much then why have you waited so long to tell me that I have a daughter? I mean, she must be what…?' He did a quick mental calculation. 'Ten, eleven months?'

'Eleven months,' she said stiffly. 'And I did want to tell you. I tried looking for you when I was pregnant, and then again when she was born. But the only Ragnar Steinns I could track down weren't you.' She shifted in her seat again. 'I probably would never have found you if you hadn't been on the TV.'

He looked at her again, and despite the rush of righteousness heating his blood he could see that she was nervous, could hear the undertone of strain beneath her bravado.

But then it was a hell of a thing to do. To face a man and tell him he had a child.

His heart began to beat faster.

Years spent navigating through the maelstrom of his family's dramas had given him a cast-iron control over his feelings, and yet for some reason he couldn't stop her panic and defiance from getting under his skin.

But letting feelings get in the way of the facts was not going to help the situation. Nor was it going to be much use to his eleventh-month-old daughter.

Right now he needed to focus on the practical.

'Fortunately you did find me,' he said calmly.

'Here.' She was pushing something across the table towards him, but he carried on talking.

'So I'm guessing you want to talk money?'

At that moment a group of young men and women came into the café and began noisily choosing what to drink. As the noise swelled around them Lottie thought she might have misheard.

Only she knew that she hadn't.

Ever since arriving in London that morning she'd been questioning whether she was doing the right thing, and the thought of seeing Ragnar again had made her stomach perform an increasingly complicated gymnastics routine. Her mood had kept alternating between angry and nervous, but when he'd walked out into the street her mood had been forgotten and a spasm of almost unbearable hunger had consumed everything.

If she'd thought seeing him on TV had prepared her for meeting him again then she'd been wrong. Beneath the street lighting his beauty had been as stark and shocking as the volcanic rock of his homeland.

And he was almost unbearably like the daughter they shared. Only now it would appear that, just like her own father, Ragnar seemed to have already decided the terms of his relationship.

'Money?' She breathed out unsteadily. The word tasted bitter in her mouth. 'I didn't come here to talk to you about money. I came here to talk about our daughter.'

Her heart felt suddenly too big for her chest. Why did this keep happening? Why did men think that they could reduce her life to some random sum of money?

'Children cost money.' He held her gaze. 'Clearly you've been supporting her alone up until now and I want to fix that. I'll need to talk to my lawyers, but I want you to know that you don't need to worry about that anymore.'

I'm not worrying, she wanted to scream at him. She wasn't asking to be helped financially, or fixed. In fact she wasn't asking for anything at all.

'I've not been alone. My mother helps, and my brother Lucas lives with me. He works as a tattooist so he can choose his own hours—'

'A tattooist?'

Glancing up, she found his clear blue eyes examining her dispassionately, as if she was some flawed algorithm. She felt slightly sick—just as she had in those early months of the pregnancy. Only that had been a welcome sickness. A proof of new life, a sign of a strong pregnancy. Now, though, the sickness was down to the disconnect between the man who had reached for her so frantically in that hotel room and this cool-eyed stranger.

She stared at him in silence.

What made this strange, unnerving distance between them a hundred times harder was that she had let herself be distracted by his resemblance to Sóley. Let herself hope that the connection between Ragnar and his daughter would be more than it had been for her and her own father—not just bones and blood, but a willingness to claim her as his own.

But the cool, dispassionate way he had turned the conversation immediately to money was proof that he'd reached the limit of his parental involvement.

She cleared her throat. 'I know you're a rich man, Ragnar, but I didn't come here to beg.' She swallowed down her regret and disappointment. 'This was a mistake. Don't worry, though, it's not one I'll make again—so why don't you get back to the thing that clearly matters most to you? Making money.'

Ragnar reached across the table, but even before he'd got to his feet she had scraped back her seat and snatched up her coat, and he watched in disbelief as she turned and fled from the cafe.

For a moment he considered chasing after her, but she was moving fast and no doubt would already have reached the underground station on the corner.

He sat back down; his chest tight with an all too familiar frustration.

Her behaviour—having a child with a complete stranger, keeping that child a secret, turning up unannounced to reveal the child's existence and then storming off—could have come straight from his family's playbook of chaos.

Glancing down, he felt his pulse scamper forward as for the first time he looked at what she'd pushed across the table. It was a photo of a little girl.

A little girl who looked exactly like him—Sóley.

Reaching out, he touched her face lightly. She was so small, so golden, just like her name. And he was not going to let her grow up with no influence but her chaotic mother and whatever ragtag family she had in tow.

He might love his own family, but he knew only too well

the downside of growing up in the eye of a storm and he didn't want that for his daughter.

So arrangements would have to be made.

Picking up the photo, he slid it into his wallet and pulled out his phone.

CHAPTER TWO

HITCHING HER SLEEPING daughter further up on to her shoulder, Lottie glanced around the gallery.

Groups of people were moving slowly around the room, occasionally pausing to gaze more closely at the sketches and collages and sculpted resin objects before moving on again. It wasn't rammed, but she was pleased—she really was. She was also exhausted.

'Nearly over.'

She turned, eyes widening, and then began to smile as the woman standing beside her gave her a conspiratorial wink. Slim, blonde, and with the kind of cheekbones that grazed men's eyes as they walked past, Georgina Hamilton was the gallery's glamorous and incredibly competent co-owner, and despite the fact that she and Lottie were different in as many ways as it was possible to be, she had become an ally and fierce supporter.

Lottie screwed up her face. 'Do I look that desperate?'

Her friend stared at her critically. 'Only to me. To everyone else you probably just look artistically dishevelled.' She glanced at the sleeping Sóley. 'Do you want me to take her?'

Their eyes met and then they both began to giggle. They both knew that Georgina's idea of hands-on childcare was choosing baby clothes in her cousin's upmarket Chelsea boutique.

'No, it's okay. I don't want to risk waking her.' Lottie looked down at the top of her daughter's soft, golden-haired head. 'She's been really unsettled the last couple of nights.'

And she wasn't the only one.

Her cheeks were suddenly warm, and she tilted her head away from Georgina's gaze. It was true that Sóley was struggling to fall asleep at night, but it was Ragnar who had actually been keeping her awake.

It wasn't just the shock of seeing him again, or even his disappointingly predictable reduction of their daughter's life to a financial settlement. It was the disconcerting formality between them.

She pressed her face into her daughter's hair. The disconnect between her overtly erotic memories of the last time they'd met and his cool reserve in the coffee shop had made her feel as if she'd stepped through the looking glass. He had been at once so familiar, and yet so different. Gone was the passion and the febrile hunger, and in their place was a kind of measured, almost clinical gaze that had made her feel she was being judged—and found wanting.

Her heartbeat twitched. And yet running alongside their laboured conversation there had been something pulsing beneath the surface—a stirring of desire, something intimate yet intangible that had made her fingers clumsy as she'd tried to pick up her cup.

She blinked the thought away. Of course what had happened between them had clearly been a blip. After all, this was a man who had turned people's need for intimacy into a global business worth billions—an ambition that was hardly compatible with empathy or passion.

Her jaw tightened. What was it he'd said about that night? Oh, yes, that it had been a 'dummy run' for his app. Well, *she* was a dummy for thinking he might have actually wanted to get to know his daughter.

From now on she was done with doing the right thing for the wrong people. She was only going to let the people she could trust get close—like the woman standing in front of her.

'Thanks for staying, Georgina, and for everything you've done. I honestly don't think I would have sold as well if you hadn't been here.'

Swinging her cape of gleaming blonde hair over her shoulder, Georgina smiled back at her. 'Oh, sweetie, you don't need to thank me—firstly, it's my job, and secondly it's much better for the gallery to have a sold-out exhibition.'

'Sold out?' She blinked in confusion. 'But I thought there were still three pieces left—those sketches and the collage—?'

Georgina shrugged. 'Not any more. Rowley's contacted me at lunchtime and bought all of them.'

Lottie felt her ribs tighten. Rowley's was a prestigious art dealer with a Mayfair address and a client list of wealthy investors who flitted between Beijing, New York, and London, spending millions on houses and cars and emerging artists.

They also had an unrivalled reputation for discretion.

She opened her mouth, but Georgina was already shaking her head.

'No, they didn't give me a name.' She raised an eyebrow. 'You don't look very pleased.'

'I am,' Lottie protested.

After finding out she was pregnant, working had been a welcome distraction from the upheaval in her life, but it had quickly become much more.

She glanced at the visitors who were still drifting around the gallery. 'I just prefer to meet the buyers directly.'

'I know you do—but you know what these collectors are like. They love to have the cachet of buying up-and-coming artists' early work, but they love their anonymity more.' Georgina tutted. 'I know you hate labels, but you are up-and-coming. If you don't believe me then believe your own eyes. You can see all the "Sold" stickers from here.' Watching Lottie shift her daughter's weight to her other arm, she said, 'Are you sure I can't take her?'

Lottie shook her head. 'It's fine. They must be on their way. I mean, Lucas was supposed to meet Izzy at the station and then they were coming straight back.'

Georgina sniffed. She was not a huge fan of Lottie's family. 'Yes, well… I expect they got "distracted".' She smoothed the front of her sculpted nip and tuck dress, and then her eyes narrowed like a tigress spotting her prey. 'Oh, my…' she said softly.

'What's the matter?' Lottie frowned.

'Don't look now but an incredibly hot guy has just walked into the gallery. He has the most amazing eyes I've ever seen."

Lottie shook her head. No doubt they were fixed on the woman standing beside her.

'Ouch.' She winced as Georgina clutched at her arm.

'He's coming over to us.'

'To you, you mean—and of course he is,' Lottie said drily. 'He's male.'

Georgina had the most incredible effect on men, and she was used to simply filling the space beside her.

'He's not looking at me,' Georgina said slowly. She sounded stunned. 'He's looking at *you*.'

Lottie laughed. 'Perhaps he hasn't put his contact lenses in this morning. Or maybe he—'

She turned and her words stopped mid-sentence. Her body seemed to turn to salt. Walking towards her, his blue eyes pinning her to the floor, was Ragnar Stone.

She stared at him mutely as he stopped in front of her. He was dressed more casually than when she'd stopped him outside his office, but such was the force of his presence that suddenly the gallery seemed much smaller and there was a shift in tension, as though everyone was looking at him while trying to appear as though they weren't.

His blue eyes really were incredibly blue, she thought weakly. But Georgina had been wrong. He wasn't looking at her. Instead, his eyes were fixed on his daughter. For a few half-seconds, maybe more, he gazed at Sóley, his face expressionless and unmoving, and then slowly he turned his head towards her.

'Hello, Lottie.'

She stared at him silence, her heartbeat filling her chest, her grip tightening around her daughter's body. In the café there had been so much noise, but here in the near museum-level quiet of the gallery his voice was making her body quiver like a violin being tuned.

It was completely illogical and inappropriate, but that didn't stop it being true.

'Hello, Ragnar,' she said stiffly. 'I wasn't expecting to see you.'

She wasn't sure what kind of a response he would make to her remark, but maybe he felt the same way because he didn't reply.

'So you two know one another, then?' Georgina said brightly.

'Yes.'

'No!'

They both spoke as one—him quietly, her more loudly.

Lottie felt her cheeks grow warm. 'We met once a couple of years back,' she said quickly.

'Just shy of two years.'

Ragnar's blue eyes felt like lasers.

There was a short, strained silence and then Georgina cleared her throat. 'Well, I'll let you catch up on old times.'

Clearly dazzled by Ragnar's beauty, she smiled at him sweetly and, blind to Lottie's pleading expression, sashayed towards an immaculately dressed couple on the other side of the room.

'How did you find me?' she said stiffly. Her heart bumped unsteadily against her ribs. She was still processing the fact that he had come here.

He held her gaze. 'Oh, I was just passing.'

Remembering the lie she'd told, she glared at him. 'Did you have me followed?'

Something flickered across the blue of his pupils. 'Not followed, no—but I did ask my head of security to locate the exhibition you mentioned.'

A pulse was beating in her head. His being here was just so unexpected. Almost as unexpected as the feeling of happiness that was fluttering in time to her heart.

'Aren't you going to introduce me?'

For a moment she gazed at Ragnar in confusion. Was he talking about Georgina? A mixture of disbelief and jealousy twisted her breathing. Was he really using this moment to hit on another woman?

'Her name's Georgina. She's—'

'Not her.'

She heard the tension in his voice before she noticed it in the rigidity of his jaw.

'My daughter.'

Her heart shrank inside her ribs.

In the twenty-four hours since she'd left Ragnar, and his unsolicited offer of financial help, she'd tried hard to arrange her emotions into some kind of order. They hadn't responded. Instead she had kept struggling with the same anger and disappointment she'd felt after meeting her father. But at least she had been able to understand if not excuse Alistair's reluctance to get involved. Meeting an adult daughter he hadn't even known existed was never going to be easy, but Sóley wasn't even one yet.

Okay, at first maybe she would have been a little cautious around him—although remembering her daughter's transfixed gaze when Ragnar had come on the television screen maybe not. But even if she had been understandably hesitant it would have passed, and he could have become a father to her.

Only he'd immediately turned their relationship into a

balance sheet. Or that was what she'd thought he'd done. But if that was the case then what was he doing here, asking to be introduced to his daughter?

There was only one way to find out. She cleared her throat. 'What do you want, Ragnar?'

'Exactly what I wanted yesterday evening,' he said softly. 'Only instead of giving me the chance to explain you used the moment to have some kind of temper tantrum.'

She stared at him, a pulse of anger hopping over her skin. 'I did give you a chance and you offered me money,' she snapped. 'And if that's why you're here then you've wasted your time. I told you I didn't want your money and nothing's changed.'

'That's not your choice to make.' He held her gaze. 'I mean, what kind of mother turns down financial help for her child?'

She felt her cheeks grow hot. He was twisting her words. That wasn't what had happened. Or maybe it was, but it hadn't been about her turning down his money as much as proving him wrong about her motive for getting in touch.

'I wasn't turning down your money—just your assumption that it was what I wanted,' she said carefully. 'You made me feel cheap.'

His face didn't change. 'So what did you want from me?'

His question caught her off-guard. Not because she didn't know the answer—she did. Partly she had wanted to do the right thing, but also she knew what it had felt like to grow up without any knowledge of her father, and she had wanted to spare her daughter that sense of always feeling on the outside, looking in.

Only it felt odd admitting something so personal to a man who was basically a stranger.

'You're her father. I wanted you to know that,' she said finally. 'I wanted you to know her.' Her voice shook a little as she glanced down at her still sleeping daughter. 'She's so happy and loving, and so interested in everything going on around her.'

'Is that why you brought her to the gallery?'

She frowned, the tension in her stomach nipping tighter. 'Yes, it is,' she said defensively.

He might simply have been making polite conversation, but there was an undercurrent in his voice that reminded her of the moment when she'd told him that Lucas was a tattooist. But how could a man like Ragnar understand her loving but unconventional family? He had made a career of turning the spontaneity of human chemistry into a flow chart.

'I'm an artist *and* a mother. I'm not going to pretend that my daughter isn't a part of my life, nor do I see why I should have to.'

His eyes flickered—or maybe it was the light changing as a bus momentarily passed in front of the gallery's windows.

'I agree,' he said, his gaze shifting from his daughter's sleeping face to one of Lottie's opaque, resin sculptures. 'Being a mother doesn't define you. But it brings new contours to your work. Not literally.' He gave her a small, tight smile. 'But in how it's shaping who you are as an artist.'

Lottie felt her heart press against her ribs. The first time they had met they hadn't really discussed their careers. It felt strange to admit it, given what had happened later in the evening but they hadn't talked about anything personal, and yet it had felt as though their conversation had flowed.

Perhaps she had just been carried along by the energy in the bar, or more likely it had been the rush of adrenalin at having finally gone on a date through the app Lucas had found.

She'd had boyfriends—nothing serious or long-lasting, just the usual short-term infatuation followed by disbelief that she had ever found the object of her affections in any way attractive. But after her meeting with Alistair she had felt crushed, rejected.

Unlovable.

Perhaps if she'd been able to talk to her mother or brother about her feelings it would have been easier, but she'd already felt disloyal, going behind their backs. And why upset them when it had all been for nothing?

Her biological father's panicky need to get back to his life had made her feel ashamed of who she was, and that feeling of not being good enough to deserve his love had coloured her confidence with men generally.

Until Ragnar.

Her pulse twitched. Her nerves had been jangling like a car alarm when she'd walked into the bar. But when Ragnar had stood up in front of her, with his long dark coat curling around his ankles like a cape, her nerves had been swept away not just by his beauty, but his composure. The noisy, shifting mass of people had seemed to fall back so that it was just the two of them in a silence that had felt like a held breath.

She had never felt such a connection with anyone—certainly not with any man. For her—and she'd thought for him too—that night had been an acknowledgement of that feeling and she'd never wanted it to end. In the wordless oblivion of their passion he had made her feel strong and desirable.

Now, though, he felt like a stranger, and she could hardly believe that they had created a child together.

Her ribs squeezed tightly as Sóley wriggled against her and then went limp as she plugged her thumb into her mouth.

'So why are you here?' she said quietly.

'I want to be a part of my daughter's life—and, yes that includes contributing financially, but more importantly I want to have a hands-on involvement in co-parenting her.'

Co-parenting.

The word ricocheted inside her head.

Her throat seemed to have shrunk, so that suddenly it was difficult to breathe, and her heart was leaping erratically like a fish on a hook.

But why? He was offering her exactly what she'd thought she wanted for her daughter, wasn't he?

She felt Sóley move against her again, and instantly her panic increased tenfold.

The truth was that she hadn't really thought about anything beyond Ragnar's initial reaction to finding out he was a father. The memory of her own father's glazed expression of shock and panic had still been uppermost in her mind when she'd found out she was pregnant, and that was what she'd wanted to avoid by getting in touch with Ragnar while their daughter was still tiny.

But had she thought beyond the moment of revelation? Had she imagined him being a hands-on presence in Sóley's life? No, not really. She'd been so self-righteous about Ragnar's deceit, but now it turned out that she had been deceiving herself the whole time—telling herself that she'd got in touch because she wanted him in her daughter's life when really it had been as much about rewriting that uncomfortable, unsatisfactory scene between herself and Alistair.

And now, thanks to her stupidity and short-sightedness, she'd let someone into her life she barely knew or liked who had an agenda that was unlikely to be compatible with hers.

'I don't know how we could make that work—' she began.

But Ragnar wasn't listening. He was staring as though mesmerised at his daughter's face. And, with shock, she realised that Sóley was awake and was staring back at her father. Her heart contracted. Their blue eyes were so alike.

'Hey,' he said softly to his daughter. 'May I?'

His eyes flickered briefly to hers and without realising

that she was even doing so she nodded slowly, holding her breath as he held out his hand to Sóley.

Watching her tiny hand clasp his thumb, she felt the same pride and panic she'd felt back in the cottage, when her daughter had been transfixed by Ragnar's face. Whatever *she* felt for him they were father and daughter, and their bond was unassailable.

His next words made it clear that his thoughts were following the same path.

'We need to sit down and talk about what happens next.'

'What happens next...?' she repeated slowly.

He nodded. 'Obviously we'll need to sort out something legal, but right now I'd like us to be on the same page.'

From somewhere outside in the street a swell of uncontrollable laughter burst into the near-silent gallery. As everyone turned she glanced past Ragnar, feeling the hairs on the back of her neck stand to attention as she spotted the hem of her mother's coat and her brother's familiar black boots stomping down the steps of the gallery.

Panic edged into her head, pushing past all other thought. This wasn't the right time or place for Ragnar to meet her family. She wasn't ready, and nor could she imagine their various reactions to one another. Actually, she could—and it was something she wanted to avoid at all costs.

Her mother would walk a tightrope between charm and contempt. Lucas would probably say something he would regret later.

'Fine,' she said quickly. 'I'll give you my number and you can call me. We can arrange to meet up.'

'I think it would be better if we made a decision now.'

Watching Lucas turning to flirt with the gallery receptionist, Lottie felt her jaw tighten with resentment. Ragnar was pushing her into a corner. Only what choice did she have?

She glanced despairingly as the inner door to the gallery

opened. She couldn't risk them meeting one another now, but clearly Ragnar wasn't leaving without a date in place.

'Okay, then—how about tomorrow? After lunch.'

He nodded. 'Would you prefer me to come to you?'

'No—' She practically shouted the word at him. 'People are always dropping in. It'll be easier to talk without any distractions.'

'Fine. I'll send a car.'

'That won't be—'

'Necessary? Perhaps not.' Frowning, he reached into his jacket and pulled out a card. 'But indulge me. This is my private number. Text me your address and I'll have my driver collect you.'

There was a pulse of silence. She disliked the feeling of being treated like some kind of special delivery parcel, but no doubt this was just how his life worked, and refusing seemed childish given what was really at stake.

'Fine—but right now I need you to go. The exhibition will be closing in ten minutes and I want to get Sóley home,' she said, watching with relief as Georgina sped across the gallery to intercept her mother and her brother. 'So if you don't mind—?'

His gaze shifted to her face. 'Of course.' He gave her a smile that barely curved his mouth. 'I'll see you tomorrow.'

Gently he released his grip from Sóley's hand. For a moment he hesitated, his eyes locking with his daughter's, and then he turned and strode towards the door. She watched, her heart in her mouth, as he skirted past her mother and Lucas.

'Sorry we're late!' Her mother ran her hand theatrically through her long dark hair. 'We bumped into Chris and your brother insisted on buying him a drink—'

'I felt awkward.' Lucas shook his head. 'The poor guy practically lost his mind when you dumped him.'

'But never mind about *him*.'

Lottie winced as her mother grabbed her and kissed her on the cheek.

'Who was *that*?' Pivoting round, Izzy gazed after Ragnar with narrowing eyes.

Lottie shrugged. 'He was just passing,' she said quickly.

Lucas frowned. 'I feel like I've seen him before…'

'Unlikely,' Lottie said crisply. 'I don't think you move in the same circles—and don't try and distract me.' She raised an eyebrow accusingly. 'You were supposed to be here an hour ago. But now that you are here, do you think you could take Sóley for me?'

She watched with relief as Lucas reached out and scooped Sóley into his arms. It wasn't quite as terrifying as the thought of Ragnar meeting her family, but her brother making any kind of connection was something she didn't need. He might just put two and two together and come up with four—and then she would have to lie to his face or, worse, admit the truth to their mother.

There was no way she was getting into all that in public. She'd already over-complicated everything enough by letting a cool-eyed stranger into her life.

But if Ragnar thought her hasty acquiescence to his demands meant that he could set the boundaries for his relationship with their daughter he was wrong—as he was going to find out tomorrow.

Were they her family?

Mounting the steps from the gallery two at a time, Ragnar felt the onset of a familiar unease—that same feeling of being sucked towards a vortex that usually went hand in hand with spending time with his own family.

The scruffy-looking man with Day-of-the-Dead skulls tattooed on his neck and the dark-haired woman wearing an eye-catching red faux-fur coat must be Lottie's brother and mother—and the thought was not exactly reassuring.

He knew from dealing with his own family that eccentricities might appear charming to an outsider but usually they went hand in hand with a tendency for self-indulgence and melodrama that was exhausting and time-consuming.

But at least with one's own family you knew what to expect.

Remembering his daughter's hand gripping his thumb, he felt his jaw tighten. Had he been in any way uncertain as to whether he had a role to play in Sóley's life that doubt had instantly and completely vanished as her hand gripped his. Children needed stability and support from the adults in their lives, not drama, and it wasn't hard to imagine exactly what kind of circus those two could create.

No wonder Lottie had been so desperate for him to leave. The sooner he got this matter in hand the better.

Yanking open the door to his car, he threw himself into the back seat. 'Take me home, John,' he said curtly.

Home. He almost laughed out loud. What did he know about the concept of home? He'd lived in many houses in numerous countries, with various combinations of parents and step-parents. And now that his wealth had become something managed by other people he owned properties around the globe. Truthfully, though, despite their scale and glossy interiors, none was somewhere he felt relief when he walked through the front door.

No, there was only one place he'd ever considered home, and ironically the person who owned it was not related to him by either blood or marriage.

But he would make certain his child had the home he'd been denied.

The next morning Ragnar woke early.

It was still dark when he got up, but he knew from experience that he wouldn't get back to sleep. He dressed and made his way downstairs to the gym, and worked the machines until his body ached.

An hour later, having showered and changed, he lay sprawled on a sofa in one of the living rooms. There were eight in total, but this was the one he preferred. He let out a long, slow breath. Outside it was raining, and through the window all he could see was the dark glimmer of water and the occasional crooked outline of antlers as the red deer moved silently across the lawns.

The deer had come with Lamerton House, the Jacobean mansion and forty-acre estate that he used as a stopover when he was meeting bankers and investors in London. His gaze narrowed. They were less tame than reindeer, but the grazing herd still reminded him of home.

Home—that word again.

He stared irritably out of the window into the darkness. Normally it was a word that just didn't register in his day-to-day vocabulary, but this was the second time in as many hours that he'd thought it. His refocused his eyes on his reflection—only it wasn't his face he could see in the glass but his daughter's, so like his own and already so essential to him.

He might only have discovered her existence forty-eight hours earlier, but his feelings about Sóley were clear. She deserved a home—somewhere safe and stable. Somewhere she could flourish.

His fingers clenched against the back of the sofa. If only his feelings about Lottie were as straightforward. But they weren't.

At first he'd wanted to blame her for so carelessly unbalancing his life, and then for keeping the truth from him, only how could he? He was as much to blame on both counts. Nor could he blame her for resenting his heavy-handed offer of money. Having managed alone for the best part of two years, of course she'd feel insulted.

But acknowledging his own flaws didn't absolve hers. She was stubborn and inconsistent and irrational. His mouth thinned. Sadly acknowledging her flaws didn't change the facts. Being near Lottie made his body swell with blood and his head swim. He had felt it—that same restless, implacable hunger that had overtaken him that night. A hunger he had spent his life condemning in others and was now suppressing in himself…

Six hours later he stood watching the dark blue saloon move smoothly along the driveway towards the house. From the upper floor window he watched as his driver John opened the door. His heart started a drumroll as Lottie slid from the car and, turning, he made his way downstairs.

As he reached the bottom step she turned and gazed up at him.

There was a moment of silence as he took in her appearance. She was wearing jeans and a baggy cream jumper. Her cheeks were flushed and her hair was tied back with what looked like a man's black shoelace. For no accountable reason he found himself hoping profoundly that the owner of the shoe in question was her brother. Raising his eyes, he turned towards John and dismissed him with a nod, so that his voice wouldn't give away the sharp, disconcerting spasm of jealousy that twisted his mouth.

'You made good time,' he said.

She nodded, her soft brown eyes locking with his—except they weren't soft, but tense and wary. 'Thank you for sending the car. It was very kind of you.' Her gaze moved past him and then abruptly returned to his face. 'So what happens next?'

It wasn't just her voice that upped his heartbeat. Her words reverberated inside his head, pulling at a memory he had never quite forgotten.

So what happens next?

Twenty months ago she had spoken the exact same sentence to him in the street outside that restaurant, and briefly he let his mind go back to that moment. He could picture it precisely. The tremble of her lips, the way her hair had spilled over the collar of her coat, and then the moment when he had lowered his mouth to hers and kissed her.

His body tensed. It had been so effortless. So natural. She had melted into him, her candid words, warm mouth and curving limbs offering up possibilities of an intimacy without the drama he had lived with so long. But of course he'd been kidding himself. Whatever it was that had caused that flashpoint of heat and hunger and hope, it had been contingent on the preordained shortness of its existence.

With an effort he blocked out an image of her body gleaming palely against the dark, crumpled bedding…

'We talk,' he said simply. 'Why don't we go and get something to drink?'

In the kitchen, his housekeeper Francesca had left tea and coffee and some homemade biscuits on the granite-topped breakfast bar.

'Take a seat.' He gestured towards a leather-covered bar stool. 'Tea or coffee? Do you have a preference?'

'Tea. Please. And I prefer it black.'

He held out a cup and, giving him a small, stiff smile, she took it from him.

She took a sip, her mouth parting, and he felt his body twitch in response. It felt strange—absurdly, frustratingly strange—to be handing her a cup of tea when part of him could still remember pulling her into his arms. And another part was hungry still to pull her into his arms again.

He cleared his throat. 'So, shall we get on with it?'

He heard the shift in her breathing.

'I accept that Sóley is my daughter, but obviously that isn't going to satisfy my lawyers, so I'm afraid I need to establish paternity. It's quite simple—just a sample from me and you and Sóley.'

There was a short silence, and then she nodded. 'Okay.'

'Good.' His gaze held hers. 'Long-term I'll be looking at establishing custody rights, but initially I just want to spend a bit of time with my daughter.' And provide a structure and a stability that he instinctively knew must be lacking in her life.

'Meaning what, exactly?'

The flicker in her gaze held the same message as the rigidity in her jaw but he ignored both.

'Since everything took off with the app I've tried to take a couple of weeks off a year—three at most—just to recharge my batteries.'

'And…?' Her eyes were fixed on his face.

'And now seems like a good time for that to happen. Obviously it's just a short-term fix, but it would give me a chance to get to know Sóley and find out what's in her best interests.'

Her expression stiffened. 'I think *I* know what's in her best interests.'

'Of course. But circumstances have changed.' He waited a beat. 'This is just a first step. I understand that there's going to be a lot to work through, and naturally any future arrangements will take into account Sóley's needs—her wellbeing comes first.'

Lottie stared at him in silence. 'In that case, it's probably easier if you come to me,' she said finally. 'Coming here is quite a long way for a day trip.'

He frowned. 'I wasn't expecting you to come here, and I wasn't talking about a day trip.'

'I don't understand…' she said slowly.

'Then let me explain. The whole point of these weeks is to give me time to think, to unplug myself. That's why I go back to Iceland. It's a less hectic, more sedate way of life, and it's easier to take a step back there. I'd like Sóley to go with me.'

Her eyes slipped across his face, once then twice, as though searching for something. 'You're joking, right?'

'About getting to spend some time with my child? Hardly.'

He watched his put-down meet its target, as he'd intended it to. Colour was spreading over her cheeks.

'She doesn't have a passport,' she countered tonelessly.

'But she has a birth certificate.'

Her single, reluctant nod looked almost painful.

'Then it won't be a problem. I have people who can expedite the paperwork.'

Her face seemed to crack apart. 'No, this is not happening. She doesn't know you—and she's never been anywhere without me.'

He could hear the tension in her voice and unaccountably felt himself respond to it. How could he not? She was scared. Of him. Not physically, but of his claim, both moral and legal, on their daughter, and he couldn't help but understand and empathise with her. She had carried Sóley for nine months and cared for her on her own for another eleven. Now he was here in her life and everything was going to change.

His back stiffened. He knew exactly how that felt—the dread, then the confusion and the compromises—and for a few half-seconds he was on the verge of reaching out to comfort her. But—

But it was best not to confuse what was actually happening here. Lottie would adapt, and what mattered was agreeing the best possible outcome for Sóley.

'Clearly I was expecting you to join us.' He spoke patiently, as though to a confused child, but instead of calming her his words had the opposite effect.

'Me? Go away with you?' She shook her head. 'No, that isn't going to happen.'

'Why not? I spoke to the woman at the gallery and you have no upcoming exhibitions.'

'You spoke to Georgina?' The tightness in her face broke into a spasm of outrage. 'How dare you? How dare you talk to people behind my back?'

The note of hysteria in her voice made his shoulders pinch together. 'You're being ridiculous.'

'And you're being overbearing,' she snapped. 'You can't just expect me to drop everything.'

'Oh, but I can—and I do. And if you won't then I will have to apply a little pressure.'

'And do what, Ragnar?' She pushed up from the bar stool, her hands curling into fists, two thumbprints of colour burning in her cheeks. 'Are you going to send round your head of security? Or maybe you could kidnap us?'

How had this spiralled out of control so quickly?

He felt a familiar mix of frustration and fatigue.

'This is getting us nowhere—and in case you've forgotten, you got in touch with me.'

He stared at her in exasperation and then wished he hadn't. Her hair was coming loose and he had to resist the urge to pull it with his fingers and watch it tumble free.

He waited a moment, and then tried again. 'Look, Lottie. You go where Sóley goes. That's a given. And by pressure I just mean lawyers. But I don't want to escalate this. I just want to do what's best for our daughter. I think you do too, and that's why you came to find me the other day.'

There was a small beat of silence.

'I do want what's best for her, but…' She hesitated. 'But going away with you… I mean, three weeks is a long time for two strangers to spend together.'

There was another pulse of silence. His heart was suddenly digging against his ribs.

'But we're not strangers, are we, Lottie?' he said softly.

The silence was heavy now, pressing them closer.

Her pupils flared like a supernova and he felt his breathing stall in his throat. A minute went by, and then another. They were inches apart, so close that if he reached out he could touch her, pull her closer, draw her body against him…

And then above the pounding of his heart he heard her swallow.

'Okay. Sóley and I will come to Iceland with you.' Her expression hardened. 'And then she and I will go home. Without you.'

CHAPTER THREE

LOTTIE AND LUCAS started their walk, as they always did, by climbing over the stile in the wall at the back of the garden. After days of rain, not only was the sun shining but it was unseasonably warm.

'Usual route?' Lucas said, steadying himself on the top of the stile.

She nodded. 'But maybe come back by the river? There might be some ducks for Sóley.'

She glanced up to where her daughter sat, clapping her hands triumphantly in the backpack on Lucas's shoulders. She was wearing a lightweight purple all-in-one and a tiny knitted hat shaped like a blackberry, complete with leaves and a stalk, and in the pale lemon sunlight her skin looked as smooth and luminous as a pearl.

They trudged around the edge of the field across short, stubby tufts of grass to the lane that skirted the farmland. Instead of the usual hum of machinery, or the pensive bleating of sheep, it was still and peaceful, but Lottie didn't mind—her head was noisy enough as it was.

Ragnar had been on television again last night, on some panel show and, watching him talk about global expansion and emerging markets, she had felt a little sick. He had sounded cool, driven and utterly focused on his goals. Of course he'd been talking about his business, but she could easily imagine him applying the same focus and determination to getting what he wanted when it came to his daughter. Plus, he had all kinds of resources at his disposal. Look at how quickly and smoothly he'd acquired a passport for Sóley.

She felt her pulse jerk forward. So quickly, in fact, that

this time next week all three of them would be flying to Reykjavik.

It was difficult to say which was more terrifying. The future when her adult daughter would be able to travel outside of England without her made her skin grow tight with panic, but thinking about spending three hours with Ragnar, let alone the three weeks she had agreed to, set off a pinwheel of alarm in her chest.

To say that she didn't want to go was the mother of all understatements—only what choice did she have? She could refuse, but then he would simply make good on his threat to escalate matters through the courts. Or she could go into hiding. Izzy knew loads of people who lived off-grid in houseboats and artists' communes. Only she couldn't stay hidden for ever.

Her stomach tightened.

She was just going to have to accept that it was happening.

But it was all moving so much more quickly than she'd expected.

It wasn't that she blamed Ragnar for wanting to get things rolling. If she'd been in his position she would have felt just the same. And nor did she really regret her decision to tell him about Sóley. But even though she knew she'd done the right thing, seeing him with Sóley, feeling the imperative weight of the connection between them, was making her head spin.

She felt a longing to snatch her daughter away and hold her close, and yet at the same time a longing to be part of the golden warmth of their inner circle. It was so confusing. She wanted to feel happy for her daughter, not panicky and envious, and she knew that she was being illogical, but she still couldn't stop herself from feeling just a tiny bit jealous of their blonde, blue-eyed bond.

A bond that would never include her.

A bond she had so spectacularly failed to achieve with her own father.

'I thought we might take Sóley into town next week. They're switching on the Christmas lights.'

It was suddenly hard to breathe. As Lucas's voice reverberated inside her head she looked up at her brother's face. It was so familiar, so reassuring, and yet she still hadn't worked out a way to tell him what was happening.

In the distance she could see the broad expanse of the marshes. Above their heads the sky was pale grey, silent and immense. It felt overwhelming, and yet in another way it was liberating, for it put everything into perspective. In comparison to something so infinite and enduring, surely her problems were puny and trifling and her secrecy superfluous?

She glanced across at her brother, seeing the scuffed patches on his leather jacket and the tiny points of stubble along his jawline, and suddenly she knew that this was it. The turning point. The moment she had been waiting for and both hoping and dreading would happen.

Up until now it had all been just in her head. It had felt safe, contained, indefinite. But telling Lucas would make it real.

'That would be lovely,' she said carefully. 'Only I'm not going to be here.'

'Really?' Lucas frowned. 'I thought you were clear up until Christmas.'

She swallowed, or tried to, but the truth was blocking her throat, making it ache.

'I am—I was. But I'm…we're going to Iceland.'

He was staring at her now, his dark brown eyes trying to make sense of her words.

'Iceland? Wow, really?' He shook his head. 'That's pretty random. What brought that on?'

For a moment she was too busy trying out various sentences in her head to reply, but the need to share the truth was swelling inside her.

'We're going away with Sóley's father,' she said quickly. 'Just for a couple of weeks,' she added. 'So he can get to know her.'

Whatever Lucas might have been expecting her to say, it wasn't that. Her brother was difficult to shock. He was tolerant and easy-going. But she could tell that he was stunned by her words.

'I thought you didn't know who he was?' His eyes searched her face, trying to guess at the truth of what she'd told him in the past.

'I didn't. But then I found out by accident and I went to his office and told him about Sóley. Then he invited me to his house, and we talked.'

Lucas cleared his throat. 'When was this?'

'A couple of days ago.'

His eyes narrowed with disbelief. 'What? And he just invited you to go away with him?'

'Yes.'

'And you agreed to go?'

As she nodded a slick of heat spread over her skin. Put like that it sounded crazy, but what was she supposed to say? *Actually, he didn't so much as invite me as issue a directive.*

She could imagine her brother's reaction. He would be furious—and understandably so. From his perspective it would seem she had been backed into a corner. Only his anger wasn't going to change the facts. Ragnar was Sóley's father, and he had a right to know his daughter.

Her heart skipped forward guiltily and she felt a slow creep of colour stain her cheeks. Ragnar's desire to know his daughter was not the only reason she had agreed to go to Iceland with him. That involved a different kind of desire.

Her mind went back to that moment in the kitchen,

when the anger and tension between them had slipped into something else, and the intensity of their emotions and the nearness of their bodies had resurrected the ghost of their unfinished connection with impossible speed.

Here in the cool November sunlight she could dismiss it as the result of nervousness or an overactive imagination, but alone with Ragnar it had been impossible to deny. In that moment the truth had been irrefutable. She wanted him—wanted him more than she had ever wanted any man.

But the suffocating force of that longing was one truth she wouldn't be sharing with her brother.

She glanced up at his profile. He looked calm, but she could read the confusion in the lines around his eyes and the tightening along his jaw.

'You think it's a bad idea,' she said slowly.

She watched with a mix of regret and relief as he shook his head.

'No, I'm just sulking because you didn't talk to me about it.'

Reaching out, she took hold of his hand and gave it a quick, apologetic squeeze. 'I wanted to but I was worried about what you'd say. What you and Mum would say,' she corrected herself. 'I didn't want to let either of you down.'

Lucas frowned. 'Let us down? Sóley is your daughter, Lottie. It's up to you, not me or Mum, if you want her to know who her father is.'

'I know, but you've always been so definite about it not mattering—you know, about our dads not being around—and Mum's the same.'

She thought back to her childhood, the hours spent watching Izzy's casual intimacy with men, the cool way she seduced and then discarded them without so much as a backward glance. To a child it had seemed both shocking, and eye-wateringly brutal, but as she'd grown older she had seen it as something else—something that underlined a fundamental difference between herself and her mother.

She felt his fingers tighten around hers.

'I do feel like that, but I know you don't—and that's okay. You're just not programmed that way, and I know that makes you feel left out sometimes. But you're my sister and I'm here for you and nothing can change that.'

Feeling the knot of tension in her shoulders loosen, Lottie nodded. It was a relief to tell Lucas the truth, but his fierce affirmation of their sibling bond mattered more. It was nothing new. She'd always needed reassurance of her place in her family. But since being confronted by Ragnar and Sóley's kinship she'd felt even more precariously placed than before.

'But that doesn't mean you have to rush into anything with Sóley's dad.'

They had reached the river now, and Lottie stared down into the water, her brother's words replaying inside her head as Sóley began to crow excitedly at a group of mallards sifting through the mud for insects and seeds.

'I can totally see why you'd want to,' he said slowly. 'But it's not like there's a time limit on paternity.'

Except there was, she thought. And at a certain point time ran out.

The blood pulsed inside her head as she thought back to her meeting with her own father. She had left it too late. So late that there hadn't been any room left for her in Alistair's life.

'In theory, no,' she agreed. 'But every day that passes is a day that tests that theory, and that's why I don't want to wait with Ragnar.'

As the silence stretched out between them she could hear the booming of her voice inside her head. Lucas was staring at her, and she could sense that he was replaying her words, mentally tracing back over the last few days.

Finally, he said slowly, 'Ragnar Stone is Sóley's father.'

It wasn't a question but a statement of fact, and there was no point in pretending otherwise.

She nodded.

He tilted his head back and whistled soundlessly. 'At least now I get why you're going to Iceland.' Hesitating, he looked her straight in the eye. 'Unless there is some other reason you and Mr Stone want to spend a few weeks together.'

Her face felt hot and tight. 'Of course there's no other reason.' She knew she sounded defensive and, remembering how her body grew loose with desire whenever she thought about Ragnar, she knew why. 'There's nothing between us,' she said quickly. 'This trip is about Sóley getting to know her father.'

It was hopeless. The tangle of her thoughts might just as well be written in huge letters across a billboard by the side of the road. But that was the problem. She didn't know how she felt or how she should feel—not about Ragnar, nor about going away with him and having him in her life. But if anyone could help her make sense of her feelings, it was Lucas.

'So you still like him?' Lucas said gently.

'No.' She shook her head, hesitated. 'I don't know. Maybe—but it's not conscious. I mean, I don't actually like him as a person.'

There was a small beat of silence.

'Okay…' Lucas raised an eyebrow. 'So what *do* you like about him?'

Her heart shivered.

His skin. The curving muscles of his arms and chest. His smell. The way his hair fell in front of his eyes when he was gazing down at her. The fierce blueness of his gaze.

'I don't know,' she lied. 'It just felt good with him, that

night.' She could admit that much—although that too was a lie, or perhaps an understatement.

It had felt glorious. An ecstasy of touch and taste. She had never wanted it to stop. Never wanted to leave that hotel room. Never felt so complete or so certain. Every fibre of her being, every atom of her consciousness, had been focused on the pressure of his body and the circle of his arms around her. Nothing else had mattered. And in the flushed, perfect aftermath of that night she had been so blazingly sure of him.

But now she knew she had made hasty and hungry assumptions. And by agreeing to go to Iceland was she making them again?

'Do you think I'm being stupid?'

Much as she loved her brother, they were different in so many ways. Like Izzy, Lucas was a serial monogamist. He was single-minded, and not subject to any need for permanence or emotional bondage, but he liked women and, probably because he was always so honest, they liked him. It was one of his strengths, that unflinching honesty, and she needed him to be honest with her now.

His forehead creased, and then he shook his head. 'You made Sóley together, so something was good between you.' He hesitated. 'But you need to be careful and clear about where you fit into all this. Don't complicate what's already going to be a fairly tricky situation with something that's out of your hands.'

He was right, Lottie thought as they turned away from the river. However fierce and real it might feel, letting something as fickle and cursory as physical attraction take centre stage was a risk not worth taking. Giving in to her hunger would rob her of perspective.

She and Ragnar had had their chance and they'd failed to make it work—and nothing, including the fact that they had an eleventh-month-old daughter, would change that.

* * *

As his private jet hit a pocket of what felt like hollowed-out air Ragnar felt his pulse accelerate. But it wasn't the turbulence that was making his heart beat faster. Over the last year he'd racked up enough air miles to have overcome any fear of flying. What was making his pulse race was the tiny shift in the drone of the engines.

They were making their descent. In less than half an hour they would land in Reykjavik. Then it would be a drive out to his estate on the Troll peninsula, and then finally he would be able to start getting to know his daughter.

Daughter.

The word still felt so unfamiliar, but then he hadn't expected to become a father for a long time. Maybe not ever. Only then he'd met Lottie, and in that moment when they'd reached for one another in that dark London street his life had changed for all time.

His eyes drifted across the cabin to where she sat, gazing out of one of the small cabin windows. Opposite her, Sóley lay across two seats, with some kind of frayed cuddly toy clamped against her body, her thumb in her mouth. She was asleep and, watching the rise and fall of her tiny body, Ragnar felt his chest ache.

As predicted, his lawyers had insisted on a paternity test, and as predicted it had come back positive. But as far as he was concerned no proof had been required. Sóley was his—and not just because they were so physically alike. There was an intangible thread between them, a bond that started with DNA but went way beyond it. He might have only found out about her existence a couple of days ago, but he already felt an unquestioning, all-encompassing love for her, and a sense of responsibility that was nothing like he'd ever felt before.

He felt his heart contract. She looked so small, so vulnerable, so ill-equipped to deal with the relentless chaos of life.

For chaos read *family.*

He thought about the complicated layers of parents and children—some related by blood, some by marriage—that made up his family. They were wilful and self-absorbed and thoughtless, but he loved them—all of them. How could he not? They were a force of nature, so full of life, so passionate and vital.

But ever since he could remember they had seemed to him like whirling storm clouds battering a mountain top. Oblivious to the damage they caused, they kept on twisting and raging, and in order to survive he'd chosen—if you could call it a choice—to sit out the storm. To be like the mountain and just let the winds carry on howling around him.

That had been his response as a child. Now, as an adult, he'd embraced the role of mediator and umpire. It was exhausting, often thankless, and always time-consuming. The swooping melodrama of their day-to-day disputes and dramas required the patience of a bomb disposal expert and the diplomacy of a trained hostage negotiator, but it was the only way, for it allowed him to live a life of calm and order on the sidelines.

He shifted in his seat, pressing his spine against the leather to relieve the tension in his back.

Now, though, he felt as though he was being sucked into a new vortex—a vortex that was the unavoidable trade-off for getting to know his daughter.

Across the cabin Sóley shifted in her sleep, losing her grip on her toy, and he watched as Lottie leaned forward and gently tucked the bear back underneath her arm.

By vortex he meant *Lottie's family.*

That glimpse in the gallery had been enough of an incentive for him to call his head of security and instruct him to make some discreet enquiries. The slim folder that had arrived on his desk less than twenty-four hours later had made for depressing reading. Both Izzy, Lottie's mother, and her brother Lucas seemed to live off-grid, rarely staying in one place longer than a couple of years and with no regular partners or jobs.

At least Lottie had an address, and she owned a house, but the idea of his daughter being raised in the eye of *that* particular storm made Ragnar suddenly so tense that before he knew what he was doing he had stood up and was walking across the cabin.

'May I?'

He gestured towards the empty seat opposite Sóley.

Lottie looked up at him, her light brown eyes not exactly contradicting the slight nod of her head but reserving judgement. He wondered why he had thought her eyes were boring. Right now, in the softly lit interior of the cabin, they were the same colour as the raw honey produced on his estate.

'Of course. It's your plane.'

She spoke politely, and it was tempting to take her words at face value. But, although her voice was free of any resentful undertone, he could sense she was still chafing against what she took to be his high-handed manner.

His gaze was drawn to his daughter and he felt his own stab of resentment. Sóley was so small, and yet he'd already missed so many of the imperceptible changes that had marked her growth from birth to now. So Lottie's indignation would have to wait—just as he'd had to wait to find out he was her father.

'I thought it would be simpler and more comfortable for you both to travel this way.'

He glanced around the cabin. There was space to move around and no other passengers, but Lottie's stony expression suggested she was unconvinced.

'I just want to spend time with her,' he said mildly.

She frowned. 'I'm not saying you don't, but you have a

house in Surrey. I don't understand why we couldn't just visit you there.'

'As I told you—I like to take a couple of weeks off to recharge.'

'So we're working around your business schedule?' Her gaze narrowed. 'I thought this was supposed to be about our daughter and her wellbeing.'

He stared at her steadily, noting the paleness of her face and the dark shadows beneath her eyes. Clearly she'd been having trouble sleeping, and without meaning to he found himself diverting his thoughts away from the evidence to the cause.

Was her insomnia solely a result of this disruption to her life? Or was something else keeping her awake?

His pulse stalled. Since she'd door-stepped him in front of his office his own nights had been uncharacteristically unsettled. Either he struggled to fall asleep, his head filling with images of Lottie's pale naked body as soon as he tried to close his eyes, or he dozed off only to wake exhausted after a night spent twitching restlessly through feverish, erotically charged dreams.

Blanking his mind of everything but the here and now, he met her gaze. 'It was and it is. Iceland is my homeland. I want my daughter to understand her connection to the country where I was born.'

'But she's not even a year old,' she protested. 'She won't know where she is.'

She was angry—and suspicious. He could hear it in her voice, see it in the set of her shoulders. But did she have to escalate her irritation into a full-blown confrontation? Was this how it was going to be every time they talked?

He felt a twinge of frustration. 'But *I* will know.' He shook his head. 'Tell me, is this you being deliberately bloody-minded? Or is it just impossible for you to accept that I might have a genuine motive for bringing my daughter here?'

'I'm not being bloody-minded,' she snapped. 'Cynical, maybe. In my experience your motives seem to have a habit of being a little shaky at best.'

'Meaning...?'

This conversation was pointless. He should be shutting it down. But he could feel his control slipping. It was something that had never happened before with any woman, but Lottie got under his skin. She made him lose the thread of his thoughts so that he felt off-balance and irresolute when normally he would be all cool, level-headed logic.

'You lied to me that night,' she said flatly. 'You had a whole agenda—all to do with test-driving your app—only you forgot to mention that to me. Just like you forgot to tell me that it was *your* app—the one *you* created. So forgive me if I don't find you or your claims very genuine.'

His jaw tightened. 'You think what happened between us that night was some kind of Research and Development exercise?' He shook his head. 'Then you're right—you *are* cynical.'

Her eyes were suddenly blazing, frustration and fury lighting up their pupils. 'And you're manipulative and cold-blooded.'

He wanted to stay angry, and her absurd unjustifiable accusations should have made him see red, but as her gaze locked on his all he could think about was turning the fire in her eyes into a different kind of heat...a heat that would obliterate the tension and mistrust between them...the same white heat that had fused them together that night.

His heartbeat stalled and slowly he shook his head.

'Not with you. Not that night,' he said softly. 'You had all the power, Lottie, believe me.'

Her eyes widened and a flush of colour spilled over her

cheekbones. They stared at one another, caught in the unbidden simmering spell of those remembered moments.

'Mr Stone, Ms Dawson, we'll be landing soon.'

His heart jump-started. It was his stewardess, Sam.

'If you could buckle up…?' She smiled apologetically. 'And I'm afraid that includes this little one too.'

'Of course.' He smiled coolly—more coolly than he felt.

His blood was still humming in his ears, and with an effort he forced his mind away from those taut, shimmering seconds of madness. The strength and speed of his unravelling was not admirable, but it was understandable. He was tired, and he had let his imagination run away with him, but in some ways that was a good thing.

The overwhelming, uncontrollable desire that had led him to act so carelessly twenty months ago was still there, and he loved his daughter. Only this was a reminder that those feelings were two opposing forces that could never and would never be reconciled.

How could they be when his body's response to Lottie might unleash the kind of emotion and disorder that was incompatible with the serenity he was so determined to give his daughter?

CHAPTER FOUR

ICELAND WAS NOTHING like Lottie had imagined.

Since their arrival two hours ago the sky had changed colour so many times she had lost count. Swollen lead-grey clouds had given way to a dazzling sunlight that turned everything golden, and then moments later the sun had been swallowed up by diaphanous veils of mist.

But if the weather was capricious, the land itself was otherworldly.

Through the helicopter window, the countryside rushing beneath her looked like another planet. Huge, smooth boulders that might have been used by giants in a game of football sat in a field that appeared to be covered in what looked like bright yellow moss, and carving a path several metres wide through the field was a thundering river.

It was beautiful and alien and intimidating.

A bit like Ragnar himself, she thought, gritting her teeth and hugging her daughter closer to her chest beneath the lap strap. Except that rocks and rivers didn't continually leave you second-guessing their actions.

Gazing through the glass, she tried to concentrate on the scenery, but the feeling of apprehension that had started low in her stomach when they'd landed in Reykjavik was now pushing up into her throat.

She had assumed—naively, as it now turned out—that Ragnar's home would be near Iceland's capital city. He hadn't said as much, but nor had there been any indication that it would be at the edge of the known earth, or at least the solid part.

A panicky furtive check on her phone had confirmed the worst. His home was on the Tröllaskagi—the Troll Peninsula. Beyond the peninsula was only the sea, until you reached the archipelago of Svalbard, with a roughly equal ratio of humans to polar bears, and then there was nothing but open water until you arrived in the Arctic.

He might just as well be taking her to the moon.

She glanced swiftly across the cabin to where Ragnar sat, his blue gaze scanning the skyline. He was wearing slouchy jeans, some kind of insulated jacket, and a pair of broken-in hiking boots—the kind of ordinary clothes worn by an average man taking a break in a winter wilderness. But there was nothing ordinary about Ragnar—and she wasn't talking about his wealth or his glacial beauty. There was a concentrated intensity to his presence so that even when he was sitting down she could sense the languid power in the casual arrangement of his limbs.

He was not always so languid or casual.

Her pulse stuttered.

They had spent such a short amount of time together, and yet the memory of those few feverish hours had stayed with her.

She clenched her hands against the curl of desire stirring inside her.

Even before they'd left England the idea of being alone with him for three weeks had made her feel off-balance, but now that she was here his constant nearness was playing havoc with her senses. She didn't want to be affected by him, but unfortunately her body didn't seem to have got that particular memo.

She thought back to that moment on the plane. One minute they had been arguing and then the air had seemed to bloom around them, pushing them closer, holding them captive, so that for a few pulsing seconds there had been nothing except their mutual irresistible fascination.

She shivered. And now they were going to be stuck in

the wilderness together, with nothing to hold them in check except their willpower.

It was tempting to throw his 'invitation' back in his face and tell him that she was going home—or at least back to civilisation in Reykjavik. But she doubted he would listen. And anyway, she didn't want to give him the opportunity to accuse her of having another temper tantrum.

Her gaze returned to the window. The land was growing whiter and the sky darker—and then suddenly they had arrived.

Clutching Sóley against her body, she stepped out onto the snow and gazed mutely at the house in front of her. Without the frenetic noise of the helicopter, the silence was so huge it seemed to roar inside her ears.

'Welcome to my home.'

She glanced up at Ragnar. He was standing beside her, his blond hair snapping in the wind, a slab of sunlight illuminating his face so that she could see the contours of his bones beneath the skin. He looked impassive and resolute, more returning warrior than CEO.

His eyes held hers for a few endless seconds, and then he said quietly, 'Let's go inside. I'll show you your rooms.'

'Home' didn't seem quite the right word, she thought a moment later, pressing her face against her daughter's cheek, seeking comfort in her warm, sweet smell. This was a lair—a secluded hideaway miles from anywhere—its white walls and bleached wood blending perfectly into the snow-covered landscape.

The interior did nothing to reduce her panic.

Partly it was the sheer scale of the rooms—her whole cottage would fit into the entrance hall. Partly it was the minimalist perfection of the decor, so different from the piles of baby clothes hanging above the stove and the stack of newspapers waiting to be recycled in her home. But mostly it was having her earlier fears confirmed.

That now she was here she wasn't going anywhere.

She was effectively trapped.

Back in England, when she'd acquiesced to coming to Iceland, she had assumed that if she changed her mind she could simply call a taxi.

Of course there was a helicopter sitting outside, like some squat snow-bound dragonfly, but she certainly couldn't fly it, and nor could she walk all the way back to civilisation with a baby.

Her eyes darted towards the huge expanse of glass that ran from floor to ceiling in the main living area. In the distance jagged snow-covered slopes stretched out towards an empty horizon. There was no sign of any habitation. No other buildings, no roads or telegraph poles. Just sky and snow and a sense of utter solitude.

'This is Sóley's room.'

They were upstairs now.

'The light is softer this side, and there's a beautiful view of the mountains.'

She turned to where Ragnar was holding open a door and stepped past him, trying to ignore the ripple of heat that spiralled up inside her as she momentarily brushed against his arm.

It was a beautiful room—the kind of pastel minimalist nursery that would feature in one of those upmarket baby magazines. There was a cot and a rocking chair, and a wicker basket piled high with soft toys. Unlike the rest of the house, it wasn't painted in a muted shade of off-white but in a delicate lilac, exactly the same colour as the lavender that grew in the fields beyond her cottage.

But it wasn't the unexpected reminder of home that made her body and brain freeze as though she'd fallen through ice—it was the two framed prints on the wall.

'They're mine,' she said slowly.

For a minute she was too stunned to do anything more than stare, but then slowly her brain began working again.

'You bought these through Rowley's?'

Ragnar nodded.

She stared at the prints, her heart beating out of time. It felt strange, seeing her work here in this house. Stranger still that he should have bought them unseen. But that must be what had happened, because he hadn't arrived at the gallery until later that day.

Georgina's voice floated up from somewhere inside her head. *'You know what these collectors are like. They love to have the cachet of buying up-and-coming artists' early work.'*

And she was right. A lot of wealthy buyers treated art as a commodity, and got a buzz from seeing the price of their investment soar, but…

Her arm tightened around her daughter's reassuring warmth as a chill ran down her spine.

But those buyers hadn't had a one-night stand with the artist and got her pregnant.

Her skin was suddenly too hot and too tight, and she knew without question that Ragnar hadn't bought her work as an investment. It was something far more subtle, more insidious. He had wanted to give her money, she had refused, and so he had found another, more circuitous but less overt method of getting his own way. And he got to own a little piece of her too.

'I'll pay you back.'

Her voice sounded tense and raspy with emotion, but she didn't care. What mattered was making him understand that she was not going to be outmanoeuvred by him or his wealth.

'Maybe not right at this moment, but when we get back to England.'

His gaze skimmed her face, a muscle pulling at his jaw. 'Excuse me?'

'For the prints. I told you before that I didn't want your money—well, I don't need your charity either. Whatever it might suit you to think, I'm not some starving artist living a garret.'

As she finished speaking Sóley twisted against her, arching her back and reaching out towards the floor. She had noticed a brightly coloured octopus peeking out of the toy basket and wanted to get closer. Grateful for a reason to break eye-contact, Lottie leaned forward and let her daughter scrabble forward onto the floor.

'I see.'

There was a short silence, and then he said quietly, 'Can I ask you something? Is this how it's always going to be? Or is there the slightest chance that you can imagine a future where I can say or do something innocuous and you won't immediately put two and two together and make five?'

She looked up, her stomach swooping downwards in shock. 'What do you mean?'

'I mean,' he said softly, 'that I didn't buy your work out of charity. I came to the gallery in the morning, only you weren't there and so I had a look around. I wasn't planning on buying anything, but then I saw these, and the collage, and I changed my mind.'

Lottie stared at him in silence, her mind replaying the events of that day. There had been some kind of signal failure affecting the train on her way in and she hadn't got to the gallery until mid-morning. And when she'd arrived Jem, the gallery's co-owner, had been frantic. Georgina had swanned off to meet her latest boyfriend for a champagne brunch and he was supposed to be on the other side of London meeting a client…

As though sensing the route of her thoughts, Ragnar gave her a brief, wintry smile. 'I called Rowley's on the way back to the office,' he continued remorselessly. 'And then I was in meetings all day until I came back to the gallery in the afternoon.'

He glanced down at where Sóley sat clutching the octopus triumphantly, her mouth clamped around one furry leg, her fists clenching and unclenching with undisguised joy.

'Not that I expect you to believe me, but I bought your work for two reasons. I think they're beautiful and, more importantly, I wanted Sóley to have something of you here. I know she probably doesn't recognise your work now, but I thought that in time she will and it will mean something to her.'

Her face was burning. A hard lump of shame was sitting heavily in her stomach and she felt slightly nauseous. She had been so certain that his motives were self-serving, only now it appeared that the complete opposite was true.

But how was she supposed to guess that he would do something so unselfish? So far their interaction had amounted to one night of feverish passion and several tense stand-offs, and from those encounters she had learned what? That the man standing in front of her was a generous, intuitive lover, but that he also had a resolve as hard and cold as the ice gullies that ran through the granite hills of his homeland.

It was all so contradictory and inconclusive. But either way it didn't change the facts. She had jumped to conclusions and she'd been wrong.

Taking a breath, she made herself meet his gaze. 'I'm sorry, and you're right. I overreacted. It was a kind impulse.' She cleared her throat. 'And I'm not deliberately trying to make things difficult between us—ouch!'

Twin hands were gripping her leg and, glancing down, she saw that Sóley had discarded the octopus and was now trying to pull herself upright.

'Is she walking yet?'

She shook her head, relieved at the sudden change of subject. 'Nearly. She has a walker at home—you know, with wheels—and if I help her she can push it for a couple of steps.'

As though to prove the point, Sóley lifted up her foot and, holding it aloft, she stood wobbling unsteadily on one leg, before lowering it carefully onto the rug like a pony doing dressage. She tried the other leg but this was less successful, and she slid down onto her bottom, her lower lip crumpling.

'Come here then.' Lottie reached down, but her daughter had other ideas, and she watched, her heart bumping against her ribs, as Sóley crawled over to Ragnar and wrapped her arms around his legs.

'Here, let me,' she croaked.

'It's fine,' he said softly. 'May I?'

As he reached down and picked up his daughter she felt a mixture of panic and pride. For a moment Sóley looked uncertainly at Ragnar, and then, reaching forward, she buried her face against his neck, her chubby hands gripping the blond hair that curled down his neck.

Lottie felt a quick head-rush, and then her heart fluttered upwards like a kite caught in a breeze. It was the moment she'd imagined for so long—the father embracing his daughter for the first time—but nothing could have prepared her for the conflicting tangle of emotions inside her chest or the expression of fear and awe and eagerness on Ragnar's face.

Or the fact that she recognised how completely it mirrored her own reaction that first time she'd held her daughter.

'Through here is your room.'

She nodded dumbly as Ragnar gestured towards another door.

'I thought you'd want to be close to her at night.'

'Thank you.'

She managed to speak with a gratitude she knew she ought to feel—even with the briefest of glances she could see that it was a beautiful, spacious room, with the same jaw-dropping view of the mountains—and yet she was struggling to feel anything except a mounting anxiety.

His eyes were fixed on her face. 'And I'm only just down there if you need me.'

Her throat tightened and the floor seemed to tilt sharply. But why? It was a point of information, nothing more, and yet there was something in his unwavering gaze that made her pulse accelerate—a few spun-out seconds of shimmering shared memories of a different kind of need.

Terrified what her eyes would betray if she didn't move, she nodded briskly, her heart leaping with relief as Sóley made a grab for her.

'That's good to know,' she said crisply, and she stepped neatly past him, her body loosening in relief at having temporarily evaded his cool, assessing gaze.

The rest of the tour passed without any further awkward moments—partly because she was too speechless with shock to say much. She could hardly take it all in, and she hadn't even seen the indoor-outdoor geothermal pool yet, or the several thousand acres of land that made up the estate.

Pleading tiredness from the journey, she retreated to her bedroom and let Sóley explore the contents of the toy basket as she watched the light fade from the sky. It was a relief after their constant enforced proximity on the long journey to be free of that churning undercurrent of sexual tension.

But all too soon it was time for Sóley's dinner.

With all the other changes going on in her life, she wanted to keep her daughter's routines as regular as possible—particularly meal times. But venturing downstairs required a concentrated effort of will.

The cool grey kitchen was large and immaculate. Signy, Ragnar's housekeeper, showed her where everything was kept, and how to work the gleaming professional standard cooker.

'If there's anything you can't find, just tell me and I'll order it in,' she said in faultless English, beaming at Sóley.

'Thank you, but I think you've got everything already,' she said, picturing her own sparsely filled cupboards and comparing them unfavourably with the well-stocked shelves of Signy's larder.

Sóley was far less intimidated by the upgrade in her surroundings than her mother. Thrilled by her brand-new highchair, she behaved just as she did at home, thumping out a drum solo with her beaker and laughing uncontrollably as she blew peas out of her mouth.

Lottie was laughing too, so that she didn't notice Ragnar had joined them until he said quietly, 'I didn't know vegetables could be that much fun.'

She felt her heart jolt forward. Lost in the familiar rhythm of spooning peas and mashed potato into her daughter's mouth, she'd started to feel calmer. She had overreacted, but obviously being thrown together like this in a new environment, with a man she barely knew, was going to be confusing and unsettling. It was no wonder she'd got mixed up about what she was feeling.

And so what if Ragnar looked like Thor's body-double? Once she got used to having him around he would soon lose the power to make her blood catch fire.

She gave him a quick, stiff smile. 'Neither did she until last week. It's her latest trick.'

It was harder than she would have liked to shut him out. He was just so *there*—not just his actual physical presence, but that inner stillness he possessed, a self-contained sense of certainty that she lacked entirely except in her art.

Her fingers felt thick and clumsy as he watched her pick up the empty bowl.

'Does she have dessert? Or is that not allowed?'

'Yes, it's allowed.'

There was a small pause and, nodding reluctantly to his unspoken question, she tried not to feel resentful or, even more ridiculously, betrayed as he picked up a spoon and her daughter obediently swallowed every mouthful of the yoghurt she gave him.

They were bonding, and that was what she'd wanted to happen, so why did it hurt so much? Maybe seeing them together was a reminder of how she'd failed to connect with Alistair. Or perhaps, having been briefly the sole focus of Ragnar's gaze, it stung to be in the shadows.

Her chest felt tight.

She hated herself for feeling like this—and him too, for stirring up all these ambivalent, unsettling emotions. Suddenly she wanted to be somewhere far away from his orbit. Reaching down, she undid Sóley's safety harness and lifted her out of the chair.

'I'm going to take her up now and get her ready for bed.'

She sensed that he was waiting for an invitation to join them, and she knew that she was being mean-spirited by not offering him one, but she couldn't make the words form in her mouth. For a moment she thought he would challenge her, but instead he just nodded.

'I'll come up and say goodnight in a bit.'

Normally Sóley loved bathtime, but tonight her eyes were already drooping as Lottie started to undress her, and she had barely finished half her regular bottle of milk before falling asleep.

Turning down the lights, she carefully transferred her sleeping daughter to the cot. But where was her bear? Lottie frowned. Mr Shishkin had been a gift from Lucas—Sóley couldn't sleep without him. Quickly she reversed her steps, but he wasn't in the bathroom, or on her bed.

As she walked back into her daughter's bedroom her feet faltered. Ragnar was leaning over the cot.

'What are you doing?' Her heart was beating like a snare drum.

He straightened up, his eyes meeting hers in the semi-darkness. 'I found him downstairs.' He held something out to her, and she realised what it was. 'I noticed she was pretty attached to him on the flight and I thought she might need him to sleep. Or is it a her? I didn't actually look.'

She hesitated, and then saw a faint smile tug at the edges of his mouth, and even though she knew that there were no actual butterflies in her stomach, she finally understood what people meant by that phrase, for it felt as though hundreds of them were fluttering up inside her, each beat of their wings triggering a warm, tingling pulse of pleasure.

'No, it's a he. He's called Mr Shishkin.'

Feeling his curious gaze, she felt her face grow warm.

'After Ivan Shishkin, the Russian artist.' Her eyes met his. 'It's a long story, but when I was about fourteen Lucas went to Russia with some mates and he sent me this postcard of a painting of some bears climbing in a wood by Shishkin. And then he gave Sóley the bear when she was born, so…' She cleared her throat. 'Anyway, thank you for bringing him up.'

Smiling stiffly, she edged past him and, leaning forward, tucked the bear under her daughter's arm.

'You don't need to thank me. In fact, I should probably be thanking you.'

She looked up at him in confusion. 'For what?'

He held open the door, then closed it gently behind her.

'For letting me in. I know it can't be easy for you—sharing her with me, letting me get close to her—so thank you. And, if I didn't say so before, thank you for telling me about her. If you hadn't done that…if you hadn't put your personal feelings to one side… I would never have known about her.'

He meant what he was saying. She could hear it in his voice. But that wasn't what was making her skin tingle.

'What do you mean, my personal feelings?' she asked slowly.

He studied her for a few half-seconds. 'I mean that you don't like me very much.'

'I— That's not— It's not that I don't like you. I just don't…' She hesitated.

'You don't trust me?' He finished the sentence for her.

There was a small, strained pause. 'No, I suppose I don't.'

He waited a moment. 'I can understand that. But if this is going to work—you and me and Sóley—I want that to change, and I'm going to do whatever it takes to make it change, to make you trust me. And I think the best way to achieve that is by talking and being honest with one another.'

She stared at him mutely. The blue of his eyes was so clear and steady that she could almost feel her body leaning forward to dive into their depths.

'Why don't we make a start over dinner?'

Her pulse twitched, and she took an unsteady step backwards.

Dinner. The word whispered through her head, making her think of soft lights and warm red wine, and his fingers moving through her hair, and his mouth tracing the curve of her lips, stealing her breath and her heartbeat…

'I was planning on getting an early night,' she said carefully. 'It's been a long day.'

His eyes fixed on hers.

'Not for Iceland,' he said softly. 'Please, Lottie. We can eat and talk at the same time. And Signy has already prepared the food.'

Lottie hesitated, but who could resist an invitation offered up so enticingly?

An hour later, with the entire uninspiring contents of her suitcase lying on the bed, she was starting to regret her decision. It wasn't that she cared what Ragnar thought—not really—it was just hard working out what to wear. At home in her draughty cottage with Lucas she just put on more layers, but Lucas was her brother. Then again she didn't want to look as if she was trying too hard.

In the end she settled for pale grey skinny jeans and a black cable-knit sweater, smoothing her hair into a slightly more glamorous version of her usual low ponytail.

She had thought they'd eat in the kitchen, but instead she found a table set for two in the dining area of the huge living space. The table was striking, made of some kind of industrial material—carbon fibre, maybe. It looked more like a piece of an aircraft than something you would dine around. But clearly it was a table, and it was set for dinner.

She breathed out unsteadily.

Dinner for two.

Only not some heavy-handed, candlelit cliché.

There was a soft, flickering light, but it came from a huge, slowly rotating, suspended black fireplace that she didn't remember seeing before, although obviously it must have been there. But maybe her mind was playing tricks on her, because the furniture looked different too—less angular and stark, more enticing…

She shivered. Of course everything familiar looked a little different in the shadows.

Ragnar was standing at the edge of the room. He looked like a monochrome portrait, his black jeans and sweater contrasting with the bleached gold of his hair and stubble, and she felt her body loosen with desire as he walked slowly towards her.

'Are you hungry?'

She stared at him, dry-mouthed, her unspoken hunger for him blocking out the ache in her stomach, and then she nodded. 'Starving.'

His eyes met hers, the pupils black and the irises blue like bruises. 'Then let's eat.'

The meal was simple but delicious.

Mussels with butter and birch, lamb with caramelised potatoes, and a burnt bay leaf ice-cream. She wasn't usually bothered about wine, but Ragnar's wine was exceptionally drinkable.

They both made an effort to avoid conversational pitfalls, so that despite her earlier reservations she found herself relaxing. Ragnar really wasn't like any other man she'd ever met. In her experience men either had no small talk at all, or pet subjects which they returned to again and again like homing pigeons. But, although his responses were brief, Ragnar was happy to talk about anything.

Mostly, though, he wanted to talk about their daughter.

As Signy cleared away the plates, he leaned back against his chair, his blue eyes resting on her face. 'It must have been hard, bringing up a baby on your own and being a professional artist at the same time. But I want you to know that you're not alone any more. I'm here to support you in whatever way I can.'

Trying to ignore the prickle of heat spreading across her skin, she met his gaze. An hour ago she had been feeling threatened by how easily Ragnar had been accepted by their daughter, but now it felt good to know that he would be there beside her.

'Thank you. But please don't think it was all bad. Like I said before, my family have been great, and Sóley's very easy going. She's more like Lucas than me in that way.'

His face stiffened, and her stomach clenched as briefly she wondered why, but before she had a chance to speculate he said softly, 'So how is she like you?'

She felt her face tighten. It was a question that had never occurred to her. Raising Sóley as a single parent, she'd never thought about her own genetic input. It had been a given. Now, though, she could feel that certainty slipping away. *How was her daughter like her?* Physically Sóley looked just like Ragnar, and character-wise she seemed to have Lucas's sunny, open temperament.

'I don't know,' she said slowly, flattening her hands against the table to stop them from shaking.

Her heart was beating too fast, and she felt a slippery sense of panic, as though she was looking through the wrong end of a telescope, watching herself shrink.

'I do.'

She glanced up, Ragnar was staring at her steadily.

'She has your focus. She even has the same little crease here…' reaching across the table, he touched her forehead lightly '…when she's concentrating.'

Her heart was still beating too fast, only this time not in panic but in a kind of stunned happiness. Ragnar was right. She did screw up her face when she was concentrating. And the fact that he'd made the connection made her breath catch in her throat.

'She doesn't just look at things, or people, she really gives them her whole attention. It's like she's already realised that there's something else there—some kind of "other" that she can't see.'

His fingers moved gently through her hair, then lower to her face, and his touch felt so warm and solid and irresistible that suddenly she was pressing her cheek against his hand.

She felt his hand tremble and, looking up into his face, she saw herself in the black of his pupils, saw her need and want reflected in his eyes and the same desire reflected back into hers, so that it was impossible to separate her hunger from his.

Her pulse scudded forward.

Behind her and around her the lights seemed to be spinning like a carousel, and she felt both warm and shivery. She must have drunk too much wine. But, glancing down, she saw that her glass was full. And then she looked up at Ragnar and felt her breathing change tempo as she realised that he was the source of her intoxication.

She reached shakily for the carafe of water but he was too fast.

'Here let me.'

He handed her a glass and she took it, being careful not to let her fingers touch his.

'I'm sorry… I think I must be tired.'

'We can leave dessert if you want.' As she nodded, he reached into his pocket and pulled out an envelope. 'I want to give you this. It's not urgent, but I'd like you to take a look at it when you've got a moment.'

She stared dazedly at the envelope. 'What is it?'

His eyes were a chilling, glacial blue. 'It's a letter from my lawyers—a kind of synopsis of my future relationship with Sóley.'

Her lungs felt as though they were on fire. Slowly she gazed across the room, seeing the soft lighting and glowing log fire as though for the first time.

She was such an idiot. All that talk about her seeing beneath the surface and here she was, oblivious to what was going on in front of her nose.

Her hands clenched around the stem of the glass. He'd even told her his plans.

'I'm going to do whatever it takes to make you trust me.'

And, like all successful businessmen, he'd identified her weak spot and then used the most effective weapon he had to exploit it and so achieve his goal. It just so happened that they were one and the same thing. *Himself.*

She felt numb. She had let her guard down, and all the

time he'd been cold-bloodedly pursuing his own agenda. He might have talked about support, but he wanted control.

She thought back to when he'd showed her Sóley's bedroom. Distracted by the sight of her own artwork, she'd missed the bigger picture.

The beautifully decorated room had been a message, spelling out the future—a future in which her daughter would be picked up by a chauffeur-driven car and taken by private jet to spend time with her father. Trips that would not include her.

Her heart contracted. Why did this keep happening? She had gone to meet her father and found she was superfluous. And now, having introduced her daughter to Ragnar, he was trying to push her out of Sóley's life.

Her heart began to beat hard and high beneath her ribs.

Well, he could think again.

Plucking the envelope from his hand, she stood up. 'I'll pass it on to my own lawyer.'

She was bluffing, of course. She didn't have a lawyer. But she wanted him to feel what she was feeling—to experience, if only for a moment, the same flicker of panic and powerlessness.

Watching his face darken, she turned and walked swiftly out of the room, trying to stifle the jerky rhythm of her heart, wishing that she could walk out of his life as easily.

CHAPTER FIVE

WATCHING LOTTIE STALK out of the room, Ragnar felt as though his head was going to explode. Had that just happened? He couldn't quite believe that it had, but then it was all a completely new experience for him.

Not someone flouncing off like a diva. That had been practically a daily occurrence during his childhood. Only back then, and even more so now, he had never been a participant in the drama.

Although with Lottie he kept getting sucked in and dragged centre stage.

And now she'd walked off in the middle of everything, leaving him mouthing his lines into thin air.

A part of him was desperate to go after her and demand that she act like the grown-up he and their daughter needed her to be—but what would be the point if he didn't know what he was going to say? And he didn't.

What was more, he had no idea how an evening which had started so promisingly had ended with her turning on him like a scalded cat.

Leaning back in his chair, he rubbed his hand over his face. Her reaction made no sense.

Earlier, outside their daughter's bedroom, when they'd talked about the future, he'd made it clear that he wanted to be honest with her and she'd seemed completely on board. In fact it had been the first time since their lives had reconnected that the conversation had felt ordinary and less like the verbal equivalent of a boxing match.

Agreed, his timing with the letter could have been better, but he had thought that she'd actually started to relax a little over dinner.

He glanced across to her empty chair. He had liked it that she had started to relax, for it had reminded him of the evening when they'd first met.

His pulse quickened.

It was strange. In real terms they had spent such a short time together—so short, in fact, that it could be comfortably counted in hours. And yet the memory of it had been imprinted in his head, so that it already felt as if he'd known her a lifetime.

His mind went back to the moment he'd first seen her. She had looked just like her profile picture on the app, and yet nothing like it. Her hair was a kind of mid to light brown, but the camera lens hadn't picked up all the lustrous threads of gold and copper, and nor had it caught the softness of her eyes or the sweetness of her tentative smile. But mostly, because of course it was only a photo, it had failed to capture that mesmerising husky voice.

Frankly, she could have been reading the phone book backwards to him and he wouldn't have noticed. And it had been the same earlier, as she'd talked about their daughter.

He hadn't wanted to break the spell. In fact, he hadn't been able to break it. Truthfully, he had been fighting himself all evening not to lean across the table and kiss her. But there was no point now in imagining how it would feel to have those soft lips part against his and, picking up his wine glass, he drained the contents.

Standing up, he switched off the lights and made his way upstairs. As he reached the top step he hesitated.

His rooms were to the right, but from where he was standing he could see a thin line of light beneath Lottie's door. Instantly he felt his breath clog his throat. She was awake, and they definitely had unfinished business. Before he had a chance to finish that thought, he was turning to the left and walking towards her room.

He reached her door in three strides and raised his

hand—but as he did so he caught sight of the illuminated numerals of his watch and something…a sharp memory of nights spent listening to the sound of raised voices and doors slamming…stayed his hand. Instead of knocking, his knuckles brushed soundlessly against the wood.

It was after midnight. The house was in darkness.

More importantly, this wasn't him. He watched, he waited, but he didn't participate. He certainly didn't ever walk into a storm of his own volition, and there was nothing to be gained by doing so now.

Restarting their tense conversation in the more intimate setting of her bedroom had 'bad idea' written all over it in mile-high letters. It would be far better to wait until the morning to confront her—not least because their strongest motive for any reconciliation would be awake and eating breakfast in her highchair.

Turning, he walked to his room. It was late, and he was tired, and his body was aching as though it was going through some kind of withdrawal.

He needed a quick shower and a long sleep—not some protracted debate with someone who was just going to argue that black was white.

Besides, she was probably already in bed.

He breathed in sharply, his groin hardening in the time it took his brain to jump from thinking the word 'bed' to picturing a near naked Lottie between the sheets.

Was this his fault?

He couldn't see how. The evening had been going so well. They'd eaten and talked, and watching the way her eyes shone with eagerness when she talked about Sóley had made his breathing lose rhythm. Only when he'd asked her how she was like her daughter the joy had faded from her voice and her fingers had started to shake as if someone was pressing a bruise on her heart.

He hadn't thought about what he was going say or do—

in fact he hadn't been thinking at all. He had felt her pain, and he'd wanted to make whatever it was that was hurting her stop, and so he'd reached out and touched her face, half expecting her to pull away.

Only she hadn't. And then, watching her eyes soften, he had been lost, falling back to that night when the softness in her eyes had stripped him not just of his clothes but of all sense and inhibition.

His body tensed—not at the memory of Lottie's hands pulling at the buckle of his trousers, but at the dull, insistent hum of his phone.

Glancing over to where it lay on the bed, he cursed softly. It would be Marta, his nineteen-year-old half-sister. She was the youngest member of his family and for the last two months had been holding off all rivals in a crowded field to take the title of most demanding sibling in his life.

His jaw tightened. He loved his sister, but since the acrimonious breakdown of her parents' marriage her life had been spiralling out of control. She had been stopped by the police and given a warning for reckless driving, and then she and her now ex-boyfriend Marcus had been involved in an argument with some photographers, after his twenty-first birthday party. And all of it had been gleefully reported in the media.

What she needed was guidance and reassurance.

What she had was a father—Nathan, who had already moved on to a new actress-model wife, and was wrapped up in the imminent birth of their first child.

She also needed her mother—who also happened to be *his* mother. Except Elin was far too busy being placated by her entourage of hairdressers and personal trainers to deal with her difficult daughter.

Only why did that make Marta his problem?

But he knew why. He couldn't turn his back on his family, and nor could he live like them, so the only way he could make it work was by taking a step back—just as he'd done outside Lottie's door.

He thought back to when Marta was a little girl. She had always been bringing him some necklace or bracelet that was so snarled up it was impossible to see where it began and where it ended, but he'd always sat down and patiently untangled it for her. It was just what he did—what he was still doing. Only now it was her life that he was untangling.

'Marta—'

He heard her quick breath, like a gasp, and then she was speaking incoherently, fat, choking sobs interspersing every other word.

'Ragnar—Ragnar, I hate her! She won't listen to me. It's not my fault. I can't stand living with her. You have to speak to her.'

She burst into tears.

Pushing back against the surge of tiredness swirling around him, Ragnar walked slowly across the room and stopped in front of the window, wondering exactly what had triggered this latest set-to between his mother and half-sister, and whether she had even considered the possibility that he might be sleeping.

Almost certainly not, he thought, gazing up at the sky. It was a clear night, and his brain ticked off the constellations as he waited for her to stop crying. When, finally, she let out a juddering breath he said calmly, 'Better? Okay, tell me what's been going on.'

It was a fairly straightforward story from Marta's point of view. In her telling, she was the innocent victim, her mother and father were twin evil villains, and he, Ragnar, had been drafted in to play the role of rescuer.

'She's horrible all the time and I'm sick of her acting like it's all about her.'

'It's not all about her—but she has just lost her husband,' he said mildly.

His sister's tears slid into resentful fury. 'He's not dead,' she snapped. 'He's just shacked up with that hideous stick insect in Calabasas. And anyway, it's hypocritical of her to be so upset. It wasn't as though she cared when she left Frank.'

To a certain extent that was true, Ragnar conceded. Elin had discarded her fourth husband, Frank, without so much as a backward glance, but perhaps she had expected her fifth husband to be her last. Although perhaps not. His mother had the kind of blonde ethereal looks that laid waste to any man who crossed her path, and she was rarely satisfied with anything or anyone for long.

But, putting aside Marta's tears and rage, what mattered was brokering peace between her and their mother.

'I think what you both need is a bit of space from one another.'

He hesitated. Lamerton would be empty for three weeks, and in his family three weeks was the equivalent of a decade in terms of drama. Quite possibly the whole thing would have blown over by then, but in the short term getting his sister and mother on different continents would stop them killing one another.

He cleared his throat. 'Look, if you need somewhere to stay you can use Lamerton. I'm sure you'll find something to amuse you in London.' Or more likely *someone*, he thought dryly. 'And if you don't want to see anyone you can just chill out on the estate.'

'Oh, Ragnar, really? You're an angel.'

Hearing her squeal of excitement, he nearly changed his mind. An empty house miles from anywhere and an unsupervised and excitable Marta were not a good combination—but, having planted the seed, he knew that it would be impossible to dislodge the idea from her mind. He would just have to hope that her fear of getting on his wrong side would curb her worst instincts.

'This doesn't mean I don't have rules, Marta,' he said firmly. 'You will be polite to John and Francesca. They are not there to put up with your mess or your tantrums.' He paused. 'Of course ordinarily I'd tell you to treat the place as your own, but in your case—*in your case*,' he repeated over her squawk of protest, 'I would ask that you don't. And do not—I repeat, *do not*—even think about having a party. And by "party" I mean any gathering of people numbering more than you and one other person.'

There was a small sulky silence from the other end of the phone, and then he heard her sigh.

'Okay, fine. I'll be polite, and I won't make a mess, and *obviously* I wouldn't dream of having a party in your house.'

Catching sight of himself in the window, Ragnar was tempted to roll his eyes at his reflection. Instead he said calmly, 'I just don't want there to be any confusion.' Glancing down at his watch, he grimaced. It was nearly a quarter past one. 'Right, I'll leave you to talk to Elin. Just let me know when you're going over and I'll send John to pick you up.'

'Thanks Ragnar.' Her voice softened and she hesitated. 'Actually, do you think you could call her? I think she'll take it better from you.'

After he'd hung up he stood with the phone in his hand, thinking. As usual Marta hadn't asked him one question about himself, but at no point had it occurred to him to tell his sister that she was an aunt. Nor was he planning on telling her until it was absolutely necessary. He wanted to keep his daughter to himself for a while—keep her from being absorbed by his family.

He'd talk to his mother later. Now he really was going to bed.

He showered quickly, towelled himself dry and then pulled on the loose cotton trousers he wore to sleep in.

As he unfastened his watch, he heard it.

A baby crying.

He paused, his body turning instinctively towards the sound.

The wail faded and, flicking off the light, he closed his eyes and rolled onto his side, his mind sliding smoothly into sleep.

He woke with a start.

Reaching out, he found his watch in the darkness. It was just gone half-two in the morning.

But why had he woken?

And then he heard it—the same unmistakable wail as before. For a few half-seconds he lay in the darkness, listening to his daughter cry. Only this time it didn't falter. Instead it seemed to be escalating.

Had she cried like that before?

Not really. A little on the plane, but that had been more like a kind of fussing.

His chest felt suddenly leaden with tension, and he sat up and switched on the bedside light.

It was ten to three now.

Was that a long time for a baby to cry?

Why wasn't she stopping?

He tried to remember his half-brothers and sisters at Sóley's age, but all the adults in his life had always been more than happy to let a crying baby or toddler disappear with a nanny.

His pulse sped up as the baby carried on wailing. She had seemed fine earlier, but she didn't sound fine now. Her cry was changing, intensifying in pitch, so that even at this distance he could feel her distress resonating inside his chest.

And suddenly he was moving—rolling out of bed and walking swiftly out of his room.

The noise grew louder and louder as he got closer. For a

moment he stood outside the door to his daughter's room, but when the crying began again he pushed it open.

Lottie was standing in the centre of the room with her back to him, wearing some kind of robe, her hair spilling over her shoulders. She was rocking the baby gently, making soothing sounds, and as he spoke her name she turned, her eyes widening with shock.

'Is everything okay?'

It wasn't. He didn't need to be a childcare expert to see that Sóley was upset and so was Lottie.

The baby's cheeks were red and tear-stained and she was burrowing against her mother's shoulder like some little mammal, then abruptly rearing backwards, her small face scrunched up in inconsolable fury.

Lottie looked pale and exhausted. 'She's teething.'

She winced as Sóley jerked her head up and banged into her chin, and then immediately began crying again.

As her ear-splitting crescendo of rage and frustration filled the room, Ragnar took a step forward. 'Here, let me.'

'No—' Her eyes flared, and she half turned away, clutching her struggling daughter. 'I didn't ask for your help and I don't want it.'

He could hear the fatigue in her voice—and something like fear.

Only why would she be scared?

He stared at her back in silence. He didn't know the answer to that question, but he did know that he didn't like the way it made him feel.

'Lottie,' he said again. 'I know you don't need my help. Of course you don't. You've managed without it for eleven months. I'm not trying to interfere—really, I'm not. Just tell me what to do and I'll do it.'

'You can leave.' She turned, her eyes fierce. 'That's what you can do.'

He stared at her, biting down on his own corresponding

rush of anger. Earlier she'd got upset about the letter from his lawyers, and now she'd turned on him like a cornered lioness with her cub—so what exactly was the right way for him to be a part of his daughter's life?

As though Sóley had heard his thoughts she lifted her head, her blue eyes fixing on his face, and then without warning she reached out for him. Shocked, he caught her, intending to return her to Lottie, but her tiny hands were already grasping his neck and he felt his heart swell against his ribs as she tucked her face against his shoulder, her sobs subsiding.

Her body felt hot and taut, but after a moment he felt her grow heavier and automatically he began to rock her in his arms, shifting slowly from side to side, holding his breath, his entire consciousness fixed on the softness of her cheek against his skin and its confirmation of his incontestable role in her life.

'Here.' Lottie was laying a blanket over her daughter's back. 'When you put her in the cot she needs to go on her side,' she said flatly.

He leaned over and placed the baby carefully on the mattress. As he slid his hands out from under the weight of her body she shifted in her sleep, her fingers splaying out like tiny pink starfish, but then she gave a small, juddering sigh, and as he tucked her bear underneath the blanket her breathing slowed and grew steadier.

He felt a rush of relief and exhilaration and, straightening up, he turned towards Lottie. It wasn't quite a team effort, but it was the first time they had worked together as parents. He wanted to share the moment with her and, stupidly, he had assumed, or hoped anyway, that she might feel the same way.

If anything, though, she looked drawn and distant, and desperate for him to leave.

His jaw tightened.

Obviously they had parted on poor terms earlier in the evening, and he would have to be emotionally tone-deaf not to see how annoying it must have been to watch Sóley settle in his arms, but surely she could take a step back and meet him halfway.

He glanced over at her small, still face.

Apparently not.

'So, I should—we should probably get some sleep,' she said stiffly.

There could be no mistaking either her tone or the implication of her words. She was dismissing him.

The skin of his face was stretched so tight he thought it might crack, and he was having to physically restrain his temper as though it was a wilful horse.

But he'd reached his day's quota of conversations with irrational childish women, and without saying a word he turned and left the room.

Watching the door close closed behind him, Lottie breathed out unsteadily.

She wanted to scream and rage like her daughter. Her whole body was jangling, aching with misery. She knew she was being unreasonable and petty, and that she should be happy that Ragnar wanted to be a hands-on father. But she hurt so badly that there wasn't room for any other feeling.

It had been such a shock, seeing Sóley reach out for him like that. Her daughter had always wanted *her*, before anyone else. Watching him settle her, she'd told herself that it didn't matter. That it was what was meant to happen and what she'd wanted to happen and that she didn't mind.

Except that she did mind.

It made her feel empty and cold, as though a huge dark cloud was blocking out the sunlight.

You're being stupid, she told herself. *You're just tired and it's making you think crazy thoughts. Sóley was exhausted. If he hadn't been there she would have settled with you.*

But that wasn't the point.

She had been there and her daughter had still chosen Ragnar. If he'd been in her life from birth she would never have questioned it, or cared. Only having grown up without a father herself, she'd assumed that she took precedence and that his role was secondary…inferior. Optional.

She bit her lip. But those were her mother's values, not hers, so why was she behaving like this? Why invite his involvement and then keep him at arm's length?

It was all such a mess.

If only she was at home. She would go downstairs, where the range would be warm, and she would lean against it, absorbing its heat while she waited for the kettle to boil. And maybe Lucas would wake up and come and sit at the table and tell her some crazy story about his day…

She pushed back against the swell of homesickness in her throat. Thinking about family and her cottage wasn't going to help. She needed to sleep, but the thought of lying in the darkness and just waiting for her body and brain to relax was appalling. Maybe if she made herself some tea? It would mean going downstairs, but it was what she would do at home and right now she needed something familiar.

Clutching the baby monitor and using her phone as a torch, she made her way to the kitchen. Thankfully, she remembered where the light switches were.

Signy had shown her how to use the stainless steel state-of-the-art coffee machine. But coffee was the last thing she wanted or needed.

'What are you doing?'

An electrical current snaked down her spine and her head snapped round. Ragnar was standing at the other end of the kitchen, watching her steadily.

She stared back at him, her heart bumping against her

ribs. Upstairs, with Sóley screaming and her nerves in meltdown, she had not really noticed what he was wearing—or rather not wearing. Now, though, in the quiet intimacy of the kitchen, it was difficult to drag her gaze away from his smooth, muscular chest, and the trail of tiny golden hair that disappeared into the waistband of his trousers.

But never mind what he was wearing, what about her? She glanced down at herself, her skin suddenly prickling. Had her robe shrunk or did it always show this much leg?

'I'm trying to find tea bags. Signy did show me, but I can't remember.'

'I know where they are.' He walked across the kitchen. 'Any particular flavour?'

She shrugged. As soon as his back was turned she jerked the robe tighter, tugging the hem lower over her thighs. 'Chamomile. Or peppermint. I can make it myself.'

There was a moment's silence.

'I'm sure you can,' he said.

She watched as he filled a teapot with boiling water from the coffee machine.

'Here we are.' He slid a teapot onto the counter. Her eyes darted to the cups—the *two* cups.

'I thought I'd join you.' His eyes rested on her face. 'Unless you've any objections?'

Taking her silence as consent, he slid onto one of the bar stools and she jerked her eyes away from the flex of his stomach muscles. 'Would it matter if I did?'

He held her gaze. 'That would depend, I suppose, on your objection.'

She swallowed. 'You sound like a lawyer.'

He didn't flinch. 'You're not on trial here, Lottie.'

'Really?' She shook her head. 'That's not how it feels to me.'

He leaned backwards, his arm draped casually against

the counter, but she caught a flash of blue and knew that he was watching her intently. 'I disagree.'

She blinked. 'Right. So you're telling me how I'm feeling?' she said slowly.

Her fingers twitched against the handle of the cup. There was something about his words that made a veil of red slide in front of her eyes. His arrogant assumption that he knew better than her. That he knew her better than she knew herself.

'That's not what I said.'

'And yet that's exactly how it sounded.' She glared at him.

He sighed. 'You know, if anyone's on trial here it's me—although I have to admit I'm not exactly sure what it is you're accusing me of doing.'

She was suddenly simmering with anger. Surely he was joking? 'Other than backing me into a corner and threatening me with lawyers at every opportunity.'

'There was nothing threatening in that letter—which you would know if you'd bothered to read it. But then why read it when you've already made up your mind?'

He spoke quietly, but she could hear a thread of exasperation weaving through his voice.

What did he have to be frustrated about?

She was the one losing control of her life and her daughter. And it was disingenuous of him to say that the letter wasn't threatening. Maybe it wasn't, but the fact that he had lawyers on call who worked out of office hours to protect his interests was intimidating, and he knew it.

'You said that you didn't want to escalate things,' she said accusingly. 'That you just want what's best for Sóley—'

'I don't.' He cut her off. 'And I do.'

'Well, I disagree.' She met his gaze, feeling a small rush of satisfaction as she threw his words back at him. 'You want what's best for you. Everything is on your terms.

Where we met, *when* we met. *This holiday.* You even went behind my back to Georgina.'

'Out of courtesy.' His blue eyes were like chips of glacial ice. 'And if I hadn't—if I'd left it to you—I'd still be waiting to meet my daughter.'

She stared at him, open-mouthed, a beat of anger leapfrogging across her skin. He was unbelievable. How could he be so unfair? So self-righteous?

'In case you've forgotten, I was the one who got in touch with you.'

'I haven't forgotten,' he said tersely. 'I just don't understand why you bothered.'

Her hands balled into fists. 'You know why. So you could get to know Sóley.'

'Except you don't want me to get to know her.' He shook his head, his blue eyes hard and uncompromising. 'What exactly is it you want from me? You gave me such a hard time for even suggesting that I help you financially, but every time I so much as offer to hold my daughter you can't get away from me fast enough. Look at tonight,' he carried on remorselessly, 'I wanted to help and you kept pushing me away.'

Her heart was pounding. He was right. She *had* pushed him away, and from his perspective it probably didn't make sense. But why did she have to see anything from his point of view? It wasn't as though her needs were high on his agenda.

She took a deep breath. 'Do you think that was the first time she's been like that?'

'No, of course not. And I'm not questioning your parenting skills. I know you can cope, but I don't know why you think you need to cope alone.'

She felt a buzzing in her ears. Out of any question he could have asked, it was the one that hurt the most. How could she explain to this cool-eyed stranger who didn't need anyone how she felt?

Her daughter's birth had made her feel whole and necessary. It had taken the sting out of her father's rejection and eased her ever-present sense of being 'other' to her mother and brother's dark-eyed autonomy.

And then she had seen Ragnar on television and, prompted by guilt and a desire to do the right thing, she had got in touch. Maybe it had been the right thing to do, but it felt like a mistake—only it had taken until tonight for her to see how big a mistake.

'It doesn't matter.'

Her throat tightened and she pushed back her chair. Her voice was shaking…her hands too. She wanted to leave, to crawl somewhere quiet and dark and hide from the terrible ache of loneliness that was swallowing her whole.

'It does to me.'

He was standing too now, but that wasn't what made her hesitate. It was the sudden fierceness of his words, as though they had been dragged out of him against his will.

'I have to go,' she said.

She felt his hand brush against hers.

'What is it?' he asked.

'It's nothing.' She shook her head. 'I'm just tired.'

'Tired of what?'

The gentleness of his voice as much as his question itself surprised her. 'I don't know,' she lied, lowering her face.

She couldn't tell him the truth. How could she explain the convoluted, chaotic journey that had brought her here, to this kitchen, to this man who lived his life by numbers?

But if she'd thought her silence would answer his question she'd been wrong. Glancing up, she saw that he was waiting, willing to wait for however long it took, and the fact that he was prepared to do that for her seemed to ease the tightness in her throat.

'It's stupid really…and unfair.'

'What is?' he said softly.

'It's not their fault. It's not my mum and Lucas's fault that I feel like an outsider when they're together.'

He studied her face. 'I thought you were close to them?'

'I am.' Her mouth trembled. 'I love them, and they love me, but we're so different.' She frowned. 'I know it sounds ridiculous, and I'm not expecting you to understand, but it feels like even though they're my family I don't fit in.'

For a moment he didn't reply, and then his eyes met hers. 'No, I do understand.'

She took a breath. 'I thought for a long time that I must be like my dad. My mum never told him she was pregnant with me, and I was convinced that if I met him there would be this moment of recognition, this connection between us.'

Her voice faltered, the memory of that stilted meeting catching her unawares, the feeling of failure and disappointment undimmed by time.

'But it didn't?' he asked.

She shook her head. 'It was too late. There was nothing there. We were like damp firewood.' Clenching her hands, she forced her mouth into a stiff smile. 'That's why I wanted you to meet Sóley now, when you still had room for her.'

'It wouldn't have mattered when you told me. I would always have made room for her,' he said simply, and her heart thudded hard as he caught her hands, uncurling her fists and slotting his fingers through hers. 'But that doesn't mean there isn't room for you too.'

She was about to protest, to pretend that he'd misunderstood, but then she thought back to how it had felt when her daughter had reached out to Ragnar. 'I don't want to lose her.'

'You won't.' Letting go of her hands, he gripped her shoulders. 'You can't lose her. She loves you and needs you more than anyone else in the world. You're her mother.'

'And you're her father.' Her face tightened. 'And I'm sorry that I've pushed you away.'

His gaze was the clear deep blue of an Arctic sky. 'I'm right here. And I'm not going anywhere.'

'But I've made everything so difficult—and that's not what I wanted to do…not what I want to do—'

She broke off, her insides tightening as they both listened to her words reverberate around the silent kitchen.

A minute passed, and then another.

'So, what is it, then?' he said hoarsely. 'What do you want to do, Lottie?'

She stared at him dazedly. Her tongue was in knots and she couldn't seem to breathe right. The air around her was shifting and swelling, pressing closer. She was losing her balance.

Reaching out to steady herself, she laid the palm of her hand against his chest. He breathed in sharply, his shoulders tensing, and the sudden acceleration of his heartbeat made her whole body tremble.

'What do I want?' she whispered.

For one intense, dizzying second they stared at one another, and then she took a small, unsteady step towards him.

'I want this,' she said and, leaning forward, she kissed him lightly.

His mouth was warm and firm, and she felt her limbs turn to air as he wrapped a hand around her waist and pulled her closer, moulding her body against his.

Heat was seeping through her robe, spreading out beneath the insistent pressure of his fingers, and she moaned softly, her arms circling his neck, her hands grasping his hair as he parted her lips, deepening the kiss. She felt his hands sliding smoothly over the bare skin of thighs, and then he was lifting her up onto the counter.

The granite was hard and cold, but she barely noticed. She could feel his lips moving over her neck, his tongue circling the pulse beating at the base of her throat, and then his hands cupped her breasts, and as his fingers pushed aside the thin fabric and found her nipples she gasped into his mouth.

Her head was spinning, her abdomen aching with a tension that made her stir restlessly against him. She was so tight and damp and, grabbing his arms, she curled her legs around his thighs, drawing him closer, pushing against the solid length beneath his trousers, trying, wanting, *needing* to appease the ache—

The sudden burst of static was like a thunderclap.

They both froze, jerking backwards from one another as though they'd been stung.

Lottie clutched at the counter as the kitchen swam back into focus. What were they doing? *What was she doing?*

'Lottie—'

Ragnar was standing beside her, but her eyes were fixed guiltily on the baby monitor.

'I have to go.'

She glanced up at him. His eyes were narrowed and he was breathing unsteadily. He looked as dazed as she felt, but right now she wasn't up to sharing anything with him—particularly her shock at their sudden mutual loss of control.

She shook her head. 'I can't.'

And, still shaking her head, she snatched up the monitor and fled.

CHAPTER SIX

STANDING IN FRONT of his bedroom window, Ragnar gazed unblinkingly into the lemon-coloured light. At some point it had snowed heavily, and an eiderdown of sparkling untouched whiteness stretched away from the house as far as the eye could see.

He had woken late—so late, in fact, that in the first few seconds after he'd opened his eyes he'd struggled to remember where he was, even when it was. The last time he'd slept in late he'd been about fourteen years old.

He breathed out against the dull ache in his groin. And that wasn't the only similarity with his fourteen-year-old self. His body hardened as he rewound his mind back through the early hours of the morning, pressing 'pause' at the moment when Lottie had reached out and touched his chest and then leaned in to kiss him, or had he lowered his mouth to kiss her?

She had been wearing some kind of soft cotton robe and, catching a glimpse of her trying to smooth the fabric so that it covered more of her thighs, he had completely lost track of what she saying, for it had been all too easy to imagine those same hands smoothing and caressing his body.

But had he known what was about to happen?

He considered the question. Not in terms of seconds and minutes maybe. And yet it had been out there waiting to happen since the moment their lives had reconnected outside his office.

They'd both been fighting it, using anger to deflect their desire, but each time they'd quarrelled their hunger had edged out their anger a little more, until finally it had been too tempting, too inevitable, too impossible to resist.

Their unfinished connection was like that feeling when you found a loose tooth and couldn't leave it alone and kept probing and jiggling it with the tip of your tongue. Hardly surprising then, that they had ended up kissing.

The kiss had been fierce and tender and beyond any conscious control. A kiss driven by a need and hunger that had burned like a molten core deep inside him.

It had lasted sixty seconds at most, and yet it had felt like an admission of everything that had gone on between them. And everything that was still pulling them together now.

He breathed out unsteadily. It was the first time he'd really acknowledged that fact—that this pulsing thread of longing was as much about the present as the past. Although why it had taken him so long to figure that out was a mystery, given that he seemed to think about Lottie in all the pauses in his day and in the dark silence of the night.

To put it in its simplest terms, he wanted her—and she wanted him. But where would that wanting take them?

His heart thumped lightly against his ribs. Sex was supposed to be simple, and at its most simple it was just bodies connecting and intertwining.

He felt his body harden more.

But, of course, in reality sex was rarely that straightforward. How could it be? There were billions of people on the planet. Even if you eliminated vast numbers of them on the grounds of age, geography, or mutual attraction, that still left a lot of potential hook-ups out there—and, realistically, what were the chances of two people who felt exactly the same way about sex and commitment finding one another and then continuing to feel the same way until death parted them?

He grimaced. Judging by his family's track record: slim to none. But he already knew that. It was the reason he'd created *ice/breakr* in the first place. To mathematically optimise the odds of couples finding a match. And the numbers clearly worked. According to the latest data from his team, the app was making about twelve million matches a day.

There was just one small problem. According to his own algorithm, one night should have been enough to satisfy both himself and Lottie—and they'd already shared a night. Yet just hours ago, the strength and speed of their desire had been mutual and irresistible.

So what happened now?

He sighed. He was back where he'd started and no nearer to finding an answer.

The dull, insistent ring of his phone made him glance away from the window and the confusing, circuitous path of his thoughts. Walking over to his bed, he picked up the phone and looked down at the screen, his face stilling. It was his mother.

He'd called her earlier and left a message, suggesting that Marta should go over and stay at Lamerton. No doubt she was returning his call. He was about to answer her when something pulled at the edge of his vision—a movement, the shape of a person, a woman…

His pulse began to beat faster, his heart leaping against his ribs as though trying to reach her.

It was Lottie, holding Sóley in her arms. Maybe it was her clothes—she was dressed for the weather in a black fur-trimmed parka and dark jeans—or maybe it was her loose ponytail and chunky dark boots, but she looked more like a student than a professional artist and mother.

He stared at her, transfixed. In the margins of his brain he knew that his phone was still ringing, but for the first time in his life he ignored it.

There was something so beautiful and tranquil about the scene outside his window, and he didn't want to risk spoiling it by letting an episode of his family soap opera play out in the background.

He felt his phone vibrate in his hand as his mother left a message. But that was fine. For once, she was going to have to wait.

His shoulders tightened. Outside the window, Lottie was holding out a handful of snow for his daughter to inspect.

His daughter.

He frowned. He should call his mother back, tell her about Sóley. Forming the words inside his head, he tried to imagine saying them to his mother. But, just as when he'd been talking to Marta, he checked himself—and immediately felt guilty, but relieved.

At some point he would tell everyone, but right now he wanted to keep his daughter to himself for a little longer—to defer the moment when she would be absorbed by his chaotic, wonderful, exhausting family.

He walked slowly beside the window, shortening his strides to mirror Lottie's as she picked her way slowly across the snow-covered lawn like one of the deer at Lamerton.

She stopped, and he stopped too. Holding his breath, he watched her lean forward and lower the little girl onto the snow. Sóley was wearing an all-in-one snowsuit, and her bright golden curls were hidden beneath a tiny hat shaped like some kind of fruit. Holding both her mother's hands, she teetered unsteadily on the spot, but even at this distance her excitement was tangible, and he felt a smile pull at the corners of his mouth as she tugged one mittened hand free and crouched down to pat the snow.

It might be the first time she'd ever seen it, and he felt a buzz of elation at witnessing her delight.

He stared intently through the glass, enjoying this unexpected opportunity to observe mother and daughter together, all the more so because Lottie had no idea that she was being watched.

His mouth twisted.

That made it sound like he was spying on her—but was it really so bad to want this one small moment to himself? Obviously it wasn't the first time he'd seen the two of them together, but he knew his presence set Lottie's teeth on edge.

Although maybe that had changed now, he thought, remembering how she had opened up to him in the early hours of the morning.

When she'd first started talking about feeling tired he'd assumed she was referring to all the sleepless nights involved in having a small baby, but then she'd told him about her father's rejection, and her feeling of being different from her mother and brother.

Her honesty had surprised and touched him—the more so because he still regretted the lies he'd told her that first night.

But it was not just her honesty that had got under his skin.

His sisters and brothers, even his parents, poured out their hearts to him on a regular basis, but always his first instinct was to blank out the emotional drama and concentrate solely on the facts. Only with Lottie there had been no drama. She hadn't wept or raged, and yet he'd found it impossible to block out the quiet ache in her voice as she'd told him her story.

It was an unsettling discovery to meet someone who could slip beneath his defences, and for it to be Lottie was even more unnerving. Only wasn't it completely understandable for him to feel that way? Logical, even?

Lottie was the mother of his daughter, so of course he cared. He hadn't liked knowing that she was upset, or that in some clumsy way he had contributed to her distress. And it had been only natural for him to want to comfort her.

Glancing back down at the woman standing in the snow, he felt his body still, remembering the feverish kiss they'd shared. Truthfully, comforting her had been low, low down on his agenda when the blood had been pounding through his veins and he'd lowered his mouth to those sweet, soft lips.

He wanted her and she wanted him, and his heartbeat stumbled as the question came back to him—the one he'd turned away from earlier. *But where would that wanting take them?*

He wasn't a fool, and he knew that giving in to this ache, this hunger, this pull between them, would end badly. How could it not? There was too much at stake—too much to lose or damage or both. Having sex with Lottie, no matter how badly he wanted it or she wanted it, would introduce too many random elements into their relationship, and he didn't do random.

He felt his shoulders stiffen.

More to the point, he didn't do relationships.

And here in his home, the home he was sharing with her and their daughter, sex was never going to feel like just some casual hook-up. There would be consequences—tempting to ignore now, in the face of the urgency and pull of their desire, but as he knew from personal experience of unpicking his family's destructive, impulsive affairs, they were consequences that ultimately neither of them would be able to outrun.

Consequences he didn't want to take on.

Not now, not ever.

Taking her eyes off her daughter for a moment, Lottie raised her face and gazed up at the sky. She had been hoping that it would have the same effect that it did in Suffolk, and that the feelings of inadequacy and mortification she'd been carrying on her shoulders since waking would magically melt away in the face of its vast indifference.

It might have worked if the sky had been the washed-out grey of yesterday. Unfortunately she was in Iceland, and today the sky was the same brilliant blue as Sóley's eyes—Ragnar's too.

Her heart gave a thump and she felt a thumbprint of heat on both cheeks as she thought back to what had happened and what might so easily have happened in the early hours of this morning.

She still couldn't quite believe that she'd told Ragnar about her father, and about how she felt about Lucas and her mum. But that wasn't even the worst part. As if blurting out all that wasn't mortifying enough, she'd then completely lost her mind and kissed him.

Driven by the restless ache that had been turning her inside out, she hadn't been able to hold back—and she hadn't wanted him to hold back either.

She'd crossed the line. Not in the sense of winning a race, but by stepping into a no-man's land where anything could and might happen.

It was just a kiss, she told herself firmly. And yet if the baby monitor hadn't interrupted them, what then?

Short answer: nothing good.

Her skin twitched as her brain silently offered up a slideshow of herself and Ragnar, their naked bodies a perfect fit as they moved together, breath quickening in a shuddering climax.

Okay, that was a lie.

Sex with Ragnar would be fierce and tender and utterly unforgettable, but that was exactly why she should never have kissed him.

Her heart began beating a little faster. It was tempting to blame her behaviour on tiredness, or the stress of the last few days—to argue that the simmering anger between them had blurred into another kind of intense emotion and so struck a different kind of spark.

And, yes, some of those arguments were plausible, and

others were true, but none of them was the reason she had kissed him. That was much more simple.

He had been standing in front of her, close enough that she could feel the heat coming off his skin, close enough that his gaze had made her think of choices, and possibilities, and a never-forgotten night of peerless pleasure.

In other words, she had kissed him because she'd wanted to.

But then he had kissed her back, his mouth parting hers, pressing her closer, until their bodies had been seamless, until she had been frantic and twisting in his arms—

Her face felt hot, the skin suddenly too tight across her cheekbones. She knew she should regret what had happened, and yet she couldn't—not quite. But that didn't mean it was going to happen again.

Clearly she and Ragnar had 'chemistry'. It seemed like such a boring word for the astonishing intensity of their attraction, for the ceaseless craving that made her breathing change pace. But, after struggling even to be civil to one another, they had finally achieved a fragile symbiosis based on what was best for Sóley. Having sex was only going to put that in jeopardy. Whatever her body might want to believe.

Sex was never simple.

Her daughter was proof of that.

She and Ragnar had used logic and mathematical certainty to select one another, on the basis that they both wanted the same thing, only that certainly hadn't included having a baby together.

But, even without putting Sóley into the equation, she knew from her own limited and unremarkable experience that for most people, most of the time, sex was more than just bodies. There was always some kind of emotional response—regret, hope, doubt, excitement—and that response was often complex and confusingly contradictory.

Right now she didn't need any more confusion in her life, and she was going to have to find a way to express that to Ragnar.

She swore silently, and Sóley looked up at her, her eyes widening in confusion as though she had actually heard and understood the word.

'Let's go and get your lunch,' she said, and quickly, guiltily, swung her daughter up into the air and held her close, burying her face in her daughter's neck until the soft pressure of Ragnar's mouth was just a dull memory.

For the moment anyway. But she was going to have face him sooner or later.

She turned towards the house—and froze.

Ragnar was walking towards her, smoothly and steadily, his blond hair shining like bronze in the sunlight. Unlike her, he wasn't wearing a coat, just a dark jumper with jeans and boots, and suddenly her breath felt hot and slippery in her throat. He was so heart-stoppingly handsome—and, in comparison to the flickering images inside her head, as solid and unwavering as a long ship.

'Hello.'

He stopped in front of her, his eyes meeting his daughter's, his face softening in a way that made her stomach crunch into a knot of pleasure and pain.

'How was the rest of your night?'

'It was fine. She didn't wake up until nearly nine.'

Should she say something now? She hesitated. Words were not her thing, but she couldn't exactly sketch or sculpt what she needed to say to him.

His blue gaze shifted to her face. 'And what about you? Did you manage to get any sleep?'

There was a small beat of silence. Then she nodded, still tongue-tied as he stared at her impassively. And then, with relief, she saw that Signy was hurrying towards them.

'I didn't realise you were out here.' The older woman's

unruffled smile cut effortlessly through the awkward silence. 'Lunch is ready. Or I could feed Sóley if you and Mr Stone are talking? I'd be more than happy to,' she added as Lottie started to protest.

But it was too late. A hungry and determined Sóley was already reaching for Signy with her arms outstretched and, heart pounding, Lottie watched helplessly as her daughter disappeared into the house.

She had no excuse now not to say something.

But before she could open her mouth he said abruptly, 'Would you like to come and have a look at the horses with me? They're out in the paddock. I thought maybe—' He frowned and stopped speaking mid-sentence, as though he'd said more than he'd intended.

She hesitated. Yesterday she would definitely have made up some excuse and refused, but today it was easier to nod and say, 'Thank you, that would be lovely.'

The horses were beautiful, and incredibly friendly. They were all different sizes and colours, from piebald through to palomino, and their coats were thick and shaggy like reindeer fur. Peeling off her gloves, she leaned over the wooden fence to touch their velvety faces. As a beautiful chestnut put his face forward for her to rub, she realised that she was enjoying herself.

Her stomach tightened. So maybe she didn't need to talk to him after all.

Here, in the bright sunlight, with the crisp air on her skin, their kiss felt distant and dreamlike. Perhaps if they stood here for long enough the brilliant blue sky might part like the sea and swallow up the memory of it entirely.

'Do you ride?'

His voice jogged her thoughts and, glancing up, she instantly realised the stupidity of that notion.

It was nearly two years since she and Ragnar had slept together and yet she could still remember every second.

And not just his hard-muscled body or the careless beauty of his face. He had an aura, a disruptive, sensual energy beneath his stillness, and it separated him from every other man she'd ever met. And right now that aura was pinning her to the frozen ground and making her limbs flood with heat.

She nodded. 'I used to. When I was younger we lived in a converted farm building and the farmer's wife had horses. She let me and Lucas ride them in exchange for mucking them out.'

She felt his gaze on her profile and, looking over, found that he was staring at her intently.

'And now?'

She shrugged. 'I don't really have the time.'

His expression shifted infinitesimally, in a way that she couldn't pinpoint—a kind of tensing in anger, but not quite.

'But you'd like to?'

As she nodded, he seemed to relax a little.

'I'll make it happen,' he said softly.

'Thank you,' she said. 'And thank you for yesterday… well, I mean this morning. For listening to me. I'm sorry to throw all that drama at you.'

'Drama?' He seemed amused or maybe surprised by her choice of word. 'You were very dignified—not dramatic at all. And I'm sorry that I made you feel excluded. Truly it wasn't and isn't my intention to push you out of Sóley's life.'

'I know. I understand that now.'

She glanced past him. There was nobody around. If she waited until they went back into the house she might have to seek out another private moment, and the thought of being alone with him inside was the spur she needed to speak.

'About what happened after we talked…'

She looked up, jolted by hearing the words she had been about to say come out of his mouth.

'You mean when I…?' She hesitated.

He gazed at her steadily. 'I mean when we kissed.'

For a second her vision blurred. It felt significant, him choosing those particular words, for he could have made it sound like her sole responsibility. Instead he was admitting his own desire had played a part.

'I thought you might want to pretend it hadn't happened,' she said.

There was a small silence, and then he shook his head. 'I don't want to do that—and even if I did I'm not sure that I could.'

His gaze fixed on her face and she felt her blood thicken and slow at the hunger in his eyes…a hunger that seemed to reach through the layers of her padded jacket so that she could feel heat spiralling up inside her.

'I know I haven't given you much reason to trust me, but trust me on this: I wanted to kiss you every bit as much you wanted to kiss me. I was just waiting for permission.' He gave her a small, taut smile. 'Look, Lottie, there's something I need to say to you. I want you to know how sorry I am for lying to you the night we met. I hope that maybe one day you'll believe that's not who I am.'

She stared at him in silence, processing his statement. He made it sound as though he'd acted out of character—but then why had he lied to her?

It was on the tip of her tongue to ask, but what had happened early this morning had to take precedence over the past. 'Why are you telling me this now?' she asked.

'I want us to be honest with one another,' he said simply. 'About what happened and why.'

'I don't know why it happened.' She paused. He had been open with her, so he deserved honesty in return. 'Or maybe I do…' Her face tightened. 'I know it's been twenty months since we—'

There was a small silence.

'I thought you might have forgotten,' he said quietly.

She wanted to laugh. Forget him? Forget that night? 'No, I didn't forget you, Ragnar. I can't.'

'You mean Sóley—?'

The sun was in her eyes, making his face unreadable. But she hadn't been talking about her daughter, she thought with a mix of shame and panic. She had been talking about *him*, and about how he had made her feel, and the soft, urgency of his mouth, and her own quickening gasp as she arched against him.

'There hasn't been a day when I haven't thought about you,' he said.

Looking up at him, she let her gaze search his face and, seeing the heat in his eyes, she nodded, acknowledging the truth of his words and the fact that they were true for her too.

His hand came up and she breathed in sharply as his fingers traced the curve of her cheekbone. Without knowing it was what she wanted to do, or that she was going to do it, she rubbed her face against his hand.

'I thought it would pass,' he said simply.

She stared at him, hypnotised by the ache in his voice—an ache she shared. 'Me too.' With an effort she slid her head away from his hand. 'And it will… But in the meantime I don't think acting on it would be—' She stopped.

'A good idea?' he finished for her.

'It would be a very bad idea,' she agreed.

She could hardly believe she was talking to him like this, but what were the alternatives? To pretend that it was a figment of their imaginations? To listen to their libidos?

Of course she could see the appeal of both—but, while she didn't know the limits of the man standing beside her, she knew her own limits, and there was no way she could play happy families with Ragnar and have no-strings sex with him at the same time.

'We're here to be parents and I think we should concentrate on that,' she said.

'I'm glad we're on the same page,' he said quietly.

Her fingers tightened against the fence and she winced as something small and sharp dug into her skin. It was just a splinter, but it stung more than it should, and she welcomed the pain—for it gave her something to focus on other than the hollowed-out feeling in her stomach. But however much it hurt, she knew her regret at stopping things before they got started would be inconsequential compared to the fallout from a self-indulgent affair.

Straightening up, she met his gaze. 'I think we should probably get some lunch.'

'Then let's go and see what Signy has cooked for us,' he said slowly.

Lunch was a beautiful fish soup with fresh sourdough bread and the most delicious butter she had ever eaten.

After lunch, Sóley almost fell asleep in her highchair. Transferring her smoothly into his arms, Ragnar took her upstairs to bed.

Lottie watched him go. It was getting easier to let him be involved now, and it was also a relief to have a few minutes without her body being so intensely aware of exactly where he was in relation to her.

She glanced around the empty kitchen, and then wandered into the huge living space. It was a beautifully proportioned room, and the light was truly incredible. As it shifted in depth and colour it was like a kind of ever-changing art installation that perfectly complemented the striking mobile spinning and shifting in the invisible air currents.

Her pulse twitched. Mobiles were supposed to be calming, and yet she felt anything but calm.

Restlessly she moved around the room. Ragnar's taste was minimalist. Everything was pared back to its essence, each piece selected on the basis that its beauty equalled its functionality.

Surprisingly, given its stark beauty, it was still a comfortable, welcoming space—perhaps because it so clearly embodied the personality of its owner. She glanced over to the amazing rotating suspended fireplace. The room certainly didn't feel cold. She could feel the heat from the fire seeping into her blood.

Collapsing onto one of the huge leather sofas, she leaned back against the cushions and gazed upwards—straight into Ragnar's blue eyes.

'Are you tired?'

He dropped down beside her, and instantly his nearness made her breathe out of time.

'A little bit.'

The light from the fire was playing off his face and for a moment she stared at him in silence, transfixed by the shifting shadows. And then her pulse tripped over itself as he put his hand on her shoulder and pressed down lightly.

'You're tense here…'

Was she? She didn't feel tense. In fact her body felt as though it was melting.

Pull away, she told herself. *Move.*

But her limbs wouldn't respond. Instead—and completely unforgivably, given what she'd said to him at the stables—she could feel herself wanting to arch against him like a cat.

'You need to relax…'

His voice vibrated through her shoulder blade and a prickling heat spread over her skin.

'Have a bit of down-time. Maybe unwind in the pool. We could take a dip after dinner.'

Her head was spinning. There were so many dangerous words in that sentence. *Relax, unwind, pool, dip, after dinner...* And yet the idea of a relaxing swim in a hot pool was so tempting. Her eyes roamed briefly around the exquisite room. Really, when was she ever going to get a chance to live like this again?

'That sounds lovely.'

'You won't regret it.' His gaze met hers. 'In fact, your body might even thank you.'

There was no moon but it was a cloudless night and, staring up through the glass ceiling of the pool house, Ragnar allowed himself a moment to tick off the constellations in the dark sky before wading into the steam-covered water.

He breathed out slowly. It was like slipping into liquid velvet. It was incredibly warm—blood-hot, in fact—and as he lowered himself down he felt his body grow heavy with a languid, almost boneless weight.

On any other night he would have simply floated on his back and watched the stars. Now, though, he moved slowly through the water, his narrowed gaze tracking the progress of the woman making her way along the edge of the pool like a nervous gazelle at a watering hole.

His heartbeat accelerated as she slipped off the thick towelling robe and dropped it onto one of the fur-covered loungers at the side of the pool. Underneath she was wearing a caramel-coloured swimsuit, a shade darker than her eyes, which hugged her body in a way that was completely understandable.

Watching her step down into the pool, he mentally thanked Signy for reminding him to suggest that she bring one.

As the water closed over her shoulders he felt a sharp twinge of regret that no amount of geothermal heat was going to fix but, ignoring his quickening pulse, he swam towards her.

'How does it feel?'

'It feels wonderful.' Her gaze followed the steam rising up from the water. 'And a bit crazy.'

'Why crazy?' He swam a little closer, drawn in by the surprise and excitement in her face.

'I don't know—it just seems mad for there to be snow everywhere and yet the water in here's so hot.'

'Well, it is the land of fire and ice.'

'The land of fire and ice?'

She repeated his words slowly and, feeling his body respond to the eagerness in her voice, he cursed himself silently. If anything was crazy it was his suggestion that he and Lottie take a dip together beneath the stars. But of course he'd been slowly going crazy for days, his feverish brain torturing his body with images of a naked, gloriously uninhibited Lottie.

They swam slowly in silence. He usually swam alone, and when he was away from Iceland he craved his solitary moments in the pool, but with Lottie beside him he felt an entirely different kind of craving, and he was shocked by how badly he wanted to give into it.

His stomach clenched. It made no sense after what he'd said earlier, and what she'd said, and yet it was there—a need, a hunger, a heat that had nothing to with any geothermal activity.

'Do you use the pool a lot?' she asked softly.

He nodded. 'Usually once a day. Sometimes twice. During the day you can see the sky reflected in the water and it's like you're swimming among the clouds.'

She turned towards him, her eyes wide and unguarded, and he felt something squeeze in his chest at the surprise he saw there.

'I didn't have you down as a poet,' she said.

For a moment, he was captivated by the softness in her voice, and then he felt an almost vertiginous rush of panic.

Glancing upwards, he felt his body loosen with relief.

'I know my limits. If you want real poetry, you just need to look up.'

She gasped. Above them, the sky seemed to be melting. Colour was suffusing the darkness, lighting up the night, and swathes of green and amber and amethyst were swirling and shifting like oil on water.

It was the Aurora Borealis—the Northern Lights—but Ragnar barely noticed the dazzling display. He was too busy watching Lottie.

He breathed out unsteadily. His body was alive with need, worse than before, and his heart hammered in his ears so that thinking was impossible. But he didn't need a conscious brain to know that he still wanted Lottie.

And then, just like that, the show was over.

'We should go in,' he said quietly.

She nodded, following him reluctantly out of the pool. 'Did you know that was going to happen?'

He held out the robe. 'Only in that it's a clear night and it's the right time of year.'

He hardly knew what he was saying, but what he did know was that he still regretted those lies he'd told her that first night. And if he didn't tell her what he was thinking now, wasn't that just a different kind of lie? One he would regret for ever?

So tell her the truth. Be honest, like you said you wanted to be.

He met her gaze, felt his pulse stilling. His home here in Iceland was his sanctuary. A place of calm and order. If he said what he was thinking then he ran the risk of unleashing chaos and passion here.

But if he didn't, what then?

The chaos would still be there, underneath the surface, and it wasn't going anywhere.

And now, finally, he understood why. Ever since that night in the hotel room he hadn't felt whole. The panic that had led him to slip away while she slept still haunted him, and only by owning this hunger was he going to restore balance to his life.

'Earlier…when I talked about what happened… I think I was wrong. Actually, I *know* I was wrong.' He frowned. 'What I'm trying to say is this thing between us, I know it's complicated and confusing…but it's also real, and pretending it isn't would be a lie. I think you feel the same way. But if you don't, that's okay. I just need you to tell me and then I'll never—'

'I do.' She swallowed. 'I do feel the same way.'

His eyes dropped to her mouth. Had she spoken or had he just imagined it?

'Are you sure?' he said hoarsely.

'About wanting you? Yes.'

She looked away and, reaching out, he gently framed her face with his hands. 'We don't need to have all the answers, Lottie.' He was surprised to find that he meant what he said. 'We can work it out together.'

She breathed out shakily and his own breath stalled in his throat as she let the robe slide from her fingers to the floor. For a few pulsing half-seconds she stared at him in silence, and then she took his right hand from her cheek and pressed the palm against her breast.

He felt his pulse accelerate, his body hardening with a speed that almost made him black out, and then, leaning forward he kissed her. Only not in the way she'd kissed him in the kitchen. This was a raw and urgent kiss, a kiss without restraint, a kiss designed to satisfy the hunger in both of them.

'You have no idea how much I want you,' he murmured against her mouth. 'I haven't been able to get you out of my mind.'

'Me too,' she whispered. She was leaning into him so

that their foreheads were touching, their warm breath mingling. 'It's like you're in my head…'

Her voice, that beautiful husky voice, made his body loosen with desire. Beneath his hand he could feel her nipple tightening through the damp fabric of her swimsuit and, breathing raggedly, he began caressing the swollen tip with his thumb, liking the way it made her arch into him and the sudden quickening of her breath.

Her hands were clutching him and tugging him closer, pulling at the waistband of his shorts, and then she pressed her hand against the hard ridge of his body and he groaned.

'Let's go upstairs—' He was fighting to get the words out.

'No.' Her voice was husky with need.

He tried to protest, but it turned into another groan as her fingers slid beneath the waistband. Recognising defeat, he picked her up and dropped her onto the nearest lounger. As she sprawled backwards on the fur he took a step away and, keeping his eyes trained on her face, he slid down his shorts.

CHAPTER SEVEN

HIS HEART WAS slamming against his ribs like a door in a gale.

Had any woman ever looked sexier? She was sprawled against the fur, her eyes wide and feverish, her damp hair spilling over her shoulders. Like the ice in spring, he felt his blood start to melt as his gaze dropped lower. The wet fabric of her swimsuit looked so much like melted caramel all he could think about was how it would feel to lick it off the curves of her body.

It was suddenly difficult to swallow past the hunger swelling in his throat, and without even really knowing that he was doing so he moved swiftly to join her.

Her skin was hot to touch, and dotted with drops of water like tiny transparent pearls. Leaning forward, he touched the one closest with the tip of his tongue and then, keeping his eyes fixed on her face, he traced a path to the next one, and the next, feeling her tremble at his touch.

'Ragnar…'

She murmured his name, and it was the sweetest sound he'd ever heard. He stretched out over her and kissed her hungrily. She cupped his face with her hands and kissed him back. They broke apart to catch their breath, and then without a word he reached out and slid first one and then the other strap away from her shoulders, peeling the damp costume away from her body until she was naked.

He breathed out unsteadily, staying his hunger to admire her high, firm breasts and slightly rounded stomach. 'You're so beautiful,' he whispered and, lowering his face, he ran his tongue over her nipples, tasting the salt from the water as she arched upwards, pressing against him, offering herself to the heat of his mouth.

And then she was jerking free, her eyes dark and fierce, and he breathed in sharply as she reached for him, wrapping her fingers around his hard length. His hand gripped hers but she batted him away, bending over him to brush her lips against him. And then she was taking him into her mouth and he was groaning, his fingers grasping her hair, his body gripped by a pleasure so intense it was almost painful.

He was fiercely aroused, his body tight to the point of breaking. The feel of her mouth was turning him inside out. He was so close, *too close—*

Clenching his teeth, wanting, needing to be inside her, he pulled away, moving with panicky suspended hunger to fit his body against hers.

'Ragnar…'

Her fingernails dug into his back, but it was the urgency in her voice that cut through his heartbeat.

'I'm not protected.'

Not protected.

He stared down at her, blood roaring in his ears. His preoccupied overheated body was making it hard to think clearly and her words were bouncing off his dazed brain like hailstones on a roof.

And then he swore silently—not just at the implied consequences of that statement, but at his own near-adolescent loss of control. Had he really been so caught up in the moment that he'd forgotten all about contraception?

Catching sight of her small set face, he put his shock and shame to one side and, blanking out the relentless ache in his groin, captured her face between her hands and kissed her gently. 'It's okay…we don't have to—'

He breathed out against her cheek, fighting to contain the desperation in his voice. He would rather wait than put her under pressure.

Her fingers tightened against his arms. 'I want to, only I don't have any condoms.'

'It's okay,' he said again. 'I don't either—well, not here, anyway.'

He didn't want her to think that he wasn't careful, and nor did he want it to look as if he'd made assumptions about what would happen here tonight.

She bit her lip. 'There hasn't really been anyone since… That's why I'm not…why I haven't…'

He didn't know why but her words made a warm ripple of relief spread over his skin, and without meaning to, he said softly, 'There hasn't been anyone for me either.'

Her eyes widened. He wasn't sure if she believed him. Hearing it out loud, he found it difficult to believe too, but it was true. After what had happened with Lottie he'd buried himself in work, too unnerved by the failure of his mathematical certainties to test them again in person.

She breathed out unsteadily. 'We should probably go inside.'

The prospect of returning to his room alone made his body tense—with hunger, not misery—but he managed to nod. 'Yes, we should.'

He felt her lean into him, and hesitate, and then she said shakily, 'My room or yours?'

The air swelled around them, swallowing up her question and retreating. He stared down at her in confusion. 'I don't— We don't— I'm not—'

Her wide-eyed, panicky gaze met his. 'Have you changed your mind?'

Hope fought with fear, and he gripped her tightly. 'You know I haven't. I can't. There's nothing inside my head except you.'

He heard her slow intake of breath.

'My room then,' she said quickly, and this time his relief was swift and sharp.

* * *

They dressed and he led her back into the house, moving purposefully through the darkness. Her heart was beating out of time and too fast, the aftershocks of their feverish almost-coupling mingling with a leaping panic. She was scared of leaving the starlit heat of the pool house, scared that the shift in mood and pace might introduce a change of perspective.

But as they walked upstairs she felt his hand tighten, and then he was pulling her against him, his mouth blindly seeking hers, kissing her with such blazing urgency that she forgot where she was and who she was, and there was nothing but the darkness and their staccato breathing and the insistent pressure of his mouth.

They made it to her bedroom—just. She had left the curtains open and, using the light from the pool house, they stripped again and kissed their way to the bed.

And then any fears she'd had about coming upstairs were forgotten as he raised her hips and gently nudged her legs apart. She felt his breath on her skin, and then her own breath seemed to stick in her throat as his tongue found the pulse between her thighs and began to move with slow, sure precision.

A moan of pleasure rose to her lips and her eyes slipped backwards. And then she was clasping his head, pushing him deeper, then pulling back, wanting more, but not wanting it to end. She felt weightless and her head was spinning. Heat was spilling over her skin in waves, each one faster and stronger than the last, so that her whole body was vibrating. And then she was tensing, pressing against his quickening tongue, her hands jerking through his hair.

She felt him move up the bed and then his mouth was on hers, pushing and parting her lips, probing her mouth and then dropping to lick her throat, her collarbone, her nipples.

Her breath caught in her throat. He felt solid, harder and bigger than before. Was this how it worked? It had been so long she couldn't remember.

'It's okay,' he whispered, his lips brushing her mouth, his fingers sliding inside her, oscillating back and forth until her skin was tightening, her body melting against him.

She found her voice. 'Do you have the—?'

'Are you sure?' He spoke through gritted teeth and she knew he was holding himself in check.

'Yes, I'm sure.'

He rolled off the bed and moved swiftly to the door. Watching him leave, she curled her fingers into the sheet. His absence felt like an actual physical loss—like the sun dropping behind cloud—but suddenly he was back, tearing open the packet and rolling on the condom with smooth, precise care, then sliding back down beside her.

He pulled her against him, and as his mouth found hers she pulled him closer still, her hands pressing against his back, reaching down to hold his hips, and then she was guiding him into her body.

His eyes were rapt and unblinking in the half-light, his face taut with concentration and a need that mirrored her own as he moved against her in time to her accelerating heartbeat. And then she felt him tense, and he was thrusting into her, filling her completely, his groan mingling with her soft cry as her muscles tightened sharply around his hard, convulsing body.

He collapsed beside her, pressing his face into the curve of her collarbone, and she clung to him weakly. They were both breathing raggedly, their bodies slick with sweat, but she wanted to lie there for ever. Finally, though, he shifted his weight and pulled out of her. For the briefest half-second she thought he'd pull away completely. Instead, though, he drew her back against him.

'I was careful…'

'I know,' she whispered, surprised but grateful that he had understood her nervousness about contraception.

His arm curved around her back, and he kept it there as his breathing slowed.

And that was how they must have fallen asleep.

She wasn't sure what woke her, but even before her eyes were properly open she was aware of the solid warmth of his body beside hers and her body's instant and unqualified response to it. Her heartbeat slowed. For a moment she kept her eyes shut. She just couldn't bring herself to open them, for to do so would mean having to return to reality, to clothes, and to being composed and civilised. She wanted to stay here in his arms for ever—to be the woman she had become in his arms.

Her body felt loose and languid, and yet she had never felt more alive, more at one with herself and the world and her place in it. If only she could freeze time…just until she was ready.

She shivered. But ready for what?

There was only one way to find out.

Opening her eyes, she felt her pulse scamper forward. Ragnar was watching her, his gaze more grey than blue in the predawn half-light.

'Morning,' he said softly.

Her eyes had adjusted to the light now, and she gazed up at him, trying to read his expression. Not once during the night had she felt that he was regretting their decision, and nor did she feel any regret for what they'd done. But cocooned in darkness, sheltering in one another's arms, it had been easy to feel as if they were in their own little world, outside of time and answerable to no one.

'What time is it?' she asked quietly.

'About six.' He hesitated, his face stilling as though he

was working something through in his head. 'Sorry, did I wake you?'

Shaking her head, she met his gaze. 'No, I'm nearly always awake by six.' She gave him a small, swift smile. 'Sóley doesn't really do lie-ins yet.'

There were three beats of silence.

Her right leg was curled over his left, and she could feel the prickle of his hair against her skin, but what did this physical closeness really mean?

Inside her head, a nervous round of questions began firing off like party poppers. What was he thinking? Had the night changed things for him as it had for her?

The questions, or maybe the thought of his possible answers, made her stomach tighten.

Was having sex really that big a deal?

She felt her face grow hot at the stupidity of her words. Yes, it was—and not because there had been nobody since that first time with Ragnar. Last night had been about more than satisfying her hunger. It had felt like an admission of something other than sex.

Her heart began to pound. Or was she just doing what she'd done with Alistair? Building castles in the air? Letting her imagination play fast and loose with the facts?

'About last night—'

They both spoke at the same time.

Her chest tightened as his eyes lifted to her face. 'You think it was a mistake?' he said.

'Do you?' she prompted. Her heart was beating so loudly now she felt sure that it must have moved from her chest into her head.

He stared at her for what felt like half a lifetime and then he shook his head. 'No, I don't.'

'I don't either.' She spoke quickly, relief making her words run into one another like a runaway train's coaches hitting the buffers.

There was another beat of silence, and then he reached out and pulled her close, kissed her with the same urgency he had in the darkness. Her heart was still pounding, but with his lips on hers the tightness in her chest began to ease.

Finally, he raised his mouth and rubbed his face against hers, so that she could feel his warm breath on her skin. 'So, what happens next?'

It felt strange, hearing her own words come out of his mouth, for asking him that question had been a defining moment in her life. It was as if they had come full circle.

Only back then everything had been possible. Standing outside the restaurant, pressed up against the heat of his body and with his blue gaze resting on her face, she had felt as though they had a limitless number of futures, some too distant to fully imagine, others too fragile to be considered seriously, but all of them had been out there.

Now, though, too much reality had come between them—good and bad—for her to feel like that.

But what was she feeling? Did she even know?

Closing her mind to the confusion of her thoughts, she let her eyes drift over the hard muscles of his chest and stomach, then lower to where the hair grew most thickly.

What she did know was that she didn't want to walk away just yet.

'Lottie?'

His blue gaze was searching her face, only she didn't know what to say. She was more confused than ever, but it seemed incredibly important not to offer up something less than the truth.

She looked up at him and swallowed. 'I want this. I want you.'

His eyes locked with hers. 'And I want you too. Emphatically. Completely. Shamelessly.'

His fingers traced the curve of her hipbone as he spoke, so that suddenly she was squirming against him.

'And I don't want to turn away from this thing between us. Not yet.'

The certainty in his voice was captivating, and she stared at him spellbound.

'Let's give ourselves these three weeks.'

He was spelling it out for her, making it simple for both of them in a way that had been beyond her, and she was grateful that one of them had managed to put it into words.

'And afterwards you'll still be Sóley's mother and I'll still be her father—just like we agreed.'

'So we just carry on as we are?' she said slowly.

He nodded. 'Until we stop.'

His blue eyes were clear and calm and irresistible. Breathing in his warm scent, she nodded slowly, and as she leaned into him they began to taste one another all over again.

'How do you feel about taking the horses out after lunch? I'd like to show you the estate while you're here.'

Keeping his eyes fixed on Lottie's face, Ragnar leaned forward and refilled her water glass. They were having lunch alone today. Sóley had already eaten and gone upstairs for her nap, and they were eating in the dining area.

It was a glorious room, with a glorious view, and normally he simply sat back and enjoyed the contrast between the restrained luxury of the interior and the stark wilderness outside the glass. Today, though, his gaze kept returning to the woman sitting opposite him.

It was easier between them now. She was still quieter than any woman he'd ever met—certainly quieter than any in his family—but her quietness no longer felt like a show of defiance. Now that he wasn't so on edge himself, he realised that if she was quiet it was because she was concentrating, really listening to what he said.

And not just listening. When her gaze was on his face it felt as if her soft brown eyes were reaching inside him.

'What about Sóley?'

He stared at her blankly. Caught in the honeyed trap of her eyes, he'd lost track of the conversation.

With an effort, he refocused his thoughts. 'We'll only be out for an hour or so at the most before we lose the light, and Signy is desperate to spend some time with her.' Sensing her uncertainty, he changed tack. 'But if Sóley isn't happy to be left then we won't go, obviously.'

'I'd really like to see the estate, and I'd love to go riding.' She glanced longingly through the glass, and then her face creased. 'But I don't have any jodhpurs or boots or a helmet.'

'That won't be a problem. When you said you liked to ride I had one of my people pick up everything you need.'

She frowned. 'But how did you know my size?'

He held her gaze, feeling his body respond in about fifty different ways to her words. 'I know how you fit against me, so I just scaled down.' His eyes flickered over the high curve of her breasts. 'With a few adjustments.'

Signy chose that moment to come and check their plates and find out if they wanted coffee or tea, and he took the opportunity to make sure she was happy to look after Sóley.

When they were finally alone, he looked back across the table at Lottie. The curve of her cheekbones was still pink and, watching her fingers slide up the stem of the glass, he felt his body stiffen to granite hardness. It was all too easy to remember her hand moving in just such a way but for a very different purpose.

Picking up his own glass, he drank some water. It was refreshingly chilled, but unfortunately its cooling effects ended at his stomach and didn't extend to his blood. He was starting to think that where Lottie was concerned nothing was going to change the way his body felt about her.

Earlier, as her hot skin had fused with his, desire as raw and potent as moonshine had driven all conscious thoughts and most unconscious ones from his head. He'd never been so perfectly out of control in his life, and Lottie's unrestrained, passionate response had left him craving more.

Only, was that *all* he was craving?

His heartbeat accelerated.

At any other time in his life, with any other woman, his answer would have been an unequivocal yes. But, remembering how he had felt when finally he'd forced himself to leave her bed that morning, he felt his chest grow tight.

Whatever he had said to Lottie, did he really believe that they could just stop and go back to their own lives at the end of three weeks? More importantly, did he want them to?

He tensed. The answer to that was an unequivocal no. And it wasn't just sex. Living with Lottie and Sóley felt right; they were a family now.

And that was great—except he already had a family, and the idea of introducing one to the other was just not something he could handle right now.

Maybe not ever…

Thirty minutes later Ragnar zipped up his jacket and gazed at the sky. The sun was rising at a shallower angle every day, and today it was barely visible behind a low, bleached grey bank of cloud, but at least it wasn't raining or snowing.

There were any number of possible routes he could have chosen for today's ride, but he'd said that he wanted Lottie to see the estate, and that meant heading up the hillside.

He might have made a different decision if Lottie had been a less experienced rider but, although it was true that she was a little rigid at the start, once she'd relaxed on Orvar, the beautiful chestnut gelding he'd chosen for her, he could see that she had perfect balance and an easy, open riding style.

Turning his own horse—a bay mare called Camille—away from the jagged iced-up edge of a stream, he moved steadily with her towards the ridge, letting the horses choose the pace, trusting them to pick their way across the uneven ground.

Feeling his phone vibrate inside his jacket, he gritted his teeth. The ongoing saga between his mother and half-sister had now sucked in his ex-stepfather Nathan and his other half-sister Freya, and he was desperate to find a resolution.

Glancing over at the expression of unguarded sweetness on Lottie's face, he felt his heart beat faster. Right now, they could wait.

'How are you doing?' he asked.

'Fine.' She smiled shyly. 'I think that's more down to Orvar than me. I mean, he's a strong horse, but I just have to switch my weight a little and he does exactly what I want. He's so quick to react, so responsive.'

He turned to look across at her, a pulse beating down his spine. 'Not with everyone. He is a strong horse, but you're not fighting his strength. Your hands are gentle, and that's why he's not pulling.' His eyes locked with hers. 'Like a lot of powerful males, he just needs the right handling. I think he's okay with you being the boss.'

He watched her fingers curl against the reins.

'Probably because he knows it's only going to be a short ride,' she said quietly.

His phone vibrated again and, watching the curiosity in her eyes, he realised that he would have to answer it after all.

'Sorry. I'm going to have to take this,' he said and, unzipping his jacket, he pulled out his phone.

Watching Ragnar edge his horse away, Lottie breathed out unsteadily.

She had thought that getting away from the house and out into the cool air would be a good idea. Obviously it was going to be difficult to make sense of how she was feeling in Ragnar's home, and with Ragnar himself so distractingly close.

Mounting Orvar, it had been easy to persuade herself that the way she was feeling was normal for someone who had just had sex after nearly two years of celibacy. Not just take-it-or-leave-it sex, either. Ragnar made her head swim. And, after thinking about it for so long, it was only natural that she was going to have some kind of emotional response to his relationship with Sóley.

But now, out here in the pale grey light, with the cool wind in her face, they weren't having sex, and Sóley was back at the house, and yet the feeling of her world turning upside down persisted.

She glanced over to where Ragnar was talking. It was impossible not to catch occasional snippets of his conversation and it was clear that he was comforting someone—someone female.

'Okay, I will talk to Nathan, but you have to apologise. Because she's our mother—'

Her pulse jumped a beat.

Not just someone—his sister.

Her head was spinning. So was this Nathan his brother?

Shifting against the saddle, she breathed out slowly. She didn't even know he *had* a sister or a brother—in fact, given the lack of any photos around the house and his reclusive lifestyle, she'd assumed he didn't have a family. But clearly he did, and clearly he cared about them—a lot. So why hadn't he said anything about them before?

Her pulse jumped again. Probably because he hadn't trusted her any more than she had trusted him.

It was a disconcerting thought, but before she could pursue all its implications she realised that Ragnar had hung up and was riding towards her.

'Sorry about that.'

His face was unreadable, probably intentionally so, but

now that she'd got past the shock of discovering he had a family she wanted to know more—for the obvious reason that Ragnar's family was also Sóley's.

'Is everything okay?'

For a moment she thought he wasn't going to answer her, and then he stared past her, his eyes fixed on the horizon. 'It will be.'

She took a breath. 'So was that your sister?'

His hesitation was so brief she might not have noticed it but for the slight tensing along his jaw.

'Yes—Marta.'

Holding her breath, she waited.

Finally, he said stiffly, 'She's had a row with our mother. It's nothing really… It's just my mother has rules and Marta pushes back. But it'll blow over—it always does.'

She nodded slowly. 'At least she can call you if she needs someone to talk to.'

'Yes, I suppose she can.' He nudged Camille forward. 'Come on, it's not far now.'

And that was that.

They reached the top of the ridge ten minutes later.

Pulling up her horse, she stopped and stared. It was an incredible view.

In the distance, she could just see the blue glint of a glacier. Closer than that, snow-covered fields bumped up against twisting towers of haphazard jagged rocks in every shade of grey and silver, and then, nearer still, twin one-hundred-foot waterfalls cascaded down black basalt cliffs.

'Can we get closer?' she asked.

He nodded. 'We can walk underneath them, if you want.'

It took them another fifteen minutes to reach the waterfalls. They left the horses by the edge of a small geothermal pool. Steam from the water had melted the ice, revealing some surprisingly green grass, and both horses instantly lowered their heads and began to graze.

Behind the falls the noise of the water hitting the rock was ear-splittingly loud, and after a moment of neck-tilting admiration they moved far enough away that they could speak without having to shout.

She frowned. 'I should have brought my camera.'

'Here.' He handed her his phone. 'Use this.'

'Thank you.'

Clambering up onto a rock, she took her time to frame the picture, conscious of his gaze and of the questions building up inside her head.

'So, how many siblings do you have?' she asked as she slithered off the rock.

She felt him tense at her question. Then, 'Seven.'

'Seven!'

She turned towards him, not bothering to hide her surprise. As a child she'd desperately wanted to be part of a big family—mainly because she hadn't always felt as if she belonged in her small one—and she could feel herself falling for a different version of the same fantasy now.

'Wow, you're so lucky. And do they all live in Iceland?'

'Sometimes.' A muscle ticked in his jaw.

'So why did you choose to live out here miles from anyone?'

He shrugged. 'Why does anyone choose to live anywhere?'

Ragnar let out an uneven breath. His chest felt as though a band of steel was wrapped around it, getting tighter and tighter.

He always found it stressful talking about his family, but here, now, with Lottie, and with that stupid conversation about giving themselves three weeks still ringing in his ears, he felt as though he might fly into a thousand pieces.

But it was ridiculous to feel that way. She was only asking him what any normal person would ask, so why was he reacting as if she was conducting an inquisition?

His shoulders tensed. He was making such a mess of this. Why didn't he just tell her what he was thinking? Why didn't he just say that he'd got it wrong? That, waking this morning—no, even before that, holding her last night—he'd felt something shift inside him, so that now he didn't want her to disappear from his life at the end of three weeks.

Shoving his hands into his pockets, he felt his knuckles bump into his phone and he felt the tension in his shoulders spread to his spine.

What was he supposed to do?

He only knew one way of managing his life, and that was to keep all the different parts separate—and up until now it had worked just fine. His family had nothing to do with his business, and his private life was private. But Lottie and Sóley would have to meet his family, and then what?

His brain felt as though it might explode. He didn't know the answer to that. But it was impossible to see the hurt expression on Lottie's face and not know that he was the reason for it. And he didn't like how that made him feel. Or the fact that she'd had exactly the same expression when she'd been talking about her useless father.

She deserved to know the truth, or at least an edited version of the truth, but he couldn't explain the messy, melodramatic dynamic of his family out here on this beautiful, tranquil day. And nor did he want to expose her to the mesmerising pull of their drama just yet. He knew what would happen if he did. Lottie and Sóley would be absorbed into the chaos and he couldn't bear for that to happen.

Only he wanted to give her something.

He couldn't change the past, or give her the father she deserved. But he could give her a part of himself he'd never shared with anyone else.

'My mother's family had a house not far from here. We

used to come every holiday and one summer, when I was about eight, I met a boy about my age—Daniel. He was with his father, fishing in the lake over there.'

It had been the holiday before his parents had divorced—six months before his father had found out about his mother's affair—and the rows had been volcanic in their scope and ferocity, and seemingly endless in those long days of summer.

'They taught me how to fish and I caught a salmon—my first.' He grinned at the memory. 'Then we went back to their house and cooked it. It was the best meal I'd ever eaten.'

And not just because of the freshness of the fish or the fact that he'd caught it. Daniel's house had been small and simply decorated, but his parents had been so calm and patient, and it had been so relaxing he'd actually fallen asleep.

'And that's why you like coming here?'

She looked confused, and something in her soft brown gaze made him reach out and pull her against him. He could see how his words would make no sense to her, but there was no way to recreate his childish astonishment at discovering there was another way to be a family—a way without drama.

He couldn't reveal how, sitting in that quiet, ordinary little house, he'd made up his mind to live his life in just such a way, and how living that kind life meant never giving in to the unnamed feeling in his chest.

Already he'd let her get too close—closer than he should. He'd felt her happiness and her pain as his own, and he couldn't let that keep happening. He couldn't risk being swamped by emotions he couldn't handle and didn't want to feel. He needed to keep his feelings under wraps and then everything would be fine.

And if that was what he had to do to keep Lottie and Sóley in his life then that was what he would do.

What other choice did he have?

CHAPTER EIGHT

LEANING FORWARD OVER the banister, Lottie felt her heart jump guiltily against her ribs. Sóley had decided to pull her socks off and push them into her breakfast cereal, and she'd only come upstairs to grab a clean pair for her. But as she'd been walking back along the galleried landing she'd heard an irresistible squeal of laughter, and then a deeper, definitely male laugh, and she'd had to flatten her body into the cool brickwork to even out her breathing.

Now she was smiling. In the living area below, Ragnar was playing hide and seek with their daughter, and she watched, transfixed, her smile widening, as he allowed himself to be found, much to Sóley's giggling, appreciative amusement.

A week ago she would have found it impossible to enjoy this moment. She would have wanted to, only her fear of being pushed out would have overridden her good intentions. Now, though, she felt differently. She knew that the father-daughter bond wasn't a threat to her own relationship with Sóley.

She inched backwards, concealing herself in the shadows, feeling a knot of nervous uncertainty tightening beneath her diaphragm.

She felt differently about other things too.

Instead of feeling as if she was trapped in a villain's lair, out in the wilderness, she felt almost as much at home as she did in Suffolk. And, rather than counting down the days until she could leave, she was trying to stretch out every minute.

Mostly, though, she felt differently about Ragnar.

Oh, she could remember her resentment and her scepticism, but they seemed to have broken up and melted away like spring ice on a lake.

She thought back to their conversation the morning after that first time they'd yielded to the burning, incessant pull of their desire. It had been a little nerve-racking, waking in *his* arms in *her* bed. She'd had no idea of what to expect, knowing only that she didn't regret what had happened.

But then they'd talked—or rather he'd talked—and she'd agreed with him that she didn't want it to be just that one night and that they should give themselves these three weeks.

Only down by the waterfalls she'd started to realise that wasn't what she wanted either—or at least not *all* she wanted.

That phone call from his sister had made her want to learn more about this man who was Sóley's father, whose touch turned her inside out but about whom she knew next to nothing.

The knot in her stomach tightened. But, judging by his terse, oblique answers to her questions, and the shuttered expression on his face, he clearly didn't trust her enough to give her more than a glimpse into his life—a glimpse that had confused more than clarified her understanding of him.

But could she blame him for being reluctant to open up?

Even her decision to tell him about Sóley had been framed as much by her failed relationship with her own father as by a need to do the right thing.

She'd been so preoccupied by her fears of being pushed out that she'd relegated his feelings, and his family, to second place—to the point of never even actually asking him a single question about them.

Her stomach muscles clenched. He was clearly the pole-star of his family. Marta had called again twice, and his mother once, and listening to him talk to them, patiently and calmly, she had felt both moved and almost envious that they had a permanent right to his attention, and she—

She pushed the words away, letting them be pulled into the swirling centrifuge of emotions she couldn't seem to unpick or understand.

Downstairs in the living area, Sóley was gratifyingly excited to see her. Kneeling down on the rug, she let her daughter climb into her arms.

'She missed you.'

Turning towards where Ragnar sat, slouching against one of the huge leather sofas, she felt her heart slip sideways. He was wearing a thin blue V-neck sweater a shade darker than his eyes, and a lock of blond hair was falling across his forehead. He looked calm and relaxed and incredibly sexy.

'Sorry for taking so long.'

He shifted against the sofa, stretching his leg out so that his thigh was next to hers, and instantly the heat and pressure of his body made her breathing change rhythm.

'You really don't need to keep apologising to me every time I look after her. Otherwise I'm going to have start retrospectively apologising to you for the last eleven months.'

'I just don't want to take you for granted.'

His eyes rested on her face, the blue suddenly very blue. 'How *do* you want to take me?' he said softly.

Behind the sudden insistent thud of her heartbeat she heard her phone vibrate on the sofa. It could be her mum, or Lucas, or even Georgina to say that the gallery had burned down, but she couldn't seem to make herself care enough to pick it up and find out.

'Here.' He reached across and handed her the phone. 'It might be a commission. Just because I'm on holiday it doesn't mean you have to be too.'

Thankful for being given a reason to lower her face,

away from his steady stare, she glanced down at the screen as her mind nervously tried to interpret his words.

He was talking about being on holiday from his job, not commenting on their affair. Or was he?

She wanted to ask him so badly that words filled her throat and mouth. *Is this just a holiday romance? Is that why you don't want to tell me anything about your family?*

But she wasn't brave enough to find out for sure.

Glancing down at the screen, she saw that it wasn't a commission—just a message from Lucas telling her that he'd fixed the leak in the workshop and asking if she thought a swing would be a good idea for Sóley's birthday.

She laid her phone down on the rug, pushing Lucas's question to the back of her mind. It should be the biggest date in her calendar, but right now she didn't want to think about her daughter's first birthday, for that would mean planning for the future—a future in which she would no longer wake to find Ragnar's warm body beside hers or fall asleep in his arms.

'All okay?'

Blocking the hollow ache in her stomach, she looked up and nodded. 'Yes, it's just Lucas.' Afraid that he might read her thoughts, she turned towards her daughter. 'Right, you, let's get these socks—'

But before she had a chance to finish her sentence Sóley had wriggled off her lap, snatched the phone off the rug and begun crawling across the floor at great speed.

'You little monkey!' Laughing, Lottie chased after her, scooping her daughter into her arms and burying her face in her stomach until Sóley was squirming and giggling uncontrollably.

Having retrieved her phone, she lowered her still giggling daughter to the rug. She could feel Sóley straightening her legs, steadying herself as she had been doing for last few weeks, pulling impatiently against her mother's restraining hands.

'Okay—you can stand by yourself.'

For a few seconds or more her daughter swayed on the spot, finding her balance, and then she raised her arms, cooing breathlessly towards where her father was kneeling in front of the huge suspended fireplace.

Watching him toss in a couple of logs, Lottie felt her heart begin to pound.

'Ragnar…' She spoke his name softly, and as he turned towards her, her eyes met his and she smiled. 'She wants you,' she prompted.

He started to get up, but she shook her head. 'No, say her name.'

A flicker of understanding passed across his face and he stayed crouched down, his eyes fixed on his daughter as Lottie lifted her phone.

'Sóley.'

His voice was raw-sounding, and she could tell that he was struggling to hold on to his composure.

'Sóley, come to Daddy.' He hesitated and then repeated himself in Icelandic.

Holding her breath, Lottie watched as Sóley teetered towards his outstretched hands, taking one wobbly step after another like a tiny astronaut, and then she stopped, weaving unsteadily on the rug. And as she tipped forward he caught her in his arms.

Lottie switched off her phone camera, tears burning her eyes as Ragnar got unsteadily to his feet, still holding his daughter close, pressing his face into her loose blonde curls. And then suddenly he was walking across the room and pulling her into his arms, pulling her close.

Burying her wet face against his shoulder, still clutching her phone, she breathed out unsteadily.

'Thank you,' he said softly.

Her hands gripped his sweater. 'For what?'

'Her first steps.'

She felt his emotion in her own chest. 'I'm just sorry it took me so long to let you be her father, and for being so wrapped up in myself. I should have asked you about your family before—especially after burdening you with what happened with my father—'

His arms tightened around her. 'You didn't burden me with anything. I'm glad you told me. And, just for the record, I think your father made the biggest mistake of his life giving up the chance to know you. You're an incredible person, Lottie.'

She shook her head. 'I'm not. I've been selfish and self-absorbed.'

'And I've been overbearing and manipulative and cold-blooded.' His eyes were gleaming, but his voice was gentle.

Recognising her own words, she smiled. 'Did I say that?'

He smiled back at her—a sweet, slow smile that made her insides loosen.

'I probably deserved worse.'

Lottie laughed. 'I definitely *thought* worse.' She took a breath. 'I'll send you that video and you can share it with your family.'

Maybe her daughter's first steps might be *her* first step towards making amends.

'I've got other videos,' she added. 'I can send those too.

He was silent for a moment, and then he said, 'I'd like to see them.'

Her eyes flicked to his face. There was something different about his voice… Only before she had a chance to consider what had changed, or why, Sóley leaned forward and grabbed her shoulder, pulling all three of them into an embrace.

Her heart was suddenly thumping hard inside her chest, as she pictured the three of them in her garden in Suffolk:

she and Ragnar were taking turns to push their daughter in her swing, their eyes bright, their faces flushed with the chilled air and with something less tangible that she couldn't name—

She cleared her throat. 'I was thinking… I know you're already taking time off work now, so don't worry if you can't,' she said quickly. 'But I was just wondering if you'd like to come to Suffolk for Sóley's birthday? It's not a party, or anything, but I know she'd love you to be there.' She hesitated. 'I'd love you to be there too.'

He was staring at her steadily, and she felt heat rise up over her throat and curl around her neck like a cashmere scarf.

'I'd like that very much.'

'Excuse me, Mr Stone— Oh, I'm so sorry—'

It was Signy.

Lottie felt her cheeks grow warm. She had no idea whether or not Ragnar's housekeeper had detected a change in their relationship, but she didn't want to make the older woman feel in any way uncomfortable.

'No need to apologise, Signy,' Ragnar said calmly. 'Sóley just started walking and we were celebrating.' He hesitated. 'In fact, why don't we celebrate properly? We have champagne, don't we, Signy?'

'Yes, we do, Mr Stone.'

'Good.'

Lottie watched as he gently kissed his daughter's forehead, and then the air was squeezed from her lungs as he lowered his mouth and brushed his lips against hers.

'Then let's celebrate.'

Leaning back in his chair, Ragnar stared down at his laptop, watching the cursor blink on the pitifully blank screen. On the desk beside him he had a neatly stacked pile of unread business plans and magazines. But it didn't matter how neatly they were stacked—he already knew they were definitely going to stay unread.

Two years ago, when his business had been starting up and he'd felt as if a hosepipe filled with data was pumping non-stop into his head, he'd followed the example of other successful CEOs and taken a couple of 'think weeks' out of his schedule.

He found them incredibly productive, and now he was following the same rules as he always did. Web-browsing was forbidden, he could only check emails once a day, for no more than fifteen minutes, and he could take no business calls whatsoever. The idea was to remove all distractions from his life and allow his mind the space and freedom to reset his goals, so that when he did return to work he would hit the ground running—and in the right direction.

He glanced again at the blinking cursor.

But clearly some distractions were just way more distracting than others, he thought, his body hardening as a slow-motion replay of the morning shower he'd shared with Lottie slid unprompted into his head.

He gritted his teeth. No wonder he was finding it difficult to focus his thoughts.

Except that wasn't true. His thoughts *were* focused—only not on the future direction of his business but on the woman who had managed to get so far under his defences that he'd actually told her about that fishing trip with the boy Daniel.

He flipped his laptop shut, moving his eyes involuntarily to the window and through the glass, to the fractured outline of a small, wooden cabin that was just visible from where he was sitting.

His shoulders tensed. When Lottie had asked him about his family he'd told her part of the truth.

Maybe he hadn't expressed it very eloquently, but he'd wanted her to know that meeting Daniel and his family had been a transformative moment for him. Like falling down a rabbit hole into Wonderland, except in reverse, for in his family there had been no end of mad tea parties and pools of tears.

In Daniel's family cabin he'd found a bolthole from the drama, and every minute he'd spent there had only made it clearer to him that one day he would need a separate space, away from his family. He loved them, even when they exhausted and infuriated him, but he couldn't live with them.

His fingers tapped impatiently against the desktop.

But he could *live with Lottie and Sóley.*

He was already doing so, and he wanted the situation to continue—even more now, after what had happened yesterday.

Suddenly he felt as if some invisible force was squeezing his chest. Watching his daughter take her first steps towards him, then catching her as she fell, he had felt something crack inside him as the swell of pride at her reaching the milestone of walking had battled with panic that one day he might not be there to catch her when she fell.

Three amazing, overwhelming, unrepeatable minutes of his life—Lottie's gift to him.

Only he hadn't wanted it to be his alone. He'd needed to share it with her. As he'd pulled her into his arms he'd been on the verge of asking her to stay longer, but then she'd offered to send him the video of Sóley walking, so that he could share it with his family, and something had held him back from speaking his thoughts out loud.

And it was still holding him back now.

Fear.

The word tasted sour in his mouth.

He didn't like it that fear was dictating his actions, but truthfully he was scared of what would happen if he asked her to stay on. Maybe if it had just been sex, as he'd told himself it would be, or if he simply respected her as the mother of his child it would be okay, but as he'd watched, felt, listened to her quiet devastation as she talked about her father's rejection his anger had been monumental.

Only what if, like the rest of his family, his emotions got too big to be contained?

He pushed the thought away uneasily.

They won't, he told himself firmly. He had a lifetime of experience in separating himself from his feelings—why should dealing with Lottie be any different?

His eyes snagged on the title of the topmost document in the pile on his desk. Even without the double distraction of Lottie and his daughter, he would find it perilously hard to be distracted by a report on *Strategic Pre-interaction Behaviours Using Emerging Technologies*. But it was the suggested date of a meeting to discuss the report that made his fingers stop tapping against the smooth desktop.

December twenty-first.

Sóley's birthday.

His gaze returned to the view outside his window. This time, though, his eyes were drawn upwards to the sky.

After days of pale grey silvery cloud today the sky was a limitless ice-blue, stretching out above the snow-covered fields like the ceiling of a Renaissance cathedral.

It was a perfect day.

He breathed out slowly. Maybe he had found a way to reset his goals after all. It would be a first step for him—a different kind of icebreaker from the one they'd first shared, but something he could give to Lottie.

With the determination of having finally made a decision, he pulled out his phone and punched in a number. 'Ivar. I need you to be ready in about an hour. No, just a short trip. Thanks.'

Hanging up, he glanced at the watch. Now all he needed to do was talk to Signy.

* * *

Pressing her face closer to the curved window, Lottie gazed down at snow-covered land, half-heartedly trying to imagine what it might look like in summer.

It was her second flight in a helicopter, and once again she had no idea where she was going, but this time, with Ragnar's fingers wrapped around hers, her feelings were very different. Instead of being tense with nervous apprehension, her stomach was tingling with excitement.

She watched as Ragnar leaned forward and tapped Ivar on the shoulder.

'Just over the ridge will be fine, if that works for you.'

The pilot nodded. 'Yes, sir.'

The sound of the helicopter made normal speech impossible and both men were having to raise their voices.

Dropping back into his seat, Ragnar gave her hand a quick squeeze, and then her heart picked up speed as he bent closer and she felt his warm breath on her throat.

'Just another couple of minutes.'

She felt her body soften as his mouth found hers. Her head was swimming, and she had to lift her mouth from his to stop herself from deepening the kiss and tearing at the layers of padding that separated them from one another.

'Until what?'

'Wait and see.'

Ivar landed the helicopter exactly three minutes later.

Flecks of snow whipped up by the rotor blades whirled around them as Ragnar climbed out and then lifted her down. As she pulled her hood up over her hair she looked up at him questioningly.

'So where now?'

He took her hand. 'This way.'

They crunched steadily through the snow, up a curving bank, and then abruptly the snow ended and she felt her feet stall. She pushed her hood back from her face. In front of her a lead-grey sea stretched out to a horizon that looked as though it had been drawn with a ruler.

And next to the sea was the beach.

Only this beach was nothing like the pale, biscuit-coloured sands of home—it was black.

Lottie let Ragnar lead her down the shifting dunes.

'It's lava,' he said as she reached down and picked a handful of tiny black pebbles. 'When it reached the sea it stopped and cooled instantly. That's the dull, scientific explanation, anyway.' His mouth curved up. 'But I still can't stop myself from looking for dragons every time I come here.'

The pull of his blue gaze was intoxicating and irresistible. She smiled back at him. 'So what are we waiting for? Let's go see if we can find one.'

It was the most amazing place, Lottie thought as they made their way across the gleaming wet sands. Apart from the noise of the waves hitting the shore at regular intervals, the only other sound was the occasional seabird crying as it swooped above the water far out at sea.

'Do you like it?'

His blue eyes rested steadily on her face and she nodded, her vocal cords suddenly paralysed by the intensity of his gaze.

'Enough to stay for lunch?' he said softly.

Lunch? She frowned. 'Where are we going to eat lunch?'

And then she saw it.

At the back of the beach, where the white snow met the black stones, was a huge fire pit filled with burning logs. Around it, fat kilim-covered cushions were spread out invitingly over a collection of shaggy sheepskin rugs, and a picnic basket was sitting on top of what appeared to be a table made out of snow.

Lottie breathed out unsteadily. Something was wrong

with her. A shard of ice seemed to be lodged in her throat, but her eyes felt as though they were burning.

'I don't understand…' she whispered.

He pulled her against him, brushing the tears from her cheeks. His jacket was quilted, hers was too, but she could still feel his heart beating through the layers of fabric and insulation.

'It's my way of saying thank-you for yesterday. For letting me share Sóley's first steps.'

Cupping her face with his hands, he kissed her fiercely and she kissed him back, relieved to have an outlet for the dizzying intensity of her longing for him.

Finally, they drew apart.

'How did you do all this?'

He glanced away. 'Signy and Ivar did all the hard stuff.'

She swallowed. There was a fluttering fullness in her chest she didn't understand, like happiness mixed with nerves—only she didn't feel nervous.

'But it was your idea?'

'I didn't just want to say what I was feeling, I wanted to show you,' he said.

Taking his words into herself, she leaned into him and kissed him again, until he groaned against her mouth and pulled away from her. Catching sight of the expression on his face, she smiled.

'Later,' she said softly, catching his hand. 'Come on—let's eat.'

There were soft rolls filled with sticky pulled pork or buttered lobster, and a creamy artichoke dip with crisp vegetable *crudités*. To follow there was hot mulled cider and some delicious *kleinur*—an Icelandic pastry that was like a twisted cinnamon-flavoured doughnut.

'Signy is a genius,' Lottie said when finally she couldn't eat another mouthful. 'Are you feeling better now?'

She spoke playfully, liking the way his eyes gleamed

in response to her teasing, but liking the weight of his arm around her waist more.

He pulled her closer. 'No.' His eyes locked with hers. 'But *you* feel wonderful.'

Her heart skipped forward. She felt wonderful too. Lighter, calmer. Happier. For the first time since her father's rejection she didn't have the nagging sense of being inadequate. Ragnar made her feel special and secure. He made her feel differently about herself.

A tic of uncertainty beat in time to her pulse.

But it wasn't just *her* feelings that mattered—her father had taught her that—and right now Ragnar had given her no reason to think this was anything more than just a thoughtful gesture.

'Is it always this empty here?' Glancing across the deserted beach, she frowned. 'Where I live there's always someone on the beach. Dog walkers, or teenagers having a bonfire party, or windsurfers.'

He took a moment to reply. Then, 'People don't come here because it's a private beach.'

It took a moment for his words to sink in. 'Is it *your* beach?'

He nodded. 'It came with the estate. There's a lot of protected wildlife up here, so it's probably for the best that there aren't hordes of people traipsing all over it.'

His eyes met hers, and she could see he was weighing up something in his head.

'Actually,' he said slowly, 'you're the first person I've ever brought here...and you and Sóley are the first people to stay at my house.'

She stared at him in confusion. Was that true? And if it was, why were they the first? And why was he telling her now?

His skin was taut over his cheeks, and she could feel a tension in him that hadn't been there before—a kind of rigid pose, as though he was bracing himself before jumping off a high-dive board.

Her own stomach tensed, but the question was waiting to be asked. 'Why hasn't anyone stayed at the house before?'

He stared past her. 'I didn't want anyone else before you,' he said finally. 'I come here to escape.'

Of course—he came to recharge, to rethink his business goals. Only she knew from the forced steadiness in his voice that he wasn't talking about work, and she thought back to when she'd asked him about living here.

'Was that why you went to Daniel's house when you were a child? Because it was an escape.'

His eyes were still watching the horizon. 'Pretty much.' His mouth twisted. 'It was difficult at home. My parents were arguing a lot. They got divorced shortly after that holiday.'

It seemed to Lottie that her head had never been so full of questions. She picked one at random. 'What happened then?'

'They remarried—both of them—quite a few times, actually. I have four stepfathers and three stepmothers, two full sisters and one brother, and the rest are halves and steps. It's all quite complicated and full of drama.'

He'd used that word before. 'What kind of drama?' she asked.

He shrugged. 'Oh, you know…the usual hallmarks of a good soap opera. Jealousy. Infidelity. Power. Pride.'

She stared at him in silence. His voice was calm and even, but for some reason it jarred with the mocking smile that accompanied his statement.

'But you love them?' Watching his eyes soften, she felt the same fluttering fullness in her chest as earlier.

'Very much. But this place—' he glanced back down the beach to the dark, jutting rocks '—is dramatic enough as it is.' His gaze returned to her face. 'Does that make sense?'

She nodded.

Truthfully, she didn't fully understand what he was trying to say, but she did understand how hard it could be to try and express yourself. Just like her, words weren't his thing—but the fact that he'd opened up to her was what mattered.

'I do understand.'

His arm tightened around her. 'I was hoping you would.' He hesitated. 'And I was hoping, too, that you might consider staying on here with Sóley a little longer.'

Her heart was thumping against her ribs. 'How much longer?'

His eyes were suddenly very blue. 'I thought maybe you might consider staying here for Christmas.'

'Christmas?'

He misread the shake in her voice. 'I know it's a lot to ask, and you've probably got other plans, but I really want to spend it with—' His face tensed into a frown and he paused. 'I really want us to spend it together. The three of us…as a family.'

His admission made the breath slip down her throat . Beneath the jerkiness of her heartbeat she felt a fluttering moth's wing of hope, even though she knew it was ridiculous to wish for something she could never have.

'You don't have to make up your mind now.'

He was right. She should give it some thought, but there was no point. It was what she wanted.

'I'd like that. A lot,' she said simply.

His fingers pushed through her hair, tipping her face up to meet his lips. 'I don't know where this is going with us, but I don't want it to be over yet.'

Something stirred inside her chest, moving stealthily, swelling against her ribs so that breathing was suddenly a struggle. She pushed against it, but this time it wouldn't go away.

'I don't either,' she said.

Not yet, not ever.

Her pulse was pounding in her head. He wasn't offering her permanence. He wasn't offering her a future beyond Christmas. But that didn't seem to matter to her heart.

She had fallen in love with him anyway.

She grabbed the front of his jacket to steady herself. Of course she was in love with him. Somewhere deep inside she knew that she'd always been in love with him—ever since that first night in London. But closer to the surface she felt panic.

She was unbearably conscious of being in love. But there was no need to tell him what she was feeling. She'd done that before—told a man what she was thinking and feeling too quickly, without filters—and she wasn't going to do it again. She couldn't risk the swift sting of rejection.

Right now what mattered was that incredibly, miraculously, he wanted her to stay.

But with Ragnar so close, and with his words echoing inside her head, the urge to blurt out her feelings was almost overwhelming.

She was desperate for the oblivion of his mouth on hers and, pulling him closer, she kissed him fiercely, losing herself in the heat of his response, letting the synchrony of their desire stifle her need to confess her love.

CHAPTER NINE

'ARE YOU COLD?'

Tilting her face, Lottie gazed up at Ragnar and shook her head. They hadn't made it into the bed—instead were lying on top of a luxurious white fur throw, her limbs overlapping with his, his arm around her waist.

'No, I'm not,' she said truthfully.

Heat was radiating from his body into hers, and the fur beneath them was incredibly warm and soft. Only…

She twisted against him, pressing closer. 'Actually, I was going ask you, just out of interest, what exactly am I lying on?'

In the heat of passion the sensation of fur against bare skin was intensely erotic, and usually she was too spent afterwards to speak, much less formulate a question. There had always been a kind of frenzied intensity to their lovemaking—maybe because they both knew that there was a time when this would end, and their imminent separation was at the back of their minds. But now they had given themselves more time they could allow themselves to savour these moments of exquisite easy intimacy.

She thought back to yesterday's conversation on the beach. It still didn't feel quite real, but it *was* real—it had happened, Ragnar had asked her to stay on with him in Iceland, and even though she knew it was just a couple more weeks, his hesitant words were making her dream of something she'd always thought life would deny her.

He shifted against her and, dragging her attention back to the present, she met his gaze—or tried to. But he was looking anywhere but at her.

'I was hoping you wouldn't ask that.' His gaze met hers.

She stared at him uncertainly. 'Why? What is it?'

He sighed. 'It's fake.'

'Oh, you.' She punched him on the arm. 'I thought you were going to say it was a polar bear, or a seal or something.'

But she wasn't angry with him. She couldn't be. Not when she could hear the smile in his voice. Shaking her head, she moved as if to roll away, but he grabbed her and, pulling her beneath him, he stretched her arms above her head, capturing her wrists with his hands.

A beat of heat ticked through her blood as he stared down at her, his blue eyes gleaming. 'I'm not a complete barbarian.'

Her body twitched as she met his gaze. They were teasing each other, using the intimacy of sex to test their relationship. 'And you're happy to say that lying naked on a fur rug?'

His lips curved upwards and she felt her heart begin to beat unsteadily. Now she couldn't just hear his smile, she could see it. Her breath caught in her throat. He might not smile much, but when he did it was as miraculous and warming as the first rays of midwinter sunlight on her face.

'I'm not lying on a fur rug,' he said softly. 'I'm lying on you.'

He shifted against her, and as the hard muscles of his chest brushed against her nipples she felt her body stir. 'Yes, you are…but I'm not sure how that disqualifies you from being a barbarian.'

Holding her gaze, he drew the tip of his tongue softly over her bottom lip, pulling at a thread somewhere deep inside her.

'What are you thinking?' he asked.

She stared at him dazedly. 'That I want you,' she said hoarsely.

His eyes narrowed, the pupils flaring, and he rolled over,

taking her with him so that suddenly she was on top. Her eyes drifted hungrily over the muscular contours of his chest and she felt his hands move from her waist to her hips, his fingers biting into her skin as she pushed down against him.

He gritted his teeth and his hand caught hers. 'Give me a minute.'

His eyes were dark and glazed, and she felt his fingers tighten around hers as he fought to gain control. Glancing down, she saw that he was watching her, and his blunt expression made heat unspool inside of her. She started to move against him, wanting, needing to still the insistent ache between her thighs.

Her body was losing its bones…she could feel herself melting… Leaning forward, she clasped his face in her hands and kissed him frantically. He kissed her back deeply, licking her mouth until her body was shaking and hollowed out with desire.

'I want to feel you inside me…' she whispered.

His jaw clenched tight and, taking a breath, he rolled off her on to the fur and reached into the drawer by the bed. She watched impatiently as he rolled on a condom, and then he took her face in his hands again and kissed her fiercely, catching her hair as her searching fingers closed around him.

He sucked in a breath as she began to stroke, and then he was moving against her hand, his dark, glazed gaze watching her steadily as he reached down and lightly touched her breasts. Her nipples tightened and she moaned softly, and then his hand moved from her breast to her stomach, then lower still, his fingers tangling through the triangle of hair, teasing a path between her thighs so that she was raising her hips, seeking more of his tormenting touch.

'No…not this way—'

His fingers found hers and he freed himself from her

grasp. Then he turned her gently but firmly so that she was facing away from him. Leaning into her, he reached under her stomach to caress her nipples, his fingers pulling at the swollen tips, and then he was parting her thighs, stroking the slick heat, making sure she was ready for him.

'Yes,' she whispered. 'Yes...'

Pushing back, she guided him inside her and began to move against him in time with the pulsing urgency of her heartbeat, heat spreading through her like a fever as he thrust up inside her, his body jolting into climax in time with hers...

Breathing out softly, Ragnar inched backwards, making sure that he didn't wake the woman sleeping beside him. It was early—too early to get up—but his brain was brimming with unasked and unanswered questions.

Away from the distracting warmth of her body it would be easier to think straight—or at least think instead of feel.

His phone was on silent, but he picked it up anyway, in case its vibrations or flickering screen inadvertently disturbed Lottie.

Closing the bedroom door softly behind him, he made his way quietly through the silent house, moving instinctively in the darkness. Downstairs in the living room he made his way across the rug to where the still glowing embers of the fire spread a soft red light across the walls.

Crouching down, he picked up a couple of logs and pushed them into the amber-tinged ashes. Watching the flames creep over the dry wood, he leaned back against the sofa, stretching his legs out towards the fire's reviving warmth.

It had been long time since he had woken so early, and more specifically woken with his eyes feeling so heavy in his head that it was as though he hadn't closed them at all. Nearly twenty years, in fact, since that day when he'd gone to Daniel's house and realised that he could step back from his parents' explosive marriage.

His spine tensed against the sofa cushions.

Maybe it would have been different if he'd been the second or third child, but as the firstborn there had been no diluting the impact of their relationship on him, and his parents had been fiercely in love. Every encounter for them had been an emotional collision. Even their kisses had looked like a form of fighting to him, and as a child he'd often wake early, with his head still ringing in the aftermath of yesterday's feuding.

Going downstairs, he would huddle up in front of the remnants of the fire from the night before. It had been cold and dark, but it had been the only time of the day when he could find the silence and solitude he craved.

And now he was here, in his own home, doing exactly the same thing.

His phone screen lit up and, picking it up, he glanced down automatically to check his notifications.

It was a text from his mother, and there were four missed calls from Marta. His mouth twisted into a reluctant smile. He could imagine his sister's outrage at being asked to leave a message. She wasn't used to such treatment—particularly from him—but he didn't have his phone on at night now that he was with Lottie.

The words echoed inside his head. *Now that he was with Lottie.* It was a simple sentence, but what did it mean?

He let out a long, slow breath.

He knew what it meant now and up to Christmas. It meant the three of them living as a family, eating meals together and playing in the snow, and it meant that at night he and Lottie would retreat to her room, moving inside and against each other's bodies until that dizzying mutual moment of swift, shuddering release.

But what would it mean after Christmas?

He swore softly. That was what had woken him this morning.

Out on the beach it had seemed to make perfect sense. Of course he wanted to share Sóley's first birthday and spend Christmas with her as a family, and inviting Lottie to stay on had felt like an obvious step. Now, though, he couldn't understand why it had felt like such a big deal—or why he'd chosen to make it about his daughter's birthday instead of what it was really about.

His hand tightened around the phone.

He'd told Lottie that he would be honest with her, but how could he be when he wasn't even being honest with himself.

So be honest!

This wasn't just about playing happy families for the sake of their daughter—in fact it wasn't really about Sóley at all. He had a relationship with his daughter now, a bond that would endure beyond any fabricated deadline, and he wasn't going to let anything come between them.

But what about Lottie?

Where did she fit into his life in the long term?

Leaning forward, he picked up another log, and edged it carefully into the embers.

If he'd asked himself that question at any point up until the night in the pool house, when he'd handed her the robe, his answer would have been *nowhere*—except as Sóley's mother, of course.

He'd had casual affairs throughout his twenties, but no serious relationships, and he'd never wanted anything more—never wanted anyone for more than sex. To do so would mean getting out of his depth and too close for comfort.

But he wanted Lottie.

Maybe at the beginning their hunger had just been an

urgency from which neither of them could turn away. Only now it was different.

Now, after the shortest time, she felt essential to his life—and yet he was still shying away from what that meant.

He gazed into the red core of the fire. Given what he knew about people's behaviour when they went from casual to committed, that was completely understandable. To him, relationships were unpredictable and challenging. His family had proved that time and time again. There were so many risks—so many unknowns for which there was no neat algorithm.

His mouth twisted. Or perhaps it wasn't the unknown that scared him but the acknowledgement of his own shortcomings that was making him hold back.

The fact that his parents and siblings acted as though they were living in a modern-day Asgard had never impacted on anyone but himself before now, but Lottie was unsure of her place in the world—could he really risk introducing her into the chaos of his family life?

He had no right to expect or ask that of her.

More importantly, he couldn't introduce her to them because he hadn't actually told his family about her or Sóley yet.

His spine tensed.

Telling them was not as simple as it sounded. Not because his family would judge—they wouldn't—but because they would want to be involved, and being involved on their terms would mean being consumed. In an instant he would be fighting for control.

He would tell them soon. But on his terms. Calmly, quietly, individually. But for now he wanted to keep Lottie and Sóley to himself, for just a little longer.

Maybe that thought had been in his head when he'd asked her to spend Christmas with him. At the time, on the beach, with panic swirling up inside him like spindrift off a snow-covered mountain, he'd justified it to himself as a first small step, a baby step…

His mouth curved upwards and he felt the rise of fierce pride and happiness as he pictured his daughter moving towards him with slow, unsteady certainty. His smile faded.

Except he wasn't a baby.

He was a grown man, and he needed to start acting like one—because for the first time in his life he was more scared of losing someone than of letting them get close to him.

Rolling onto her front, Lottie lowered her face and closed her eyes. Sóley was having her nap and Ragnar was holed up in his office, reading through business proposals. She hadn't felt like sketching today. Instead, she had sneaked out to the pool house and, after a quick dip in the steaming water, she made her way to the sauna and was now stretched out on one of the slatted wooden benches.

Beneath the towel she felt warm and weightless.

Of course that was due in part to the voluptuous heat of the sauna. But it was Ragnar's invitation—and this time it *was* an invitation—to stay on in Iceland that had wiped all tension from her body.

Her heart swelled against her ribs.

It wasn't a big deal, she told herself for perhaps the tenth time since waking. It was just a couple of weeks. Only she could sense that the words hadn't come easily to him. And he hadn't had to say them at all, so surely that did make it into some kind of deal.

They would be together, properly together, so his inviting her to stay must mean that he liked her. The thought made her pulse dart forward and she allowed herself a moment of pure, incredulous happiness.

She was growing drowsy now. And as her limbs grew

heavier she felt the air currents shift and knew that someone had come into the sauna. Even without looking she knew it was Ragnar.

Opening her eyes, she looked sleepily up at him. He was wearing a towel, knotted low around his hips, and as her gaze skimmed his powerful body her sleepiness vanished instantly and her nerves started to hum like an electricity substation. Against the soft fabric the lean muscles of his chest and stomach looked like burnished bronze, and as he walked towards her she felt her insides tighten around a ball of hard, pulsing heat.

'I thought you were working.'

'I was.' Sliding onto the bench beside her, he dropped a kiss on her half-open mouth. 'I got through it quicker than expected.' His eyes slipped slowly over the bare skin of her shoulders. 'But then I had an incentive…'

She bit her lip. Her skin was prickling, and she could feel the tips of her nipples pressing into the towel. 'Incentive? Is that how you see me? As some kind of carrot on a stick?'

His long dark lashes flickered up and, blue eyes narrowing, he reached out and hooked a finger under the knotted towel above her breasts. 'That's not what I was picturing in my head, no.'

Pulling her closer, he tipped up her head and ran his tongue lightly along her lips. She moaned against his mouth, arching her body upwards, blindly seeking more contact.

'Have you got a condom?'

'No…' He groaned softly and kissed her hard, his lips parting hers, and then slowly he released her. 'I was so desperate to get down here I didn't think.'

Her stomach flipped over at the sweet look of regret on his face. It was flattering to know that she affected him so strongly, but there was a tension beneath his skin as though he was bracing himself, or building up to saying something that was on his mind.

Her heart began to thump inside her chest. 'Let's just go upstairs,' she said quickly.

'No. I don't want to go upstairs.' His voice was hoarse, but it was the tension in his arms that made her stop talking and stare at him uncertainly.

'I didn't mean that.' Gritting his teeth, he reached out and touched her cheek. 'I do. It's just there's something I want to say to you. About you and Sóley staying on for Christmas. When I asked you on the beach I made a mistake—'

In other words he'd changed his mind.

She stared at him miserably. Beneath her legs the solid bench felt suddenly as though it was made of paper. He'd had time to think and of course he'd changed his mind—but she wasn't going to let him know about the stupid hope in her heart.

'It's okay—I get it,' she said woodenly. 'You're a busy man and you've already taken three weeks off.'

'No, that's not what I meant.' His face was taut. 'I asked you to stay on here, but what I really meant to ask—what I should have asked you—was will you move in with me when we get back to England?'

She stared at him in mute disbelief, stunned by his unexpected miraculous question.

He stroked her face gently. 'I'm not good with words, and I didn't make myself clear yesterday, so I'm going to try a little harder this time. I want *you* to move in with me, Lottie. Sóley too, of course, but I'm asking *you*.'

Lottie pressed her hand against her mouth. Everything was spinning out of reach, her breath, her heartbeat, her thoughts. He wasn't saying that he loved her, but he wanted her—and not just for sex, but for herself. And right now that was enough.

'I want that too, but are you sure?'

His hands tangled in her hair and he drew her forward. 'More sure than I've ever been.'

And, tilting her face up to his, he kissed her.

Warmth flooded her body and she felt her bones start to soften. He was wrong, she thought. He was good with words—but he was even better at kissing.

For Lottie, the rest of the day passed in a kind of bubble of invulnerable happiness. At first she could hardly believe what had happened, but then Ragnar told Signy, and she'd finally allowed herself to accept that for once the hopes and expectations of her imagination had matched up with real life.

The following morning they woke early, reaching for one another in the darkness, making love slowly, taking their time. Afterwards Ragnar held her close to him, so that it felt as though his blood was pulsing through her veins.

As the sun started to ease into the room they could hear Sóley, gabbling to herself from next door. Lottie inched away from Ragnar's warm, solid body.

'No, I'll get her,' he said.

She shook her head. 'I want to—you always get up first.' Leaning forward, she kissed him softly on the mouth. 'Why don't you grab some more sleep?'

His gaze drifted slowly over her naked body and she felt her breasts start to ache.

'I'm not actually feeling that sleepy…'

They stared at one another, a pulse of desire rebounding between them—and then there was a short, imperious shout from the other side of the wall.

His eyes locked with hers and then the corner of his mouth curved upwards. 'It's fine. I'll go and hit the gym for an hour.' Shifting against the bedding, he grimaced. 'Maybe two.'

Lottie fed Sóley her breakfast and then had a piece of

toast herself. Signy had taken the morning off to visit her sister, so it would be a treat to cook breakfast for both of them. Imagine cooking breakfast being a treat. She smiled. It was just one small example of how her life had changed over the past few weeks.

The biggest and best change was that she and Ragnar had both managed to overcome the false start they'd made twenty months ago in London. Okay, he hadn't said that he loved her, but then she hadn't said it either—and besides, she smiled, neither of them were good with words.

Picking up Sóley, she glanced down at her daughter's cereal-splattered dungarees. 'How did you get so mucky?' She sighed. 'Come on, then, let's go and clean you up.'

They were less than halfway up the stairs when she heard the sound of a car in the driveway.

It must be Signy. Except Signy would let herself in, she thought, frowning as there was a sudden frantic knocking on the door, followed almost immediately by someone pressing the doorbell insistently.

She stared at the door uncertainly.

Ragnar hadn't said anything about visitors, and the house was so off the beaten track it couldn't be anyone looking for directions. It was probably just another delivery of work papers for him.

She glanced up at the discreet security video screen in the wall and felt her spine stiffen. That didn't seem very likely. Standing in front of the camera was a young, very beautiful woman with white-blonde hair, wearing ripped jeans and some kind of shaggy astrakhan coat.

A young, beautiful, weeping woman.

Heart pounding, Lottie punched in the security code and opened the door.

'Oh, thank goodness—I thought there was no one here.'

Storming past her without a word of explanation or even a nod of acknowledgement, the young woman pulled out her phone and with tears still pouring down her face began frenetically typing.

'You can bring that in,' she called shakily over her shoulder.

Lottie watched in stunned silence as a slightly apologetic-looking taxi driver carried in an expensive, monogrammed suitcase.

'Oh, you need to pay him. You *do* understand English, right?'

Still too stunned to speak, Lottie nodded.

After paying the driver, she closed the door and turned to face the young woman. She had stopped typing into her phone, but she was still crying, and yet her smudged mascara and swollen eyes didn't detract from her quite extraordinary beauty.

Lottie stared at her in confusion. *Who was she?*

The question was barely formed in her head when the woman finally looked at her straight on and her arresting blue eyes instantly and unequivocally provided the answer.

'You must be Marta.'

The woman frowned. 'Yes, I am.' Despite her tears she spoke disdainfully, as though her identity should be a matter of common knowledge. 'Is Ragnar here?'

Lottie nodded. 'He's in the gym.'

Marta sniffed. 'He must be in holiday mode.' Her eyes narrowed on Sóley, as though seeing her for the first time. 'I'm surprised he lets you bring your baby to work.'

'Oh, I don't work for Ragnar,' Lottie said quickly. 'I'm Lottie—Lottie Dawson. And this is Sóley.'

She hadn't been expecting to meet Ragnar's sister, so she hadn't given much thought to how Marta would react to her words, but blank-eyed bewilderment probably wouldn't have been high on her list—or on her list at all.

'Who?' Marta stared at her, her lip curling.

'Lottie…' She knew there was a slight tremor in her

voice, but there was something unnerving about Marta's cool, dismissive gaze, so like her brother's and yet not. More unnerving still was the stinging realisation that Ragnar's sister had no idea who she was, or what she was to him.

The happiness and certainty of earlier fell away. She felt as though she was gripping on to a cliff-edge.

Breathing in against the feeling of vertigo filling her head, she held her daughter closer, taking comfort in the tight grip of her arms.

What should she say? Even if she had the right words, the thought of saying them out loud was just too daunting—for how could she reveal what Ragnar had so clearly decided to keep secret? Only why would he keep his daughter a secret from his sister? And was it just his sister or his whole family?

'Marta—'

Lottie turned, her heart pounding. Ragnar was walking down the stairs and clearly he'd dressed in a hurry. His hair was wet from the shower and his shirt clung to his body, where his skin was still damp.

'What are you doing here?' he said softly.

Bursting into tears, Marta bolted towards him and, watching his arms pull her close, Lottie felt suddenly like an intruder. Whatever it was she needed to ask Ragnar, right now he needed to take care of his sister.

'I'll leave you two to talk,' she said quietly and, sidestepping Marta's sobbing back, she forced herself to walk upstairs.

For the next two hours she tried hard to distract herself from what was going on downstairs. It helped that Sóley was extra demanding, refusing to be put down for a moment and wanting her mother's full attention. Probably she'd been upset by Marta's distress, but thankfully she was too young to have understood Ragnar's deceit by omission.

Lottie shivered. A lump of ice was lodged in her stomach and she could feel its chill spreading outwards. Why hadn't he told his sister about their daughter? It didn't make any sense. He'd spoken to Marta countless times—how could he not have mentioned her?

Maybe he hadn't wanted to tell her when she was so upset. Then again, he had a big family, so maybe he was telling them one at a time.

Glancing down, she saw that Sóley had fallen asleep. Even with her blue eyes out of the equation, the family resemblance between her daughter and Marta and Ragnar was unmistakable. It was there in her jawline and the shape of her mouth.

Turning, she felt her heart stutter. Ragnar was standing in the doorway, his gaze resting on her face. He looked tired. Instantly she forgot her own fears and, walking across the room, she pulled him against her. She felt him breathe out, and the lump of ice in her stomach started to melt.

'Shall I put her down?' he asked.

She nodded and, lifting his daughter up, he laid her gently in the cot.

'Let's go downstairs,' he said quietly.

The hall was empty and silent, the kitchen too.

Lottie watched as Ragnar poured two glasses of water and handed her one.

'Is Marta okay?'

He nodded. 'She will be.'

'She probably needs some food. I can make her some lunch—'

'You don't need to do that.'

'Oh, I don't mind—'

'No,' he said firmly. 'You don't need to do that. She'd not here.'

She frowned. 'Not here. Where has she gone?'

'To Reykjavik. To a hotel.'

'But she was so upset. She shouldn't be on her own—you should go after her.'

His face stilled. 'That would be a little absurd as I was the one who sent her there.'

She stared at him, not understanding. 'You sent her away? But why?'

'This is my home. I have rules. And Marta broke those rules. She knows I don't have people to stay here.'

His answer both irritated and confused her. 'She's not "people". She's your family.'

He shrugged. 'I know—and I particularly don't have my family here. This is a place of calm and order. I don't want their drama under my roof.'

Rules. Drama. What was he talking about? She could feel panic clawing up her throat. 'But you love them.'

'Yes, I do. And I show that love to them in many different ways, twenty-four-seven. All they have to do in return is follow my rules, and the first and most important rule is that they don't turn up unannounced.'

He sounded as though he was explaining a scientific law, like gravity, not talking about his family.

'But love doesn't have rules…' she said slowly.

'Which probably explains why so many people are unhappy.'

She felt a chill as his blue gaze met hers. His eyes were hard and unreachable.

'I love my family but I can't—I *won't*—live with them. I keep everything separate and contained. That's how it works. That's how I live.'

The hurt in her chest was spreading like a blizzard.

'Is that why you didn't tell Marta about me and Sóley?'

She saw the truth in his eyes before he even opened his mouth, and it hurt so badly she had to grit her teeth against the pain in her heart.

'Yes.'

'Have you told *anyone* in your family?'

This time he shook his head.

She breathed out unsteadily. It had happened again—just like with her father. They had met too late. Ragnar, the man she loved, the man she so badly wanted to love her, was someone who couldn't be what she wanted or give her what she needed. Only she'd been too busy painting pretty pictures in her head to see what was actually in front of her nose.

'What if I tell you that I love you?' she whispered. 'Would that change anything?'

As he shook his head the distance in his eyes made her almost black out.

'I want to go home.' The words left her mouth before she knew they were there. 'I want to go back to England—now.'

He glanced away, and there was a long, strained silence.

'Then I'll go and speak to Ivar,' he said finally. 'I'll leave you to pack.'

And without meeting her eyes he turned and walked out through the door.

CHAPTER TEN

STANDING BESIDE THE fire in the middle of the living room, Ragnar breathed out unsteadily. This was his home, and yet he felt adrift—disconnected and dazed.

He didn't know which was more unbelievable. The fact that Lottie and Sóley were gone or that he had stood and watched them leave.

He fumbled with the equation in his head but nothing he did would balance it.

He shivered. He felt cold, and the house was so quiet. No, not just quiet—it was silent. The silence of reproach and regret.

His eyes flicked across the empty room to something square and yellow, poking out from beneath a cushion on the sofa. Slowly he walked towards it, his heart pounding as he saw what it was.

Lottie's sketchbook.

He picked it up, his hand shaking as he turned the pages, an ache flowering like a black orchid inside his chest.

What had he done?

Or rather what hadn't he done?

Why hadn't he stopped her leaving?

Why had he just stood and waited while she packed?

It made no sense. He'd only just asked her to move in with him, and she'd agreed, and for the first time ever he'd been thinking about a future that offered something other than lives lived separately with clearly defined borders. For the first time ever he'd been looking at a hazy rose-gold sunset of a future, with Lottie and his daughter.

And then Marta had arrived, crashing into his ordered, tranquil life, trailing snowflakes and suitcases and disorder in her wake, and instantly the sunset had been blotted out by the need to act quickly and decisively.

Of course he'd taken care of her, but there had been no possibility of her staying. And he'd tried to explain that to Lottie. Tried to explain that he couldn't let his family into his home with all their tears and traumas.

Only she hadn't understood, and she'd kept on pushing and pushing, and then—his breathing faltered—then she'd told him she loved him.

He could still see her face now—the expression of shock and hurt when he'd more or less told that her love didn't change how he felt. He gritted his teeth. Except he hadn't said anything. He'd just shaken his head like a robot.

But he hadn't been able to make his voice work. Marta's random appearance was such an unsettling reminder of what would happen if he allowed the separate strands of his life to overlap, that her astonishing words and his own feverishly joyous response to them had been silenced.

Of course, seeing Lottie upset had hurt—badly—but not enough to blank his mind to the fear, so that when she'd told him she wanted to go home he'd told himself that it was for the best.

But it wasn't.

It was the biggest mistake he'd ever made.

The next few days were interminable, and he realised that time was *not* a great healer. Being alone in the house—or worse, in his bed—was like pressing against an open wound, and after one more day of agonising solitude he went down to the stables and led Camille out into the yard.

He rode blindly, seeing nothing, caring about nothing, just trying to put as much distance between himself and his silent home as he could. But when they reached the top of a hill Camille slowed and, leaning back in his saddle, he gazed down at the waterfalls. His eyes blurred—and not because of the freezing wind.

The sky was dark and low and the wind was bitterly cold against his face. Any rational, sane person would be happily sprawled out on the sofa in front of a log fire. But he didn't feel rational or sane or happy. And that was why he was here, roaming the freezing hills.

It was ridiculous and illogical to act like this.

Signy certainly thought so.

Probably Camille, too, but thankfully horses couldn't talk.

Only he didn't know what else to do.

For years he'd relished coming here. Even before *ice/breakr* had gone global it had been a place of sanctuary—somewhere he could take a breath before the next storm hit.

His hands tightened against the reins.

But not any more. Now his house was an empty, echoing reminder of his stupidity and cowardice. For so many years he'd had to fight to keep his life orderly and tranquil, and now he had succeeded in achieving his ideal. After expelling Marta from his home, even his family were keeping their distance—only instead of relishing his solitude he hated it.

He missed Lottie and Sóley.

Without them life had no purpose, no value.

But she deserved a better man than him.

So be that man, he told himself. *Be the man she needs you to be. Find her and fight for her.*

And, turning away from the waterfall, he pushed Camille down the slope towards the only future he wanted—a future he was not going to let slip away again.

Looking up at the Suffolk sky, Lottie flinched as a few flakes of snow landed on her face. She was standing in the back garden of her cottage, supposedly trying to decide where to put Sóley's swing. All week it had been threatening to snow, but of course it had to wait until today, her daughter's birthday, to actually make good on its promise.

As if she didn't have enough reminders of Ragnar Stone already in her life.

All the shops were filled with fur throws and cushions for Christmas, and when Lucas had finally managed to drag her to the pub one evening she'd caught sight of a blond man crouching in front of the open fire and, ignoring her brother's exasperated protests, had simply reversed back out through the door.

But of the man himself there had been nothing.

Not a word in nearly three weeks.

No phone call.

No text.

She swallowed against the ache building in her throat.

Not even a birthday card for their daughter.

A mixture of misery and anger flared inside her. She still couldn't accept that he was acting like this—punishing Sóley for what had happened between the two of them. It seemed so small-minded and cruel, so not like Ragnar.

Or maybe it *was* like him.

Remembering the cool, almost clinical expression on his face when she'd told him she loved him, she shivered. After hearing him talk so dispassionately about his family, and his ruthless dismissal of Marta, she'd been mad to tell him that. But then she'd naively been assuming that her words would mean something to him, that they would matter—that *she* mattered.

Her mouth twisted. But they hadn't—and she didn't.

And now she was here, back in Suffolk, it was difficult to see why she had ever thought he cared about love *or* her.

Truthfully, she barely knew him—she'd just made herself feel that she did, letting the intoxicating power of their lovemaking weave a spell not just over her body but her mind too. She'd been so flattered, so desperate to believe in the story she'd told herself in her head of two people separated by circumstance but destined to be together.

She bit down on a sudden choking swell of tears. She was stupid. And selfish. For it was her fault that her daughter—her beautiful, sweet daughter—would never have a father in her life. But clearly Ragnar had meant what he said about keeping his life separate and contained.

'Lottie—'

Hearing Lucas's voice, she swiped the tears from her cheeks and took a quick, calming breath. If she could take one positive away from this whole mess it was that it had made her realise how close she and Lucas and Izzy were as a family.

Her brother and her mother were fundamentally different from her in so many ways, but she understood now that it wasn't just nature that mattered. Ragnar had taught her that nurture was just as important. Since she'd stumbled into the cottage, with tears pouring down her face, both Lucas and Izzy had been utterly amazing.

Those first few days back in England she had felt adrift from everything—like the survivor of a sinking ship, she had only been capable of clinging to the wreckage. Then, when the shock had faded, she had been ill, stricken with cramps, immobilised by the crushing weight of failure and disappointment.

And all the time, despite everything that had happened, she'd missed Ragnar. The nights were bad, but waking was worse, for each morning she had to work through her grief and her loneliness all over again.

It was her family who got her out of bed, and dressed, and she was so lucky to have them.

Forcing her lips into a smile, she turned towards Lucas.

He sighed. 'Oh, Lottie, we agreed. No crying today.'

'I'm not crying.' She met her brother's sceptical gaze. 'Honestly. It's just the cold. I'm fine, really.'

'So, did you decide where you want it?'

She gazed at him blankly still lost in thoughts of Ragnar. 'Want what?'

He groaned. 'The swing, Lottie. Remember? I said I was going to put it by the vegetable patch and you didn't want it there—'

Without warning, she felt her face crumple. 'Sorry, I forgot.'

'No, I'm sorry.' Reaching out, he pulled her against his battered leather jacket. 'I'm just feeling cranky, but I shouldn't take it out on you.'

She pressed her face into her brother's chest, breathing in his familiar smell. 'You didn't—you've been great, Lucas.'

Looking up at him, she watched his jaw tighten.

'I want to kill him, you know. For how he's treated you and Sóley.'

'Well don't.' She smiled up at him weakly. 'We need you here—not in prison.'

His face creased into a reluctant smile. 'Is that your way of telling me you know where you want the swing?'

It took over an hour to make the frame and fix it into position but, despite the numerous setbacks, Lottie found it strangely relaxing. At least trying to make sense of the comically inadequate instructions took her mind off Ragnar, and the swing was lovely. Made of wood, it had two seats—one for a baby and one for an adult.

Lucas took hold of the frame and tried to jiggle it. 'Look at that.' He grinned at Lottie. 'Rock-solid.'

'Oh, well done, darling.' Izzy was standing by the back door, holding Sóley in her arms. 'It looks fantastic. Shall we give it a try?'

But as she tried to put Sóley into the baby seat her bottom lip protruded and began to wobble.

'Here, let me try, Mum.' Reaching out, Lottie took her daughter.

'Look what Lucas has made. Isn't he clever?' she said softly.

She felt Sóley relax at the sound of her voice but when she tried to lower her into the seat the little girl just grabbed her neck and refused to let go.

'I'm sorry, Lucas.' Looking over at her brother's disappointed face, Lottie felt her stomach twist with guilt.

Since getting home, Sóley had stopped being the easy-going baby she had always been. She was clingy, and often woke several times in the night. It was tempting to tell herself that it was just her age, or her teeth, or even the change in routine, but she knew that Sóley was missing Ragnar as much as she was, and that only added to her feelings of guilt.

'You'll be okay, you know…' Her mother leaned forward and kissed her cheek. 'You're stronger than you think. Strong enough to survive this. And Sóley will be okay too. Children are very resilient.'

'I don't *want* her to have to be resilient,' she said hoarsely.

'I know, darling.' Izzy smiled. 'But that's nature's way. You have to be tough to survive. Look at everything I put you and Lucas through. No father figures, let alone actual fathers, and all those different homes and schools, and always having the wrong clothes.'

Her mother was looking straight into her eyes, and in that moment, the calmness of her expression made Lottie realise that she had focused too much on their differences instead of how much they were alike.

She shook her head. 'It wasn't that bad.'

Lucas caught her eye and grinned. 'It was pretty bad—especially the clothes.'

Lottie smiled. 'But whatever happened you were always there, Mum. And we were lucky to have you.' As she spoke, she wondered why she had never said that to Izzy before and why it felt true now. 'I'm lucky to have you, then and now.'

'Me too,' Lucas said, his eyes gleaming. 'Only don't go getting the wrong idea and start thinking that this love-in means you get to wear any of your weird kaftans to the party.'

Izzy and Lottie both laughed.

'Right, darling,' said Izzy. 'I'm going to take my granddaughter home with me so she can have a nap. No.' She held up her hand imperiously as Lottie started to protest and then gently pulled Sóley into her arms. 'She needs a nap and you need a little time on your own to make your peace with today. Come on, Lucas.'

After the car had driven off Lottie went and sat on the swing. It was starting to snow again, but it wasn't that cold, and it was calming just to sit and let her feet scuff against the ground. Glancing up at the sky, Lottie breathed out, trying to find the peace her mother had mentioned.

Her emotions were not out of control now. She felt sad—but not the crushing misery of those early days, just a lingering emptiness that she couldn't seem to shift. And that was okay, because her mother was right. She was strong and she was going to survive.

And because she was strong she was going to put her sadness aside this afternoon for the sake of her family—especially her daughter.

Ragnar Stone was not coming to this party so she certainly wasn't going to let the memory of him ruin it for her or anyone else.

Her body stilled. From beyond the hedge she could hear the sound of a car making its way up the lane. No doubt her mother had forgotten something crucial, and sent Lucas to retrieve it. As she swung gently back and forth she heard the car stop in front of the cottage, and then the crunching sound of footsteps on the path. Then the click of the garden gate. Definitely Lucas, then. Her mother could never open it without a huge tussle.

'So what did you forget?' she called out. 'I'm going to go with either your phone or Mum's bag.'

'Actually, I didn't forget anything. I let it slip away.'

Her heart turned to stone. She stared across the garden, her breath dissolving in her lungs. Ragnar was standing at the edge of the path, his clear blue eyes fixed on her face. He looked just as he always had, and the pain of seeing him again made her feel lightheaded.

'What are you doing here?' Her voice sounded small and unfamiliar in the sudden echoing silence.

'I came to talk to you.'

Her throat tightened. He made it sound as though he was just dropping in, when the reality was that he hadn't been in touch for weeks. Two weeks and six days, to be precise.

She swallowed, pushing back against the ache in her chest. 'In case you've forgotten it's our daughter's birthday, so I don't really have time for a chat.'

He didn't move. 'I know it's her birthday, and I want to see her. But I have something I need to say to you first.'

'I don't want to listen to anything you have to say, Ragnar.' She stood up abruptly, letting go of the swing so that it banged into the back of her legs. 'Do you really think you can just turn up here for her birthday? It's been nearly three weeks.'

'I know. And I'm not proud of myself.'

'Well, that makes two of us.'

He sucked in a breath as though she'd slapped him. 'You have every right to be angry with me.'

Angry? *Angry?* She stared at him, the word spinning inside her head like the ball in a roulette wheel.

'You think I'm angry?' She shook her head. 'I'm not angry, Ragnar. I'm hurt.'

Crossing her arms in front of her chest, she clenched her teeth. She was not going to cry in front of him.

But as he took a step forward she felt her eyes fill with tears.

'I'm sorry,' he said softly, and the softness in his voice hurt more than anything else, for that was what she missed most. 'I'm sorry,' he said again. 'I never meant to hurt you. I would never hurt you.'

'You're hurting me now.' Her arms tightened around her ribs. 'You had no right to come here. I was just starting to feel okay.'

'I had to come. I had to come and see you.'

'And now you have—so you can go.'

He didn't move. He just stood there, with snowflakes spinning slowly around him.

'Ragnar, please.' The hurt broke through her voice, and as she pressed her hand against her mouth he was walking towards her and pulling her close. She pushed against him. 'You have to leave.'

'Please give me a chance.'

'To do what? Throw my love back in my face?' She shook her head. 'It's too late, Ragnar. Whatever you think is going to happen here, it isn't.'

'I love you.'

'No.' She shook her head. 'You don't get to say that. That's not allowed.'

'I thought love didn't have any rules?' he said quietly.

His voice was strained, and now that he was closer she could see dark smudges under his eyes, and he looked as if he'd lost weight.

Blanking her mind to the idea that he might be suffering too, she shook her head again. 'You don't love me,' she whispered. 'And more importantly I don't love you. Not any more.'

His eyes were steady on her face.

'I don't believe you. I think you do love me, Lottie. And I know that I love you.'

Reaching out, he caught her hand, but she pulled it away.

'You think that's all it takes? Just three little words. Well, I've got three words for you. Separate and contained.'

'But I don't want to be separate from you.' He took her hand again, and this time the fire in his voice stopped her pulling away. 'I can't be separate from you. I thought I could—I thought that was what I wanted, what I needed. But I need *you*.'

'So why did you let me leave?'

Leaning forward, he pressed his face against her. 'Because I was stupid and scared.'

'Scared of what?'

She was holding her breath.

'Of feeling. Of how you made me feel.'

The shake in his voice made her eyes burn.

'My family feels everything so intensely, and when I was kid it used to scare me, being around that kind of intense emotion. And then, when I met Daniel that summer, I realised there were other ways to live. All I needed to do was take a step back, keep my distance.'

She felt him breathe out unsteadily.

'I shouldn't have let you go. It hurt so much, but I kept telling myself that I was doing it for the right reasons. That I couldn't be the man you needed and so I'd just end up hurting you.'

Remembering his tense expression when he'd found Marta in his house, she thought her heart might burst with understanding and relief. So it had been fear that had made him put his sister in a taxi. Fear, not indifference, that had stopped him from telling her what was in his heart.

'So what's changed?' she said softly.

His hands were shaking. 'I did. I realised that I didn't

have a choice. I can't live without you or Sóley. I'm going crazy without you.'

He was laying his heart bare, saying the words she'd longed to hear, and yet she was scared to hope, scared to believe that they were true.

She felt his fingers tighten around hers.

'I didn't believe it could happen to me. I didn't think I could fall in love. And then it came so quickly and completely—and that scared me, because I didn't think I was capable of giving you the love you deserve.'

His eyes softened.

'My family are crazy when they're in love, and I didn't want to be like them. And then I realised that I'd been so fixated on all the ways I didn't want to be like them that I'd stopped seeing all the ways I did. Like how brave and generous and loving they are.'

'I know what you mean,' she said slowly. 'I did the same thing with my mum and Lucas, reading too much into our differences.'

He stared at her uncertainly. 'Did you mean what you said? About not loving me.'

She shook her head slowly. 'I want to mean it, but I can't.'

Sliding his arm around her waist, he kissed her. She felt him breathe out shakily against her mouth.

'I love you,' he said.

'I love you too.'

His eyes locked onto hers. 'Enough to be my wife?'

Looking down, she felt her heart swell. He was holding a ring with a sapphire as blue and clear as his eyes.

'Let me try that again,' he said hoarsely. 'Will you marry me, Lottie Dawson?'

She was nodding and smiling and crying all at the same time.

'That *is* a yes, isn't it?'

She nodded again. 'Yes, it is.'

As he slid the ring onto her finger she pulled him closer. 'So what happens next?'

He smiled. 'This…' he said softly.

And, tilting her face up to his, he lowered his mouth and kissed her.

EPILOGUE

Six months later...

GLANCING OUT OF the window, Lottie bit her lip. Why was it taking so long? Surely they must nearly be there.

But the scenery scudding beneath the helicopter's whirling rotor blades was no help at all—mainly because it looked nothing like it had the last time she'd seen it, just over six months ago. Then, it had been covered in snow, but now the snow was gone, and the land was a patchwork of colours and textures—a bit like her sixth form art project, she thought, a bubble of laughter squeezing out of her chest.

'What's so funny?'

Meeting her brother's gaze, she shook her head. 'Nothing, really. I was just thinking about an art project I did at school.'

'Okay…' He raised an eyebrow. 'You did eat breakfast, didn't you?'

'Yes, I did. I had muesli and yoghurt and fresh fruit.' She poked him gently in the ribs. 'So, what do you think?'

It was Lucas's first visit to Iceland, and she was desperate to hear his thoughts—to find out if he felt the same way as she did about this incredible country that was now like a second home to her.

'Of your breakfast?' He grinned. 'Oh, you mean of all this.' Shaking his head, he blew out a breath. 'What can I say? It's right out there… I mean, look at this place!' He leaned forward, his eyes widening as they flew over a huge vivid green field of moss. As he looked back at her, his face softened. 'I can see why you love it so much.'

She smiled. 'It's just so beautiful and rugged and remote.'

His eyes gleamed. 'Are you talking about Iceland? Or Ragnar?' he said softly.

Looking down, she stared at the sapphire ring on her finger. 'You do like him now, don't you?'

She thought back to the moment when she and Ragnar had walked into her mother's garden together, after he'd proposed. Lucas hadn't liked him at all then, but thankfully Sóley's babbling open-armed excitement at seeing her father had meant that his disapproval had been limited to a stiffness of posture and a murderous scowl.

Her pulse skipped forward. It had been a shock, seeing her normally easy-going brother like that, but it hadn't lasted. Ignoring her panicky protests, he and Ragnar had gone for a walk the next day, and when they'd returned they hadn't been brothers-in-arms, exactly, but Lucas had welcomed him as a brother-in-law.

She felt him shrug beside her.

'Yeah, he's not the worst. I mean, I wouldn't ask him to join the band, but he's pretty handy with a pool cue.' As she looked up to meet his gaze, he rolled his eyes. 'I like him, okay? He knows a lot of stuff but he's not boring about it, and he's generous with money but not flash.' His mouth twitched. 'Oh, and he's got some *extremely* hot sisters.' He hesitated, his face suddenly serious. 'But mainly I like him because I can see how much he loves you, and I know that he makes you happy.'

She swallowed against the lump in her throat. 'He does…he really does.'

Her heart contracted. Ragnar had worked so hard these last six months to turn his life around. He'd started by introducing her and Sóley to his family, and he hadn't stopped there. He'd talked to each of them in turn, explaining how he'd felt as a child and then as a man. It had been really difficult for him, but he'd been determined to deal with his fear and committed to their future—his and hers and their daughter's.

She'd been scared of meeting his family, and it had been terrifying. They were all so glamorous and emphatic. But almost immediately she'd realised that beneath all the drama there was a solid core of unbreakable love and, even though they'd been at loggerheads for months, the first time she'd met Ragnar's mother, her ex-husband Nathan, his new wife Kim and their new baby had been there too.

It had been surreal, but kind of wonderful.

A bit like his family.

The family who had welcomed her into their hearts.

Lucas frowned. 'Hey, you promised no crying.'

As Lottie swiped at her eyes she felt the helicopter start to slow. 'We're here,' she said softly.

Her heart gave a thump as they landed, and then he was sliding back the door and climbing out, holding up his hand to help her down.

'Here.' He took her hand and slid it through his arm. 'Let's go find your man.'

Her man. Her Ragnar.

Her chest squeezed tight and, gripping Lucas's arm to steady the trembling of her heart, she started to walk towards the beach, to find the man she loved without limits.

The man she was going to marry today.

'She's here.'

Glancing up, Ragnar felt the twist in his stomach muscles loosen. Behind him, his brother and best man Rob gave his shoulders a reassuring squeeze.

'Shall I get the bridesmaids?'

Ragnar glanced over to where a giggling Sóley was holding hands with his sister Marta. Their blonde hair was gleaming in the sunlight, their faces tipped back as they fled from his brother, Gunnar, across the black sand.

'No, it's okay. They're having fun.'

Turning his head, he gazed at the rest of his family. They were standing in a casual semi-circle, and his eyes moved slowly from one smiling face to the next.

It was true—everyone was having fun. There had been no arguments or tears or sulking. He felt an ache around his heart. They were all trying so hard, because they loved him. And he loved them as he always had, only now it felt so much easier to love and be loved.

He felt his gaze pulled back across the sand to where Lottie was walking towards him.

And that was down to her.

Lottie had made this happen.

She had made him stronger. And kinder. She and Sóley had made loving as simple and natural for him as breathing, so that now he found it difficult to understand how he'd survived for so long living as he had.

But everything was different now—particularly him. He no longer kept those he loved most at arm's length—and, incredibly, now that they could come and go at will, his family seemed like different people too, less intense, less demanding.

More fun.

That word again.

It was so not what his life had been about before, but now he had fun every day.

A flicker of heat skimmed over his skin. He had passion too. And tenderness. But most of all he had a love that was as warm and bright and unending as the summer solstice—and that was why he'd wanted Midsummer's Day to be their wedding day.

Straightening the cuffs of his dark suit jacket, he breathed out unsteadily.

Lottie stopped in front of him, her hand trembling against her brother's arm, her face soft and serious.

He stared at her, his pulse beating in time to the waves curling onto the beach.

She looked amazing. Fitted to her waist and then spilling out in layers of tulle, her white dress was perfectly offset by the black of the sand beneath her feet. She was holding a bunch of wild flowers picked by Sóley and Marta from the fields surrounding the house, and her hair was loosely caught up at the base of her neck.

She had never looked more beautiful. And, meeting her gaze, he felt the ache in his chest intensify.

Her eyes were shining with tears of emotion, and the same emotions that were shining in his eyes were filling his heart. A happiness like no other, and a gratitude that life had let them find one another not once but three times—a statistic that had no basis in logic and was just the beautiful, disorderly, topsy-turvy mathematics of love.

'You look beautiful,' he whispered.

The celebrant stepped forward and smiled. 'Shall we begin?'

As they spoke their vows tears were sliding down his face—tears he would never have allowed to fall before meeting her.

Finally, they exchanged rings, and the celebrant smiled again. 'And now you may kiss, as husband and wife.'

They each took a step forward and then, as he lowered his mouth to hers, she leaned towards him and they kissed, softly at first, and then more deeply, to the appreciative applause of their watching families.

'I can't believe we're married,' she whispered, gazing at the gold band on her finger.

'I can't believe I made us wait so long.' Cupping her face in his hand, he brushed his mouth against hers. 'But it had to be this day.'

Her heart swelled with love as she looked up at him curiously. Ragnar had chosen the day, and at the time she'd assumed he'd picked it because Midsummer was a day of celebration for Icelanders. But the shake in his hand now told a different story.

Reaching up, she stroked his cheek. 'Tell me why you chose it?'

'It's the summer solstice.' He hesitated, struggling to contain the emotion in his voice. 'That means the sun will never set on our wedding day. I just liked the idea of that.'

'I like it too.' Tears filled her eyes and throat and, pulling him closer, she kissed him softly. 'I love you.'

'And I love you. So very much.'

For a moment neither of them could speak, but as Ragnar lowered his mouth and kissed her again Lottie knew it didn't matter. Sometimes words were irrelevant.

* * * * *